ALSO BY SIERI

SALT KISS

SIERRA SIMONE

Bloom *books*

To Christa, for helping me bloom.

Published by Bloom Books, an imprint of Sourcebooks
P.O. Box 4410, Naperville, Illinois 60567-410
(630) 961-3900
sourcebooks.com

Cataloging-in-Publication data is on file with the Library of Congress.

Printed and bound in the United States of America.
VP 10 9 8 7 6 5 4 3 2 1

When I set out for Lyonnesse,
A hundred miles away,
The rime was on the spray,
And starlight lit my lonesomeness
When I set out for Lyonnesse
A hundred miles away.

—Thomas Hardy

PROLOGUE

In Washington, DC, even the moon looked like a lie.

The man stood on the balcony and stared at the red disc that looked painted right onto the night. His sister came and joined him at the railing. The sounds of wedding laughter and dancing filtered in from behind them.

"Well?" she asked.

"My plans haven't changed."

She didn't think so. She wondered how much he knew. Him, the man who knows, who's made his business knowing. But it was her business to know too, and the fact that they were twins only made them perfectly matched for the contest. Not that they were always at odds, of course, but her brother played his own game, with his own rules, and with stakes raised higher than any sane person would accept.

She didn't like to think of the consequences if he ended up losing. She had a wife to keep safe after all, a whip-smart chatterbox who wanted to save the planet with wind turbines and low-carbon diets. She had people at her job who counted on her. She had her own legacy to think about.

"Blanche can't be hurt by any of it," she said finally, turning back to gaze at the wedding through the open doors of the ballroom. Their older sister, Blanche, was dancing with her new husband, her face glowing with joy, her fingers twisted in her husband's jacket. Although she'd fallen for Ricker Thomas, a hawkish brigadier general, she was as soft and gentle as they came. She was a pediatric nurse who spent her weekends socializing shelter dogs and doing thankless river cleanups, and she was the kind of doting, generous person that invariably had park benches dedicated to them after they died.

Unlike the twins, she was good, and they'd recognized this from an early age, forging a unspoken pact to keep her as free from the shit of the world as possible. It was unusual for younger siblings to protect an older, but Blanche shone like a candle in winter, and the twins would kill anyone or anything that made the flame gutter.

Including each other.

"Blanche will be safe."

She didn't believe him, but he already knew that.

"Your plan is stupid," she told him instead. "And if it hurts Ricker's son, it will hurt her too."

Her brother joined her in turning now, and she knew who he was looking for.

Tall, dark-haired, fair skin that had been suntanned by four grueling deployments to Carpathia. He had a straight nose, high forehead, dark slashing brows, and a mouth that was unfairly pout shaped. Even though he was only in his late twenties, his forest-green eyes held a lifetime's worth of sadness and anger.

Tristan Thomas. Blanche's new stepson. No longer a soldier as of two weeks ago. A hero, according to the news, and a skilled and valiant warrior, according to the medals and ribbons pinned to the jacket of his dress blues.

She looked over at her twin, not that it mattered. His ruggedly handsome face was unreadable, as usual.

"You could find someone else," she pointed out.

"It needs to be him," her brother said.

She didn't bother arguing with him. He already knew all of what she would say. "And if you succeed? If all this works and you stab Ys through the heart, what then? What of Tristan? Your future wife?"

Her brother, Mark Trevena—owner of DC's wickedest kink club, and once the most feared operator in the CIA—straightened up and buttoned his tuxedo jacket. "There's time yet to think about it. The wedding isn't for several months."

She narrowed her eyes. "A lot can happen between now and then." Mark of all people should have known that people weren't pawns. Not that people weren't meant to be *used* as pawns, no, no, she didn't mean that. She was a deputy director of the CIA, had come up as an officer gathering human intelligence. People were meant to be used.

But the trouble with people was that they weren't inert pieces willing to stay where they were put. They had their own thoughts, however paltry and cliché, and they had their own tender little hearts, and their own little loyalties and patriotisms and gods. Mark might think he could move Tristan Thomas across the board like a pout-mouthed little knight, but Tristan himself might have other plans.

This mysterious future wife of Mark's might have other plans too.

But Mark wouldn't move on this, and maybe she wouldn't have either in his shoes. Tristan *was* very pretty. And if she'd lost what Mark had lost, she would burn the world down too.

"Just promise me you'll be the one to answer to Blanche if you corrupt her new stepson," she said finally.

"Why, Melody," her twin brother said, his teeth flashing white in the dark, "I would only ever corrupt someone who wanted it."

CHAPTER 1

On paper, I'm already the perfect candidate for the job.

I entered West Point at age seventeen and gave the army eight years after that. I've been in diplomatic environments and war zones and my last deployment in Carpathia was spent guarding its new president, and Carpathia's beloved former First Lady Lenka Kocur from rebel attacks. There is a Distinguished Service Cross sitting in a box in my dresser, next to a valor device and some metal oak leaves; it's under a neat whorl of dress socks. I'm trained in risk assessment, surveillance and countersurveillance, armed and unarmed combat, defensive driving, and advanced first aid.

I have no partner, no lover—just a handful of friends who no longer know how to talk to me.

I have no job. No direction.

No point.

The email gave me an address, clear as day, but when I pull my father's modest, American-made hybrid into the parking garage, I see the building I'm meant to go to is on an island in the Potomac. I park and get out of the car, buttoning my suit jacket with one hand while I get my bearings. There is a bridge—narrow, pedestrian only—arcing from the shore to the flat stretch of land. On the island is a building, five stories tall, its exterior clad in glass and its shape like something between a castle and a ship with a sharply angled roof and a prow-shaped front.

The sun glitters off the glass as I finish my survey of the parking lot—five cars, none of them nice enough to belong to my would-be employer, security cameras mounted to the light poles—and then I take the bridge over the water to where my new uncle-in-law works.

Lyonesse.

That's what this place is called.

An island kingdom that sunk beneath the waves, according to Wikipedia. The ultra-exclusive home for the elite sinners of the world according to internet chatter. With the kind of guests Mark is rumored to entertain here, it's no surprise this place is impressively secure.

A woman greets me from behind a low desk. I stride forward, reminding myself to smile, because for so long smiling hasn't been part of the job. I used to smile a lot, I think, before I went over there the first time. I can't remember anymore.

As I walk to the desk, I clock the pertinent details of the space, the narrow doors set into the light-wood-paneled wall behind the desk—one leading to something mundane, like a coat closet, the other probably connected to a security office or something similar—and the metal stairs leading up to a glass-walled walkway. There is an elevator and some low, leather-clad benches.

The woman is wearing something almost like normal receptionist's clothes, but there's a latex collar wrapped just above the tie-neck of her purple blouse. My step hitches, my pulse gives a thready surge. Her throat is long and slender, and the gleaming latex is so smooth around it, and she's wearing it so naturally, so casually. Like it's something utterly normal.

Maybe it is here.

"I'm here for an interview," I say, recovering. It's not only the collar—it's that she's pretty, with soft hair and high cheeks and a silk blouse that would slip frictionlessly from her shoulders, and I'm still not used to anything silky or soft or tailored. I'm still not used to lovely things, expensive things, indulgent things.

Carpathia was cold and muddy, our uniforms rough, everyone in helmets and MCEP glasses, our world shrunk down to dirt, plastic, and metal. When I'd walked down the aisle to join my father at the front of the sanctuary last week, I'd nearly fallen over at the scent of incense lingering in the air. At the reception, I stared at my slice of cake like I thought it was a lie, fairy food to trick the mortal boy into staying in fairyland.

I am embarrassed at how easily my deployments broke me. Even if I'd never fired a gun, never trembled on freezing pine needles waiting for the shot that would kill me, I'd still have been broken by the sheer fucking monotony of it all. The boredom. The deprivation.

And they call me a hero.

"Of course," the woman says, coming to her feet and leading me to the elevator in heels a mile high. I keep my eyes on those heels as we go, refusing to leer. We take the elevator up to the topmost floor, pass through a set of glass doors into what seems to be a waiting room. One wall is glass; the rest are pale wood. The floor is polished concrete. I catch reflections of myself all over, and I don't recognize the tall, suited man as me.

"He's ready for you." The woman gestures toward a

cracked door in one of the wooden walls. "And I'll be in the lobby if you need anything. My name is Ms. Lim."

"Thank you, ma'am," I reply, and she smiles, like I've said something funny. Then she's pushing her way through the glass doors, and I'm left alone to enter Mark Trevena's office for my interview.

I smooth my jacket, take a breath. My father would hate my being here, but he's on his honeymoon and can't stop me. My mother would have hated it too if she were still alive—before she died, she'd been a respectable suburbanite with a city council seat and plenty of pet causes she volunteered for. No way would she have wanted her son tarnishing his important medals with something as tawdry as working for the owner of a kink club.

I don't know how I feel about it either, honestly. When the email came from Mark a few days ago, inviting me to interview for the position of his new bodyguard, I nearly deleted it. I didn't know much about him other than what my father had told me, that he was a murderer and a liar and a deviant on top of it. Not to mention that even the idea of a kink club made me feel like I couldn't breathe.

But I didn't delete it.

I reread it. I wandered around my father's empty farmhouse much as I had wandered around it for the past few weeks—aimless, hungry, a shadow—and I wondered how many more aimless weeks were ahead of me. I couldn't stand to be in the army anymore—not deployed, not behind a desk, not somewhere in between—but the shapelessness of civilian life was a slow-dawning horror. Not since before West Point had there been days upon days of nothing, with no routine, no discipline, no structure.

I needed…something. And something more than a *job*. Something more than hours of boredom followed by slack, empty nothing at the end of the day. Something more than a compressed vessel of civilian life with its small horrors and even smaller stakes. I needed something that would swallow up my time and my thoughts, keep me busy, give shape to my now shapeless life.

And everything in Mark's direct email promised that. Long hours, little autonomy. I'd be a shadow with a gun.

I decided to take the interview. I could always say no after, and I probably would. I didn't care much for men like Mark, men who killed without facing their enemies. Agent. Spy. Assassin. There were soldiers who cheered them on, soldiers who *became* them even, but I couldn't respect anyone who killed without a fair fight, who deceived to get what they wanted, even if what they wanted was to serve the same country I served.

Where was the loyalty in that? How could you trust the fidelity or allegiance of someone without integrity, decency?

But also…what did it matter now?

I knew from my father that Mark had been out of the CIA for years; I knew from online gossip that Lyonesse was a BDSM club of sorts. He'd moved from death to sex, and Lyonesse was his. If he was going to be loyal to anything, it would be this world of his own making, and I could understand that. Maybe even trust that.

Still undecided, I walk through the door of his office, which is nestled proudly at the building's prow. Sunlight lights the space—glass; concrete; pale, pale wood—along with two chairs and a large glass desk. The chair behind the desk is empty, the entire office is empty, and I hesitate for a moment, unsure if I should wait here or go find Ms. Lim again.

But upon a closer inspection of the room, I see a cracked door in the wall behind me and a hallway beyond. Deciding that I have little to lose by walking through it, I push it all the way open and step inside.

If I expected another, more interior office, I'm quickly

enlightened—the doorways I pass seem to lead to suites of rooms. I see glimpses of wood floors and low-slung sofas, bookshelves. Maybe Mark lives here. Or wants people to think he lives here.

But it's the door at the end of the hall that catches my attention. It's held open without a prop, like it's designed to stay open when needed. Stairs lead up to a glowing well of early spring sunshine. I take them and emerge onto the roof. There's a shimmering pool at one end, and at another, there's a large sunshade stretched over a table with two chairs. Underneath it sits Mark Trevena, my new uncle-in-law and my potential employer.

He stands up as I approach and extends a hand for me to shake.

"Tristan, good to see you again," he greets me, his voice cool.

"Likewise, sir," I say as I take his hand. His grip is strong enough that my nerve endings spark, and a strange heat lingers after he lets go. The breeze moves over the roof just then, and I can smell—

Clean skin and—

Rain, maybe. Fresh rain with thunder in the air.

The scent hits me harder even than Ms. Lim's latex and silk, than the cake at the wedding. It's so subtle…and yet…

I try to shake it off as Mark gestures for me to sit and then returns to his chair with an easy, muscular grace, but it becomes harder, not easier, to keep my mind on business as I'm able to get a good look at him.

He is everything that I missed while deployed.

His suit, a casual blue, is tailored so perfectly that I can see the suggestion of powerful shoulders and biceps, the narrow taper of his waist. His tie is a silk that gleams softly, expensively, while his shirt is a creamy white that begs for someone to touch it. A large watch, the kind that would reflect light and get you killed on a mission, glints from underneath his jacket sleeve. Even the way he picks up a rocks glass of something cold and clear—it speaks of time. Luxury. Sensuous enjoyment.

And his face...

I look down for a moment, at the table setting laid out and waiting for me on this rooftop, almost incredulous with myself. I've seen him before, at the wedding; I already knew about the dark blond hair and the jaw dusted with the same tarnished gold. The blue eyes and straight, thick brows and strong nose with a subtle bump, like it's been broken before.

His mouth is shockingly full but also geometrically drawn. Hypnotic.

I'm grateful when someone approaches us, a slim young man in black trousers and a corset, his red hair pulled into a ponytail. He sets down salads before us both, leaves us with goblets of water, and asks if I'd like anything stronger. I refuse. Mark gestures for another of whatever he's drinking, and the young man gives a graceful nod.

I pick up a fork on instinct—a soldier eats when he can—and pause. The salad is like nothing I've ever seen before, a green-and-purple-and-yellow creation designed to look like a butterfly's wings. The dressing is painted in delicate lines to make antennae along the top. Chopped chives are scattered in arcs, as if emulating the wafts of air coming from beating wings.

There's no need to have a salad this beautiful, this eerily lifelike, and when I look up, I have a moment when reality feels subtly *un*real.

This is a job interview at a sex club, with a man known to be a killer. Everything about this should have been tawdry, cheap, and gritty. Instead, I'm sitting atop a glass bower, the low slung view of the capitol in front of me, the river all around, with a salad that is somehow more finely worked than a piece of jewelry. And the man in front of me...

It's a mistake to look at him again. At the wedding, he'd been a figure in the shadows, only in the light once, to walk his older sister down the aisle to my father. I'd been my father's best man, watching his new bride with whatever hope I was capable of mustering these days. It had been a good thing, that wedding. But I'd no longer felt good things the way I should anymore, and the moment I caught sight of Mark in his tux, his strong, tan neck above the crisp lines of his collar and bow tie, his long lashes framing eyes the color of night, I'd looked away until Blanche was in front of my father and Mark was gone.

I can't look away now. This is an interview, and I need to focus.

I just—wish I couldn't smell that rain scent of him. I wish the salad weren't so beautiful. I wish my impression of this place weren't now tied to light, water, air. It will make it harder to say no later if I want.

"I promise it's not too pretty to eat," says Mark.

I finally drag my eyes to his. The sunlight makes no secret of his strong features or the small things that mar them. The barely there gold stubble, the broken flare at the bridge of his nose. A thin scar disappearing into his hair.

"I didn't realize there'd be food," I say, trying to claw back a sense of normalcy. It's strange that I should be unsettled by a man, a pretty salad, a far view.

It's the years in scratchy canvas and cold, foreign mud that have ruined me.

"I thought this was an interview. Sir."

"You can learn a lot about someone from the way they eat," observes Mark as he lifts his own fork. With the side of a silver tine, he presses into one of the butterfly wings until there's the crisp sound of it breaking in half. Something bright red oozes out. A sauce made with beets, I think. "Something I learned as a soldier."

"You were a soldier?" This surprises me. My father had talked about Mark like Mark had sprung from the low-piled carpet of Langley fully formed. I know that sometimes soldiers are recruited into the CIA's paramilitary arm, but it hadn't occurred to me that Mark might have been one of them once upon a time.

"I was."

"And what were you after that?" I think I'm asking to make a point, or to separate us maybe. Make it clear that we are not the same.

Mark's mouth moves as if he can guess what I'm thinking. It's almost like a smile. "Something worse."

It's the honesty that unnerves me. And him, he unnerves me. Sitting across from him is like walking through the trees in Carpathia, my rifle at the ready.

I look down at my plate for something to do and grab my fork. The butterfly wing crunches as I cut into it. I take a bite and bright flavor explodes on my tongue. The salad is crisp, tender, well dressed. The edible flowers mixed in are sweet.

I look up to see Mark watching me.

"I told you," he says. He sounds satisfied.

"It's very good," I admit.

"Tell me about your duties in the army," Mark says. He leans back to take a drink, his eyes never leaving my face. He's watching me chew and swallow. I swipe a knuckle over my lower lip.

It suddenly feels like something more charged than a job interview, but I can't say why. His face is neutral, his voice contained, polite.

But it *is* an interview. I have to answer, and so I do. I outline my four deployments as objectively as I can, their locations, their purposes. I don't talk about the ARCOM from the second deployment or the Bronze Star that they've nominated me for from the last. Surely Mark knows all that. And anyway, it doesn't mean I'm better at a job.

It just means I lived while others died.

Our salads are replaced with charred duck breast and pickled celeriac. Crescents of pureed parsnips and potatoes, creamy and tender. It's the best food I've ever eaten, and it's on top of a glass palace built on debauchery. Maybe anything tastes good after so many months of DFAC food, of MREs in a grubby outpost, but I don't think that's it.

Mark sips his drink as I finish telling him about my duties and assignments. He's on his third and is remarkably steady. I get the sense that he must drink often, and I log that away for the conditional future. *If* I take this job, I'll need to know his habits, his mental state. It's easier to keep sober men alive—something I learned the hard way while on diplomatic escort duty.

After I stop talking and set down my fork, Mark assesses me. And then he sets down his drink.

"I'll be brief. You are the only candidate. I need a new primary bodyguard, someone who can be with me almost constantly. There will be relief shifts, of course, and time off, but not as much as would be ideal. It will necessitate travel and living proximate to me."

The server comes and removes our plates, but instead of presenting us with dessert, he sets a slim leather folio in front of me, and then hands a thicker one to Mark. A pen comes with mine. Expensive, gleaming, nothing like the pens I carried with me on deployment, which were cheap and plastic and came in boxes of twenty.

I open the folio as Mark speaks.

"This is a nondisclosure agreement before our

14

conversation goes any further. It's not an agreement to anything other than your silence; you'll see the usual niceties there."

Niceties. It is five pages of thinly veiled legal threats. On the other hand, being in the United States military has inured me to threats. When the stakes are being court-martialed, you get good at keeping your mouth shut as a matter of course.

I uncap the pen and sign, watching the ink bleed into the paper.

"Wonderful," says Mark. He takes the folio from me, hands it to the server without looking at him. The thicker portfolio takes its place. I open it up and then I cough.

I'm greeted with words like *anal hook* and *cock and ball torture.*

I look up to Mark, who returns my gaze with a mild one of his own.

"I see why you had me sign the NDA first."

"Surely, you're not shocked by what happens in a kink club," says Mark. "But either way, it's best you acquaint yourself with the possibilities before you take this job. Being on my security team means you'll be inside Lyonesse and my own…habits. I'll need to know what limits you have when it comes to witnessing kink. I'll also need to know how much flexibility there is to those limits. I cannot always predict, for example, what might be happening in the private rooms when we walk down a hallway. What you might hear or see through the windows. What might be happening in the booths around the dance floor."

"And your…habits? Sir?"

"You would be my personal bodyguard," says Mark, as if the problem is obvious. "There would be no one closer to me."

"Do you really need this?" I ask. I look around us at

the rooftop, the serene blue sky, the corseted server coming toward us with plates of something colorful and sweet looking. "This place is for sex, right? Why would you be in any danger running a place for people to have sex?"

Mark's jaw moves the tiniest bit, like he's pressed his tongue to the roof of his mouth while he thinks about answering. Then he says, "Kink and sex aren't always the same thing, firstly. Secondly, I think you must have a very charmed view on sex if you think the mere presence of it precludes danger. And thirdly, Lyonesse is in rather a special situation. We invite only the famous and the powerful to be members, and we take their membership payments only in information."

It takes me a minute to understand. When I do, I feel something between disgust and admiration. "Payment in information. And then you use it for what? Blackmail?"

Mark lifts his drink as the server sets the desserts down. I don't take up my spoon just yet, watching Mark swirl the ice in his glass once and then take a practiced swallow. The server leaves, and Mark swirls his glass again.

"Yes, blackmail," he answers. "Sometimes."

"Sometimes."

"Blackmail is an axe. No matter how sharp the blade, you can't expect it to work as delicately as a scalpel. There are much better uses for my information than cracking apart logs."

"But axes and scalpels alike can make enemies, sir."

"Just so."

I pick up the folio. "I'll need time to think about it."

"You have a week," says Mark. He hasn't touched his dessert yet either. "I want it to be you, but I can't wait much longer than that. To my regret."

I nod and stand. He stands as well and shakes my hand again, and once again, sparks spray up my nerve endings at his touch. *Touch-starved*—that's what the combat stress counselor said after my last mandated session. *Skin hunger.* She recommended hugging my dad, getting a pet, and downloading a dating app. I dismissed all three at the time, but if I'm having to catch my breath after a handshake, then maybe it's necessary.

"I'll let you know, sir," I say, and then I walk down through the glass fortress of Lyonesse with the folio under my arm and my mind replaying the crunch of his fork against the butterfly's wings over and over again.

Chapter 2

I'm aware of two things as I flip through the portfolio that night, beer in hand, my father's empty Virginia farmhouse creaking and sighing around me.

The first is that this job should be everything I hate. I hate lying, thieving, manipulation—and Mark doesn't even do that for our country anymore; he does it for *himself*. That's greed; that's selfishness. And that's even on top of how Mark makes a living, which is with his kingdom of vice.

I flip through page after page of acts of sex and pain and humiliation, having to Google half the things I come across, even with the helpful descriptions printed after each term. I know nothing about this world; I barely know anything about sex that hasn't come from porn. Porn that apparently was limited in scope if I'm having to research this much.

I'm a walking punch line: a twenty-nine-year-old combat veteran who's also a virgin. And I'm going to shadow someone who's made a living out of screwing?

But the second thing is wholly and incontrovertibly

this: I can't live another day as Tristan Thomas, unemployed former soldier.

I can't stay in my father's farmhouse, even though I know he'd let me, since he's moved in with Blanche in the city. I can't spend my hours trying to read, trying to watch TV, driving around the not-quite-suburban, not-quite-country roads instead. Running until my lungs feel like they're made of broken glass. Jerking off with my teeth clenched together as if I'm still afraid of waking my teammates.

I have to *do* something.

Or rather—God help the soldier left in me—someone has to *tell* me to do something.

It only takes me until midnight to email and accept the job. I don't bother countering the salary or benefits—after the army, they both look embarrassingly good to me. Probably to make up for the meager time off, but I don't care. I don't want time off.

After I send the email, I take a shower and go to bed in my teenage bedroom, which still smells faintly of cheap cologne and deflated basketballs. I fall asleep to a cold wind blowing against the old house, dreaming instead of wind against new tents. Of a long convoy, a coffee-stained paper map. Bullets spraying through ferns and, just once, through a carotid artery.

Dream me already knows they'll write up a citation for that bullet, nominate me for something. They'll say I'm a hero; they'll talk about courage and valor like they're lucid, uncomplicated things.

But dream me knows it'll be a lie, just as I know it's a lie every moment that I'm awake.

There's nothing simple about killing. Not ever, but especially when they want to give you a medal for killing your best friend.

———

The next Monday, I'm back at Lyonesse. Ms. Lim, wearing no collar this time but instead a set of keys at her narrow waist, takes me behind the desk to a hallway. To my validation, it does indeed lead to a security room, albeit one much bigger than I imagined.

She leaves me with a giant of a man named Goran, who has deep gold-tan skin, black hair buzzed short, and a tattoo of an insignia featuring a grim reaper on the back of his neck, peeking above the collar of his suit jacket. Before he turns to greet me, I catch the lettering around the edges of the insignia—First Battalion, Ninth Marines. The Walking Dead.

"Hello, new guy," he says cheerfully. He's older than me by a couple of decades, with plenty of lines around his eyes and a starburst scar on the side of his mouth. He has a broad face with a lantern jaw, and a dark, twinkling gaze. He looks like the kind of guy whose laughter fills a bar—also the kind of guy a bartender looks to for help with an unruly patron. But I don't miss the quick, efficient flick of his gaze over the wall of screens in front of him. A former 1/9 like him would be more than a gentle giant. And Mark doesn't strike me as the kind of employer to hire someone for their genial personality alone.

"I'm Tristan Thomas, sir," I say, taking his offered hand and then sitting in the chair next to him. "Ms. Lim said you'd be showing me around today?"

"Kink club orientation, right, right," Goran says, reaching for a sheaf of papers. "We have a bit of an unusual situation with your position."

"A bit of one?" I ask as I accept the papers and then a pen. I use the long desk in front of the security screens to start flipping through everything. My employment contract. Another NDA. A direct deposit form. "Everything in this place is unusual."

Goran laughs, and I'm right, it's a sound that fills a room.

It almost makes me smile, it's that nice to hear. "Damn right it is, but you'll like it. You just got back from Carpathia, right? Well, the food is better, and the view too. Plus you'll never meet a more unhinged son of a bitch than Mark Trevena—never a boring day with him around."

"Right," I say. I start signing my way through the papers without giving them more than a cursory once-over. Like I said, the military has ruined me for signing my life away.

"But your position is unusual even for here. See, I'm the head of Lyonesse's security, but as his personal bodyguard, you'll report to Mr. Trevena directly. Or put another way, he's your boss but come to me with all the boring shit, and I'll handle it."

"Got it. Are there other people on Lyonesse's security team?"

Goran leans back in his chair. "There's ten of us—eleven including you—and then an outside team we contract with for larger events. Since Mr. Trevena's primary residence is here, the team is available for your relief shifts whenever Mr. Trevena is in DC. But when he travels, you'll be on call twenty-four-seven. All done already? You don't waste too much time reading the fine print, huh?"

I slide the papers his way, pen placed neatly on top. "Nothing's worse than where I've been." I mean it in a gallows humor sort of way, like *ha-ha, isn't it funny that I spent the last eight years of my life getting yelled at, shot at, getting scared and scorned and was somehow still lonely even around sixty other people?* but Goran's face goes still when I say it.

"Yeah," he says, and something in his voice makes me wonder if he was in Carpathia back when President Colchester was there, when the war was still a *war* and not a *conflict*.

The Walking Dead re-earned their nickname several times over in Carpathia—highest killed-in-action ratio of any marine battalion. And for a minute, the difference between marine and soldier disappears, and we're just two men hiding scars on the insides of our thoughts, scars in the shape of mountains and forests and too-empty villages.

"Yeah," he says again, heavily, and then stands. "Come on. We'll find someone to man the cameras, and then I'll take you for the nickel tour before I give you to the boss."

———

I'm given a laptop, earpiece, gun, and harness. Then I meet two of the other security team members and get acquainted with the shift rotations—skeleton crew during the day, with increasing shift coverage toward the evening. The club is busiest from dinner till two or three in the morning; Fridays and Saturdays are the busiest of them all, with members drinking, fucking, and making use of private rooms until dawn. I get the impression that Goran runs an amiable but tight ship, and the two team members I meet seem to respect him immensely.

On an upper floor, we stop by some glass-walled offices and meet the club's manager, Dinah—a slender woman with dark, jewel-toned skin, undercut purple curls, and a cell phone that won't stop chiming with club business as we make introductions— and Sedge, a fair and freckled young man with nearly colorless eyes, who's Mark's administrative assistant. We also meet a pale woman with a wary expression and dark hair in waves over her shoulders. Andrea, the club's treasurer. I don't know if she is the treasurer of the club's money or of its hoard of information. I wonder if she helps Mark with his sometimes-blackmail.

She doesn't seem to like me.

But Goran's cheerfulness bulldozes through any awkwardness, and then we're touring the building: the large open hall in the center, ringed with balconies and with a stage at the front; the private rooms, furnished in the most luxurious depravity and outfitted with panic buttons and cameras for the safety of guests and club employees alike; the decadent, speakeasy-style bar on the second-highest floor.

"They'll tell you in some corporate bullshit seminar that you can only have one priority," Goran says as we take the elevators down past the ground floor and to a subfloor. "But you're better than that, so I can tell you that we have two priorities here at Lyonesse. The first is to keep everyone here safe—guests and employees. The second is to keep this floor locked down at all fucking costs."

The elevator doors open not to a dank concrete corridor but to a spacious vestibule lit with blue lights. Glass double doors are opposite our elevator doors, and beyond them, I see a second set. I also see a thumbprint scanner, a retina scanner, and a surfeit of cameras.

I don't need Goran to tell me what's down here. "The information."

"Membership dues," Goran says, sounding pleased at my deduction. "Servers are down here. All sorts of fancy stuff to keep them cool and air-gapped and whatever else. We don't need to know all the tech shit, but it's our job to make sure no one comes down here except Mr. Trevena, Dinah, and Andrea. It's rigged up pretty tight against someone trying to get something, but it's not foolproof."

"Rigged up?"

Goran nods at the locks. "Any attempt to open the doors without a valid thumb and retina scan will trigger an alarm. The floor around the servers is built with weight sensors—if there's any kind of unauthorized approach to the machines, the room responds by sealing itself off with aluminum shutters, and the servers will power down. Nothing online and no way out until we let you out."

"And that's not foolproof?"

He scratches his neck. "There's a lot of machinery to shut down, and it has to go offline in the right way so nothing is corrupted, or something—I don't know. The upshot is that someone conceivably could have nearly a full minute to connect with the servers and try to get something."

"But then they'd still be locked in the room."

"Yeah. Unless they rolled out from under the doors before they came all the way down—but you have less than sixty seconds from triggering the sensor to the room being sealed off. So it's unlikely someone could get what they wanted and then make it back out in time, but unlikely isn't impossible, and we'd do well not to forget that."

I look through the two sets of doors again, able to make out a larger room beyond, lit with more blue light. I wonder what kind of information people surrender when they come—and if it's worth it, knowing someone has the potential to blackmail you at a moment's notice.

As if knowing where my thoughts are, Goran says, "It doesn't have to be information about yourself, you know."

I glance back at him, confused. "What else would people give, sir?"

"Oh, my sweet army puppy," Goran laughs. "Information about *other* people, of course. Or information they've gotten from whatever jobs or positions they have. We have a Moldovan diplomat here, for example—he's not telling Mr. Trevena about the time he cheated on his college girlfriend. He's telling Mr. Trevena about arms deals. New mercenary groups. Cabinet members who sympathize with the continuing rebellion in Carpathia. That sort of thing."

I look back at the server room with a new respect...and a new wariness. When Mark and I spoke of blackmail the other day, I suppose I had been thinking of all the shallow and tawdry peccadilloes that people would be desperate to buy silence for. Not state secrets. Not whispers of martial movements, governmental shifts, and all the other tesserae that come together to form a mosaic of a world still dragging itself back from the edge of war.

"Now," Goran says, shepherding me back to the elevator. "Let's see your new digs."

Part of my employment offer is to live here at the club, and it's something I've accepted, since commuting in from the farmhouse would be a pain in the ass, and this place comes rent free. Mark is paying me enough that I could afford a decent apartment nearby, but it seems like a waste to pay for a home I'll barely be in.

And when I see my apartment on the third floor, I know I've made the right decision. It's in the prow of the building like his office above me, with glass walls overlooking the river, a small but expensive kitchen, and equally expensive furnishings. I walk over to one of the glass walls while Goran explains parking and a few other details to me. The prow doesn't face the city, but the Potomac itself, pointed like a ship about to sail to sea. For a minute, I imagine it is, that the whole building is moving to the open ocean, spreading massive sails above it.

"...and he'll be expecting you in his office within the hour. I expect you'll go over his rules and requirements then and what he'll need from you."

I nod, my eyes still on the place where river meets sky, thinking of Chesapeake Bay and the Atlantic beyond.

"...and you should know that no one will think any differently of you. You can't work at a place like this and not have it change the way you think about things, and if any one of us were in your shoes, we would probably end up doing it too. Mark has that way about him, and this place has a way about it too, gets into your bones. Makes you want things you thought you would never." A pause and then a cheerful: "And his last bodyguard never seemed anything but over the moon with the arrangement."

I turn away from the view and stare at the former marine, utterly lost. "Pardon, sir?"

Goran's eyebrows lift and then his mouth slowly closes as his hands come up. He's the picture of someone saying *oh shit, never mind.* "You know what, I shouldn't have said anything," he says, seeming to fumble a little. "It's nothing. You'll hash all that out, I'm sure. Or not. Either way, none of my business."

I open my mouth to tell him to stop, to explain himself, but he's already beating a hasty goodbye, surprisingly brisk for such a large man.

Mark has that way about him.

Makes you want things you thought you would never.

Maybe Goran just means working here in general. Here, where the mundane is made of blindfolds and ropes and the extraordinary is kept locked away below the waterline, trapped behind two sets of glass doors.

With a final look around my new home, I make to go upstairs to Mark. To the start of my new life as his shadow.

CHAPTER 3

"Ah, my new bodyguard," says Mark as I'm let into his office by Ms. Lim.

He's standing up from his chair and his suit jacket is off, thrown over the side of his desk, next to a laptop, a folder, and his seemingly perennial glass of vodka or gin on the rocks. The other day on the roof, I saw his proportions under the immaculate tailoring of his suit, but without the jacket, with only the expensive cotton of his button-up shirt, I can see that he's more than just well shaped. The neat lines of his waist leading into his trousers and the curves of his arms and shoulders are those of a man in his prime. Goran had showed me a gym here—available for all club guests and employees—but strangely, I can't picture Mark in it, fussing over the kinds of muscles that are for show.

He'd be more into running and calisthenics, maybe. Push-ups in the morning, squats and sit-ups after.

I tell myself I'm only noticing because I may need to help scout running routes when we travel. His habits are my business now.

"Good afternoon, sir," I say, coming to stand in front of his desk.

"I take it Goran has taken care of the paperwork and the essentials. He explained the dress code to you?"

"Yes, sir." It isn't much of a dress code—suits in black or gray, an issued firearm, and a leather shoulder harness for wearing said firearm. But there is a stipend for the suits at least.

Mark looks at the suit I'm wearing now, his gaze trailing from the slightly too-short trouser cuffs to the tightness at the shoulders. It's a suit my father bought me after I graduated West Point, saying that a man always needed at least one suit for the occasions he couldn't wear his dress uniform to. It's eight years old now.

"I'll give you the name of the tailor I'd like you to see." He holds up a hand, as if forestalling any protest. "I'll make sure the club covers it. You are mine now, so I'll need you to look the part."

"Yes, sir."

"Those army manners," he says, "they'll fit in well here. Did you meet Sedge?"

"Yes, sir."

"He will email over my schedule each day, along with travel itineraries. I'll try to give you as much notice as I can with travel, so you can make whatever security arrangements you'll need to make, but many of my trips are unexpected, so my promises are cheap. When we're here at the club, most of my meetings will be here in my office—and for most of those, you will be asked to wait outside, as a show of privacy and discretion for my members."

I nod.

"In the evenings," Mark says, taking his jacket off the desk and shrugging it on, "if I'm not traveling or having dinner in the city, I'll generally eat in the club and then make my presence known after. I'll take meetings there too, more informally. Unless I'm in a private room or unless I explicitly dismiss you, I'll expect you to be close."

He tugs at the cuffs of his jacket sleeves with crisp efficiency. I see that silver watch again and think of how it would glitter through the trees or from the window of an abandoned building. I was able to return fire at someone in a dark alley once because they were wearing a watch just like that.

How strange life is now, that wearing something that can reflect light feels unbearably and ostentatiously reckless.

Mark's hand drops to the folder on his desk, his fingertips skimming the front. "You emailed over your consent to what you might witness at the club and your limits."

My eyes drop to the folder. He gave me the folio filled with terms and explanations. He sees stuff every day I can't even imagine; what's more, he *facilitates* it. It should not feel like such a private thing to share, what I can withstand watching in a professional setting.

"No waterworks or scat," says Mark, not flipping open the folder, as if he already has the salient points of its contents memorized. "That's quite all right, as we don't do that here at Lyonesse. You seem comfortable potentially witnessing everything else, which I'd expect from someone with your record overseas. Watching someone happily being caned is certainly better than watching someone's fingers get blown off because they lit a cigarette after dusk. Although…"

I know what's coming. When I'd walked in, I'd automatically shifted into a parade rest position, my feet planted and my hands behind my back, and now I feel the tiniest impulse to fidget, to rub my thumbs together. I resist.

"You've annotated *wax play* here," continues Mark. "Not as a hard limit but as something you would find hard to watch."

His blue eyes lift to mine, and I feel the penetrating force of his gaze.

"Normally, I wouldn't interrogate someone on limits, but we're in a special circumstance and wax play is exceptionally common. And"—a small tilt of his head—"rather initiatory-level stuff when it comes to kink. So I admit I'm curious. And for work purposes, I do need to know if this is a mild aversion or if it's something more painful than that."

"No," I say before I can think about how I want to phrase my explanation. "Not painful. And not an...aversion."

And then I flush. Embarrassingly, humiliatingly.

I'm twenty-nine and I'm hot-cheeked about wax.

A beat passes as Mark studies me. "I see," he says. "And so the other thing you've marked here—*breeding kinks*—"

I have to look down at the floor. "Also not an aversion," I manage to say. My jaw is tight, my face is on fire. "I just wanted to tag that I might struggle to stay professional if we were watching something. Like that."

I hear footsteps; when I'm able to force my eyes up, Mark is in front of me. He's shaved since I saw him last, and his face without stubble is like something from a magazine. Too handsome, too striking, too entrancing to be hidden under a helmet and protective eyewear. No wonder the CIA poached him and sent him out to woo and lie and kill.

"Breeding," he murmurs. The word on his lips is sinful.

"Sir."

"Is it about pregnancy? Procreation?"

I want to die. "It's not about pregnancy." I have to dredge the words out of my chest. It's the first time I've ever spoken about this. Ever. "I like...I like the closeness," I add with some difficulty. "The idea of leaving part of yourself inside someone."

"So it's about the fluid itself. Like a creampie kink."

"Yes, but—" I'm struggling. It's so much easier to type

breeding into a porn site and let the search engine do the work than frame this in words spoken out loud. In front of my boss. "It's more than that. More than unprotected sex."

It's the ownership, the claiming. The idea of being used...or using someone myself.

"It's not about actually making babies," I repeat, just so to make it extremely clear. "I, um. The breeding kink is for me too. Not just for what I'd like to do to someone else."

Mark's expression doesn't change, but his pupils do. They bloom.

"Good to know," he says after a minute. "In that case, rest assured that I don't expect you to be made of stone when it comes to the things that happen at Lyonesse. In fact, I'd be rather disappointed if you were."

"Sir," I say. It takes more willpower than I'm proud of to hold that sharp, perceptive gaze.

The corner of his mouth indents. "Well, with that settled, I have a meeting in the city. You may as well come and begin getting acquainted with the little chores that make up my day."

CHAPTER 4

"THEY WILL BE CURIOUS ABOUT YOU," MARK SAYS LATER THAT night as we take the elevator up to the central hall of the club.

"Who?"

"Everyone" is the reply as the elevator comes to a stop and the doors open.

I'm doubtful as I follow Mark down a glass-walled corridor. After spending the day in the back seat of a car and standing outside two different doors—one of them at an office for a company that sells weighted blankets of all things—I'm already settling into being a silent, nearly inanimate shadow, and I find the idea of being the subject of anyone's curiosity faintly ludicrous.

I suppose if they knew who my father is, there might be the tiniest flicker of interest—at least for any DC natives familiar with the higher-ups in the American military. Or perhaps for international guests who might look to leverage such a connection.

Even though he can't see my frown, Mark seems to know which way my thoughts are tending and says over his shoulder, "I suppose I should have asked this earlier, but would you like to work here under a pseudonym? On account of your father?"

I think a moment. "No, sir."

I'm not famous, and in the world of generals, my father barely ranks as anyone of note. And if Mark can stride around his club with everyone knowing he used to work for the CIA and that his twin sister currently does—well, I can handle the tiny chance that someone might connect Tristan Thomas to General Ricker Thomas.

"As you wish," Mark replies, and then we walk through a secure door to the titanic central hall at the heart of the club. The ceiling, a few stories above, is a pitched tent of glass and steel. During the day, it gave the space the feeling of a cathedral. At night, it's a canopy of purple-streaked clouds and whichever stars are bright enough to burn through the city's glow. It stretches over the space as if to say, *yes, night children, the time for sinning is now.*

And sinning they are, dancing, drinking, probably more, judging from the amount of skin I see. I flick my eyes quickly over the crowd on the floor, seeing nothing dangerous, and then return my attention to the balconies. Above us are two more and then a floor with windows overlooking the space—the upper story of the club, where Mark lives. Our own balcony is made up of nooks, some filled with chairs and some with leather-upholstered booths.

I follow Mark to the largest one, in the center of the balcony, with an unobstructed view of the stage and a black leather armchair surrounded by other armless chairs. By some sort of architectural genius, the nook is not nearly as loud as the hall itself. When I take my place at the back, several paces behind Mark's armchair, I can hear Goran's genial tones in my earpiece clear as day.

"Well, kid? What do you think?"

"It's busy, sir," I say, using our new stationary position to more carefully take in the room and the club's guests.

"Yeah, and it's only a Tuesday. Just wait until the weekend."

"I can't imagine."

I really can't. The place seems full to bursting now. It must be a zoo then. A nightmare to continually assess risk in. I think of the parades and rallies I had to work in Carpathia while doing diplomatic escorts, and anxiety flicks hotly across the skin of my nape.

"Don't worry about it," replies Goran easily. "Club duty will be a piece of cake because no one is suicidal enough to take on Mark Trevena on his home turf. It's mostly just reminding the people wasting his time that he's invulnerable."

"Wasting his time?"

"You'll see," Goran says, and then the line clicks off.

Dinah, the club manager, joins us soon after, wearing not the tailored pantsuit I saw her in earlier but a strapless leather jumpsuit, tight and corseted, baring her gleaming shoulders. When she sits next to Mark, I hear Mark say, "Well?"

"He's mollified for now," Dinah says. With the nook the way that it is, I can hear them easily, even while standing behind them. "But we need to tread carefully. If he's recognized…"

"I'm aware of what he's risking. We've given him every allowance Lyonesse can offer. Does he think he needs more privacy than the president of the United States?"

The president of the United States… I'm glad no one is looking at me just now because I'm certain my expression is betraying my shock. I think about how long Lyonesse has been open, and then I have to wonder which president came here—the late President Maxen Colchester, who died in a Carpathian terrorist attack two years ago, or the current president, Embry Moore, who married Colchester's widow.

From behind them, I can only see Dinah's arm lift as if in a shrug. "He seems to think so."

Their conversation is cut short when they're joined by three more people—Andrea the treasurer, still wearing what she was wearing earlier today, and a suited man I don't recognize with dark olive skin and long, dark hair leading a shirtless man on a leash. He sits next to Mark, greeting the others, while the leashed man sinks to a graceful kneeling position next to his chair.

I blink a moment. There is plenty of fetish clothing on the dance floor tonight—and a nonzero amount of nudity—but this is the first time I've seen someone explicitly...submitting. Even after all the research I had to do to get through Mark's consent forms, it's jarring to see a grown adult, a man tall and layered with muscle, allowing himself to be led around like a dog.

After eight years in the army, and the four before it at West Point, the very idea is taboo. Strength and pride—they run as rigid through my concept of masculinity as wrought iron, as sharp as barbed wire.

And yet I think of the army. Of standing at attention, of marching in straight lines. Of the sweet relief of being told where to go and what to do there, even if it was only dropping to the ground and busting out push-ups until our arms gave out.

I shake it off.

It's entirely different.

But as Goran's predicted time-wasters begin coming to the nook, I find my eyes returning to the kneeling man over and over again. To the broad frame held in perfect docility, the muscled limbs quiescent, his head bowed with long hair covering his face like a curtain. He's larger than the man who leashed him; he could easily stand up and wrench the handle of the leash from his partner's hand. But he never does. There's no tension in his frame, no stiffness in his shoulders as his partner reaches over to stroke his head. On

35

the contrary, the minute he does, the kneeling man melts pliantly into him. If he were a cat, he'd be purring.

Watching it makes me feel… It's the wrongness—it's the wrongness of it that's making me restless inside my own skin; it's the transgression. This isn't the mutual exchange of bodies, not the slow and tender reciprocity I know is good and healthy to want. This is *control*.

This is shame.

And why is this man letting it happen? Rubbing his face against his Dominant's leg, tilting his face up for the idle kisses dropped there?

I ignore the hook in my stomach, try to ignore them. The person sitting across from Mark at the moment wants a new private room, and Dinah and Andrea are listening intently. From what I can see of Mark's sprawled legs and tapping fingers on the chair, he is not.

Next, there's someone who's furious that their ex-wife is still a member of the club. After them is someone who'd like to do a vampire glove demonstration next month, and then after that is someone whose appointment is spent bitching about the space exploration bill about to pass Congress, as if NASA funding were under Mark's control.

Mark's legs are spread and his head is tilted to the side for all of it, the picture of someone in the throes of professional boredom. I can't see his face, but I can imagine the inscrutable expression on it. The one that gives nothing, promises nothing, and yet still makes you try for more.

Only one visitor does Mark straighten up for, a woman with creamy skin and blond hair waved over one eye. She looks to be in her early forties, with a thin but lovely mouth and cinnamon-colored eyes. Lady Anguish was what Mark called her when she first sat across from him, a nom de kink as it were. And even with the scant knowledge of BDSM that I have, I know she is a Dominant. I can see it in her posture, the assured way she speaks without raising her voice or leaning forward, trusting that everyone else will come to her to be heard.

She wants to invest in Lyonesse, wants a share of ownership in exchange for helping the club expand to Los Angeles and London. She makes a good case, and Mark listens attentively, nodding and asking her questions, and then finally promising her a meeting later in the month.

After she leaves, Dinah says, "That was a mistake."

Mark leans back in his chair. "You think so?"

"I know so. You can't possibly be thinking of splitting ownership."

"You think I'll open myself up to a takeover."

"With Anguish? Yes, Mark, I do. We barely know her, and the only thing we *do* know is that she's hungry."

Mark's voice is musing when he speaks. "Hunger isn't always a bad thing."

"Speaking of hunger," says the man next to Mark. I gleaned earlier that his name is Arjun, and that the man kneeling next to him is Evander. "Where did you find this wonderful specimen of a bodyguard?"

As one, Arjun, Dinah, and Andrea look back at me. Mark doesn't, and neither does Evander, who remains still and relaxed on his knees.

"My sister's wedding," Mark finally replies, and everyone laughs like this is a joke.

"And will he be available to attend to others?" asks Andrea.

Attend to…

I flush as I take her meaning, and stare straight ahead, trying to pretend like I didn't hear.

"Tristan is here only for me, I'm afraid," Mark replies, crossing his feet at the ankles. "Strictly *look but don't touch* as far as you're concerned." His voice is mild, but there's something firm underneath the mildness. Steely, even.

I stare at the back of his chair. Is it possessiveness? He doesn't want to share me because I'm his? Or is it because he knows that I'm only here as a bodyguard and not to *attend* to anyone?

Out of the corner of my eye, I see Arjun's wide smile. "But not as far as you're concerned, eh, Mark?"

"We all know about Mark and his bodyguards," Andrea says.

There's a knowingness in her cool tone that digs at my control. I keep my eyes ahead, my face neutral. Bodyguards are meant to be invisible, barely there, and I'll be damned if I fail at it my first day here.

I remind myself that I heard far worse before I'd even had my morning coffee in the army—and my fellow soldiers had been a lot more creative and disgusting when it came to sex-themed insults than the people here. Even the good-natured ribbing was enough to strip the paint off a building, much less what came when someone was actually trying to get under your skin.

I can handle people insinuating I'm some sort of... *companion*...for Mark. My job isn't to prove them wrong; it's to keep him safe.

"Never fear, Tristan," my boss says now as he stands up and buttons his suit jacket. "Your virtue will remain intact."

At *that*, I fight a blush. He can't possibly know that I'm still a virgin. He's making a joke, using a turn of phrase.

It means nothing, and even if it did, it's not like... It doesn't change anything.

"Maybe Mark's brought that little blond back to him," Andrea says. There's something pointed in her voice, and Mark doesn't miss it.

"Yes, maybe," he says. There's something equally sharp in his voice now, sharper even, and Andrea looks away. Something about the blond is a point of contention between them. I wonder if the blond is a woman and then shake off the twinge the thought brings. Even if the blond *is* a woman, that doesn't mean Mark only likes women. And anyway, it has nothing to do with me.

"What Mark does with his submissives is his business," Dinah says, and Andrea gives a tight smile.

"I never said otherwise."

"Good night, all," Mark says before this exchange can go any further, and then he looks at me. "Tristan?"

I follow him as he turns and leaves the hall—a hall which has gotten more raucous and indecent as the hours crept by—and survey the people dancing, crawling, writhing in each other's laps as we walk to the doors leading out. It will take some getting used to, assessing a place like Lyonesse for threats rather than a city street or a mountain village, but the challenge is also a little thrilling. Very different kinds of dangers await here.

I think of Arjun's long fingers sifting idly through Evander's hair.

When we get to the elevators, Mark stops. "I can see myself up," he says.

"Yes, sir."

"What did you think of tonight?"

I hesitate. I think Mark is the kind of man who appreciates an honest answer, but I still want to be diplomatic. "It was different," I finally reply.

"Of course," he says with something like a smile. And then, with his eyes a brilliant blue in the light of the glass hallway, he says, "There will be worse than Evander kneeling on the floor, you know."

I don't ask how he knows watching Evander made me uncomfortable. Either he looked at me without me noticing *or* he's guessing and seeing what his words draw out. At any rate, the safest answer seems to be "Yes, sir."

He watches me, and I see an infinitesimal flex in his jaw,

like there's something he wants to say but is deciding against it. "I only ask that you keep an open mind," he says finally. "You strike me as a romantic person. There's romance here too, in letting go. In surrender."

He turns to face the elevators, his profile suntanned and hewn against the blue and black glass of the hallway beyond. "I was in the army too," he adds. "I can guess what you might think about Evander. I can even guess how you might feel if you saw a woman kneeling next to Arjun tonight, looking delicate and helpless."

I haven't thought of that, but the minute he speaks, I feel a wave of protectiveness, of worry for this imaginary woman. It's one thing to read about dominance and submission online, but when it's happening in front of you, when the reality of the coercion is *right there*…

"I promise that no one at Lyonesse, aside from me, needs a knight in shining armor," Mark goes on. "Everyone else is winning a game they've chosen to play, no matter how it might look. Everyone here—whether they're being caned or electrocuted or simply fucked into next week—is here because they want to be." He presses the elevator button and then looks at me. "An open mind, that's all I ask."

"Yes, sir."

The elevator chimes and the doors open. "And, Tristan?"

"Yes?"

"Good work today." Mark smiles and steps into the elevator.

The unexpected praise lights me up.

I'm glowing the entire way back to the farmhouse.

CHAPTER 5

I'M GIVEN A HALF DAY TO MOVE MY THINGS TO MY NEW apartment at Lyonesse—not that I need it. After years of bouncing between deployments and bachelors' quarters, all I've got are a few boxes of clothes, a handful of books, and a service cross I've only taken out of the case once, to wear to my father's wedding. For a moment, I finger a picture from my graduation from West Point, a clump of eight of us, grinning in our grays and whites, slender cadet swords dangling from our waists.

We couldn't wait to graduate, to join our compatriots in Carpathia, to go *make a difference*, whatever that meant. In Carpathia, a new country that had been carved out of the mountains a decade before, no one actually knew what a *difference* looked like or how anyone could tell if they'd made it. Because while peace had been won there once, it had only lasted until a man little better than a dictator came into power. And then after he'd been deposed, the American military had flooded back in to help the Carpathian government hold on to their own country.

We were there to keep the peace, to build infrastructure, to train their new soldiers and airmen—but the enemy wasn't some outside force wearing brightly colored uniforms. They *were* the Carpathians, or rather a minority of them: zealous Carpathians wanting to see their country as the most violent and hostile version of itself. They were willing to kill their neighbors and friends to see it happen.

All of us, in our West Point grays, had been walking into the last place on earth it felt possible to make a difference.

My touch lingers over McKenzie Reed, all flyaway red hair and freckles, who I was too late to save on our first deployment. I'd dragged her and three others to the end of an alley while exchanging fire with unseen enemies at the end of it. She'd died anyway, and if I'd managed to kill any of the fuckers, I never found out because there were no bodies there when we finally had enough soldiers to secure the alley for good.

I got the service cross for that, for the two others I'd saved, even though McKenzie had bled out into a puddle, her green eyes vacant behind her eyewear and her mouth open, like she'd been trying to call our names.

But it's Sims whom my fingertips stop on, Sims whom I look at the longest.

Aaron Sims, who was alive four months ago and isn't anymore.

I close the picture back in the book where I found it, put the book in a plastic tote, and then carry it out to my dad's car. I lock up the farmhouse and give a cursory look around. I've said goodbye to this place so many times that saying goodbye now feels like playing to an empty theater.

I don't look back as I start the traffic-choked drive to the city, two podcast hosts chattering about the proposed space exploration bill as I go.

"Who wouldn't want to see this country enter its second golden age of space-faring?" one host demands.

"Forty-seven senators apparently," the other dryly replies.

———

"Have you told your father about your new job?" asks Mark as his driver, Jago, takes us to a late lunch in Foggy Bottom. It's only Mark and me in the back, Mark sitting with one leg out, his elbow braced against the side of the car. He's the picture of dilatory ease.

I wonder how many glasses of clear liquor he's had so far today.

"I sent him an email," I answer after a minute. It was a short email, only a couple sentences long, because there was no way I could tell my father I took a job being his new brother-in-law's bodyguard without it leading to a *conversation*, and there was no point in giving him more ammunition to work with before the conversation was inevitably sprung on me. It's an Alpha Charlie waiting to happen; I have no illusions about that. I'm just grateful he'll have to wait until he's home from his honeymoon.

"I can't wait to hear from my dear sister's husband about it," Mark says, moving his elbow down.

"I'm sorry, sir," I say.

Apologizing for my father is a reflex by now. He's a good man. He's just very much General Thomas first, everything else second, and it's been a pain in my ass since kindergarten, when he made my favorite teacher cry during parent-teacher conferences.

Mark waves a hand. "You don't have to apologize. Or call me sir. We're family now."

"What else should I call you? Uncle?"

A small, private smile. "Maybe later. Otherwise, call me what you like."

43

"Yes, sir."

He huffs out a laugh as we roll to a stop in front of the restaurant. Familiar with the routine after yesterday, I step out first, do a quick scan of the area, and open Mark's door.

Mark emerges from the car, any traces of the smile on his face gone. His eyes glitter as he straightens and buttons his jacket. He gives me a curt nod, and then I trail him to the restaurant entrance, where we're shown right away to a table, despite him not speaking a word to the host.

I'm a little unsettled by this sudden mood of his, but I tell myself it's nothing to do with me or anything I've done. It's probably something to do with this lunch and who he's meeting.

A banker, Mark said in the car. *Bounces between London and New York. Geoffrey Laurence.*

The name meant nothing to me, and Mark's mouth had quirked.

Don't worry. It's a good thing not to know him.

I'm given a small table behind Mark's, where I can see the entrance to the restaurant and most of the people walking in or out. I can also see Geoffrey Laurence himself, a short, pale man with silvering hair and cleft chin. His suit is the kind of expensive that hides itself in texture and immaculate tailoring rather than flash. Money so established it's ceased to even be aware of itself.

Mark's demeanor stays the same for most of the lunch. I can't hear what he and Geoffrey are saying, but when he speaks, the words seem to be brief and direct. He doesn't gesture when he speaks; he doesn't look away from Geoffrey when he listens. His posture is so effortlessly controlled that even the way he yields his fork has something of a sniper's precision about it. Only once do I catch a scrap of conversation:

You're sure about the safety report?

The information will be leaked next week.
Then I'll see it all sold before then.

I wonder what kind of safety report, what kind of leak Mark could be talking about that would have him so rigid and cold, so utterly different from he was last night at the club, as languorous as a lion after a meal. And then I wonder which Mark is closer to the real one: this contained vessel that gives nothing away or the sprawling lord of the underworld from last night?

And after the lunch has concluded—which is the minute the entree is finished, there's no lingering over clear liquor or dessert today—Mark stands to leave with an expression on his face that's something more than unreadable. It spells danger, maybe, although in a way I can't explain. His eyes aren't narrowed, his mouth isn't set in a snarl or even a hard line. It's just that there's a watchfulness to his expression, a patience.

Patience that should make anyone wary.

But the banker doesn't seem deterred. Either he's used to Mark, or he wants something and wants it badly enough that he doesn't care what the consequences are of him getting it.

I knew people like that in Carpathia. The local politicians looking for clout, the marines looking for glory or at least a good fight, the wholesalers and middlemen swooping into a town the minute supplies got scarce to make deals and scrape the last bit of money out of the civilians there. It would be easy to believe that things ended miserably for them, but that was only true like a third of the time. Maybe Geoffrey Laurence will get what he wants from Mark and never have to discover what's behind that aloof expression.

For Geoffrey's sake, I hope so.

Mark is in a strange mood as we get back in the car and Jago takes off. His fingers are tapping against his knee, and his jaw tightens occasionally as we pass ugly college apartments and bland State Department buildings.

45

"I'm sorry, sir," I say, and then regret saying anything when his dangerous gaze moves to me.

"What for?" he asks.

It's too late to take anything back now without making his mood worse, so I force myself to reply. "For whatever safety report issue has made your afternoon so frustrating."

He looks at me a moment and then looks away. "It wasn't the report that ruined my afternoon, Tristan. Only my company."

The banker? I suppose I could see that—there had been that indefinable air of avarice to him, and while I think Mark thinks fondly of sin, I don't know if he thinks fondly of all sinners.

"I offered him a business deal some years back," he says after a minute. "And I've never forgiven him for his answer."

"He refused?"

"No." Mark's voice is hard. "He agreed."

I have no idea how to interpret this, and I don't get the sense that Mark is welcoming questions about the topic. At any rate, he shifts, sitting up and turning to look over at me.

"What did you hope for when you came back?" he asks.

I'm looking out of the window, but I can still feel the simmer of his gaze on my skin. "Back, sir?"

"Yes, Tristan, back." In my periphery, I see his fingers flex over his knee. "From the war."

"It's not a war anymore," I say automatically. "We were there on a—"

"A coalition counterterrorism mission, yes, I know what they called it in the briefing room, and I know what they still call it. Indulge an old man and let me call it a war."

"You're not old—"

"So what did you hope for? When you were over there, tired and cold and scared shitless or bored to death? There must have been something. Something you held on to and built entire palaces in your mind around. Something you promised yourself you'd have within days of stepping off the plane."

Something I'd hoped for?

I know what I would hope for now, in my right mind, with the horror—however freshly congealed—behind me.

For Sims not to be dead.

For McKenzie not to be dead.

For all of us to graduate from West Point and then decide we wanted to sit behind computer screens somewhere or embed ourselves like pointless burrs somewhere in administration, where our biggest headaches would be paperwork and space heaters that didn't get warm enough.

For me to wake up and once again be the Tristan Thomas everyone used to know, the boy who liked books with dragons and hot summers and honor choir and basketball practices so grueling he couldn't even walk after.

But while I was there? In it?

I think back. I'm sure I wanted a steak dinner at some point. The kind of steak dinner that made your stomach hurt it was so filling, with two different kinds of potatoes and fresh rolls and pie.

I wanted sex, I know that much, although it had been hard to conjure up specifics, since my imagination when it came to sex was blurry and mostly informed by porn. I wanted to nap for hours and hours, nap long enough and hard enough that I made a Tristan-shaped impression in a mattress so soft it barely met the legal requirements for the word *mattress*.

And then I remember.

I remember sitting on a cot once we'd returned from the outpost to the base for the last time. I'd stared at my hands. The hands which had killed Sims and so many other people besides that it no longer mattered how many they'd also saved. Someone had propped an old iPad against a rucksack on a cot, and a few soldiers were watching some movie about driving and crime, and at some point, I looked up and the two characters were kissing in an elevator. Kissing so slowly and tenderly that it felt like a fairy tale kiss even though the movie was the furthest thing from a fairy tale.

I thought of that kiss as I'd gone to bed that night, as I waited for the lengthy, formal debrief the next day. As I sat in a folding chair, the cold metal biting through my uniform jacket, watching the major trying to pretend he wasn't freezing his ass off after being used to the comforts of the permanent base near Uzhorod.

I thought of how lovely that kiss must have felt for those actors, how soft their lips must have been, how tender their mouths. Soft like nothing in my life, tender like something could only be outside of a war, in the real world, in real life. Real life where you didn't kill your best friends.

And I remember thinking that if I could only have a little of that softness, that tenderness, I'd be whole again. I'd be fixed, healed. I knew it.

Touch-starved. Like the counselor had said.

"A kiss," I say softly.

"A kiss?"

I'm too lost in the memories of those last days at the forward operating base—of the shuffle back to Uzhorod, and then to Stuttgart, and then home—to watch my words. To notice how much I'm talking. "I've only been kissed a few times before," I say. "But I remembered how good it could feel. We watched a movie with a kiss one of my last nights at the FOB, and it was all I could think of. How nice it would be to have someone's mouth against mine, their hands on me."

Mark's fingers have gone still. "Who was kissing you in these thoughts? A girl from home?"

"There was no girl from home," I admit. "No boy either. I'm not good at starting things, no matter who the person is. And when someone starts something with me, I—" There are no words for what I do. Even *obsession* doesn't capture the swiftness and intensity with which I can fall in love. And like an infection, my obsession needs only the tiniest cut, the shallowest scrape to take root. A single glance, a kind word as I'm handed a cup of coffee.

I think of it as a kind of curse, one I've had since birth, and the only cure I could think of when I was younger was transferring that curse to an entire country rather than to a person. A country, at least, was big enough to hold an obsession, and the army was more than happy to nurse utter devotion inside my chest.

"I get attached," I say finally.

"You're telling me that a soldier as beautiful as you, as strong and stupidly noble as you, can't find someone to kiss because you *get attached*."

I become aware that his attention is still fixed on me. And the word he used—*beautiful*—feels stuck and quivering in the ground like an arrow at my feet. He called me beautiful.

"It's a problem," I answer distractedly, my mind on that arrow of a word. *Beautiful.*

"I find that hard to believe," he says. "Who wouldn't want you to get attached to them?"

He says it so casually, so mildly, that I know he doesn't understand. Falling in love at the smallest provocation…no, most people don't want that. In fact, nobody I've ever met. It's smothering. Cloying. I can be those things and often was in high school.

And I feel a little embarrassed now, having revealed this unwanted flaw of mine when I typically do everything I can to keep it hidden. There's a reason I lean on army discipline so much, on silence. If given the smallest opening, the worst of me will burn its way out, a fever no medicine can contain.

"What did you hope for, sir?" I ask, hoping to redirect the conversation away from myself. "When you got out?"

"Of the army? I don't suppose you'd call it getting out, since I left to join the CIA."

"Of the CIA, then," I say. "What did you want when you left?"

A serrated laugh as he looks out the window. "I wanted to kill a lot of people."

I don't know what to say to that. Especially because from the way he says it, I know he means it.

His fingers are tapping his knee again, and his jaw is tight as he stares out at the city. I get the feeling he's not really looking at the world beyond his tinted reflection.

We pass the rest of the ride in silence.

CHAPTER 6

"I'M NOT GOING INTO THE HALL TONIGHT," MARK SAYS AS WE walk across the bridge into Lyonesse. "So your services won't be needed."

"At all?" I ask, glancing up at the bright afternoon sun. I've barely worked at all today.

The glass doors open for us as we step inside, both of us nodding at Ms. Lim behind the desk, who is wearing the keys at her waist again.

"Some days will be twenty-four hour days, Tristan, and I can't help that. So enjoy the easy days when they come." Mark presses the button for the elevator and we both get inside, me hitting the button for the third floor and then hitting the button for the top floor on his behalf. "Besides, I'm sure you have more moving and unpacking to do."

I don't, but confessing that feels a little pathetic. Who wants to admit that their entire life can fit into a stack of totes?

"Yes, sir."

And when the doors open on my floor, I step off like I have something to do with my afternoon.

I do manage to fill a few hours. I unpack all the totes— clothes and books mostly—and take a good inventory of the kitchen, which is already stocked with utensils, small appliances, and even some food staples. As a club employee, I can order a meal from Lyonesse's impressive kitchen whenever I want, but I'm too much of a soldier to crave butterfly salads that look like they bleed. I go to a grocery store instead and stock up on food that's half teenage boy and half the kind of bullshit you eat when you want to stay in shape. My cupboards are now bursting with sugary cereal and macaroni and cheese, and my fridge is full of eggs, vegetables, and fruit.

My father calls just as the sun decides it's done for the day, and I only hesitate a moment before I pick up the phone.

"Hi, Dad," I say, realizing that my free hand is gripping the polished concrete counter like I'm braced for battle. Which I am.

I make myself let go as he answers.

"Blanche is packing for the trip home, so I thought I'd take a moment and call."

I don't respond. If he wants to make this a fight, then he has to be the one to start it.

He's smart enough to know what I'm doing, but he's also the one who has a new wife he wants to keep happy and who might walk back in at any moment so he finally gives up and speaks. "Of all the jobs, Tristan. Of all the bosses."

"I thought you'd be happy that I'm working with family," I say.

"You know I'm not. First of all, he owns that *business*." My father has a gift for keeping his voice inflectionless and still managing to convey layers of meaning inside a single word. "Secondly, you know what he used to be."

I do know. "It's not my job to approve of his résumé."

"His résumé." My father does the thing again, the word

résumé coming out evenly but still carrying with it a wealth of disapproval. "We are soldiers, Tristan. We fight fair fights. *His* résumé is a résumé of death."

"It's in the past."

"Hardly in the past for the families of those he's murdered. You've heard about Chişinău?"

"I don't think so."

"He found a nest of Carpathian terrorists in an apartment. He was supposed to bring their leader in, arrest him formally, and instead every single one of those men went missing. There was nothing there for our Moldovan military partners to find, not even blood spatter. They just vanished into the darkness. The next month, we're all suddenly privy to a huge packet of intelligence on terrorist cells in Eastern Europe."

"That's hardly proof of—"

"And Brussels? Three diplomats found dead in their beds on the same morning, all three of apparent heart attacks, all three of them set to vote on a crucial EU bill that next day?"

"You can't know—"

"Rome, the month before he left. They found a priest torn apart in his own sacristy. A priest, Tristan. I was told that they had to rip out the floor and the walls because the blood had soaked the grout and stained all the plaster."

"Dad, stop." I'm gripping the counter again. "It doesn't matter."

"You're protecting a man who murdered people, tortured them, priests and politicians and people that deserved a fair trial at least. And that's who I *know* about—Tristan, there's a reason most of what Mark did was never written down."

"I'm not apologizing for what he's done, or condoning it. But I need a job, and this is something I can do," I say.

There's a pause, and I know what's coming. I know what's coming because it's come before.

"If you hadn't left the army—" my father starts.

And for a minute, all I can see is Aaron Sims, standing in front of me, his gun aimed at my head, his eyes desperate and pleading. Sims hadn't wanted to kill me.

I think…I think he wouldn't have.

But I still had to kill him. Kill him where the mountains were high and the trees were thick and where we were so, so far away from where we'd been born.

I had to kill my best friend, and my father thinks I should still be in the army.

"I have to go. I'm on duty right now," I lie. "I'll call later. Love you."

I hang up as quickly as I can and then brace both hands on the edge of the counter and lean over it, breathing hard. The combat stress counselor told me to breathe in a special, count-to-four way when the memory of Sims got like this, when I could see him and smell the evergreens and feel the cloying winter mist on my cheeks.

Sims is dead and I killed him and I have to breathe now.

After a minute, I can stand up straight, and after another minute, the memory is just a memory again.

A hero. My father called me that when he greeted me as I stepped of the airplane. *You did a hero's job, Son. Stand proud.*

Here I am shaking in a near-empty apartment instead.

I need something to do. Something to—

I can't be here alone with my thoughts a second longer. Before I can think better of it, I'm shrugging on my ill-fitting jacket and taking the elevator upstairs.

If the door is closed, I'll know for sure he doesn't need me. I'll do push-ups until I can't think anymore. I'll walk across the bridge and then go for a run so long that I nearly lose my way in the dark. Something.

But the door to Mark's office is cracked, and so is the door inside that leads to the hallway and his suite beyond.

I tell myself I'll just peek in, just to satisfy my very natural, very professional concern that he might need me for security and then go back to my apartment.

But the door to the roof is propped open. Mark's up on the roof.

I'm just doing my job. He could be with more of those supplicants from last night or meeting with strangers who would benefit from knowing he isn't unprotected before they get any ideas. But my certainty evaporates as I emerge from the stairwell and see him leaning against the far railing, a glass in hand.

He's alone. Alone and clearly deep in thought, and I'm intruding.

I take a step back, meaning to retreat before he can see me, and then I hear my name.

"Tristan," he says. He doesn't raise his voice, and so my name comes with the slow wash of water against Lyonesse's shores. "Come here."

Regretting the impulse that led me up here in the first place, I straighten my shoulders and walk toward him. He turns as I approach, taking a drink of his whatever-it-is on the rocks and then leaning backward against the railing. Watching me.

"Sir," I say, getting ready to apologize. "I wanted to make sure that you didn't—"

He waves a hand. "It's fine. Stay with me a minute. The sunset is wonderful from up here."

"Yes, sir."

"Do you want a drink?" he asks. "There's a little bar over that way."

"No corseted waiter tonight?" I say before I can stop myself.

But I'm not punished for my sarcasm. There's a something almost like a smile to his voice as he says, "There's only you. And alas, no corset. Yet."

I must not hide my expression fast enough because he does laugh now, a low noise that ripples through me like the ending note of a song.

"Go fix yourself a drink, Tristan. But be quick, the sun's about to set."

I shouldn't make myself a drink in front of my boss, not while I'd normally be working, but the thought of going back down to my empty apartment and staring at the ghost of Sims isn't any more appealing. So I remind myself that I'm not in the army anymore, and I venture into the small, roofed area that serves as a bar and staging station for food. There's an excellent selection of European beer—something I did enjoy about my deployments very much—and I help myself to a Żywiec porter.

I go back to the railing and Mark looks at my drink. "I have a small fortune's worth of single malt back there, and you brought back a beer."

"I like it."

Even if it does remind me of Sims. Of R & R in Warsaw, drinking until we stumbled down to the river and passed out. Of another R & R island-hopping in Greece, until we found ourselves standing in front of the temple of Poseidon outside Athens and cracking open the cold drinks we'd smuggled in, daring each other to duck under the ropes to find Byron's name chiseled onto one of the pillars.

Mark clinks his glass to the neck of my bottle and then we both take a healthy swallow.

"You don't have whiskey either, sir," I point out.

"Juniper berries are a superfood, which basically makes gin a cold-pressed juice," he says. "I'm looking out for my health."

"Yes, sir."

"Now watch."

We watch, the silence easier than it should be, given how

restless and strange the silence had been in the car earlier. The sun sinks in slow splendor over the flat river and the city beyond, the horizon broken by the Monument and the Capitol and the cranes against the sky like predatory birds perched in wait. Orange and pink fade into violet and blue, a few brave stars try to burn their way through the city's glow, and all of it is rendered in duplicate by the river stretching before us.

The traffic and the river make a kind of soothing symphony to it all, and the beer is good, and Mark next to me makes me feel—aware, I guess. Of the breeze tugging gently at my jacket and of the way my clothes feel on my skin. Of how often I lick my lips and swallow.

When I turn to look at him, to tell him he was right about the sunset, he's set his glass on the ledge and is already looking back at me. Watching me. I don't know for how long.

"Hold still," he says, voice low. "I can see the sky reflected in your eyes. It's quite arresting."

I am fixed by his words, by his attention. I don't think anyone has ever said something like this to me. I don't think anyone has ever murmured *hold still* to me as a directive purely for their pleasure.

I...I don't dislike it.

If I were thinking clearly, I might say it was to be polite, to placate my new boss, to figure out what, exactly, was going on. But I'm not thinking clearly right now. All I'm thinking is that he's so close and that the last of the sunset's behind him, framing perfectly the rugged cheeks and jaw, the high forehead and long eyelashes, the bluntly gorgeous features that make him equally hard to look at and hard to look away from.

That smell—clean summer rain—is all around me.

Mark's hand lifts to the lapel of my jacket; I feel his

touch wisp up to the lapel's notch and then trace down. His fingers curl into the fabric, holding me.

I can't see the lingering sunset in his eyes, only the sparkle of countless city lights. His full lips are parting.

His head tips toward mine.

The kiss is soft, *so soft*, for how firm his lips are. They brush against mine once, twice, before slotting with unutterable pliancy against my mouth. His hand continues fisting in my jacket as our lips part together, in tandem, and I hear him pull in a long breath through his nose, as if scenting me.

The idea is so crudely physical that it has me shuddering, even before his tongue dips into my mouth with excruciating skill, grazing against mine in measured demands until I open even more.

His fingers tighten slightly in my jacket and there's a small release of air from his nose—he's pleased. Pleased that I opened for him. His tongue reaches deeper, demands more, until we are kissing fully now, nothing held back. He tastes like juniper and citrus and cinnamon.

Instinct has me reaching for him, reaching for more, but he releases my lapel and catches my wrists before I can touch him.

The kiss breaks wetly, abruptly, and we stand there, breathing hard with his hands tight as manacles on my wrists.

He lets go of me suddenly, with a hard shake of his head, like he has to make himself.

"What—" My voice is hoarse, shaky. I want to reach up and touch my wet mouth, but instead one hand goes to rub at my wrist. "What was that for, sir?"

Mark says, finally, "It seemed right that at least one of us should get what they'd hoped for."

What they'd hoped for.

I'd hoped for a kiss.

And then he takes his glass from the ledge and leaves the roof.

I stay there in the dark, trying to pin thoughts and logic to what just happened. Reminding myself that I'm standing on top of a building where a kiss is the most innocent act possible, that Mark probably kisses people as often as he shakes their hands.

Reminding myself that he is my *boss*. My new stepmom's brother. Possibly an evil man.

But when I finally go down the stairs, past the closed doors of Mark's suite and down to my own floor, I can't remember any of it. I can only remember how his mouth felt against mine and how that kiss was even more tender and silky than I'd imagined a kiss could be before I came home.

CHAPTER 7

"—STARTING TO THINK IT'S A MYTH AT THIS POINT, NOT A fucking word from the wedding planner. Oh, hey, new kid, come on in."

Four days after my boss kissed me on his roof, I walk into the security office to start my first full, real week as Mark's bodyguard. Goran and his assistant head of security—Nat, a tall woman with medium-brown skin, short twists, and a Semper Fi tattoo on the inside of her forearm—are sitting at the table in the office, laptops open in front of them.

"Club schedule for the week," Goran says, sliding a paper across the table to me as I sit down. For the main security team, the weeks start on Tuesdays, our weekends consisting of the club's slow days, Sundays and Mondays. A smaller relief team can more easily cover the club then, and can cover Mark's movements too.

Not that I much enjoyed my weekend. The day after the kiss was taken up with my suit fittings downtown, and by the time I could get back to Mark, he was eating dinner with some visiting guests. Then came his usual hours in the hall, continuing to entertain said visitors. There'd been a shibari demonstration, and two club submissives had come and made themselves pliantly available until his guests happily took them to private rooms to continue the night.

And then we were walking back to the elevators, Andrea with us the entire way, deep in conversation with Mark about some budgetary problem—and by the time it was just him and me alone in the elevator, we only had a single floor together before I had to get off.

"Sir," I said, not sure what I wanted to tell him. That I'd thought of nothing but the kiss since the moment he left the roof, that I hadn't been able to sleep? That for the first time in months, I didn't dream of war but of sunsets and warm mouths?

That I spent the entire evening trying not to stare at him, trying not to trace the harshly handsome features of his face, the sharp, cool flicks of his gaze?

That I was worried that the curse of mine, the obsession, the *getting attached*, was quickening? That I was so scared—so fucking scared—that it was already too late?

My doors had opened before I could speak anyway. Mark regarded me with a gaze that was far too level for the amount of gin I'd seen him drink.

"The kiss was a gift, freely given," he told me. His voice was still that lazy, cool drawl he used in the hall. "If you're worried that I'll expect more, please don't be."

I had to step off, and so I'd said, "Yes, sir," but the minute I got inside my apartment, I wanted to fling myself headfirst into the river, because…because I didn't know.

I just knew that his dismissive *please don't be* had stung, along with the implication that he wouldn't expect more— wouldn't *want* more.

Even though that was for the best.

Yes.

I had to spend the next few days reminding myself of that. That I shouldn't want more kisses from my step-uncle slash boss.

But the opening had been cut, the rift torn, between the curse and the rigid control I forced over my life.

I had to admit that I noticed him, his mouth and hands, the long lines of his body.

I had to admit that when I closed my eyes, I thought of his fingers curled in my jacket and his mouth on mine.

I tried not to think of anyone in particular as I gave myself release, but even with my phone playing porn in front of me, my mind was pulled back to him. To Mark Trevena, who didn't want more from me.

Hold still, he'd said.

It was a long weekend.

But I'm nothing if not a believer in the cleansing power of routine, so here I am, ready for work to make everything right.

Nat and Goran discuss the planned kink demonstrations happening in the hall and all the notable guests who have rooms booked this week. Two of the guests have their own security teams that will liaise with Goran; one of the demonstrators will need our narrow electric truck to get their vacuum bed across the bridge; there's a costume party on Friday that Nat wants better staffed because costumes generally equal more jackassery in her experience.

Sedge has already emailed Mark's itinerary for the day, as well as a look ahead at his calendar—I see trips to Bishop's Landing, Singapore, and England coming up—and after Goran and Nat finish with the weekly meeting, I sit at the table and use my new laptop to review everything Sedge sent over.

"It looks like there are already safety plans made for his upcoming trips," I say aloud to Nat and Goran, who've started clicking and typing on their laptops after the conclusion of their costume party argument.

"Yeah, that would be Strassburg," Nat says without looking up from her screen.

"Strassburg?"

Goran also doesn't look up from his laptop but points a finger at the far wall. I get up and walk over to the corkboard, pinned with the weekly schedule, mandatory workplace safety notices, and several pictures. One of them is the whole security team with a very famous movie star, another is Goran beaming over a birthday cake in the shape of a unicorn, and the next one I see is a Polaroid of the team, this time with a husky man with bright red hair and a beard. He stands behind Mark, shoulder harness visible under his open jacket as he wraps an arm around Goran next to him. Mark has the small indent at the corner of his mouth that sometimes passes for a smile, and everyone else in the picture is grinning. The white part of the instant photo is labeled *club anniversary*.

"The one behind Mark?" I ask, even though I don't think I need to. He's the only person in the picture I don't recognize.

"That's the one. Great bodyguard. Got poached by a bossy little peach of a pop star."

"I think he was smitten," Nat says. "No way that pay raise alone was enough to leave a rent-free apartment and getting split open like a fence pos—" She breaks off abruptly.

I look back to see Goran has shoved her shoulder with his.

"Well, it's a kink club, who wouldn't want to work here?" she asks, although I don't think that had been anything like what she was going to say.

We all know about Mark and his bodyguards. That was what Andrea had said my first night in the club.

I am about to ask more, but something about Goran's red cheeks and the studious way Nat is staring at her laptop makes me shy. And there's no relevance in the question, is there? Even if Strassburg and Mark had…well, Mark had already made everything clear.

If you're worried I'll expect more…

We finish our security prep work for the morning, and I leave for Mark's floor. I'm joined by Sedge in the elevator, who murmurs a quiet hello and then slips out ahead of me the minute the doors open. The assistant even *moves* in a murmur somehow, his steps thoughtful and wary.

I enter Mark's office to find him propped on the front of his desk, Sedge already explaining something in a low voice.

"And the total amount?" asks Mark as Sedge hands him a stylus. He is holding out his tablet for Mark to sign now.

"Close to six hundred thousand dollars, sir."

"Not bad for an afternoon's work," Mark says, signing. "And imagine how happy our friend the congresswoman is going to be when her committee will be in the spotlight for the next six months."

"I don't have to imagine, sir. She's very active on TikTok. Will there be anything else?"

"Not that I'm aware of," Mark says, and his eyes slide to me. They drop once, quickly, to my mouth, and it's like a fist to the stomach.

Oh god, please let me get through this first full week without embarrassing myself.

———

Three days later, I'm sitting in an office in Baltimore while Mark meets with someone in a corner suite. There's a TV turned to a financial news channel, and even though the sound is muted, the chyron at the bottom declares that Wall

Street's been rocked by the news that a weighted blanket company's latest product—a blanket that gently vibrates as you use it, something that went viral immediately and smashed sales records—apparently has a tendency to catch fire while its users sleep. Worse, the company *knew* about this before the product launch and failed to disclose the risk. The talking heads on the TV are going wild about it, waving their hands and interrupting each other if the fragmented captions are any indication. There's talk of recalls, potential bankruptcy. A congresswoman has already sworn to investigate it—the same one I presume Mark and Sedge were speaking of the other day.

I glance down the hall to where Mark is, the suite door firmly shut, and I quickly pull my cell phone from my suit jacket pocket to confirm my suspicions.

When Mark emerges from the meeting thirty minutes later and stops in front of the TV, there's an amused quirk to his eyebrow.

"You knew about it, didn't you, sir?" I say later in the car on the way back to DC. "You knew when we visited their offices on my first day."

"The company's former COO is a member of Lyonesse. Last year, his payment was information about the blanket and anticipated sales, so I invested. This year, his payment was that they'd lied about the safety tests, so I sold my shares. As did any member at Lyonesse who'd invested with them."

"So the visit…?"

He stretches his legs, crossing them at the ankles. "I wanted to make sure the CEO knew it would be pointless to fight this—or to punish the former COO."

"Was the former COO the one who leaked the safety results?"

A quick exhale, like a laugh. "No, that was me."

"Why?"

"Why leak it? You don't believe I'm passionate about consumer safety? Tristan, I'm wounded."

"I'm sorry, sir," I say, and that earns me a press at the corner of his mouth.

"No, you're not, but I rather think you would be if I were really hurt, which is good of you. But alas, you are right to suspect my motives. I wasn't happy with how they'd treated their COO—my club member—before he quit, and I felt a little vengeful on his behalf. It's a happy accident that people are safer in their beds now."

"I suppose giving your friend in Congress a nice soapbox was a happy accident too, sir? And the extra six hundred thousand dollars?"

"I forget you grew up here. Well then, you already know how often these happy accidents seem to occur in the Beltway."

"It seems like they happen more often when Lyonesse is involved," I point out.

The curve of his mouth widens, almost a real smile now. "As you say, Tristan. As you say."

————

I throw myself into work, into running and push-ups and sit-ups when I'm not shadowing Mark, and when I am shadowing Mark, into the full, attentive minutiae of being a bodyguard.

I learn his work habits; learn the times he prefers to run, exercise, and eat; the restaurants he likes to frequent for working lunches; the manner in which he receives the more notable and preeminent guests of his club. I study the safety plans for the upcoming trips and begin to make my own for the few trips marked further out on his calendar; I study each and every person he meets with and commit them to memory.

And if his cool voice still works its way into my chest, if I find myself tracing the fullness of his mouth when it's pressed into its usual inscrutable shape during meetings, then I hope I hide it well enough.

I can't want him. And it would be foolish anyway, since he treats me with the same lazy remove as he did our first two days together.

If you're worried I'll expect more…

Five weeks into working for him, we make a trip to Manhattan and then to Bishop's Landing outside of it, a Hamptons-esque area with Edwardian mansions aplenty. It's a masquerade, and while I assume I'm meant to stay with the car and let the event security take point, Mark gives me a domino mask and makes me go inside after I help Jago secure the car.

"I need you to dance with me whenever I say," he says as I find him again. "For protection."

"Protection? Sir?"

The masque is a sumptuous revel of wealth and luxury, with costumes that look like they cost thousands and thousands of dollars, not to mention the flowers and candles and food. It's like being inside a fantasy novel. East Germany in the sixties, it is not.

Mark wraps a strong hand around mine and pulls me out onto the floor. "You see, Tristan," he says as his other hand finds the small of my back and pulls me closer. I instinctively lay my right hand at his shoulder and feel the warm convexity of muscle there. "When you're in the business I'm in, a party like this is a chance for people to schmooze their way into your good graces. My good graces, unfortunately, have to be paid for, but it's not polite to say so. Being fond of dancing, with a conveniently available dance partner, makes a lovely little escape hatch from these overtures."

The business I'm in—information, not kink. And he

doesn't need protection from violence but from awkward networking.

"This wasn't in the job description, sir," I mutter as I do my best to remember how to waltz. *One two three, four five six. One two three, four five six.*

"The job description is whatever I say it is." A sigh. "You dance like you're following orders."

It's only eight years of military experience that keep me from shooting a glare at him. "I am following orders, sir," I point out.

His eyes flash blue under his own domino mask. "Follow them better, then," he says, and pulls me even closer. Our hips are pulled in, his hand unyielding at the small of my back, his fingers tight around mine. "Feel what my body tells yours to do. Stop counting."

With a deep breath, I do as he says. I watch as his shoulders dip, feel as his thigh brushes mine as he steps. The hand at the small of my back moves ever so slightly, a signal forward or backward or to the side, and the minute I stop thinking and let him lead, the dance becomes as natural as breathing.

And then awareness burns through me like a brushfire: the rainlike smell of him, the firm length of his legs moving so close to mine. The stretch of sun-bronzed throat above his bow tie. Our hips are close enough that it would only take a missed beat, a hesitation, for him to feel the erection lengthening in my suit trousers.

I have to look away, pretending I need to keep my gaze to the side so I don't misstep. I don't want him to see what I'm failing at stopping.

I'm trying not to, I wish I could explain. *But I think of you too much. I think of your last bodyguard, who you might have fucked, and I think the ache in my throat is jealousy.*

At some point, the music ends, and we move off the

floor. And despite Mark's earlier words, and although he does keep me close, he engages in conversations the rest of the night, leaving me free from his touch and craving it all the more.

CHAPTER 8

TWO DAYS AFTER WE GET BACK FROM BISHOP'S LANDING, I take the elevator up from the security office to the top floor, doing my morning check-in with the object of my blooming obsession.

For some of the meetings Mark takes, he wants me in the room or just outside it; for some, he doesn't want the presence of security to upset whatever delicate transaction is about to take place. And for yet others, he wants me visible down on the server floor, a human manifestation of how safe their secrets will be at Lyonesse. Each day is slightly different, but I don't mind because each day is set by what he needs, and so there's a reassuring logic to that. All I need are my orders, and I'll march wherever I'm told.

Today I'm also holding a cappuccino fresh from the club kitchens because I noticed on our trip to Bishop's Landing that it's Mark's morning drink of choice. Which surprised me a little—I suppose I expected a precisely pulled shot of espresso or even just black coffee, the lifeblood of the U.S. military machine. But a cappuccino takes time to make, time to drink. It invites stirring and savoring. Hardly the drink of a former special activities officer.

It's the kind of knowledge about someone that raises more questions than answers, and maybe if I find him in the right mood, already switched into the charming club host from the controlled autocrat he usually embodies during the day, he might tell me why he likes cappuccinos. He might arch his eyebrow at me, the line of his mouth moving just so—the small gestures that would be an earsplitting grin on any other man.

Instead, I walk through the empty vestibule to his office door and push it open to find him taking off his jacket behind his desk. Which has a naked woman tied to the top of it.

I stop, cappuccino hot in my hand, the wooden door swinging shut behind me. The skills I learned in battle and sharpened as a diplomatic escort serve me unexpectedly here. I take in the entire scene in seconds.

The woman, curvy and pale, has bright red ropes knotting her thighs to her calves, and her wrists are bound and lashed over her head. She is tied to the edge of the desk, knees apart, so that anyone who stepped up to the edge of the desk would have easy access to her open, flushed cunt.

And Mark has already taken advantage of that access: a Hitachi wand lays next to her, and a flush is staining its way up her soft stomach to her face, all the way to the roots of her strawberry-blond hair. Her nipples are cherry red and stiff enough to look like they ache. They're wet too, like they've just been sucked on. And even from here, her pussy glistens.

I notice the white latex gloves on her hands just as Mark looks over at me.

"Ah, Tristan, good morning." His eyes drop to the cappuccino in my hand, a pleased expression on his face. "Is that for me?"

He asks this as he's unzipping his pants.

The woman tied to his desk stares dreamily at me.

My eyes are drawn to Mark's large hands as they make efficient work of the clasp and zipper, of the waistband of the dark boxer briefs underneath. His cock, when it emerges, is long and thick. Cut, with a large crown and a visible vein twisting down the side. I watch him tear open a condom packet with the same curt efficiency as he used to free his erection, and he rolls the sheath over himself in three brisk movements.

"You can stay. This won't take long," he says to me.

"I—"

He's already sinking his latex-shiny cock into her swollen core, one hand guiding himself in as the other comes to spread over her sternum, holding her still for his entry.

My breathing comes faster as I watch her arch against the ropes tying her down, as I watch her being held down for him to penetrate.

Two things come to me just then.

The first is that I consented to this. I signed a document; I agreed that I would willingly witness acts of sex and kink at my place of employment.

The second is that the document, the consent, none of it matters right now anyway. Because I don't want to stop watching.

I don't want to leave.

Mark strokes in and out of her with the expression of a connoisseur savoring something that meets their approval, and I want to know how it feels. To be him or to be her. To have a soft pussy held still for my taking or to have his thick shaft working in and out of me with slow, powerful drags.

I'm hard now.

I'm aching with wanting…everything. Everything in front of me, and the cappuccino is forgotten, and the day is forgotten, and there's just my boss fucking a woman tied to his desk like it's as much a part of his day as reading the news.

Mark picks up the Hitachi, and the woman whimpers.

"No, Mr. Trevena, *please...*"

"Hmm" is all Mark says. And then he proceeds to turn it on anyway.

She pulls against the ropes as if in protest, and despite the heat in blood, I step forward instinctively. She said *no*—

"Never fear, my knight," Mark says mildly. The hand not holding the Hitachi is sliding under the knots around her plush thigh, tugging on them with something like fondness in his expression. He's still inside her. "What's your safeword, flower?"

"La mer," she pants.

"And what do you say if you want to stop?"

"La mer."

Safeword. That term was in the folio, in the comprehensive glossary included with everything else. I stop, one foot still forward and my eyes on her, making sure she's okay.

She smiles at me and then presses her lips together, as if to show me that wild horses couldn't drag the word from her lips right now. And then Mark presses the vibrator to her clit. Even from here, I can see that it's rosy and swollen, and I put that together with the flush staining her skin and guess that she has had an orgasm already.

Maybe more than one—maybe so many that yet another sounds like torture.

And I can see the diabolical genius in it. Mark hasn't beaten her with a crop or a cane, he hasn't clamped her, he hasn't done any of the stuff I've witnessed in the club, but it doesn't matter. She's squirming, whimpering, *reacting*, as he tortures her with pleasure, as he strokes himself into her center.

By now, I've given up all hope of making myself leave. I stand there, frozen, breathing nearly as hard as they are, having to reach down to adjust the bulge in my pants. My hand lingers there after I'm done, the heel of my palm grinding mindlessly against the stiff flesh there.

I have to force myself to drop it. I can't masturbate. I can't take his place. I can't take her place. No matter how badly I want to.

She climaxes with a scream that leaves no doubt how deeply she's feeling her pleasure. Between the toy and Mark's relentless thrusts, I have to imagine it's as deep as her blood, as deep as her bones.

"There we go," mutters Mark, spearing into her. Even through his suit trousers, I see the moving muscles of his thighs, his backside, and through his shirt, I see the flex and strain of his back and shoulders as he drops the wand and wraps his hands around her soft waist to hold her still.

Because he's driving into her so hard now that even the ropes can't keep her from being literally fucked away from the edge of the desk.

He ducks his head, and his hair leaves its carefully styled tousle and falls forward over his face. Silhouetted against the sun coming in through the floor-to-ceiling windows, I see it perfectly. I see his lips part too, and I hear a muttered curse.

He drives in a final time, so deep that I almost feel it all the way over here, and then he holds himself completely still as he pumps his release into her body. She's still coming down from her own peak, breathing hard and half whimpering, and he keeps his hands tight on her waist as he finishes.

It takes me a minute to realize that he's looking over at me. Watching me as his balls drain.

A surge of heat so urgent I worry I'm going to ejaculate right then and there yanks at my thighs and belly, and I have to bite the inside of my cheek to keep myself from going over the edge. And the moment ends anyway, Mark closing his eyes once and then withdrawing.

After sex like that, no one could fault him for collapsing in his chair and catching his breath, but Mark is already disposing of the condom and buttoning himself up by the time the thought finishes flickering across my mind. He drops a kiss on the woman's stomach and starts unknotting the ropes with a practiced deftness that reminds me that Mark is the original here. The founder and king of this kinky kingdom.

Soon she is sitting up with a blanket around her shoulders, a glass of water in her hands. Mark tucks a knuckle under her chin and lifts her face to his. He murmurs something to her that I can't hear, and she murmurs back, equally low.

Even though I can't hear what's exchanged, I can see her expression as she looks up at him, and it's one that borders on worshipful. After a few more words, she slides off the table and disappears into the small bathroom just inside the hallway which leads to his private apartments. She's shorter than I'd initially thought, and then suddenly Andrea's words from my first night come to me.

Little blond.

Mark is wrapping the ropes into neat coils as she does, and then with a look at me that clearly says *stay put*, he disappears into his apartments with the rope and the vibrator.

The submissive emerges dressed in a bright yellow sundress which should clash with her Titian hair but doesn't at all. She still has the white latex gloves on, utterly incongruous with the small gold necklace at her throat and delicate leather sandals on her tiny feet.

"Thank you again, Ms. Beroul," Mark says, taking her hand and dropping his head down to brush his lips over her knuckles.

Even through her gloves, she must feel it because she gives a small shudder. "Anytime, Mr. Trevena," she says huskily, and then she leaves, her topaz-brown eyes flashing once to me in an interested glance, which I return.

"Well, Tristan?" asks Mark, heading behind his desk and

putting his suit jacket back on. "You wanted to go over the schedule, I presume. And bring that here. I want to drink it before it's completely cold."

———

Thirty minutes later, I leave Mark's office with as much dignity as can be expected. I didn't cream the inside of my pants, I didn't stammer and flush while we went over the schedule, and in fact, the only time I found myself unable to speak was when Mark took the mug from me and saw it was a cappuccino and not just a regular coffee. The expression on his face had been so pleased then that I was grateful I was already about to sit down.

It could bring a man to his knees, that expression on Mark Trevena's face.

But even though I've mostly got my hard-on under control, I'm still restless from the morning as I make my way down to Andrea's office to return a folder Mark just finished signing his way through.

"Couldn't find Sedge, could he?" Andrea asks, extending her hand to take the file and not bothering to look at me. She's in her uniform of a pantsuit and a low, sleek ponytail, and her expression is the usual one she wears around me—like I'm about to disappoint her.

"I was already in his office," I explain. My voice is a little hoarser than normal, and she looks up. Something deep in her expression shifts.

"Was Mark with someone this morning?"

I don't know how closely I need to guard his privacy from her, but I suppose my silence is enough of an answer.

"First time you've seen him in action, then?" she asks, leaning back in her chair a little.

Again, I don't answer, and again, it seems to be its own answer.

She looks down at her desk, and for once, there's nothing sharp or dismissive in her tone. "There aren't a lot of dominants like him," she says after a minute. "Even here. Mark could make someone kneel for him in the brightly lit aisle of a grocery store. He could gag them with a dirty radish, and they'd thank him for it."

Yes. They would.

"It was the little blond submissive you mentioned," I say, passing a hand over my face. I'm still too hot, my clothes too tight. The minute I have a break in the day's schedule, I'm running to my apartment to rub away the need still fussing against my zipper.

"The little blond submissive… Oh. No," Andrea says, shaking her head. "She's not in the city, or I guarantee you that we'd know about it."

It's strange to me that Mark has a submissive that's not *here*, but then again, he might have many at Lyonesse to play with in the meantime. Although I haven't seen as much.

I also haven't seen as much as a hint of a romantic relationship, long-distance or otherwise.

"This must be someone new," Andrea continues, her tone musing. "But I'm glad he's found a way to blow off steam. He's too busy playing the king of the castle in the evenings to make use of our club subs, and now that Strassburg's gone, I don't know how he's managing. Or how we're going to manage in the long run because he's a fucking monster when he's not able to scene. Or screw."

She looks up and sees me staring at her.

"So it's true, then," I say. "He and Strassburg…"

"Oh yes. Not publicly, because Strassburg was worried about how being a submissive would affect his reputation as a bodyguard. But for private needs, yes. Mark used him."

Used him. The words nearly make my knees buckle. God, what is happening to me?

"I see," I manage faintly.

Andrea eyes me for a moment, and I see the subtle twist of her mouth to the side, like she's thinking of saying something. But then she just shakes her head and flips open the folder I brought her.

I'm clearly dismissed.

I go back to Mark's office and post myself outside, knowing in ten minutes or so, Ms. Lim will lead up his first meeting of the day. But my thoughts are so tangled and troublesome that I can barely focus on the day's schedule.

Does Mark want me to do for him what Strassburg did? Despite what he said to me the day after our kiss, would he want that if I offered it?

Do I want to offer it?

I've never done—that. Sex. But it doesn't mean I couldn't. That I wouldn't be good at it. And I'd want to be good at it, just like I've been good at everything I've tried in my life. Singing, basketball, soldiering…this could be something else to add to the list.

Being used by him.

And as the day wears on, what I keep remembering is not the agonized pleasure of the Titian-haired submissive or even the way he gazed at me while he came.

Instead, I think of Arjun's hands moving through Evander's hair, petting and stroking and praising, and even as I bristle just thinking of it, my mind helpfully substitutes Mark for Arjun and puts me in Evander's place.

Kneeling with long fingers toying possessively with my hair. Kneeling for him.

I think I'm fucked.

CHAPTER 9

IT IS AN ESSENTIAL PAIN OF MY NEW JOB THAT THERE IS TIME
for my mind to wander. Even with preparing new security
plans, even with cataloging every restaurant and office we
visit, studying every person Mark meets with, there are too
many moments of nothing, of waiting, of standing outside
his office or behind his chair in the hall, my mind free to
drift to its new, all-encompassing preoccupation.

Him.

Imagining myself tied to his desk in that woman's place.
Kneeling next to him, his fingers in my hair.

It's all I can think of, all I can imagine. In the early hours
of the morning after Mark has held court with his camarilla
in the hall, I come back to my apartment and jerk myself
thinking of his hand on my head. In the morning when I
wake, it's the same.

I think of the scenes we see in the hall night after
night—people tied down, held in place to be punished
or outright used—and I have to accept that I found the
sight of Evander kneeling that first night unsettling not

because it was something I didn't want but because it was something I *did* want. Something I hadn't known I wanted until I saw it, and then even after I saw it, I was terrified of what it all meant.

Every time I masturbate, I sit on the edge of my bed afterward, trying to reconcile the Tristan of six weeks ago with the Tristan of right now.

The morning we're set to leave for Singapore, my father calls again, and I make myself answer, since I've been dodging his calls for nearly a month now, responding only via text.

Sorry I missed your call, it was a busy night.

Sorry I couldn't talk, was on duty.

Yes, I did see that the space bill is finally getting its senate vote next week. I hope you and Blanche are well.

But there's only so long Ricker Thomas will stomach going without a sitrep, and so I know it's time to talk, however pointless the conversation will be.

"Son," he says after I answer. "It's about time."

"It's been busy here." I open my dresser and pull out several rolls of socks, tuck them in a neat line in the open suitcase on my bed. "How's Blanche?"

"Perfect," my father says simply, and despite myself, I smile. Blanche is everything he isn't—open, warm, compassionate—and she's kindled something in him I wouldn't have thought impossible.

My smile is short-lived, because he says next, "You know, we're planning on staying in her town house for the time being, but I don't have plans to sell the farm. You could still live there if you wanted. I wouldn't expect rent, Tristan. Ever."

"Dad—"

"And if it's just any kind of work you're looking for, you know I can help."

"I know."

There's a pause, one that I know from long experience is the pause of a general changing strategy. "There's a rumor that the intelligence side is looking for someone. An NSA agent has disappeared while on the trail of a hacker."

I don't respond, knowing my father will forge on anyway.

"And the last person we know for sure the agent talked to was Mark Trevena."

I'm getting my toothpaste now, along with my other toiletries, zipping everything into a small and worn leather bag. A surge of defensiveness on Mark's behalf temporarily makes it difficult to think. "All right?"

"Tristan," my father says impatiently. "The rumor—the rumor is that Mark Trevena is involved with the disappearance of this agent. That he's working with this hacker and colluding to sell classified information to whoever's willing to pay."

I drop the leather bag in my suitcase and drag in a slow breath. I can't let my preoccupation with Mark make it so I fight with my father over this. I have to be careful. "Dad. If you think accusing my boss—your brother-in-law, by the way—of treason and murder because of some agency rumor is going to make me quit—"

"Just consider it," my father cut in. "You know his club deals in secrets, you know that the caliber of secrets he's getting has to stretch to the highest level. Surely there're meetings you don't sit in on, surely there are times he goes missing that you can't account for—"

It's my turn to interrupt. "He's not sneaking around doing murder, Dad. He watches people get flogged and he takes meetings with people who would also like to watch people get flogged. That's it."

"You don't know him," my father says firmly. "No one does. That's the point. No one *really* knows who Mark Trevena is, what he's done, what he's doing. He's a ghost; even in the most classified of records, he's barely there. The only thing anyone can say for sure about Mark Trevena is whatever they can learn from his sisters, which isn't much. Even Blanche can't tell me anything beyond their childhood."

I zip up my suitcase, ready to argue. *I* know him; I'm with him as much as someone can be with their boss.

But as I'm about to speak, I realize I don't know as much about Mark as I think I do.

I know that he likes cappuccino in the morning and gin on the rocks every other time. I know that he runs five miles every day, that he swims another few miles on the rooftop pool after. I know how he sits in the club, head braced on his fingers, long legs kicked out, a devil waiting to be amused, and I know how he sits in meetings with potential clients and business partners, with danger glinting off him like the moon glinting off sea ice in the dark.

I know he likes his food delicate, creative, strange. I know he wears the same silver wristwatch every day. I know when he looks at the river, there's something in his face that makes me think he's far, far away in his thoughts.

I know what he sounds like when he comes.

But I don't know what he believes, what he wants. What he's willing to fight for. I don't know when his parents died and if they were kind to him and if he misses them. I don't know why he still goes to Mass some Sundays and I don't know why he left the CIA and I don't know why he built Lyonesse after he left.

So I can't argue with my father. And I don't.

Eventually the call ends, and I take my suitcase downstairs, ready to travel to the other side of the world with someone who's still a stranger to me.

I expect Mark to fly on a private jet, so I'm surprised when we get to the airport and make our way to a commercial flight.

"I do care about the planet a little," says Mark, seeing my face. "Well, enough not to fly privately. Also it's very useful to fly commercial sometimes. Makes you easy to be searched for, if anyone were looking for you."

"Do we want to be easy to be searched for? Sir?"

He gives me that expression where his mouth pushes in at the corner. An almost smile. It makes what he says next sound playful and not ominous. "You never know when it might come in handy."

We fly to New York, and I can't hide my excitement when we're at the front of the plane. The flight attendant brings us chocolate chip cookies, and the only time Mark looks up from his laptop for the short flight is to snort at me asking for his cookie if he wasn't going to eat it.

At JFK, we are escorted right onto our next plane, and I almost run into the back of Mark when he stops in front of a section the size of a lounge. The attendant is showing him inside, and then I realize that the lounge is his *seat*, a plush leather armchair in a small room with a closing door, full-sized television, table, and separate bed. And a vase of fresh flowers.

It's…slightly nicer than the C-17s that took me to Carpathia.

I could stare at the vase of flowers for the entire flight. Flowers in the air. Pointless. Lovely.

"You're here, Tristan," Mark says right as I'm glancing down at my ticket, expecting to see a seat in the normal, non-vase-of-flowers section, and I look up to see the attendant lowering the far wall of Mark's cabin to reveal an adjoining suite.

"The beds will fold out together to make a double bed," the attendant says with the air of a thoughtful host, and I flush so deeply my cheeks burn.

"Oh, we don't—I don't—"

"We'll start with the Krug," Mark tells the attendant before I can finish stammering out that we don't need a double bed. The attendant nods gracefully and leaves.

I step hesitantly from the aisle into my suite and stare at Mark from across the lowered wall. He's already setting his briefcase down and shrugging his suit jacket from his well-made shoulders. I watch for a minute, my face flushing hotter as his shirt pulls tight over his body, and then tear my gaze away, deciding to follow his lead. By the time my jacket is hung in the narrow suite closet and my small messenger bag stowed, the champagne has arrived and we give the attendant our orders for dinner and for breakfast, since the flight is over eighteen hours long.

"Shall we toast?" asks Mark after the attendant leaves and closes Mark's door behind him.

"To what, sir?"

He thinks for a minute. "To lucky guesses."

"Have you made any lately?" I ask.

"You," he says without hesitation.

I blush anew.

And then his mouth presses in at the corner. "I hope to be making more very soon."

"To lucky guesses, then," I manage to say normally, lifting my glass.

Mark catches my gaze, his dark blue eyes burning into mine. "To lucky guesses," he echoes softly, and then drains his champagne before reaching for his laptop and opening it.

I resist the temptation to pull out my own laptop again. I have the particulars of the trip already memorized—the people, the places, the purposes. Mark is meeting with the owner of a kink club in Singapore to discuss a mutual membership option and is meeting with the CEO of a shipping conglomerate who is a member of Lyonesse due to pay his membership fee. A fee he'll only deliver privately to Mark, in person, which I've noticed is very common. People feel safer giving up secrets when they can see your face, when you're giving them expensive drinks and assurances the information will never ever be connected to them should it get out, unless they want it to be.

It should be an easy trip, with plenty of time between the two appointments, and that's why I chose the trip to talk to Mark.

About Strassburg.

About…me.

But as I watch him refill his champagne glass, I remember my phone call this morning.

You don't know him. No one does.

Can I really offer to do what Strassburg did when I still know next to nothing about him?

Yes, my body sings; *yes*, my heart sings too. But my head reminds me of all the times I've fallen hard—of how foolish I felt when I learned the object of my desires was already in a relationship or wasn't interested. In high school mostly, but also at West Point once or twice. The idea of falling again terrifies me.

I'm already immersed in Mark. If I add sex to the mix, I might be lost.

Lost and unable to come back.

Mark sets aside his laptop when dinner comes, and after the first course is served, he glances up at me, long fingers grasping the stem of his wineglass. He doesn't drink yet.

"Well, Tristan?"

I'm suddenly nervous that I've forgotten something

crucial, made some error of bodyguard etiquette during our first international trip. "Yes, sir?"

"You've been sneaking glances at me for the last two hours. Out with it."

"With what?"

"Whatever question you're burning to ask. I promise I'll answer."

I shouldn't be surprised that he noticed me looking at him, but I am. I have an abrupt and unhinged vision of me blurting out that I'll take Strassburg's place, and then panic. I'm not ready, I don't even know if I—

Mark has taken a drink and is now studying me calmly. "Would you like me to start guessing? We do have fifteen and a half hours left of our trip. I'm sure I'll land on the right answer before we land."

I desperately cast around for something, anything, to say that isn't the only thing I've been thinking of for the last week. Because I'm not ready, not here in an airplane, no matter how private the suite is.

"I…"

Think. Think.

"I was wondering why you made Lyonesse," I say quickly, grabbing onto the first thing I can think of. "Why not a regular job after you left the CIA?"

Mark gives a small exhale. A laugh. "Do I seem like the regular job sort to you?"

I can't say that he does. "Well…no. Sir."

He sets his glass down and looks at it for a minute, as if considering. And then says, "Do you know the legend of Lyonesse, Tristan?"

"I saw snippets online when you first offered me the job. A sunken kingdom."

"A drowned kingdom. The legends say the sea took it after King Arthur's time; archeology suggests it's a folk memory from Neolithic times, when sea levels around Cornwall rose and submerged fertile fields and forests." Mark looks up at me. "The legends also say Lyonesse was drowned for its sins. Similar to a kingdom in a Breton legend—Ys."

I pick up my spoon and sample the soup. Sweet corn and crab, with a bite of whiskey and lime. It's delicious with the white wine they served with it, and even after weeks of eating at the city's finest restaurants with Mark, eating the club's culinary masterpieces, I have another moment of dizzy appreciation for how strangely beautiful life can be outside of a war.

"Ys was also drowned for its wickedness," Mark goes on. "Celtic Christians saw both legends, Ys and Lyonesse, as analogies for Sodom and Gomorrah."

"And is that why you named a club after it? A tribute to wickedness and all that?"

Mark gives me a real laugh. "No, no, I wasn't that clever. My grandfather was Cornish and would tell me and my sisters tales of Lyonesse at bedtime. I loved them. The idea of a place unbearably lovely and also unable to last. And the story is a warning, I think, for those who need to listen. Power can be lost, the ground under your feet can founder, and only the just will survive. An important reminder for anyone delving into the world of pain and pleasure."

He pauses a moment, long fingers twirling the stem of his glass, slowly, slowly, the wine rippling faintly from the plane's vibrations. "When I left the CIA, I left very disillusioned. I'd lost—something. Getting it back was impossible. I had to find another way to live, and I couldn't live in the world as it was."

"So you built your own?"

His eyes dip down, the long lashes resting briefly on his cheeks. "Something like that." He looks back up to me. "Do you like it? The world I built?"

Answers crowd on my tongue.

I hate it and I love it.

It's all I think about.

I want to kneel for you.

"It's still very new to me," I reply diplomatically.

"Hmm," Mark says, looking down at his soup, and the conversation lapses into silence as we eat.

CHAPTER 10

TWO ATTENDANTS COME AND MAKE THE DOUBLE BED.

"Tristan," Mark says, standing and unbuttoning his shirt after they leave. I realize he's about to change into the provided pajamas *right then*, and my heart flips. "Stop looking at the bed as if it will bite. I promise I won't kick you in my sleep."

"I don't think it's big enough for both of us," I hedge, although it's true that the bed does seem a little narrow for two former soldiers. "I can sleep in my seat—"

Having unbuttoned his shirt, Mark strips it off and then opens his belt. I stand and turn to give him privacy, the stretch of tan, muscle-etched stomach burned into my mind.

"Tristan," Mark says again, this time in an amused voice. "You've seen me put on a condom. Surely me changing into pajamas is tame stuff by now."

"I didn't want to intrude, sir."

"I hired you to follow me day and night, to be near me while I conduct business and more personal affairs. I'm not shy."

Swallowing, I turn back around. Mark is wearing the pajama pants, but *only* the pajama pants. His chest and shoulders are bare; hair like dark, tarnished gold glints softly from his chest, and more stretches from his navel to the drawstring waistband of his pajama pants. His nipples are a muted pink, the inside of a seashell seen at dusk, and there is a tattoo of a bird in flight on his left forearm. I've seen part of it before, when he's had his sleeves rolled up, but now I can see all of it: precisely drawn feathers and a sharp beak and a single closed eye, all rendered in black ink.

The pants hang low enough that I can see another black tattoo on his hip, just above the waistband. It's two words, small enough that I can't read them from here.

"Tertia optio," says Mark, noticing the direction of my gaze.

"The third option."

Mark looks surprised. "That's right."

"My father," I explain. He was familiar with the adage that if diplomacy fails and war isn't a possibility, a third option should be chosen. The third option being any plausibly deniable thing the CIA deems necessary, of course. "He didn't believe in it. To him, if diplomacy fails, then transparent conflict is the answer. Not whatever it is the Special Activities Center does."

Mark pulls back the covers on his side of the bed. "Spoken like a soldier" is all he says.

I don't know why, but I bristle. "He thinks any fight should be a fair one. Soldiers fight fairly, honestly."

"Okay," replies Mark, and that amused tone is back. He gives me a look, and I get the distinct impression that he thinks I'm being *cute*. It makes me bristle even more.

"He's not wrong," I say stubbornly. "Special 'activities' is just a euphemism for murder—"

"There are things worse than murder," Mark interrupts,

like a teacher who's had enough of a student getting an answer wrong. "Lots of murders, for example. Isn't it better that one or two people die rather than hundreds or thousands? If one or two deaths stops months or years of killing, torture, rape, famine, utter misery?"

"But it's not *right*," I say stubbornly. "It's not a fair fight to come through a window and just *kill* someone—"

"We didn't always kill people," Mark cuts in impatiently. "Special activities is a lot more than that. And as for fair fights… if you consider drones and Hellfire missiles against rebels armed with forty-year-old guns and their great-grandfathers' bayonets a fair fight, then I'm not sure what to tell you."

He's wrong, I know he's wrong, but I struggle for the words to tell him so.

He lets out a soft breath.

"You should change into your pajamas," he says. "Even if you sleep in the chair." And then he climbs into the bed, arranging himself on his side, facing away from me.

I quickly change, pulling on the pajamas—top and bottoms—and then go back to my recliner. It's been a day of nothing but sitting, and I doubt I'll be able to fall asleep, but this will be my best chance, here on a secure flight with a door closed to the rest of the plane. Once we land, I'll need to be alert and watchful, awake, and if I learned anything while deployed, it was to sleep while I can.

A fair fight…

Mark is wrong, of course he is, but when I close my eyes—just for a moment—I see Sims. Sims framed by trees and fog, and he's holding his gun with a shaking hand.

Everyone put your goddamn guns down, he says in the dream.

We are motionless, staring. Unable to think. We trained and trained and trained for the enemy, but with one of our own pointing a gun at us, we're lumps of confused meat, worse than boots, worse even than civilians.

This can't be happening.

Now! Sims snarls. *I'm not fucking joking!*

We got out of our escort vehicles to scout a potential rebel trap in the surrounding woods. Rebels that Sims said he saw.

But there are none and now we're out of our vehicles like fucking fools. He's going to kill the woman nominated as Carpathia's next prime minister, who will lead in conjunction with its president. He's going to kill everyone else in the car we're escorting, including her family.

I don't drop my gun.

Sims, I say, and my voice is shaking like his hand. *What the fuck are you doing?*

The fog is clammy and cold, and makes everything hazy. The children in the car are crying and I can hear them through the windows. Their father is holding them. The ministerial nominee steps out of the car, her back tall, blocking the window and her family behind her. When I give her a quick glance, she's dry-eyed and *pissed*.

Sims, I say again, swinging my eyes back to his gun. *Stop it right the fuck now.*

His hand is still shaking, shaking so hard, and his eyes are begging me. *Put your gun down, Tristan. I'll make it fast for them. I'll let the whole squad go. Just put your gun down and walk away.*

Sims. My best friend. He shares his Nintendo Switch with me, steals my Pop-Tarts; he helps me hold on to the memory of McKenzie. He's kept me safe for three of my four deployments, the shield at my right when we've cleared villages, dry creeks, and damp mountain caves.

And he's about to kill the people we're supposed to protect.

I don't drop my gun.

Tristan, he says, and he's begging me now. Begging me

to let him kill a democratically elected leader and three civilians, two of whom are kids.

...my best friend wants to kill two kids.

The look on Sims's face when I raise my gun to his chest is awful. Now I'm begging him right back. *Fucking, please, man, fucking stop it.*

I have to do this is what he said, and despite the desperation in his face, the shaking hand, I hear the dead, dull certainty in his voice. I know then.

I know there's no stopping him.

It doesn't matter that he points the gun at me now. I would have had to shoot him anyway because I'm the lieutenant and Jesus fuck, *they're kids*—but it does sting, in a stupidly irrelevant way, that he would raise a gun to my chest.

I gave him my fucking Pop-Tarts.

Tristan, please, he says, eyes wild, but his voice is the same dull, inflectionless tone.

I move first, dropping the barrel of my gun as I duck to the side to put myself between him and the soon-to-be prime minister. I squeeze the trigger as I do, and my bullet strikes true—his knee. He buckles and I think, *okay, we're done now, he knows this is over*, but even as he buckles, his gun is lifting.

He's still going to try to shoot them.

The other soldiers around us—having watched the entire exchange in frozen shock—react, their own guns finally moving, but I'm faster.

My next bullet tears through Sims's throat.

And that's when dream splinters from memory. In my memories, Sims dropped like a sack of potatoes, a hand flying weakly to the side of his neck. There was blood everywhere, and I was calling for medevac, I was lunging forward and clapping my hand over his to add more pressure, I was looking down into his pale gray eyes and telling him to hold on, that we were going to save him, and his face was full of fear and he sputtered words full of blood, *family...ease... family...ease...*

I'll make sure your family is comfortable, I told him, *as much ease as they need.*

And his free hand reached up, like he wanted to grab the vest of my body armor, and then with a choked spray of blood from his mouth, it dropped back to the ground.

He was dead.

But in my dream now, he doesn't drop. Instead, blood gushes slick and crimson from his neck and he shoots the woman behind me. I shoot him again, through the eye, and he steps forward, a gaping hole in his head, and he fires at someone in the car behind me. He's killing everyone and I can't stop him.

I shoot and shoot and shoot, and he keeps coming, bloody and pulpy and horrible, a monster from a movie, a nightmare from the grave, and he opens his mouth and it's just blood and broken teeth and he says, *I hope they prick you when they pin that medal on. I hope you have to bleed like me. I hope you get to tell everyone what real heroes do.*

Stop, I whisper, but he doesn't stop.

Shards of white teeth fall from his blood-slick lips as he speaks. *How could you not know I was going to do this? How could not see me faltering, struggling—how could you kill me when you didn't even try to help me first—*

I'm crying, but I need to keep shooting him, and I can barely breathe, and I need to scream, and I can't. I'm making no sound because I can't breathe, and then I realize I'm choking on blood too, on broken teeth and the pulp of my own torn open throat—

"Tristan," comes a voice, solid and firm. "Tristan."

I'm still choking on teeth and flesh and Sims is still lumbering toward me.

94

And the voice comes again.

"Tristan." A hand is on my shoulder and then on my jaw. My eyes flutter open and it's not the nightmare-Sims, but my boss, shirtless and bent over the recliner. And I still can't breathe.

I reach for his hand, panicked, air-starved, and his blue eyes sweep over me in a cool arc, assessing. And then his hand is on the back of my neck, and I'm pushed down so my head is between my knees.

"Breathe," he says, and it's a command; I recognize it as a command.

I try to obey, my ribs working but nothing else, and I think I can still taste blood in my mouth, and then Mark snaps, "Breathe," again, in a voice so sharp and mean that I'm shocked into sucking in a breath.

And then another.

And then another.

Mark keeps his hand on my neck, and it's as cruel and insistent as his voice, and I'm shivering with relief—that the nightmare is gone, that I'm here and not in that cold, gray forest. That someone is telling me what to do and then making me do it.

When he's finally satisfied that I'm breathing, he lifts his hand. "Sit up," he commands, and I do. Something rolls down my jaw and drops—tears.

Embarrassment punctures the relief, and I try to wipe them away as quickly as possible.

Mark sits on the edge of the bed and watches me, his face in its usual neutral expression. But his eyes…there's a recognition in his eyes that makes me want to cry again.

"I saw the reports, the classified ones," he says. Quietly.

"Don't tell me it wasn't my fault," I say. My voice is hoarse, broken. "Don't say I'm a hero. I am so fucking *sick* of people calling me a hero."

"Heroes are make-believe," Mark says, and startled, I look up at him.

I didn't expect him to say that. No one says that.

As if he knows what I'm thinking, a bitter smile crosses his face. "They're all lying to you or they're all lying to themselves, and no option is better than the other. I only knew one hero, President Colchester, and surprise, he's dead now. You weren't a hero that day because you did something much harder than being hero, and that was doing the necessary thing, the fucking *hard* thing, the thing that no one else in your squad had the guts to do. And no matter how many times you wake up unable to breathe, you'll know this: you couldn't have done a single thing differently."

He stands up and goes to the table next to me. There's a clink, a glug, and a glass of amber whiskey is pressed into my hand.

"Drink," he orders, and I drink. It burns, and the scald of it anchors me to…something. Myself, I guess.

"Thank you, sir," I say.

"Next time, just sleep in the bed," Mark says.

CHAPTER 11

OUR FIRST TWO DAYS IN SINGAPORE GO PRECISELY TO PLAN, and enough so that by the time we visit the kink club, a glass-and-metal confection near the massive glowing gardens by the bay, I think I'm ready to talk to Mark.

About being available. For him.

At first, I think the certainty comes from Singapore itself, bright and busy, and still lush somehow, despite the high-rises and car-choked streets.

And then I think maybe it comes from watching Mark meeting with the CEO, walking behind them in the gardens, realizing that people are stopping to look at Mark, to stare at him. He's that handsome, that well made, that merely prowling around in a casual gray suit is enough to turn heads in one of the busiest cities in the world. And it's more than his features and athletic frame; it's the way he moves —effortless, unconscious power.

Who wouldn't want to give themselves to someone like that? Strong and lovely and sovereign?

But I know —and I think I knew it then too—that the

certainty is because of the plane. Because he helped me not with sympathy or soft, coaxing words but with sharp commands and a strong hand on my neck. Because he didn't call me a hero. Because he understood that killing Sims hadn't been something as easy as being good or being brave.

He is maybe the only person who seems to understand that.

And maybe I want to give him something in return for that gift, that understanding. Or maybe I just want him, and to hell with the consequences. So what if I fall in love with him and he doesn't fall in love with me back? I'll still be his to use. That'll be enough.

And so I wait until we're done at the club, done touring its excesses—the small indoor Ferris wheel equipped for sex, the tractable subs and terrifying Dominants, the wealth dripping from necks and fingers and liberally poured wine bottles. I wait until we get back to our hotel suite, with its two separate bedrooms, the colorful lights of the gardens at night pressing against the windows.

"Sir," I say as Mark walks toward his room.

He's already stripped off his jacket and draped it over his arm, and his fingers are on a cuff link. "Yes?" he asks. It's been a long day and his hair has freed itself from the elegant hairstyle he favors. Some of it has fallen forward over his forehead. It looks heartbreakingly soft.

I stand in the middle of the suite's living room, daring myself to say the words, to just *fucking do it* already.

"I know what Strassburg did when he worked for you," I say, hoping I sound neutral but confident and not like I'm terrified of all the potential outcomes of the next few minutes—not like I'm terrified even of the outcome that I *do* want. "I mean…on top of his regular duties."

Mark is still, watching me with eyes gone atramentous in the dark.

"You know." It's not spoken like a question.

I forge ahead. "I know he was your submissive. I know you had sex with him." I try to think of all the things I wanted to explain, make clear. "I know it wasn't romantic or anything, more of an arrangement, and I—"

It's so hard to talk when he's watching me. When he's motionless, sharp-eyed, like a chess player waiting for an opponent to walk themselves into their own trap.

"I want to do that," I finish. There's a tremble in the word *want* that I hope he didn't hear. "I want to do what Strassburg did. With you."

Mark's hand drops from his wrist, the cuff link still fastened, and I catch the small flex in his jaw before his expression becomes neutral once more. "Let me make sure I understand. You're offering yourself for me to fuck."

"Yes, sir."

"Why?"

Of all the questions, I didn't expect that one. "Because—because I think it would be good. For you. To have that." My answer is punctuated by short, shallow inhales; Mark is walking toward me now, his eyebrow lifted.

"You think it would be good for me," he repeats. He stops just a foot away, and I can smell that subtle, haunting scent of him. Rain and heat and lingering electricity. "And that's why you want to do this."

"Yes, sir."

He draws in a breath. Waits.

"No," he says finally.

Cold humiliation slides in my veins like a thick gel.

"No?" I ask in a faint voice.

"No," he confirms. "We're not doing that."

"But—"

Even in the city-lit glow of the otherwise darkened room, I see his eyes flash. "I've given my answer, Tristan."

"Because you don't want to?" I can't help but ask. It's

needy of me, insecure and miserable of me, but I have to know. I have to know if I'm not enough for him even to use.

A bitter laugh escapes his mouth and he turns away. "Strassburg offered because he already knew he was a submissive, and it was just as convenient for him as it was for me. He needed to be topped and didn't have time outside of being my bodyguard to make it happen. It was mutually beneficial."

My misery is in charge now, making me speak when I should be apologizing, retreating, escaping to my room to shove my face against my hands and let my sheer, worthless *unwantability* overtake me. "You didn't answer my question" is what the misery says, and Mark looks at me.

"Yes, I want to," Mark says. Bluntly.

My stomach lifts, drops.

"I want to shove you to your knees and fuck your pretty face whenever I feel like it," he goes on. "I want to slide into your tight hole and stroke there until I come. I've thought of almost nothing else since the wedding."

My mouth is wet.

"Oh," I say.

"But." Mark looks away. "I can't fuck someone without my needing to—*well*. Sex with me is rarely nice, let's put it that way. I will—I'll have to—"

There's a tightness to his jaw now. It's the most emotion I've ever seen from him, including at his sister's wedding.

"You saw Evander kneeling that night, and it bothered you," he says. "Strassburg saw people kneeling and was eager for the moment he could do it himself. I can only be the man I am, not someone easier, and so this is my one gesture toward goodness. I won't fuck someone unless I know they want it. All of it."

"I do want it," I say, my voice shaking.

He shakes his head. "I will use you like a toy. Like a

100

thing. I will make you cry and like it. I will take you more often than you think a person could need to fuck."

I can't breathe. I can't think. Those words in his cool voice—like a fist around my penis, like teeth on my throat.

"Whatever idea you have about being...*this* for me is incomplete, badly informed. This is not a good idea, and—" He passes his hand over his face and looks back at me. "It'll complicate things. In the future. If I'm fucking you."

"I don't care," I tell him quickly. "And I want—I want all that."

His eyes search mine. "When you first came to Lyonesse, you seemed to find the idea of submission degrading. Tristan: I will degrade you. I will enjoy it. Unless you are wired to feel more like yourself, more alive, more *human*, when someone is tearing you apart, then I would be a bad Dominant and a bad brother-in-law to Ricker to use you like that."

He steps away, and the new space between us feels like a warning. I'm losing this.

"Please, sir," I say. "I—"

My pride is gone, my reason gone. There's only desperate, lonely need.

"I want it. I promise. I promise."

"Even if I believed you really knew what you were asking for, it doesn't change anything. Fucking you would have consequences that I can't entirely predict. It would be exceptionally foolish of me to let my craving for you derail a year that's been as deeply planned as this one."

It is still a rejection, I'm still hurting with it, but my mind lights on those words: *my craving for you*. On the words that came before them.

He does want me.

He does.

Mark shakes his head and turns. "Please forget this. Find someone who will take all that lovely, selfless nobility and give you something lovely and selfless in return. It's not me."

I mean to speak, I mean to stop him, but by the time I figure how to open my mouth and tell him that I don't want anything lovely and selfless, that I want all the things he said with the using and the tearing apart, he's gone.

CHAPTER 12

THE NEXT MORNING, I WAKE WITH MY USUAL ERECTION, deciding to take care of it in the shower. Before, my mind was filled with images it had conjured from scenes at the club, from the kinky porn I'd started watching, but I don't need any of that this morning. Only Mark's face, lit by Singapore at night, studying mine. Only his voice, cold and level.

I will use you like a toy.

I will degrade you. I will enjoy it.

Normally, I masturbate like a soldier. Fast, efficient. A quick hand on my cock, the shortest road to release. But this morning, I imagine what Mark would do to me. Nothing as easy as a quick orgasm, I don't think. Nothing as obvious as steady, tight strokes. He'd touch the inside of me until I was squirming. He'd press against my prostate until I was mindlessly fucking the air. And then he'd edge me until I became nothing but swollen, aching flesh, so full of come and need that I'd let him do anything, any depraved thing he wanted to do to me.

When I finally climax, a hoarse noise tears up from my

throat, my stomach muscles seizing as semen erupts from my jerking, pulsing organ. My heart is hammering against my ribs. I press my forehead to the cold tile of this way-too-opulent hotel shower and tell myself to stop. Just. Stop.

Maybe he wants to fuck me, but there's enough in the way that he won't, and I don't know if I could handle him saying no to me again. I've been through hunger and fire, blood and death, but there's still a part of my heart that's soft and easily bruised. Offering Mark what I offered last night… it's too close to exposing that delicate, beating tissue to him.

When I dress and emerge into the main area of the suite, I find Mark fully dressed and taking a virtual meeting by the window, his watch glinting in the morning sun as he drinks his cappuccino. There is an open newspaper next to his plate, and another folded neatly by his mug. It should be quaint, the paper, the analog watch, but Mark as a man resists even the idea of quaintness.

Instead, it feels purposeful, elegant. Intentional. I think if I asked him why the physical newspaper, why the old-fashioned wristwatch, he'd have answers so obliquely logical that I'd feel like an uneducated jackass for even asking in the first place.

"So Hill, Avendano, and Hodges," Mark says. "With Collier as a possibility."

"I'll make it worth your time," says the other person in the meeting. They sound a little arrogant and also a little desperate. It only took a few weeks in combat for me to learn what a bad combination those two things were in a person.

Mark laces his hands together, his eyes leveled on the screen of the tablet propped in front of him. "There will be several favors I'll have to call in, and lots of collateral information used up in the process, so it won't be cheap. It also might not be possible."

"Ten as a down payment that you can keep no matter what, then," the man says. "Ten more for succeeding."

Mark's face doesn't change, but I notice his toe taps a little impatiently under the table. "And then thirty more in stock."

"Twenty million dollars, and thirty million in stock?" the man says incredulously, and I fight to control my expression as I realize exactly how much money is being discussed over an empty cappuccino cup right now. "Trevena, that's not possible."

"Ah, Richard," says Mark. "You know that I know it is."

There's a silence.

"Fine," the other man grinds out. He sounds furious. "But that's contingent on you getting this done."

"A problem for another day," Mark replies lightly, and then ends the call.

"Tristan," he greets, and there's no sign of anything on his face pointing to our conversation last night—no wariness, no pity. It's the same cool expression I see every morning when I go up to his office after the daily security meeting.

"Good morning, sir." I hope I appear as cool as he does and not like I just rode my own fingers thinking of him.

"Please, have some breakfast. And take your time. Today is an easy day. I only have one job for you."

I sit and help myself to fruit and coffee. "Anything you need me to do, sir."

"Tonight, I'll need you to order room service," he says, setting his tablet back down on the table. "And then receive it without your shirt on."

I stare at him, my hand frozen on the spoon I'd been using to serve myself cut papaya. "Sorry?" I ask.

I was expecting an excursion into the city, perhaps another visit to last night's club. Not whatever this was.

"Let's say"—Mark glances at his watch, seems to be doing math in his head—"at twenty-three hundred hours."

"Is the shirtless part important?"

"Very. Also, order enough food for two. With champagne." Mark thinks for a moment. "And have the shower running when they come to the door."

"Sir," I say in affirmation, although I'm still confused. I'm not above ordering room service or anything like that, but it's strange to be planning it this early in the day. *And planning to be shirtless*. But it's my job to do as I'm told, so ordering room service without a shirt it is. With the shower running.

So fucking weird.

"And there's one more thing for today…" says Mark, and that's how, an hour later, we end up at a narrow, white church tucked between apartment buildings, kneeling in the back row while the priest does the liturgy of the Eucharist.

The service is in English, as are the songs, and even though it's been years since I regularly went to Mass, I recognize the hymn from my childhood, and start singing along about one bread and one body and one Lord of all.

But I'm only a verse or two in when I become aware of a pair of dark blue eyes fixed on me.

"Sir?" I whisper.

He's looking at me like he's never seen me before. "You can sing," he says.

I don't even know what to say to Mark's observation; it's like having someone tell me that I have green eyes or freckles on my nose in the summer.

It is strange to think that I can spend nearly every moment of every day with someone and have them not know this about me, this thing that it feels like the whole world knows. Tristan Thomas can sing. He sang in high school, and he sang at West Point, and then when he was deployed, he'd sing if someone had a guitar. He can't even go to a bar that has the *potential* of karaoke without being cajoled into singing.

It's a pointless talent for a soldier. Like a sledgehammer that's also able to paint miniature oil portraits. Yes, it's interesting, but when has that ever gotten the job done?

I turn back to the hymnal, even though this song has, like, five lines to it and I've had it memorized since I was little, and start singing again.

He keeps watching me. And after we go up and get our Communion, I can feel his gaze moving back to me when we sing the final hymn.

Finally, Mass is over, and rather than get in a car back to the hotel, Mark has us walk.

"Is there a reason we went to Mass today, sir?" I ask after we're a block away from the church, knowing it's not actually my business but still curious. Mark's residual Catholicism seems at odds with his present job and maybe even his past one. That he still feels the need to come sit in Mass sometimes is strange to me. He is hardly what you expect to see in the dictionary if you were to flip the pages open to *Good Catholic Man.*

A priest torn apart in his own sacristy…they had to rip out the floor and the walls…

I shake off my dad's words, forget them. They're just rumors—rumors that seem very far away from the man who just charmed every old lady within *peace be with you* handshaking range.

Mark eases out of his suit jacket and drapes it over his arm. I don't do the same, although I'd dearly like to. The humidity here is a living, breathing thing. "I find it anchoring," Mark finally replies. "Don't you?"

"Because it's familiar? Yeah, I guess."

"You're not religious?" he asks. It's his turn to sound curious.

"Not really," I say. "I never minded going to Mass before I went to West Point. I liked it even. I liked the singing and the comfort of it and seeing everyone." And then I pause, having surprised myself.

When I look over, I see that Mark has lifted a brow. An invitation to elaborate.

"Well, I—I'd just forgotten that part," I say, feeling a little silly. He doesn't care about this. "I'd forgotten that I liked seeing people. Being part of a group."

"Being part of a group—you didn't feel that way in the army? With your platoon?"

"With *them*, yes. But when I came home after my first deployment, it was…"

I can't describe what it was. Like being a pod person. Like being an extraterrestrial. I felt like a stranger among people who'd known me my entire life.

"They didn't understand," Mark finishes for me. "They couldn't."

"Even my father—all his deployments were during peacetime, you know? He didn't seem to understand that it was different, and whenever I tried to explain it, it kept coming out wrong."

And it was never that I consciously gave up trying to explain it, but I kept telling myself that if I thought of the right words first, the right metaphors, it would be like a spell. A spell that would unlock the truth, and I could make my father see how terrifying it had been, how lonely and yet also how cramped and teeming—and I'd be able to explain how we'd see something so *deeply fucked up* and then we'd all wake up the next day and go back to business as usual, and how that turned life into something so flimsy that nothing meant anything anymore.

And if I could make General Ricker Thomas understand, then maybe I could eventually make everyone understand. Or at least understand enough that they would stop seeing me as some sort of symbol. As a stock photo of a courageous soldier, clear-eyed and valiant.

Mark nods a slow nod. He gets it. I feel like a jackass right then for forgetting that.

He gets it.

"You know what I'm talking about," I say. "That feeling of when you come back."

"I thought it would be worse after the CIA," says Mark. "But it wasn't. It was about the same. You want to tell everyone what it was like, what you saw, what you had to do, and at the same time, you can't even find a single word to start describing it that doesn't shrink the entire thing down into something smaller and easier than it was."

"Yeah." We cross a narrow street, Mark's shoulder brushing once against mine. "That's it exactly."

I see our hotel peeking above the other buildings, but Mark veers left, down another narrow street. I'm getting used to Mark's excursions when we travel, but I do wish, professionally, he'd tell me where we were going so I could get my bearings first.

"Anyway, to answer your question, sir, I'm not religious now because I don't think I ever was in the first place. I liked it, church, the building and the people in it, but God felt like part of the package and not the reason for it. He's just never felt as viscerally *there* as something like the army. Like America."

"Have you made a graven image of our country, Tristan?" Mark asks, sounding amused.

Have I? Maybe I had at one point. At any rate, I'm afraid I'm onto a new graven image now, a new idol.

He's walking right next to me.

"Not anymore, sir."

"Hmm."

We stop in front of a small storefront with a display of dusty clocks in the window. Without pausing to read the sign listing the shop's hours, Mark walks through the open door. The rooms above the store have their shutters flung wide to cajole a stray breeze, but the shop below is stifling and dim, filled with shadows and ticking clocks.

Mark approaches the counter in back, already unfastening his wristwatch with practiced movements. "I think this is running fast," he says to the man behind the counter, whose expression doesn't change. "Could you quote a repair for me?"

The man blinks behind his glasses, once, and then takes the watch and goes into the back. Mark leans against the counter, looking utterly relaxed and dashing with his jacket over his arm, and his white shirt hugging his wide shoulders and tightly muscled chest and stomach. A gentleman out for an afternoon stroll, with all the time in the world.

I almost remind Mark that our plane leaves tomorrow morning, so there's no time for a watch repair that will take longer than a few hours, but then I notice how often his eyes drift back to the doorway the man left through. Even if his expression is easy, he's very aware of the time it's taking for the shopkeeper to return.

The man comes back several minutes later, the watch and a folded piece of paper in his hands. Mark takes the watch, unfolds the paper, and reads the numbers scrawled there. He sighs, disappointed.

"It's too much, I'm sorry. I'll have to try somewhere else." He gives the man an apologetic nod, pockets the paper, and then we leave.

The shopkeeper doesn't speak a word in return.

———

After we get back into our suite, Mark hands me a bottle of water and then says he's going to take some calls in his room. I won't be needed until the shirtless room service tonight, so I'm free to do whatever I like. I go inside my room and chug the entire bottle. And then it takes about thirty seconds before I'm toeing off my shoes, taking off my jacket and tie, and draping myself sideways across the bed.

Twenty minutes, I tell myself. My internal clock is pretty decent at this sort of thing, honed under the threat of bullets and bombs, and so I close my eyes certain that I'll wake up exactly when I want to.

Except when I do wake up, it's with that abrupt and sick feeling of oversleeping. The sun is lower in the sky, and my feet are cool from where they've been hanging off the bed. I check the clock—it's close to six—and pad into the suite to see if Mark needs me.

But Mark isn't there.

I stand for a moment in the empty living area, straining my ears for sounds from his room. When I hear nothing, I go over and knock and then let myself inside.

It's also empty, as is the bathroom.

He's not here.

Except…except his phone is here, on his bedside table, next to his slim leather wallet and passport. He wouldn't go anywhere without his phone and passport, right?

Alarm skates through me, grazing my thoughts, and I go get my shoes, jacket, and phone, ready to go find him. I get all the way to the door out of the suite when I see the note wedged into the crack between the door and the jamb. I pull it out. It's written in pen on the hotel stationary.

Remember, it says in neat handwriting. *2300. Don't forget the champagne. Or the shower.*

I stop. Consider.

If Mark wanted me to go with him to wherever he went, he would have asked, and clearly he's planning on coming back to food and champagne. And me shirtless.

The thought of that makes me restless, unsure, blood pooling into my groin with hot, sporadic surges.

Maybe he's changed his mind from what he said last night. Maybe it's a test. Maybe he just wants champagne and a bodyguard peep show. Whatever the reason, I do precisely as he asks. I unbutton my shirt and leave it in my room, and then I call down for dinner when it's time. Mark hadn't specified *what* he wanted to eat, so I make a guess with steak, and then order a couple different desserts for him to try.

When the food arrives later, I feel rather silly opening the door without my shirt on, the shower running in Mark's bedroom with absolutely no one in it.

"I'll take that," I say to the person who's brought up the cart, half trying to hide behind the door as I do. Six weeks of working in a kink club, and I'm still shy about someone seeing my bare torso.

The hotel employee's eyes slide past me to the room, where the lights are low and one of the bedroom doors is cracked open. The sounds of the shower's spray hitting tile echo through the space, and the employee and I come to the realization at the same time.

Shirtless man, dinner for two. Shower running.

I suddenly understand exactly what this must look like.

"Of course, sir," the employee says, cheeks pinking. I tip him and roll the tray inside and then fight the urge to go bury myself in a pile of towels after I turn off the shower. Why the fuck had Mark wanted the hotel to think—why *plan* for that?

But I don't have the chance to ask him, not over dinner at least, because an hour passes without him coming back, and then another.

And then another.

I eat my cold steak and some dessert.

I put my shirt back on and then sit on the couch.

I fall asleep there, in front of the food and champagne I ordered, fighting the urge to feel like I've been stood up.

But I can't fight it, and the bitter loneliness of it follows me into my dreams, where I don't dream of Sims exactly but of standing with Sims in an alley, the alley where McKenzie died.

He hadn't been there, not in real life—but also in real life I hadn't been miserable over a man I hadn't even met yet. We stand there over McKenzie's body and I can't feel anything other than Mark's rejection, even with one of my dead best friends at my feet. And Sims turns to me and says, with blood running out of his mouth, *What, you thought he might change his mind about you?*

When I flutter my eyelids open a few hours later, it's to the blue haze of pre-dawn, and there's a tall figure standing in front of the couch, looking down at me.

My body must already recognize him because I don't jolt up with adrenaline. My heart speeds in a very different way than with fear.

"I hope you treated yourself to the good champagne," says Mark. He's wearing different clothes than yesterday: a T-shirt that looks brand-new and cheap, and jeans that look brand-new and expensive.

I straighten up, blinking fast. He looks faintly amused and also tired. Smudges stain the skin under his eyes and his jaw is rough with stubble. His hair is tousled and loose, hanging over one side of his forehead. It makes him look younger.

"Sir," I say. "I didn't realize you'd left until after you'd gone."

He waves a hand, stepping around me to examine the room service cart nearby. "I didn't want to wake you. I just had a place I wanted to visit while I was here."

"A place," I say, looking at his clothes again. The lettering is in Thai. I think it's advertising a brand of beer.

Mark lifts a metal lid to look at the hours-old steak

underneath and then grabs a roll. I notice that the tattoo on his arm is gone…but a smear near his elbow reveals the trick. Makeup. He's covered his tattoo in makeup.

"I haven't seen very many T-shirts in Thai here," I say.

"Hmm," Mark says noncommittally.

My father's words come back to me right then, shimmering next to the shirt, the uneaten meal. *Surely there are times he goes missing that you can't account for…*

Shirtless with the shower running, that's how he wanted me to take the food. Just enough to make the moment memorable and embarrassing for the hotel employee.

"Last night, sir…was I an alibi?"

"Technically, the person who delivered your room service is the alibi," says Mark easily, taking a bite of the roll. I've never seen him eat like this, fast and chewing hard. "And let's make sure you're packed. Our flight is in three hours."

CHAPTER 13

ABSOLUTELY NOTHING CHANGES WHEN WE GET HOME EXCEPT for one thing—sometimes, at the corners of a conversation or as he passes me as I hold the door for him or as we say goodbye after another night in the hall, I catch him looking at my mouth.

I will degrade you. I will enjoy it.

I haven't forgotten a single syllable of that conversation, and I don't think he has either. But my pride makes a delayed appearance and insists on guarding itself from future rejection. *He'll just say no again if you try*, it says, sulky and pouty in my thoughts. *If he really wanted you, he'd fuck you anyway.*

So I don't bring it up again, and neither does he, even though I sometimes can't think of anything else but long, strong fingers, the dip of his Adam's apple when he drinks his gin, the way his cock gleamed ruddy and thick under wet latex in his office.

Two nights after we get home, I hear a knock on my door, the first visitor I've had since I moved in. Curious, I go to answer it, wondering who it could be this late in the evening, and then my heart stutters behind my ribs when I see Mark through the peephole.

"Sir," I say, opening the door, "do you want to go back up to the hall?" I haven't changed out of my suit yet, so I could just grab my earpiece and go…

"No," Mark says, stepping inside, and he's not wearing *his* suit anymore. He's in dark tactical pants and a black turtleneck. Black boots and no watch. "I thought we could take a trip."

I glance down at my phone, see that it's two in the morning. Remember that it's my job to do whatever he wants.

"Yes, sir. Should I change?"

"You should. Dark clothes, and be quick."

I go and change into dark pants and a black compression shirt I wear to run sometimes, dark sneakers, and then come back.

"Leave your phone here," Mark says and then turns to leave.

Thirty minutes later, and we're parking our car at a Chevy Chase tennis court. I look at it as we get out of a beige Camry that Mark put different plates on before we left Lyonesse.

"I didn't picture you as the Camry type, sir," I say as Mark pulls out a stocking cap and uses it to cover his blond hair.

"That would be the point," he murmurs, and then he looks up at the moon and heaves a giant sigh. "Come on."

We walk through the court and a long park, staying under the trees where possible, and then we get to a row of Tudor-style houses. We stand in the shadow of one house while Mark appraises its neighbor. The streetlight makes a harsh chiaroscuro of his face; the lines of his cheek and jaw are sharply visible, along with the slopes of his mouth. I think I could count every one of his eyelashes like this.

"You're going to follow me to that house," he says as he produces a slender flashlight from his pocket, which I take. It's warm from his body. "The occupant is currently with an escort, but when he returns home, he will come through the back door. He will come as quietly as possible so he doesn't wake his wife."

I see the problem right away. "So you need me to keep watch."

"Flash the light into the upper left window three times if you see him. A taxi will drop him off at the top of the road. But I'll be quick."

"Sir, I—" I stop myself, torn. I don't feel comfortable doing something patently illegal.

On the other hand, what did I expect when I took a job with a self-admitted blackmailer?

"This isn't a murder or a theft," Mark says. "I promise I'm not resurrecting my wet-work days. And if it soothes your conscience, I'll be the only one breaking and entering."

I take in a breath. The night is brisk, and my fingers and toes are starting to get cold. I wish Mark didn't look so good in a black turtleneck.

"Okay, sir," I say, and then we make our way through the grass and trees to the house, where Mark lets himself into the unlocked back door. I see sensors for a security system mounted on the doorframe and have a momentary jolt of panic, but Mark touches my shoulder and then points to the security console on the wall. It's blinking green.

It's disarmed. For the philanderer to sneak back inside more easily, I assume.

With a nod to show I understand, I step back, flashlight at the ready, as Mark disappears into the bowels of the house. My senses are on high alert, and I hear everything, every gust of wind and creak of branches, every pop and sigh of the house. I fist the flashlight, my thumb resting on the button, my blood racing.

The stakes are so much lower than they were in Carpathia, but it's like my body doesn't understand how to calibrate danger anymore. It's like there's either zero danger *or* it's an existential fucking threat, and here in a snoozing Maryland suburb, my adrenaline is spiking like I'm about to attack an enemy camp.

But there's no enemy, no camp, and soon, there's not even any need for the flashlight. Mark emerges from the shadows of the house, closes the door behind him, and off we lope back to the car.

"What were we doing, sir?" I ask finally, once we're on the road again. "If we weren't stealing anything or hurting anyone?"

"I was leaving something behind for our unfaithful friend," Mark says. He's wearing gloves—he must have put them on inside the house—and they make his hands look larger, more powerful than ever as they move on the steering wheel.

"Are you going to tell me more than that?"

"Not until I know if it's worked and that we've done this properly, without any link back to us. The less you know until I have that certainty, the safer."

A very Special Activities Center way to think.

"At any rate," he says as we pull into the lower level of the club's parking garage, "we should know soon enough."

———

It worked. The next afternoon, the space exploration bill—the one with a comfortable margin for passing the senate chamber—fails.

I read the updates on my phone while Mark is in a meeting in his office. Two senators changed their votes without any notice. One senator claimed transportation issues and didn't show up to vote. And the last came down with gastroenteritis so violent that he can't even leave his house.

His house which is in Chevy Chase, Maryland.

The most interesting bill to pass through Congress during President Embry Moore's administration is dead, and it's because of four senators.

Hill, Avendano, Hodges, and Collier.

Mark's meeting ends, and I have my phone put away by the time the door opens and Lady Anguish steps out, giving me a small vulpine smile. Mark steps out too, kissing her hand before she boards the elevator.

"Did you see?" he asks once the elevator doors close. His voice is triumphant, and there's a boyish glint to his eye. He looks like he just pulled off a high school prank.

A high school prank that I think he might have earned fifty million dollars for.

"Did we give an elected lawmaker gastroenteritis last night, sir?"

Mark waves a hand. "We merely *infused* gastroenteritis onto his toothbrush. What happened next was out of our control. Besides, I can't blackmail everyone, Tristan. It would get boring."

"And why are we blackmailing anyone again? Around a popular bill that would be objectively a good thing?"

"My definition of objective good is more limited than yours," Mark reminds me. And then he walks back into his office as I trail behind him. "There are two companies with the ability to partner with NASA for a renewed space program. One is a clear favorite because they're ready to expand immediately. The other company has much better tech and design but isn't ready to scale up."

"So that company…"

"Asked me to kill the bill, yes. Never fear, though. It'll be back soon. It's too necessary and there's too much public interest for it to stay dead."

"And by the time it comes back, the company that hired you will be ready to compete more evenly?"

"That's right. And if they get a favorable government contract, fifty million dollars will be a drop in the bucket," Mark says. "An advisable gamble for them. A great stock opportunity for me."

He's pushing papers together on his desk now, and I think about how he fucked a curvy sub half to death on this desk. Left her nipples wet and her thighs rope-bitten, and now he's casually mentioning how he derailed federal legislation in less than three days because someone had good stock options.

Mark glances up at me, and victory still burns through his normally cool expression. "Let's get lunch," he says. "I'm starving."

CHAPTER 14

Two weeks after we get back from Singapore, I'm in the daily security meeting listening to Nat and Goran bicker about hosting a prince from Spain and what additional security precautions they need to take. I've been listening to this same fight for a week now, so I'm about to pack up and go upstairs when my daily email from Sedge hits my inbox. I open up the most updated schedule for Mark and then frown at the screen.

In a little over a month, there are three weeks shaded in, with the word *Ireland* noted above. There are literally no details attached other than the words *Philtre D'Amour*.

"*Philtre D'Amour*," I murmur out loud to myself.

"It's the yacht," says Goran, and I look up at him, surprised.

"Mark has a yacht?"

"I feel like even the word *yacht* is a little mild," Nat adds.

"What would be the right word, then?" needles Goran, who still seems to be grumpy over the prince security issues.

"Ridiculous," mutters Nat, and then Goran's face splits into a delighted grin.

"Okay, you're right. That thing is ridiculous."

Sedge would be the one handling the details, the equipping and porting and boarding, and so I'll need to talk to him to figure out next steps for a security plan. "I wonder why Ireland of all places," I say, folding my laptop shut and standing.

"Isn't *she* Irish?" Goran asks, just as Nat says, "Her mother's from Ireland."

"Who has an Irish mother?" I ask.

They both look at me, two sets of blinking brown eyes. "Isolde," Goran says, like he's telling me the sky is blue.

"Ah," I say. That clarifies nothing for me.

Nat's phone pings, and she eyes the screen like it's about to bite her. "That's the prince's team about their precious cargo. I swear if they have another fit about—"

That's my cue to leave, and leave I do, going to find Sedge before joining Mark upstairs. I find Sedge in his office on the floor below Mark's, dressed in trousers and a button-down shirt layered under a tight V-neck cardigan with birds on it. His colorless, barely gray eyes flick up to me as I enter.

"Hello," he says in that soft, wary way of his. I've learned that most of the employees on this floor fall into the same kinky categories as the members here. Dinah and Andrea are Dommes, Sedge is a submissive. Ms. Lim is a switch, which I can only measure by when she wears a collar and when she wears keys—and in the variances of her *fuck around and find out* energy as she's dealing with guests.

"Hello," I greet politely. "Do you have any more information about this trip to Ireland next month? Goran said that Mark wants to take a yacht?"

Sedge's full mouth turns down. He is very pretty when he pouts. "I know as much as you do. He won't even give me a proper set of dates for the trip, much less its purpose or if he's taking any meetings there. All I know is that he plans to fly there and sail back, but since he won't give me the dates, I can't even book the flight."

If Sedge is having trouble getting answers out of Mark, I know I'll fail for sure. I've learned that Mark seems to have no greater pleasure than giving me needlessly cryptic responses to ordinary questions—or worse, turning the questions back around on me.

But I'll still have to try; I can't allow him to take an international trip with zero precautions.

"Thank you," I tell Sedge now, and I make to leave. Sedge lifts a hand, and says, "Tristan?"

I stop. "Yes?"

He tucks a lock of chin-length hair behind his ear. "You're going to Cornwall in a few days."

I nod. The trip was on the books before I came on, and we're staying at a property Mark owns, so the passive security there is already very robust. No meetings, no excursions. If I didn't know any better, I'd call the five days in Cornwall a vacation, but I do know better.

Mark Trevena doesn't seem the vacation type.

"I've never—well, I've only been here a year and half, but I've never traveled with him. So this was secondhand from Strassburg. But Mark takes this trip every year at the same time, and Strassburg told me once that Mark likes to be left alone for it. In fact, he usually sends Strassburg away to stay at an inn nearby." Sedge looks awkward, like he thinks he's betraying Mark's loyalty somehow. "I just didn't want you to be caught unawares."

"Thank you," I say, not sure what to make of this warning. It stings preemptively, because if he didn't even want Strassburg with him—Strassburg whom he fucked, whom he dominated—then I can't imagine he'll want me there either.

And I shouldn't care. I shouldn't care.

Maybe I'll wake up tomorrow a different person, unobsessed, and I won't mind at all.

———

Mark says very little on the flight to London, and then on the second flight to Newquay. When we pick up the rental car at the airport, Mark slips a small device out of his shoulder bag and attaches it magnetically to the bottom of the car.

I stare at it and then stare at him.

"No one but Sedge, Strassburg, and the caretaker knows where this place is. And now you," says Mark. His voice is subdued. "I prefer to keep it that way."

"Does it block the car's location?" I ask, getting inside. It's a nondescript car, a small gray sedan a few years old, not the sleek sports car I still imagine when I think of Mark driving somewhere.

Except this makes more sense, actually, much like the Camry a couple weeks ago—it would be a terrible CIA operator who flashed around in a memorable car, visible and interesting.

"Something like that," Mark says, and then there's a something almost conspiratorial in his expression when he adds, "Melody got it for me. Don't tell anyone."

The drive to the property takes over an hour as we move away from the coast and into the heart of Cornwall. Mark drives, his large hands on the steering wheel and the gear shifter, making the unremarkable sedan hum to life under his capable, subtle touch.

I think I'm jealous of a car.

We pass through valleys, through moors and the occasional village, until trees begin to fringe the side of the narrow road, thicker and thicker still, until we dip into a valley deeper than the others, deep enough that it still feels like spring has only just started here while the rest of the peninsula is in full, heady bloom.

The road narrows even more as we pass through two brick posts, each topped with a roaring lion, which are weathered into lichen-spotted suggestions of themselves. The trees are thick enough now that they meet over the road, joining together in a tangle of dark branches and new leaves.

And then the road twists and the trees break abruptly to reveal a stone house of two stories, two chimneys, and plenty of glittering windows. There's a conservatory at one end, a stretch of overgrown garden, and a small chapel that looks older than everything else. Magnolia trees in full bloom dot the grounds, the breeze sending white and pink petals fluttering to the ground. Gardenia bushes with fat, white flowers spread beneath the front windows, and anxious birds flap between them and the narrow graveyard next to the chapel.

"Morois House," Mark announces as he stops the car in front of the black-lacquered door. It's the last thing he says to me for two days.

———

Through whatever cardigan magic Sedge wields, he has Morois House ready for us when we walk inside. Every room smells fresh and is free of dust, the kitchen is stocked with enough food to feed a platoon for a month, and when I find the small closet housing the thin but sufficient network of security cameras, everything is in perfect working order.

Mark doesn't even bother dropping his bags. He swipes an unopened bottle of scotch from a long buffet table in the kitchen and then stalks straight into a book-lined room I assume is the library, bringing his things with him.

He shuts the door before I can follow him in.

At least I have the dubious comfort of knowing that it isn't anything I've done, but it is still strange that first night, making sandwiches for dinner alone, my knocks to the library door going unanswered.

The next day I wake to find the library door still shut, and with nothing really bodyguard-like to do, I decide to explore the wooded area around the house and get a sense of the grounds.

I follow the overgrown footpaths up to the edges of the valley and find I can't see any other houses or buildings at all. There's only the road, barely visible under its lattice of branches, and very far off, I can see a brown smudge of forbidding moor on the horizon. In the upper reaches of the valley, bluebells are starting to press up between the trees, and they're also growing along the edges of the graveyard behind the chapel, magnolia petals caught in the tangles of their long leaves.

The gravestones are too worn and moss-covered to read, but inside the unlocked wooden door of the chapel, I see a small plaque.

In memory of Albert Trevena, who fell at the Somme, 1916.

So this is a family property, some kind of ancestral Trevena house. I read the other plaques on the wall—other Trevenas, with a handful of Tyacks and Teagues mixed in, and then note that the altar and font—while empty of religious appurtenances and water—are dustless and gleaming.

Back inside the house, I find the library door still shut, and so I start exploring the space beyond my bedroom and the kitchen.

I expect more clutter and antiques from a house passed down through generations, but the place is as impersonal and spare as a rental, although still comfortable. I find two more guest rooms, and then a larger room I presume to be Mark's when he's not cuddling a bottle of scotch in the library. A dark coverlet covers the bed, with only one pillow. It hasn't been slept in. I notice discreetly recessed rings embedded into the dark wood of the bed's posts.

Definitely his room, then.

I know I shouldn't snoop, it's not polite, it's not at all my job to scout the territory *inside*, but it's like a burning in my blood. To know him. To touch the things he's touched.

I'm over to the dresser before I can stop myself, peeking in the drawers.

They're empty, except for the bottom one, which has a sweater folded neatly inside, next to a dried rose. The rose is old and brittle enough to have left a dredge of brick-colored dust underneath it. The sweater is sealed in a clear bag, the kind of bag you put winter things in to protect them from pests.

Or to preserve a lingering scent.

You're intruding. I was expecting to see pajama pants that I could imagine hanging from his hips or rolls of ties I could imagine wrapped around my wrists. Not...not whatever this is.

I shut the drawer carefully and am about to leave when I see the bedside table has a drawer too. Sticky with shame but too curious to stop, I open the drawer. From the dangerous king of kink, I expected all sorts of perversions near at hand to his bedside: lube, toys, condoms in bulk. But it's just the remote for the TV and a picture frame, laid on its face.

I pick it up to see a handsome man with light brown hair, blue eyes, and a heart-pangingly gorgeous smile. He's looking away from the camera, his thick eyebrows down in an expression of unmitigated mischief, a giant silver watch on his wrist. I study it a moment.

It's partly out of focus, but I'm almost certain it's the same wristwatch Mark wears every day now.

There's no date on the picture, but judging from his clothes, this picture is less than a decade old. With the thin lines around his smiling eyes, I guess that he was in his thirties when the picture was taken. Close to Mark's age.

I put it together with the lonely sweater and rose, with

Mark's one-man scotch festival in the library. This man was someone to Mark. Someone he loved, and he isn't around anymore.

He either left Mark—or he died.

CHAPTER 15

I WAKE UP TOO EARLY THE NEXT MORNING AND STARE AT THE ceiling, cataloging my two options.

I can either stay here, in this strange mausoleum of old roses and new scotch, or I can leave and let Mark suffer properly. Grieve all over the house and grounds and roam drunkenly into the kitchen when he wants without worrying about running into someone else.

Having haunted my dad's farmhouse for days on end, I understand it. There are some things so miserable, so private, that even their being *witnessed* feels like an additional agony.

Also I'm worried he hasn't eaten since we got here, despite my trying to give him clumsily made sandwiches through the library door.

I shower and dress, and when I emerge, I see one of the library's doors hanging open, and the dim space beyond it empty. I think I hear a shower somewhere else in the house, down the far hallway, where Mark's bedroom is. That encourages me. If he's able to leave the library, then maybe he'll be able to have a conversation with me about whether it would be better if I left.

I wait half an hour or so, drinking a cup of coffee in the observatory and watching a slow drizzle take up on the glass, trying to give him plenty of time to get dressed. I'm restless, bothered. I don't know what by. That he has a picture in a drawer of a man wearing the same wristwatch as him? That he might indeed want me to leave?

It's all ridiculous, and I still can't help it. I want to be near him. I want to watch those infinitesimal twitches in his jaw while he's thinking; I want him to quirk an eyebrow at me in faint amusement. I want to watch those blue eyes flash when he forgets to control himself.

But it's not up to me. And maybe this is a chance to show how obedient I can be for him. How submissive. Going away when I'm told.

I go back to the kitchen and pour two cups of coffee, two glasses of water, and pile a bowl with berries and cut bananas. I load up a tray and go to the library door, which is once again closed.

I knock. "Sir?" And then I add, pointlessly, "It's Tristan."

There's no answer. I hesitate for a moment, torn between breaching his privacy and worry, and then I do what I've been good at for the last eight years, and I follow my gut. I open the door.

The library is not large, not like something from a movie, but there's something arresting about it nonetheless. An unlit fireplace yawns at one side of the room; at the far end, there is a large bay window letting in the room's only light, which this deep in the wooded valley is a low, green glow, filtered through the petaled shade of a magnolia tree. Books are stacked floor to ceiling on sturdy shelves, a mix of old paperbacks and leather- and cloth-bound books. An antique desk sits in front of the window.

Mark is behind the desk, wearing only a pair of soft lounge pants, his hair dark and damp from his shower. His hands are braced on the leather-topped surface, and his head is dropped between his shoulders.

"Sir, I—"

He doesn't look up. I set the tray down, take a small breath, and step forward. It's not so unlike a battle, approaching him right now.

Step light, breathe light. Be ready for anything.

"I brought some breakfast in," I say. "And I wanted to ask if I"—the question scalds my throat as I push it out—"if I should go. To a village or somewhere. Sedge said you might want to be alone."

He doesn't move from the desk or look up, but I see the muscle-layered sides of his rib cage expand in an uneven exhale.

I step forward again. "But I don't mind staying," I add helplessly. "If you want someone here with you."

His shoulders move with his next breath, and they're so rigid, so tense, a tension that is wrapped all around his body from head to toe. He looks like he's barely holding it together.

"Go if you want," he grinds out at last. His voice is rough, hoarse. With scotch or misery, I can't tell.

"What do *you* want, sir?" I ask, and he finally looks up at me.

I nearly take a step back at the ferocity of his stare. His eyes are scorched with emotion, nearly black in the low light of room and almost feral. As he stares at me, his cheeks grow darker. He's flushing.

It doesn't look sweet on him. It looks dangerous.

"You should go, Tristan," he says. His voice is low and not at all cold. I've never seen him like this, flushed and avid. It's intoxicating.

Literally. I feel unsteady. Buzzed.

"I don't want to go," I say. It's an admission of too much, maybe, but I can't stop it. "I want to stay."

I approach the desk slowly, and he tracks my movement with sharp, burning eyes. Even though he doesn't move outwardly, the rippling tension in his body signals his awareness, his restraint.

"Let me help," I whisper.

"You can't." His voice is flat, dead, but his gaze—it still sears. There are smudges under his eyes and there's stubble on his cheeks and he looks like a man who hasn't slept or eaten or done anything but cut himself open with memories for the last two days. "You can't," he repeats, and looks away.

Two months ago, I would have thought he was right. For someone who's been good at everything he's ever tried, I am only good if I'm following orders.

Sing this note. Throw this ball. Shoot this gun.

Follow this man and make sure no one tries to hurt him as he glides around his glass kingdom.

When there are no instructions, I'm lost. Maybe it's having a solider for a father, or maybe the army did its job too well, but whatever it is, I sometimes feel like I'm missing the *thing* that makes people act. Like I'm a wind-up toy that can only march in the direction it's pointed. Even in Carpathia when it was choice after choice, my call after my call, the overall mission was clear. Protect the civilians and officials. Stop the rebels. Keep your guys from dying.

And maybe that's why I know what to do right now, why I'm walking around the edge of the desk to Mark's side.

The mission is still clear, even if it's changed.

It started as serving as his bodyguard and now it's just: serve.

Mark doesn't move his hands from the desk, but his head turns, and he watches as I go to one knee…and then to the other. The rug laid over the wood floor is thick enough that I sink into it. My knees are close to his feet, and before I lift my face to his, I see that his bare feet are large and strong-boned, lightly dusted with hair at the top.

He turns properly now, looking down at my upturned face, and then his long fingers grip my chin, holding me still for his examination.

The sapphire burn of his stare sends a thrill of danger skating down my spine, and oh shit, what am I doing?

What if he rejects me again? Sends me away after I've made it excruciatingly plain how much I want him? Want to try *this* for him?

He could break me. And not with floggers or clamps or whatever else the rooms at Lyonesse hold, but with only one word. With a turn of his head.

I'd be broken.

But he doesn't turn his head. He doesn't tell me no. Instead the fingers on my chin shift, and I feel a thumb drag slowly over my bottom lip. My mouth opens without me telling it to, and I see his pupils bloom even darker.

"This won't be easy." And that's all he says before he uses his free hand to tug his drawstring pants down and pull out his cock.

I have to look, I can't not look. He's mostly hard, the flesh jerking as it continues to fill with blood, and light catches on the line of golden hair above it.

My mouth waters.

"I don't want easy," I whisper, and then I utter the most honest thing I've ever said: "I want you."

Mark rolls his jaw. One hand holds my chin, the other his ready erection. "You don't know what you're talking about," he says.

And then he pushes the head of his penis into my open mouth.

It's hot and smooth, and the taste of him is the taste of freshly cleaned skin with a trace of soap. I've never done this before, and there's the quiet terror that I'll be no good at it, that Mark will sneer his derision and pull back, but there's something inside me that's larger than the terror—something that's eager to please and also certain that being eager to please is enough.

I try licking, wrapping my tongue around the taut crown. His lips part.

"So pretty," he says darkly, like it's a bad thing, like it's the worst thing. "So goddamn pretty, Tristan."

My own erection kicks at the danger in his voice, straining against the material of the athletic shorts I'm wearing without anything underneath. I want to be pretty for him; I want him always to be talking in that voice, like he has plans that should terrify the fuck out of me.

Whatever's been changing inside me for the last two months has finished changing. I need to be his. On my knees, on my back, humiliated, bruised, used. Whatever he wants me to be, I want it too.

I'm so hard now, just from his presence in my mouth, just from his voice, and then he tightens the hand on my jaw.

"Hold that pouty mouth open," he says, and slides deeper in.

It's nothing like porn, nothing at all, because porn hadn't told me that it would be so wet, such a stretch, that I'd feel a strange surge of pride whenever he gets deep enough to choke me. Which he does more and more, pulling out and then sliding to the back of my throat. His hand is still on my jaw, holding me open, and then his free hand comes up and brushes something off my cheek.

A single tear.

It's purely physiological, from the steady invasion of my throat, but something about it feels good too, like crying for real, freeing and cleansing. Soldiers shouldn't cry, but I've never been able to help it much, probably because most of the time it feels right and necessary—confirmation that an invisible pain is real; it's so real that it can be touched and tasted.

And it turns out I like this, being used to the point of tears. I suck in breaths when he withdraws and try to swallow him down when he goes back in, and while he's not being easy with me, I recognize that he's holding something back too.

When I meet his gaze again through my leaking tears, I see that his restraint is not out of pity, or worry, or anything sweetly tentative. He's taking the time to study my every reaction; he's using his restraint to watch me with a newly unfettered expression. Like he knows it's my first time and he's relishing it.

I will use you like a toy. Like a thing.
I will make you cry and like it.

"Swallow it," he says, and that's all the warning I get before he pulses in my mouth. He's so deep that I barely taste him, but I feel it, hot and thick, and when I start swallowing, he slides his hand down to my throat to feel me drinking him down.

Triumph is scrawled all over his face. That expression with his hand on my throat—and knowing that my mouth was good enough to get him there within minutes—means that I'm now in an agony of lust. My cock burns against the silky fabric of my shorts, and my heart is thumping against my ribs like a sledgehammer.

He holds me still until he's finished, and I'm looking up at him with tears streaming down my face. As he pulls out, I become aware of how much *wasn't* in my mouth—God help me if he ever wants to go all the way in. But the trepidation is tangled up with lust too, with the need to be *something* for him, even if it's just an obedient plaything.

He stares down at me, his palm idly massaging my throat. He's still hard, his chest moving in controlled oscillations, and his face is still victorious.

"I knew it," he says.

"Knew what, sir?" My voice is lower, thicker, with his hand against my windpipe.

"That this is where you belonged."

Where I belong. At his feet, with my mouth open and my heart in his hands.

"Yes, sir," I whisper, and I can't help it—I want to touch him. Touch the taut, tan skin of his abdomen and the neat black ink of his tattoo. Press my palm to his chest and see if his heart is beating as hard as mine.

But when I reach, he catches my hand. "Touching is earned," he says. "A prize. And we're not done playing yet."

With strength that astonishes me—and thrills me in a sick way—he grips my arms and hauls me to my feet. I'm only barely upright when my shirt is torn off and I'm bent summarily over the desk. My shorts are ripped down to my ankles, and instinctively, I lift up, an unthinking response to sudden nakedness. His hand is on my neck immediately, pressing me back down. His bare foot kicks my ankles apart; the shorts are kicked somewhere off to the side.

"If you want to stop, tell me," he says. "But if you want this, stay down."

"I want this," I whisper. I press my hands on either side of my head, proof I'm not planning on stopping, leaving. "But. I've never—"

It's embarrassing. I'm embarrassed.

Mark isn't embarrassed at all though. There's a rough eagerness to his touch as his hands drop to the curve of my ass and he slowly spreads it apart. Cool air kisses along the delicately pleated skin of my entrance.

"Has anyone been here before?"

"No. I've—I'm—"

He crouches behind me, and one hand moves to stroke over the sensitive opening.

I shudder. Such a small place, and yet one short caress has me burning all over.

"Never?" he asks. I can't tell what's in his tone. "You're a virgin?"

"Yes," I say, so glad my face is pressed to the leather mat on the top of the desk. I shouldn't be so embarrassed, it shouldn't matter. Lots of people in their twenties are; lots of people want to be.

It's just that I never wanted to be.

Fingers stroke over my rim again, exploring. "It's such a pretty hole," says Mark in low voice. "All tight and lovely, just ready and waiting to be opened. A flower."

He presses, testing the resistance there, and my cock, trapped against the edge of the desk and hanging rigidly down, surges miserably. I reach without thinking—I have to touch it, I have to have relief—until a sharp *smack* makes me grunt.

Pain stings my wrist and it's put firmly back by my head. "That has to be earned too."

I pant a little against the leather, the pain now a sparkling heat spreading up my arm to my chest. Everything is sparkling. If you cut me open, my blood would be sparkling too.

Mark bends over me, his hard member against my ass, the linen of his pants brushing against the backs of my thighs. His naked chest is hot and firm against my back, and the feeling of being pressed down onto the desk is better than I ever could have imagined.

Having someone's weight on me harrowing in combat—is so fucking wonderful now. I think I'll dream of it when this is over.

"Having you like this is enough to make someone wild, Tristan," he says in my ear. "Bent over and exposed. Letting me do whatever I want."

"Whatever you want, sir," I echo breathlessly, nearly mindless with lust now. I want—I want—I can't even name all the things I want right now. Him inside me. Him on top of me. Him using me until he spurts and all those heavy limbs are finally, finally relaxed. "I want to make you feel good."

"So sweet of you," he says, and then his teeth sink into my shoulder. I jerk underneath him, the shock of the pain mingling with the arousal churning in my stomach. His weight leaves me, a hand pressed between my shoulder blades to keep me where he wants, and then I hear the drawer next to my hip roll open. There's the sound of searching, rustling—he's looking for something, but I don't think even he knows what he's looking for—and then I hear a pleased grunt. Before I even have the time to wonder what it is that he's found, there's a sharp, flat sound, and a stripe of fire sears along the side of my ass.

"A ruler," Mark says. Almost cheerfully. "An old one, probably from when this was my grandfather's office. They made them thicker back then." He whacks me again with it and I jolt.

"Does it hurt?" he asks.

"Yes," I say into the leather mat on the desk. "But don't stop. I—want it."

And I do, I do want it. It hurts, but it's the hurt that comes with laps or push-ups, with long drills or nights spent out in the cold, sleeping on the ground. It feels *right* somehow, like it's *for* something—except instead of being for my country, for my fellow soldiers, for goodness and bravery and loyalty, it's for him.

For Mark.

The ruler comes again and again, diabolical and hot, and Mark straightens and steps back so he can hit my ass everywhere, until I'm sucking air through my teeth, until my head is rolling on the desk. And then like he's building a sick kind of ladder, he layers stripes one above the other, from my knee to the lower curve of my ass.

The last one stings so much that my knees buckle, and I suck in a wounded breath.

"Mmm," he says. "Such a nice little spot, isn't it? So good for the strong subs who need a little bit more…effort." He strikes me there again, pausing to listen to my low groan before he moves to the other side and does it again, taking care to layer two extra stripes along the bottom of my ass.

The ruler clatters on the desk near my hand, and Mark seems to be admiring his handiwork, chafing his large palms against the welts he's left all over me.

"So pretty," he murmurs to himself. "So sweet."

I feel the slide of his hand and then gasp again as it finds my erection, giving it a tight, sharp squeeze that has me moaning. His thumb swipes expertly over the head and goose bumps erupt all over my body as he smears the slick precum everywhere.

I would have never believed before now that I could still be hard after being worked over with a ruler, but here I am, shamelessly trying to press into his touch, widening my legs. Too late, I realize that might have been his aim all along, because then he runs two fingers slick with my own arousal over my newly exposed hole. I shiver on the desk, my hips rocking mindlessly back to meet him, and he rewards me with a slight press of his fingers inside.

"Oh," I say, like he's surprised me.

He pauses.

"Don't move," he orders and then leaves the room. I see bare legs, the low light catching on the gold hair on his calves and thighs. He must have discarded his pants at some point. And I have the strange feeling that I shouldn't lift from the desk to see where the pants ended up, that I must stay exactly as he left me. I want to prove myself to him—prove that when he commands, I will listen.

He comes back, feet padding on the stone flags of the hallway and then on the wood planks and rugs of the library.

I can almost *feel* his pleasure when he sees me in the same position he left me in. And I hear it when he says, "Good boy," along with a light caress to my spine.

My toes curl at those two words. *Good boy.*

He sets something on the desk near my hip, and I hear tearing and then the noise of something slick on hard flesh. A condom.

I knew it was coming, and yet my breath catches in my chest. He's going to fuck me with his cock now. He's going to slide into a place so tight that even a single finger feels like an invasion.

His mouth drops to my shoulder and then to the nape of my neck.

"I wish you could see how incredible you look," he murmurs, and then he reaches for something. A plastic click—a bottle—the sound of liquid. Something cool and slick is painted over the tight eyelet of my ass and I shiver.

"Shh," he says. "It'll warm up in just a minute."

And then his finger circles me, slow but not sweet, more like the touch of someone savoring a first course, knowing a full meal is ahead. It breaches me with leisure; first the fingertip, then up to a knuckle, and then another.

I'm starting to sweat, my skin so flushed it feels like I'm burning. Between my legs, I feel each and every infinitesimal draft of air along the swollen and slick end of my cock.

"Have you ever done this to yourself?" he asks.

He runs a club where sometimes people sleep in dog

crates for fun. I shouldn't feel so flushy and awkward when I reply, "Yes, sir."

"Just fingers? A toy maybe?"

"Just fingers. I—I was too embarrassed to buy a toy."

There's a huff of laughter; warm air brushes past the place where my neck meets my shoulder. "Just wait until someone tells you about the internet."

His finger is thick, long, and he turns it *just so*. It brushes against the place inside that makes me wild.

"I've never—" I'm squirming underneath him now, and if I thought him lying on top of me was heavenly, it has nothing on *moving* underneath him. On writhing and bucking and being held pinned in place anyway.

"I've never had a real place of my own," I continue, and this is almost more embarrassing than anything else, but then there's another caress inside and any emotion that's not *oh god right there* vanishes. "I was nervous about ordering something and having someone find out I'd bought it for myself."

"So just your fingers, then," Mark says, and then when he pulls out and pushes back in, there's now two fingers. I'm being stretched. Dilated. This is as much as I've ever done to myself, and the angle has never been like this, it's never been this deep and adept. I make a noise as he begins to fuck me slowly but thoroughly with his hand, grazing my prostate with every stroke, working me open bit by bit, until it gets easier and easier to take.

He's moved off me, and I try to look over my shoulder at him. I can't see much, but I can see that his expression is pleased and darkly ravenous. His eyes are fixed on where his fingers move in and out, and his free hand is sliding up and down my abused flank, sending sparks of sensation all over my body.

"I used to dream about having a submissive like you," he murmurs. "Just like you."

The words sink into me like heat from a fire, and even with pleasure spiking through me, I know how dangerous it is. How dangerous words like that are for someone like me, someone who's only one breath away from falling in love with him.

"I didn't know to dream you," I admit in a whisper.

He stills behind me, and there's a pause. I wonder if he's going to speak, laugh, scoff, but instead, he lowers his mouth to my shoulder and catches the trapezius muscle in his teeth and bites down. The pain steals my breath away.

He lingers for a moment, teeth undoubtedly marking me, like he's trying to put something he can't say into the bite instead.

And then his mouth comes near my ear. "Tristan."

"Sir?"

"This part won't be easy either."

He grabs the back of my neck, and without warning I'm hauled off the desk and pushed onto the floor. I don't have time to adjust or get my bearings; I'm shoved and then pressed down, my cheek against the carpet, my left knee shoved up to expose my entrance. My erection is trapped underneath me, and though the carpet is plush, no carpet is soft enough for bare flesh to rub against repeatedly. But I rub anyway, squirming, desperate for friction. My heart is wild in my chest, and I think I might ejaculate right now. Solely from being shoved down and shoved open. Solely from the shadow of him over me, from the sight of his left hand planted by my face, large and strong.

Something big, hot, and slippery presses against me, and I shudder, closing my eyes and breathing into the floor. It's so big. So much bigger than my fingers or his, so much... *more*. And when he breaches the tight muscle that guards against intrusion, I make a low, labored noise. It feels like he's splitting me in half, cleaving me right in two.

He hisses above me, an animal sound, and my dick surges painfully just to hear it. Hear what my body is doing to him. I want to hear it again; I want to hear every noise possible.

I remember reading that I should open for this part, that I should bear down against him, and I take a deep breath and push against the invasion. With an abrupt slide that has us both grunting, he sinks all the way home.

For a moment, that's all there is. The discomfort, the stretch. The fullness, the heat. My cock like an aching bar against the carpet, desperate to rut and come, my pulse pounding in my throat.

His strong hand by my face, the fingertips digging into the carpet.

"That's good," he groans, giving an experimental thrust. "I knew it would be. I knew it would be so—*fuck*—"

He moves again, this time lowering himself so that he's all the way on top of me, his chest and stomach to my back, his legs tangled with mine. One arm slides under my stomach, hand spread possessively wide, and then his forearm braces above my head.

His head comes down and I feel his lips on the place where my jaw meets my ear.

I want to move, to turn to kiss him, but I can't. I'm pinned with his weight, his hips, his arms around me, and the feeling of it is like the feeling of the expensive rug on my needy cock: exquisite torture.

I test it a little, still trying to move, and only succeed in driving his organ deeper into my body.

Soft lips curve against my cheek. "Trying to get away, Tristan?"

No. No, that isn't it at all. "Making sure I can't," I breathe in admission, and his fingers tighten on my stomach.

"I knew it," he says, an echo of his earlier words, and I should hate that—I should hate that this is what I want, that

143

it is so obvious. That someone else can see that I don't want to be on my own two feet, being looked in the eye and kissed softly. That I don't want romantic and respectful and tender.

That I want to be pressed facedown in the carpet while my boss pumps into me from behind instead.

And yet, I am shivering, moaning, trying to fuck my cock against the same carpet that's also rubbing me raw. It feels so goddamn *right* that I think my bones are going to crack under the rightness of it.

I was always meant to be here.

I was always meant to be here.

His heavy limbs and hard torso and chest keep me still for the taking; he fucks me like he hasn't gotten to fuck anyone in years. Which I know isn't true—I can still remember the slick sound of him using the gloved submissive's cunt—but it feels true, it feels so true. In the ragged tear of his breath, in the way the hand on my stomach keeps flexing and grabbing and spreading. In the way he keeps mouthing my shoulder, my neck, the top of my spine.

In the almost desperate driving of his hips, the strain of his stomach and thighs and calves to get himself deeper, to pound harder.

And each and every piston of his hips has me seeing stars; the blunt head of him and his wide shaft rubbing against the sensitive gland deep in my body. Each thrust rocks my own hips forward, forcing me to fuck the carpet, and the knot inside my groin is so tight that I can't breathe, and his shuddering, grunting satisfaction is also mine, and the proof that I'm giving him pleasure is just as potent as a hand on my cock—*more*—and then I'm a wild thing underneath him, because it's too much, I'm feeling too much—

"Oh, so pretty," he croons as I writhe, sobbing, the orgasm clawing its way from somewhere I didn't know orgasms could come from. I'm spurting hot and thick all over his grandfather's carpet, and the contractions are clenching in my stomach and thighs, and I think deep in my core too, because his crooning breaks off into a rough, staccato grunt.

He rides me through it all, like he's trying to literally fuck the sperm out of my body thrust by thrust, and maybe it's working because the climax is wringing me out, milking me of everything I have, and then I'm crying in the rug, so dizzy I can barely see, a warm slick of ejaculate underneath me.

"You—" he says, and he swears a bitten-off oath, plunging in once more and holding himself deep inside me with all of his weight.

Even through the dizziness, I feel him swell and pulse, releasing the fullness of his pleasure into the condom. The throb of him inside me steals my breath away, and I'm still so dizzy, and I want to feel this forever, this exact thing: him on top of me, jerking inside me, his breath warm on the stinging bite he left on my neck.

Mark doesn't deny himself a moment of his orgasm, only moving to stroke himself a few more times with my body, as if to make sure every last bit of use of me is had, and I shudder with renewed longing as he finally slides free and straddles my thighs. I feel the wet length of his dick nestled against the cleft of my ass; when I muster the effort to look over my shoulder, he's looking down to where his still-condomed shaft rests on my skin, his chest heaving, his cheeks flushed.

"My god," he says, his voice hoarse with exertion. "You have no idea what a fucking prize you are."

He gets up, and I let my eyes flutter closed for a moment, knowing I need to move but unable to summon the energy to. If it weren't for the heavy hammer of my heart against my sternum, I'd believe I was dead.

I intuit more than hear Mark's steps—his tread is

always quiet, but barefoot it's nearly silent—and then there's the far-off sound of running water in the kitchen. I know he's back when there's a waft of air, and then a warm cloth is pressed against the intimate skin of my entrance. I shiver and try to move, and a firm hand comes down on my back.

"I'm not done yet," Mark says, and he takes his time running a hand over the welts on my thighs and ass, testing the bite on my shoulder with his fingertips. It all stings, but I don't think there's any broken skin anywhere; Mark must have found that wafer-thin line that maximized sensation without causing anything more serious than a florid signature which wouldn't outlive the next sunrise.

For a moment, I'm reminded of the rumors about him, the stories of Mark Trevena, Special Activities operator. That torture was something he did, something he was supposed to be incredibly skilled at doing. That the reason he knows how hard to hit me without breaking the skin might be because he'd been kinky for a very long time…or because that knowledge was very useful in his previous life at the CIA.

It should give me chills, this thought, and I think it does, except those chills are swallowed by everything else, by him rolling me onto my back and examining my face for carpet burn. He carefully wipes my cock clean, lingering triumph in his expression, along with the intense focus I recognize from his meetings. He doesn't speak.

"I think I made a mess on your carpet," I finally say. I'm coming back to myself unsteadily, a soul crawling back inside its earthly shell.

Mark's eyebrows lift in blank confusion, like I've just brought up the price of Skittles in Svalbard. "Carpets can be cleaned," he says slowly, like he thinks he might be missing something.

I hiss as the cloth works away the little flecks of drying

orgasm on my dick. When I look down, the skin is bright red, but again, not broken.

Raw enough to hurt, whole enough to be abused again soon.

"I should clean the carpet," I say. My voice is dazed. "I don't want to leave it—"

"It'll be my favorite stain," Mark says, amused. He uses the cloth to scrub at the worst of the puddle and then tosses it on the chair near the desk. He stands up and looks down at me. At some point, the weather shifted—tepid rain to angry clouds. He's all shadows now, and the little light that's left is preoccupied with caressing his jaw and strong nose, with turning those blue eyes into a dark, shimmering mercury.

Above me like this, he looks like a god, something from a myth, and it's impossible not to notice that he's still erect.

I want—

I'm not ready for this to be over.

I'm not ready to go back to the way things were.

"Is there more?" I ask in a whisper.

Something bleak passes over his face. "There's always more," he says.

CHAPTER 16

HE MAKES ME CRAWL.

In the army, humility is beaten into you, not with impact but with effort and shame. Push-ups until you want to die, insults nasty enough to make your eyes sting, drills so hard and pointless that you want to quit. And always the reasoning is the same—it's to make you strong, make you sharp, make you loyal. No matter how convoluted the logic is, it all leads back to those three things.

But here, today, the logic isn't convoluted at all. It's a short, straight line.

Why crawl?

Because he wants me to.

The floor changes from carpet to wood to stone as I make my way from the library to the rest of the house, and the shame I feel is delicately balanced by the dazzling certainty I have in this moment, by the gasping arousal that has me by the neck. My cock is a stiff pipe between my legs, swinging and aching, and the cool air reminds me of my nakedness. Of how exposed I am as one knee moves after the other.

Mark follows, lube and condom box in hand, and as we reach the main section of the house—lit by the large glass conservatory at the end, which is currently letting in the dark, silver light of the almost-storming sky—he says in a strained voice, "Stop."

I stop, unsure of what he means. Stop crawling? Stop this—this—game altogether?

But no, he's already dropping to his knees behind me, there's more lube, the tear of a condom wrapper, and then—

"Oh my god," I mumble, my head dropping between my shoulders. I'd thought earlier, on my stomach, was intense, but like this, on all fours, it's breath robbing.

"You looked so lovely crawling for me," Mark explains, one hand curled around my hip, the other making soothing passes on my spine as he forges deeper and deeper. "Your pretty hole still wet and open. I had to. I had to."

I am more yielding than I was earlier, I think, the muscle worked pliant, but it's still intense, intense enough to make me moan, to make my cock leak and leak and leak as he fits himself to the glove of my body and makes use of it.

Outside, through the glass of the conservatory, the skies open and rain begins to drop on the glass. Hard, like falling stones. It swallows up the slick noise of Mark behind me, of my choked gasps.

But the sound I make when Mark presses an autocratic hand to my throat and arches me up so that I'm upright and my back is to his chest—that carries just fine. A low, loud moan, rolling like thunder, juddering and breaking as each thrust works me from the inside out.

Mark's hand stays tight on my throat, keeping me stretched and arched, but his free hand finds my bobbing cock and gives the hot, rigid flesh a squeeze.

"Please, sir," I manage, knowing I sound pathetic, pleading. *"Please."*

149

"But why," he says in my ear, "when you are so perfectly sweet right now? Maybe I should leave you like this forever, hard and begging, so you'll offer up your body whenever I so much as look at you?"

I pant, the agony of his denial and the agony of my lust too tangled to pick apart, and he knows it, he must know it, because there's a pleased laugh in my ear, dark and low, as he drops his hand to my tightening testicles and cups. My eyes flutter shut—it's so good—it's almost enough—if he just kept fucking me, I think that alone would—

"Fuck," he grunts, and for the second time today, I feel the swell and surge of him inside me. Even though it's not my climax, I'm shivering like it is, wishing he weren't wearing a condom so I could feel his cum, so that it could make everything slick and slippery. So that I could carry around a part of him inside me. So that he'd be leaking out of me all day.

God, just the thought of it nearly breaks me.

He doesn't loosen his hold for a long minute after he orgasms, his face coming to rest in my neck as his cock stops pulsing.

"You're dangerous," he finally says against my skin. "This is why I didn't—goddammit. I can't make it twenty feet without fucking you. What are we going to do?"

My erection is a thing of misery between my legs. "I don't know," I say, almost nonsensically. I can barely think. I just want him to fuck me or let me touch myself or *anything*.

A heavy sigh as Mark pulls free and stands. A firm hand to my shoulder stops me from standing too.

"To the bedroom," says Mark kindly, as if I've forgotten.

"Sir" is my response, and this time we finish the journey.

———

The sound of rain, steady, drumming, lovely, fills the room. The first thing Mark did when he came into the bedroom was open the doors to a small, magnolia-littered balcony.

The second thing he did was tie me to his bed.

I regret begging him to jerk me off earlier, because for the last hour, he's been doing exactly that…except not letting me finish, backing off at the precise moment I'm about to crest and watching with a cruel smile as I writhe and twist against my bonds. My good manners slowly melt away too, until I'm swearing, cursing, calling him an evil motherfucker, a sadistic bastard, telling him I hate him.

Every insult only seems to delight him more. "It's a shame you're not being sweeter," he'd say with a sigh. "Only sweet things get to finish."

Or: "It's only just now that you're seeing that I'm evil? And they said you were such a brilliant soldier, my god."

And then my insults turn into worship, into reverence, as he crawls slowly over my body. The rain washes the stones and ferns and trees outside, sending in a smell that is exactly like *him*, and the muted silver light is beautiful on his naked form. Long, muscled legs, firm, etched chest and stomach. Broad shoulders that drape me in shadow.

He lays his entire body over mine, and then with his fingers on my jaw, he brushes a tender kiss over my lips. It's soft and warm like the rest of me is straining and stippled with goose bumps, and then he parts my lips with his own, dipping his tongue inside my mouth and moaning at my taste. I feel the moan tremble through his chest into mine, and I feed the moan right back into him, trying to arch, trying to chase.

His lips curve as he pulls back, waits for me to accept that he's in charge of this before he licks into my mouth again. Our tongues slide together, and it's wet, and god, it feels so fucking good to have him *kiss* me, and then his hips begin moving.

It makes me burn up from the inside out, how good his cock feels against mine, rubbing and rutting. The chafed skin of my frenulum sends little bites of pain along with it, so that every surge of pleasure is razored with a tiny bit of discomfort, and I'm suspended on the edge, dangling, helpless, keening. The building orgasm in my belly has been so thwarted, so tortured, that it almost doesn't know how to unfurl itself and bloom, and I'm crying, I realize, hot tears tracking down my face, because it hurts so good, so goddamn *good*.

And then I remember what Andrea said after I found Mark with Ms. Beroul, that he could effortlessly dominate someone in a brightly lit grocery store, and I *get it*. I get it now. He didn't have anything today but an old ruler and the weight of his body, and he's still wrecked me. Tortured me, used me. Made me want to worship him. And never more than right now, with his mouth on mine and a hand slipping down to palm my backside and keep our hips fitted tight together.

"Please," I whimper into his kiss. "Please, sir."

"If you can come like this, then you may," he says, his lower body flexing and flexing. Sweat is wet between our chests and stomachs and is damp on my forehead. I can't tell the difference between the smell of the rain outside and the smell of him. All there is, all there can be, is him.

I come, my back bowing, my mouth falling open in a silent gasp, the release tearing up my thighs, vicious and biting for all the times it's been denied. My erection swells against Mark's and then begins spurting warm jets of come between us, slicking the way for him to fuck against me even harder, even faster.

He slides both arms underneath me—one under my neck, the other under my waist—and bites my jaw as his hips give a few rough thrusts and then go completely still.

Warm release spills, adding to what's already there, and with him pressed all the way to the top of me, his mouth against my jaw, I feel every single bit of his pleasure. His harsh breath, his moving ribs. The shivering tension in his thighs and stomach as his cock finishes jerking between us.

For a minute, we stay just like this, the ejaculate trapped between our bodies, our hearts trying to collide through our chests. The rain coming down in loud, wet whispers just outside the open door.

And then he lifts himself enough to look down at me, to run a thumb over my swollen mouth. His expression is rueful.

"There go all my careful plans," he says.

I have no idea what plans he means, but I know he was right in Singapore when he said this would complicate things. How could it not?

But also how could I resist?

He unties me and checks my wrists and ankles, even though the bonds had been expertly tied—tight enough to restrain but not so tight that I lost sensation in my toes and fingers. I'm once again reminded that there is a reason why he might be good at tying people up that has nothing to do with fun afternoons and romantic Cornish rain.

He has me sit up, gives me a glass of cool water.

"How do you feel?" he asks.

I stare at him, knowing I need to speak but finding that the words are floating just out of reach. But the dizzy, aching, well-used thrum in my body needs only a few words. "The fucking best," I say honestly, and that surprises a laugh out of him. Not a dark one, not a mean one, but something unplanned and delighted. It comes from deep in his chest.

"You're high," he says finally. "On endorphins. You can't be trusted." He gets off the bed and takes the glass from me, setting it on a small tray he'd brought in. "Let's get you cleaned up."

In the shower, he's just as imperial with my body as he was on the library floor. He has me stand with my feet spread so that he can run the warm washcloth up and down the inside of my thighs, the valley of my ass, the soft place just behind my balls. He pays close attention to the aching furl of muscle that he made such use of earlier; he's careful when he cleans my abused cock, forgoing the cloth to wash me with only a soapy palm. I'm hard almost instantly from this, even though it *hurts*—it hurts to have an erection after being aroused all day, and the soap stings the sensitive skin. He only snorts to himself when I twitch and stir in his grip, but he doesn't let me come.

He washes my hair, my hands, the bottoms of my feet until I make sharp, sucked-in laughs against the tile, and then once I'm finally clean, he turns me so that my back is against the wall.

"Stay," he commands, like I'm a dog that will start shaking out its fur the minute it can, but I don't mind—it's a relief to know exactly what to do. Not to have to wonder if I'm supposed to get out or if I'm supposed to clean him the same way he just cleaned me.

All I'll have to do is listen, and I'll do the right thing. After what happened in Carpathia, I could nearly cry from the simplicity of an equation like that.

Besides, it's a lovely view, watching Mark wash himself. Suds track over the ridge of his collarbone and down the faint corrugations of his stomach. The hair on his chest is darker when it's wet, lying flat, as is the line down his stomach and the hair on his thighs. His penis, even flaccid, is thick and heavy looking, lightly veined. His testicles have lowered in the heat of the shower, some swing to them as he scrubs himself with utilitarian brevity, and his nipples have flattened some. I wonder how long it would take for them to stiffen against my tongue or fingertips.

He washes his hair, the motions efficient, not for show, but it doesn't matter, it's still a show for me, because it's him and his body is a work of art under the running water. The muscles, the neatly inked tattoos. The wet arch of his throat and gleaming rise of his cheeks.

The hair—longer when wet, longer than I thought. Long enough that I could spend hours stroking it if he ever let me.

I try not to think about this specific shower, though, or even this specific house. This house with its sweater and rose tucked into a bottom drawer, this house where Mark comes on some sort of yearly pilgrimage to lock himself inside the library and drink. I don't think I'm the first person to be in this shower with Mark nor the first to be tied to the bed in the other room.

And I promised myself that I was content being physically available to Mark with no emotional attachment; that no matter how hard I fell for him, I wouldn't expect him to reciprocate, that I'd plan on being alone in whatever cyclone of emotions this churned up. And that promise would preclude jealousy because how could I be jealous of someone who owned a club for fucking? Who fucked people on his desk like it had been penciled onto his daily agenda?

But I find the thin tendrils of jealousy twisting in my rib cage anyway, because if the man in the picture is the reason Mark comes here every year—if the memory of the man in the picture is worth that—then he must have meant so much to Mark. Been so much for him.

I want to be that much for him.

Ridiculous.

The shower stops, and Mark pulls me out onto a small rug to towel me off. I blink at the abrupt brush of cool air, and then I find myself swaying. He catches me easily with both hands, grabbing me by the shoulders and holding me so he can study my face.

I blink back at him. Water is dripping from the ends of his hair onto his shoulders.

"How do you feel now?" he asks.

I have to reach for the words. "A little…woozy."

He studies me a minute longer. "You need to eat," he says finally. "Come on."

We dress—me in some borrowed sweat pants from Mark because he seems reluctant to let me out of his sight, even for the handful of minutes it would take for me to get to my room and get my own clothes—and go to the kitchen, where Mark tells me to sit on a stool by the counter and then starts opening fridge and cupboard doors.

"Is there anything you can't eat?" he asks. He pulls out a cutting board and a knife.

I shake my head.

"Is there anything you feel like?"

"I like meat," I offer, and to Mark's credit, he doesn't make a joke of it.

"Steak it is, then," he says, and gets to work, pulling out the raw steak, butter, salt, potatoes, and greenery.

"Do you want help?" I ask, and he points at me with a potato.

"I will get that ruler and make good use of it if you move from that stool. Stay."

I stay, a little torn, because the instinct to help is pulling at every nerve in my body. But the pleasure of watching him at work is drugging in its own right: the competent way he washes, cuts, and preps; the thoughtful way he brushes his knuckles over the surface of the skillet before he spins it by the handle and sets it on the hob.

Dazed as I still am, I can't push away all the curiosity

and fascination with him that I normally hide away. I just let him see me in agonies of pain and lust both—and I'd do it again in a heartbeat if he asked—so why not let him see my curiosity too? My yearning to know him?

I take a drink of the cool water Mark pressed into my hands after I sat down, and then I ask, "Why don't you use the submissives at the club? For yourself?"

Mark has just dumped potato chunks into a pot of salted water to boil, and he turns to face me, throwing a kitchen towel over his bare shoulder. His hair, unstyled after the shower, is a tousled blond mess, the damp parts still dark, the dry parts a pale gold streaked with platinum.

He doesn't seem to find my question invasive at all. His expression is relaxed when he says, "It's bad business to fuck the people you pay."

And then he adds, with a small smile, "Except for my bodyguards, I suppose. I'm making a habit of that."

"But really," I press, not understanding. "If it's about time or convenience or any of the other reasons why Strassburg was good for you, surely the people at your club would be the best?"

He sets to stripping kale leaves from their stems with deft flicks of his knife.

"There are other considerations," he says. "No matter how transactional a scene is, no matter how straightforward the fuck, there is intimacy there, wouldn't you agree? Shared vulnerability. A part of myself I keep hidden as much as possible."

I think about his teeth in my shoulder, his surprised laugh. His admission: *I used to dream of having a submissive like you.*

It was intimate; it was the definition of intimate. No matter how desperate or unplanned it was, no matter how unemotional I'd vowed myself to be…

"And," Mark continues, now rolling the kale leaves and slicing them in a chiffonade, "I think you'd also agree that I am the keeper of quite a bit of information. Information that many people would like access to. Intimacy and information"—the thinly sliced kale is transferred to a bowl, replaced on the cutting board by cloves of garlic he peeled earlier—"do not mix. Which sounds alarmingly obvious, but you'd be surprised how many people think they are somehow immune to hormones and neurotransmitters. Limerence."

"So you're worried that you'd be compromised somehow? By a club submissive?" No matter what he says it's impossible to imagine him divulging something confidential to a club submissive just because the sex was good.

"I hear your doubt," he says, putting the minced garlic in another bowl and then going to check on the potatoes. "And I have news for you. Doubt is informed by confidence. And confidence is informed by experience. And experience is a goddamn liar almost all of the time."

"So you don't trust yourself."

"Or anyone," Mark says. The potatoes are rescued from the pot and go on a roasting pan with salt, rosemary, and garlic, and then into the oven.

He sighs, facing away from me. There's something resigned in the set of his shoulders. "Except I have decided to trust some people. Strassburg. You. You were both already as deep into my life as I'd let anyone, so there was no compounded risk." I see the grim set to his mouth when he turns back to the salad. "Although I may have risked other things. The next twelve months do not account for an... entanglement."

I don't want to encourage this line of thinking; the thought of him deciding we need to stop this, that we can't do this again, has my throat closing.

"What about Ms. Beroul?" I ask, more to ask anything,

to say anything, to pull him away from thoughts of *risk* and *entanglement*. "You don't worry that she'd compromise you?"

"Ah, Ms. Beroul. No, I don't worry. Isabella lives in Montreal and belongs to the owner of a club there who loves to share her. She's not in a position to leverage her proximity to me for more, given that the proximity is so limited." Mark juices a lemon with his bare hands, juice and pulp dripping around his strong fingers. "So you remember her, do you?"

"Hard to forget," I say dryly, and he laughs as he squeezes the other half of the lemon.

"Just wanted to make sure. Now, what about you, Tristan Thomas? How is it that you've made it to twenty-nine without some monster like myself claiming you for his own?"

I watch as minced garlic, olive oil, and grated pecorino are whisked together with the lemon juice and then tossed with the kale ribbons. "I—it wasn't on purpose," I mumble, looking down at my hands. "I wanted to. But it's like I said before, I get attached."

I'm embarrassed to say it again, in the context of what we've shared today, because I don't want him to think I will get attached to him. And yet I almost do want him to think that because I already *am* attached.

Stop. Don't he'll feel the same way about you.

The salad is set aside and the steaks are put on the pan to sear.

"I still don't understand how this is an impediment to fucking," says Mark, and that's the thing, that's what's so hard to convey about it.

I remember being interviewed once after the ceremony for my Distinguished Service Cross—the reporter had been more interested in me as an eligible army bachelor than in McKenzie's death or even in what I'd actually done to merit the award. The reporter had asked why I was still single, and

I had no way to answer that wasn't honest because I'd never been good at lying. I told him that I was ready to fall in love at a moment's notice, and what he wrote after quoting my stupid little answer was that I was a *romantic at heart*. Something that was and is true, and yet is such an easy phrase to bat around, like it doesn't come anchored to an anvil of hammered infatuation.

"I guess it was more that I craved something from a connection that I couldn't seem to find. Not love or anything like that," I say quickly, a total lie, but I don't want Mark second-guessing taking me to bed. "But just *something*. Respect or a shared intensity. I needed to know that we were"—The words feel colorless and clumsy in my mouth— "together in something. Wanting it as much as the other. I didn't think I would like to share a bed with someone and find out that they'd only said yes because they were bored or I was an easy option or because they felt bad for me. I don't like being alone in a feeling. I want to share it."

I shut my mouth, abruptly feeling like a jackass. But Mark's face after he puts the steaks in the oven and turns to study me doesn't seem like he thinks I'm a jackass. He looks thoughtful.

"I would say that the army did a number on you, but maybe it turned out that the army was ready to place all of that exactly where they wanted it—directed at itself. It was happy to be your lover, and dare I say—"

But he doesn't dare say, it turns out.

He presses his lips together. Shakes his head. "Never mind. But I'm honored it was me."

"I'm the honored one."

It's too honest, maybe, my voice too rough, speaking less of honor and more of that blood-simmering *rightness* as Mark held me down on the carpet, left welts and bites and everything else on my skin.

His eyes change at my words, darkening. There's something else mixing with the lust in his expression now. Something rigid and haunted.

I think it's grief.

"The steaks should be done," he says, and indeed, within ten minutes, we are eating the best steak dinner I've ever had in my life.

We eat in the conservatory as the long spring twilight darkens around us, a light rain still pattering on the glass ceiling. The valley is beautiful in the rainy twilight, but it's the shirtless man next to me that steals all of my attention. His long fingers on the fork, the flex of his jaw as he chews.

"This is amazing," I say, holding up a potato chunk like it'll explain something to me. "How did you get so good at cooking? Surely not in the army or the CIA?"

He cuts a piece of steak and then nudges it critically with the tip of his knife. "It *was* in the CIA, actually. A long assignment in Vienna. My SAC partner and I were posing as businessmen with ties to mercenary groups— positioning ourselves to be courted by what was then the nascent rebellion against the new Carpathian government—or perhaps I should say, a rebellion hoping to push the government into a more extreme stance. People who wanted to go even further than Melwas Kocur but still idolized him."

Melwas Kocur had been the leader of the Carpathian separatist movement, and the first president of the new country…although *president* implied he was a more benevolent ruler than he was. He hadn't been too interested in the democratic process, to put it mildly, and had instead been more interested in murdering dissidents, hoarding resources for himself and his top supporters, and agitating to start another war. And then an old video from the war had emerged of him sending children out to die on a burning boat in a lake—a ploy to divide the American soldiers' attention, which had worked at the time. The soldiers sacrificed a village to save the children, and it had been a severe blow to both morale and strategy. But years later, it had finally become Melwas's undoing. He'd been exposed, deposed, and imprisoned. It had been hoped his legacy would end there, but the radicals who had continued to fight and raid in his name grew emboldened, their small conflicts flaring into a cohesive resistance against their own government that no one could douse the flames of no matter how hard they tried.

"Anyway, they wanted what all groups like that want," Mark goes on, "money and weapons and friends in high places, and so it took some time to establish ourselves as those people. You have to start slow, you see, if you really want to manipulate people. It's no good just to appear like a mirage and expect things to go the way you want—you have to be subtle. Let them think all their ideas and feelings are their own, slowly twist things up so that they unwind in precisely the right way. And then as everything is falling apart, your hand is nowhere to be seen."

He takes a long drink of scotch, sets the glass down as his throat moves. "All that to say, the first few months of the assignment were hardly movie material. It was mostly being seen, making introductions, planting stories about my wealth and my connections, and my mission partner and I didn't overplay our hands. We went slowly, creating a depth to the identities, a history to the stories, something you can only do with time. And so we had a fair amount of free hours in those days. It was either learn to paint watercolors or cook. I hate cleaning paintbrushes. So I chose cooking."

"Did you already like doing it? Cooking?"

"I like good food, but I went straight from making ramen in my college dorm room to eating cafeteria food at basic training. I never learned how to cook much beyond spaghetti." His mouth twitches. "I think I went through about fifty pounds of butter in those early days, just trying to figure out stuff that middle schoolers learn how to bake in school. I was truly bad at it."

I try to imagine Mark fussing with measuring spoons and YouTube videos. The legendary spy in his expensive suits and perfect hair looking down at a tray of ruined chocolate chip cookies in dismay. "It's hard to imagine you bad at anything," I say, and it comes out sounding besotted. I want to punch myself in the mouth.

"I could say the same about you, Mr. Prom King and Distinguished Service Cross," says Mark mildly.

"Oh, that's —" I don't know what I want to say. Just that all of my achievements are so *contextual*, so caveated. Sure, I was prom king, but that's because the other guys were dicks that year. Sure, I have that cross tucked under a roll of socks in its new drawer at Lyonesse, but it might as well be a plastic toy sheriff's badge for all the good it does McKenzie and her family. "I'm bad at lots of stuff."

Namely not falling in love with my boss.

After we eat, I'm less woozy, but I can't stop yawning. My cock aches, and there's a sweeter, more tender ache inside my body that makes me blush to feel. Mark watches me a moment, and says, "Bed."

"Yes, sir," I say, standing, bracing myself for what comes next. He'll say that this was a good day, but that it wouldn't be smart to do it again, and he'd be right, of course, and then we'll sleep in separate beds, spend the rest of this trip avoiding each other, and then go back to Lyonesse as two polite but distant men.

"I'll take care of the dishes," Mark says. "Brush your

teeth and do whatever else you need to, and then I expect you in my room by the time I'm finished."

My breath catches as I meet his gaze. It's dark, intense. His mouth is set in a hungry, grim line.

And he wants me in his bed tonight.

I have no intention of arguing.

"Yes, sir," I say.

———

He uses me one more time that night, after he comes in and finds me kneeling on the floor next to the bed. I have no idea what I'm doing, just groping for memories of what I've seen submissives do at Lyonesse, but it must be something close to right, because when he sees me, he hisses a sharp breath through his teeth. Shirtless, I can see the quick heave of his ribs as he stares at me on the ground.

"I didn't treat you like a virgin today," he says. "I should go easy on you tonight."

"I don't want you to go easy on me."

"You keep saying this, but this isn't altruism on my part," Mark says. "It's caretaking what belongs to me, especially because"—he's very close to me now—"I'd like to fuck you again tomorrow. Come here."

He pulls me up onto the bed on my back. My pajama pants are taken off and so are his. And I think, as he's crawling over me, that he wants to use my mouth again. My blood is hot at the very idea.

"Such an exquisite mouth," he murmurs. But he doesn't move the way I think he will; he's turned to straddle me facing my feet. "You can touch me now, just for now," he says, like it's the utmost kindness he can bestow. And then he lowers himself over my face.

My hands go instinctively to his hips just as I realize

what he wants. A shiver rips through me. "I've never done this," I manage on an exhale.

"I know you haven't," he says. "Just let me have your mouth and I'll do all the rest."

And that's all he says before he's sitting fully on my face. He still smells like our shower, soapy and fresh, and when I open my mouth and kiss—gently—the delicate, muscled ring of his opening, I taste a hint of soap too. Above me, he makes a satisfied grunt, and I can feel when he takes himself in hand and starts masturbating.

I kiss his entrance again, giving him my tongue as he told me to, and I'm rewarded with another grunted exhale. When I slide my hands from his warm hips to his hard thighs, I feel goose bumps all the way to his knees. Each shuttle of his fist on his length I feel in my own body. My erection is bone-achingly jealous; it bobs against my stomach as I start swirling my tongue on Mark's skin. Precum leaks from my tip and starts wetting my stomach, and it *hurts* being turned on again after being edged so mercilessly earlier, after the carpet, but the pain feels so strangely good. Like the soreness after a long workout, earned and satisfying.

He likes when I push my tongue inside him, or when I hold it flat for him to rock against, and I find it's all unbearably arousing, having him move over me, his thighs caging my face, the firm curve of his ass pressed against me. The goose bumps betraying his pleasure, the unfairly easy way I can get this fierce man to buckle and grunt with just an indecent flutter of my tongue.

And he's letting me touch him—freely, constantly, and I can't get enough, my hands are roaming everywhere, the slim lines of his hips to his ridged stomach to the hard wings of his shoulder blades. His thighs obsess me the most. The muscles shifting under my palms as he rocks over me, the crisp hair, the grace of them. It's like stroking the flanks of a predatory cat or a wild horse. Powerful and beautiful and deadly.

He comes fast and hard riding my mouth, his hand jerking a merciless orgasm from his length. It lands mostly on my belly, but some of it streaks across my own erection, and I can barely think, my breath and my body are wound so tight. I could come from the feeling of his semen on my skin, on my cock, hot and thick and wet—

He lifts from my mouth, a large hand wraps around my rigid length. It only takes three strokes, lubricated by his own cum, and I'm gasping, twisting, trying to fuck my hips up into his hand as I throb out an agonizing climax. Pulse after pulse—tingles tracing from the soles of my feet to my fingertips—static bright and fuzzy at the edges of my vision.

He doesn't give me any quarter, jerking me through it all, not stopping until he's satisfied I'm finished, drained. I'm panting like I've run a race when he climbs off me and returns with another warm washcloth.

I gaze up at him as he cleans me, feeling like my arms and legs are made of lead. And then somehow my eyelids are heavy too, and my blinks feel slower and slower. I blink once and he's cleaning me; I blink another time and he's gone. Another time and he's moving me, moving the covers, until we're both under the crisp sheets and he's tucked me into his arms, my back to his chest. Our skin presses together everywhere.

That night, I don't have a single bad dream.

Chapter 17

The morning after our first day, I wake up to him stroking the skin around my opening. I arch instinctively.

"You're awake," he says, and nothing more as he reaches for the lube and condom box. He uses his own body to fix me to the bed while he works his way inside, and when I start moaning, he sticks his fingers in my mouth and orders me to suck. I come so much faster than him that I'm already hard again by the time he finishes.

"You're so goddamn tight," he mutters through his final thrusts. "*Fuck*. I'm going to need this so much."

We come at the same time—me for the second time—grunting and messy. The only thing that would make it better would be if it were even messier—if there'd been no condom at all. Only him, marking me, making me wet and sloppy with his pleasure.

Afterward, as he's pulling out, I tell him so, that we don't have to use a condom, seeing as he's tested so often and I was a virgin until very, very recently.

"You want to be bred, sweet thing?" he murmurs, biting my earlobe. "You want me to leave my load inside you?"

I groan, fresh desire unfurling in my gut. "Please, sir."

A kiss on the back of my neck. "I promise to think about it, my pretty Tristan."

But he never does take me raw.

He cooks for me, he washes me, he takes me around the grounds and fucks me in his favorite spots. He pushes into my body on a magnolia-petal-strewn blanket in the grave-yard, comes down my throat on a footpath near the topmost ridge of the valley. When we get caught in the rain on a walk, he shoves me against a tree and kisses my mouth like it's the only good thing left in the entire world. My lips are swollen for a whole day after.

When he's not cooking or fucking me, I'm still the entire locus of his attention. He makes me read to him while we sit under his favorite hazel tree with bottles of cold, crisp cider nearby. He annihilates me at chess and then grumbles about how my generation knows an embarrassing *nothing* of strategy, subtlety. He takes me to watch the lambs bleat and scamper in the field a mile to the north and listens while I talk about the animals back home. How we leased our farm when I was a kid but how the new farmer let me help with the calves and baby goats, how it was my job to feed them bottles of milk while they headbutted me with their tiny heads.

When the spring evenings get chilly, he lights a fire in the library and watches me with flames reflected in his stare.

I have no way of proving it to myself, of verifying it, but I can't shake the feeling that this is really him, that this is the real Mark. Not the indolent devil of Lyonesse or the cold former killer, but the man who watches me eat with a possessive interest, who scolds me for bad chess moves, who can identify all the tiny, temporary wildflowers that crowd up around the gravestones.

It's not that his eyes glitter less when he's sprawled in

a chair; it's not that he's any less ruthless. It's just that it's all there *together*, stirred up together, and it's all completely fixated on me. Playful cruelty and utter possession, and I am at the center of it all.

It's...staggering. I am undone by his attention. His notice.

Which is not to say that I don't still see the ghost of whatever haunts him here at Morois House. There are moments after the welts, the orgasms, the glasses of water put to my lips, when I see something lost in his face, the same expression I saw when I came into the library for the first time. Burning and bleak.

Dead but still dying.

I fall asleep with him trapping me to his chest, and I wake in the morning with both of his arms around me and his legs tangled in mine, his face against the nape of my neck. But sometimes in the middle of the night, I come out of sleep to find that he's sitting on the side of the bed, cradling a plastic-wrapped sweater in his hands, or that he's gone to the library and shut the doors.

Sometimes when we're in the graveyard I look over to see him rubbing a magnolia petal between his thumb and forefinger, his eyes on the fragile pink flesh of the flower, his chest moving fast.

I don't disturb those moments and I never ask about them later. Whatever I am to him, I don't think I have the right to. Even if little brambles of jealousy prick the insides of my ribs when I think about how devoted he is to a mere memory.

Mark is quiet on the drive to the airport and during the flights home. In the first-class lounge at Heathrow, he drags me into a single bathroom, shoves a wad of paper towels in my mouth, and proceeds to lash my ass with the end of his leather belt—not nearly as painful as it could be if he'd actually slid it from its loops and properly worked me over, but painful enough that I'm moaning around the makeshift gag as he fucks me after, his clothes rubbing against the newly welted skin.

He still doesn't speak after, whatever demon not fully exorcised, but he does crouch behind me and check the welts, running his fingertips over them to test how puffy they are, if the skin is broken at all. He helps me clean up and then when we emerge back into the lounge, he goes to the bar for a glass of ice water and brings it back to me, watching to make sure I drink it all.

It's a long flight home with my ass that sore, not just from the lounge but from days of punishment and sex. If I'd thought Mark needed the toys stocked in the rooms of Lyonesse to work his craft, I no longer thought so at all. Anything from kitchen towels and wooden spoons to earmuffs and painter's tape were put to work on me, and often enough, he just used his own body. His cock or fingers to gag me, his arms and legs to hold me down. His teeth to punish me until my tears brimmed over and then he licked them up like they were some kind of payment owed to him.

And always, always, I was hard and panting for it.

Always, always, I was falling deeper and deeper in love.

So healthy.

We get to DC bleary-eyed and vaguely disheveled in that hard-to-pinpoint way of long travel, and my stomach is gnawing on itself as Jago drives us home to Lyonesse.

What will happen when we get there? Will Mark want to pretend that we weren't together in Cornwall? Will things continue as they were? But even if Mark wanted to continue, it couldn't be the same, not with his schedule. It couldn't be days of doing nothing but making sure I'm so thoroughly devirginized that I can hardly walk in a straight line.

When we step across the bridge to the club and go through the doors to the elevator bank, Mark turns to me and says, "Do whatever you need to clean up. Then come to my apartment."

I nod, the gnawing feeling growing worse.

I don't know whether he's calling me up to fuck me again or to—well, *break up* is probably the wrong way to put it, since we're not truly together, but whatever the Cornish Grief Fling equivalent of breaking up is.

I drop my things in my apartment as soon as I walk in, take a quick shower to wash the plane off, and then go to brush my teeth and get dressed. As I do, I catch a glimpse of myself in the mirror. Bite marks in various stages of healing dot my skin, front and back, a particularly defined one on the place where my neck and shoulder meet. My ass and thighs are welted and bruised, as are my shoulders and upper back, from the ruler and wooden spoon and kitchen towel. I have scrapes on my knees from the times he took me in the woods, and a grass burn on my forearm from a particularly vicious screw under the branches of the hazel tree. Mark had been right that first day together. He really couldn't go more than twenty feet without needing to fuck me.

I didn't mind.

I run my hands over the marks the way I used to run my hands over battered maps in Carpathia, like I'm committing important information to memory. I need to remember every single time he touched me. I need to remember how it feels to see my body as living proof of his desire.

Even if I'll never have his love, I'll know I had that. His hot stare under the hazel tree.

Once upstairs, I move through the empty lobby area in front of his office and through the office itself, into the hallway that leads to his apartments. Despite working here almost two months, I still haven't seen the inside of his private living space; he's always in his office when I come in the morning.

One of the doors is open—I still knock, feeling strange, wishing we were back at Morois House. Things were so simple there: I was his to hurt or to fuck, and he was mine to adore. And there was nothing but time for all of those things.

"Come in," he calls from somewhere in the apartment, and I enter, momentarily surprised by what I see. I'd expected something as stark and minimalistic as his office, glass and glossy wood and then more glass, but his private rooms are the furthest thing from stark.

The floors are made of wood, running in wide, pale planks, and the walls are the green of bay leaves or dried sage. A velvet couch and two overstuffed chairs set off a living area; botanical watercolors hang on the wall. Lights are everywhere, lamps and sconces and pendants, and built-in bookshelves are crowded with books. Just beyond is the kitchen, its butcher block island covered in bowls holding oranges, onions, and apples. Well-loved copper pots hang on a rack.

It's stylish and expensive, but it's not cold. There's something of him stamped on this place, and it reminds me of who he was at Morois House—not only a hedonist nor a murderer but something more than both.

I could spend days here, just exploring his things. Him.

I start with the books, which are mostly medieval history and ancient philosophy, with a smattering of cookbooks and slim volumes of poetry. And oddly enough, there's an entire shelf of yellowing paperback mysteries that claim to be coauthored by a cat.

"In here, Tristan." Mark's cool voice comes from deeper

in the apartment, and I pass into a small hallway to find an open door to a large bedroom. The floors are the same wide-planked wood, but the walls are painted a soft white. There're more bookshelves, a large bed with a white cover, and a door out to a narrow balcony with a glass railing.

The light is tinted blue, with strange patterns waving and dancing over the floor and walls. I look up to see three skylights in the ceiling, and above them, the clear water of rooftop pool, shot through with refracting sunlight.

Mark emerges from the bathroom in gray trousers and a button-down with the sleeves rolled up, feet bare and hair still damp. When he sees me, his eyes hood a little in a now-familiar gaze, a dark and burning stare that usually precedes some humiliating command. In Cornwall, I privately thought of it as the *mine* stare, the look of a dragon gazing upon his hoard of gold, a conqueror looking over his bloodstained spoils.

It never fails to make my mouth dry, to send heat and blood down deep into my belly.

Yes, yours, I hope my gaze says back.

He rolls his lips inward, briefly, as if stopping himself from something. And then he says, "Let's have a drink on the balcony, shall we?"

After a long flight where I stayed conscientiously sober as a weak gesture toward my role as a bodyguard—as if having a constant semi and being distracted by Mark's mouth weren't just as bad as being soused on first-class champagne—a cold beer sounds great. I tell him so and he leaves to fetch one for me, returning with the Żywiec porter I like and his usual glass of gin, and then together we go out onto the balcony. It's small, but there's enough room for the two of us to lean against the railing and look out over the Potomac.

It's warmer here that it was in England, but not hot. Just warm enough that the beer is nice to drink. The air smells like water and concrete.

"I know what you're going to say," I breathe out, unable to hold it in any longer.

"You do?" asks Mark, looking over at me. His arms are on the railing, his glass dangling carelessly from his fingers.

"You're going to say that we should stop, that I don't know what I'm getting into, that this will only make things messy since I'm new to kink and was still a virgin as of last week, and then you'll say that we should go back to the way things were—and—and I don't want to go back to the way things were, sir," I finish in a rush. "I want to be yours. Like Strassburg was. Please."

It looks like he's fighting a smile.

"Tristan," he says. "I don't want to stop."

His words hang in the air like light, there but not there, and I have to breathe, have to swallow, before I can speak. "You don't want to stop?"

"I don't, however selfish that makes me." His eyes are very blue out here in the sunshine. "But I do owe you an apology."

I have no idea what he could mean. For food and orgasms and the only nightmare-free nights I've had since I killed Sims?

Maybe…maybe the stuff with the rulers and spoons and library carpet…

"Mr. Trevena, I liked everything we did. Please don't say you're sorry for it. If you say that you're sorry for it, it makes it seem like it's worth saying sorry for." And if it's worth saying sorry for, it makes me feel ashamed for having wanted it in the first place.

"I'm not sorry for what we did," he replies after a minute, his eyes searching mine. "And I want to do more of it. But I am sorry for how it was done. I should know better." A small, bitter laugh. "If nothing else, I should know better. But I wasn't thinking clearly this week."

I remember seeing him in the library, every muscle

standing out in harsh relief, bleak anger turning his face into that of a vengeful god. Haunted by whatever haunts him there.

"I used you selfishly," he goes on, "and while I am a selfish man, I prefer to be so on purpose. And whatever this week was, it wasn't on purpose." He looks away from me. The breeze lifts and pulls at his hair, streaks of gold and platinum glimmering in the sun.

"Okay, then," I say slowly. "Well, if you feel like you need to apologize for that, then I accept your apology. Although isn't this how most people do things? Not on purpose?"

"Most people don't gag their lovers with paper towels," Mark replies mildly. "We're not most people."

I roll the beer bottle between my palms for a moment. "Are you saying that it needs to be on purpose from now on?"

"Yes."

"Okay, then it's on purpose. I agree. I'm in. Whatever other consent you need, it's yours." My words are quick, eager. Now that I know he's not going to make us stop, all I can think about is getting back to it. About him dragging me inside and making me his plaything again.

He looks back at me, a small bracket on the side of his mouth like he's fighting off another smile. "You're not very good at self-preservation."

"Why would I want to be?" I whisper, staring at him. His golden skin and hair, his sharp gaze. His strong throat and long-fingered hands. The part of me that signed up to go to war, that went back to it over and over again, is his in this moment.

The rest of me already was.

"You will want to be better at it, because I can't be trusted. If I had even a shred more sense, I'd stop this, but I don't and I can't. I want it too much. But if we're going to do the wrong thing, we at least need to do it the right way. I

175

should have made sure of that at Morois House, and I'm very sorry that I didn't."

He holds up a hand when I open my mouth to argue. "You're going to say that you didn't need anything else this last week, but one day you might, so we must."

My expression goes a little mulish, and he smiles again.

"You saw me with Isabella. She liked struggling, reacting— she could do that knowing I wouldn't do anything she hadn't already agreed to do, and she could do that because she knew she *could* stop me at any time. Wouldn't you like that?" He comes a little closer, his hand on my wrist. Even through the cuff of my button-down, the warmth sinks right into my skin. "To fight me a little bit? To struggle underneath me? To have me pin you down and take something away from you?"

I'm breathing harder now. He squeezes my wrist until I gasp, my knees going soft, his eyes missing nothing. Surely not the flush blooming on my cheeks or the heavy pulse pounding against his wrapped fingers.

"I want that," I say. "A lot."

"I want to do it to you. But *on purpose* means a safeword. Limits."

"I don't have any limits," I say automatically.

"So I could peel a piece of ginger root and put it in your rectum before work tomorrow? Make you walk around with it inside you?"

My mouth is open. "What?"

He laughs. It's a small one, but it's real. "I would happily fig you if you wanted. But this is why we have to talk about limits beforehand. You remember all the terms and acts you had to review before you even worked here—how much more does it matter now that you'll be on the receiving end of things?"

"This is like the army," I mutter. "Paperwork where there shouldn't be any."

"It won't be filed away in an HR drawer, Tristan. It's just to help me."

I take a drink of beer and then look down at the river. "Fine. I'll go over the list of things again. Probably not the... the ginger thing though."

"It's four-hundred-level play, certainly. Now, your safeword—it needs to be something you can easily remember but not the kind of thing you'd say casually or spontaneously."

Isabella Beroul's had been *la mer*. The papers I read through prior to working here had used red, yellow, and green as a safe-wording system. I like the simplicity of it, but something about it feels too impersonal, too clinical. I want this to be mine and mine alone.

Magnolia petals flicker through my mind, white and pink, but with them comes the memory of Mark's fingertips on a petal, rubbing and rubbing, his eyes blank in a graveyard.

No, not *magnolia* then. But something else there, something else at Morois House.

I think of the hazel tree we sat under. How safe and lovely and adored I felt as he watched my mouth while I read him Marcus Aurelius and Musashi.

"Hazel," I say softly, and his gaze goes to my face. I see something flicker through his expression before he carefully shuts it away.

He nods. "Hazel it is. There is one more thing—"

I think I must be pouting now because there's an amused crook to his mouth again. "I promise it's short, but it will help me be good to you."

I tilt my head to show I'm listening.

"I want to know what you like about it. Us."

Being yours are the words that push against my lips, but I swallow them back. I can't say that. I don't want the humiliation of him knowing how far I've already fallen for him. I don't want his pity as he tries to find a way to tell me that he doesn't feel the same.

And I don't totally understand it myself. When I first came here, just the idea of a male submissive disturbed me. Now the thought of going even a day without Mark pushing me facedown onto the nearest convenient surface has both my chest and my dick hurting.

So I try for the next most honest thing.

"When you're with me, when you're hurting me or playing with me or using me, I don't feel heavy anymore. I feel light inside of my own skin, like…like my heart is so light it could float away."

And then I stop. I still don't know if that made sense, and I definitely don't know if that exposed too much of what I can't ever expose, and I have no idea what Mark is thinking right now as he studies me, his gaze piercing, a line drawn between his brows.

"I promise not to let your heart float away, Tristan," he says. Quietly.

And then he steps close enough for me to smell him, to smell the rain and wet earth, and it's the smell of Morois House, I think, rich and hidden, and then his mouth is on mine, driving away every other thought.

Chapter 18

My limits are more than nothing but still not extensive.

Maybe it's a soldier's hubris, like I can fucking *hooah* my way through anything, including nipple clamps and electric fly swatters, but mostly it's that everything on the list, I now imagine Mark doing to me, and I just want him to do anything to me. Anything he wants.

Also, and maybe this line of thinking makes me a bad submissive, but *anything Mark wants* so far has resulted in me having the best fucking orgasms of my life.

It's not all ensorcelled martyrdom, you know.

———

Mark and I fall into a rhythm over the next few weeks.

In the mornings, after the security meeting and my morning dose of fiber because fiber is an important part of my life now, I come up to his office where I'm shoved under his desk to suck him off or I'm dragged up to the roof so he can fuck me under the morning sky. We decide early on to be discreet-*ish*, knowing that it would be impossible to hide things forever from Jago or the core Lyonesse staff. So while I'm not servicing Mark in the hall (yet), I routinely find myself on my knees in the car while we're driving around the city. Or dragged out of the hall with an impatient hand around my wrist and shoved into the nearest playroom, shackled to a bed and then paddled or flogged or whatever new sadism Mark dreams up that night.

On Sundays, Mark keeps me in his apartment and cooks for me, makes me read to him while he effortlessly dices shallots and garlic and other wonderful smelling things. For dessert, there's me on the table, being edged or tormented or slid into.

At nights, I sleep with him, his arms wrapped around me and his legs tangled with mine. I wonder if Strassburg did all this, if Strassburg had to read him Sassoon and Owen and Rosenberg on Sundays, if Strassburg got to know the heavy weight of Mark's limbs as he fell into a dreamless sleep.

On the third Sunday, after we eat a dinner of radish greens and quail—the quail bones so tiny and delicate that I feel like a monster eating it—Mark clears the table and I kneel on the floor. It's never something he's asked me to do in these in-between moments, these moments that aren't quite kinky and aren't quite not, but it feels good to do it anyway. Settling. Like when I'm down there, I'm already lighter.

"Evander never makes eye contact with anyone but Arjun, and even then, it's only when Arjun lets him," I said one morning to Mark after I'd taken his erection in my throat and swallowed his cum. I was still kneeling after, my head resting on his thigh like he sometimes let me do, and his fingers were in my hair, toying and teasing, the one thing that never failed to make me want to purr like a cat. "Should I be doing that too, sir? When it's just the two of us?"

"I'm a little more organic than most in what I like

privately," Mark replied. "I like seeing your face. Your eyes. I like when I can see all the little desires and petulances that make having a submissive so much fun."

"Will you tell me when you want me to do something?"

He tugged on my hair. "Always."

So kneeling when we're not in a scene isn't something he's said to do, but I like it, and I also like the way his eyes flit over to me in silent pleasure as he cleans up.

I do look at him though; I don't think that's something I can ever give up. I could watch him move between the kitchen sink and the dishwasher forever. I could take in the poetry of his rolled-up sleeves and the efficient grace he uses to wipe down the counter for the rest of my entire life.

After he's done, he comes to me.

"It's your birthday tomorrow," he says, tucking a finger under my chin.

"Were you looking at my file, sir?"

"Perk of the position," he says, looking down at me. "Also my older sister texted me very stern instructions not to forget."

"She's very nice," I say honestly. I've been talking to my father as infrequently as I can manage, but I still hear all the happiness she's brought him in his voice.

"Blanche is an angel. It's very strange, given that Melody and I are not," he says. "Anyway. Setting aside the fact that our families are now legally connected and I have people reminding me of your birthday, I already had this planned for you. But we'll need to go down to a playroom for it."

We don't usually go to the playrooms, and even when we do, it's more about proximity to the hall and Mark's impatience than what's inside. He's just as happy to make me kneel on dried beans from his pantry or torture me with binder clips from his desk drawer as he is to use the special-ized tools downstairs.

My curiosity is hardly sated as we step inside the playroom and I see a plastic sheet laid over the leather upholstered platform in the middle of the space. There's a plastic sheet underneath it too. I turn to face him. He's already unbuttoning his shirt, eyeing a table against the deep green wall.

"I can't recall us needing a plastic sheet before. Sir," I say, not sure whether I sound nervous or excited.

"It's a courtesy for the cleaning team," replies Mark and takes off his shirt. "Undress and get on the table."

I automatically obey, unbuttoning my own shirt and pulling off my slacks and boxer briefs. I lay on the platform, the cool plastic crinkling under me, watching Mark's back as he prepares something at a narrow table against the wall.

"On your stomach," he says, and I obey then too, with only a little hesitation. I'm not scared, but the plastic has my mind whirring. There's no doubt that towels are useful nearly all of the time, but plastic sheets?

I'm settled with my head pillowed on my arms as Mark comes over. I brace for the first ticklish drapes of a flogger or maybe the initial stroke of a paddle, but instead, I feel only his hands, warm and large and—

slick—"Baby oil," he murmurs as I shudder underneath him. "Relax."

Strong and slippery, his hands work the oil into my back and shoulders and upper arms. More oil is drizzled onto the small of my back, and then—and then—

"*Fuck*," I groan as he works the oil into my backside and upper thighs, his thumbs sliding teasingly close to where I want them. It's so warm, the pressure so good, and his thumbs are *right there*. I arch a little, trying to push my hips up into his touch.

"God, you're easy," Mark says, but it's spoken fondly. "One short massage and you're spreading for me."

I am, I realize with my face burning on my forearms. I've got my hips lifted and my knees apart, hoping this will make an arrow to where I want his touch. My opening, my testicles farther down. The oil has made everything so slick, and then his knuckles graze against the underside of my scrotum and I gasp.

He ignores me, continuing to rub me everywhere else, and then finally he gives me a moment of kneading but slippery attention on the eyelet of muscle between my cheeks. By the time he rolls me over, I'm so hard that my cock is straining in the air above my stomach.

He makes a tutting noise, like he's embarrassed for me, and starts working the oil over my chest and stomach in short, warm passes, making sure he's left my nipples bunched into tiny points when he's done. My hips are moving, chasing, as he oils my stomach and then my hips, neglecting my erection to massage my thighs and calves and feet. The erection lifts above my stomach a little, as if trying valiantly to get his attention, its tip now gleaming with need.

"Sir," I pant, closing my eyes as his fingers work over the soles of my feet. It feels amazing, but I'm going to die if he doesn't touch my dick. "I thought this was supposed to be a birthday present."

"I don't think I ever said the word *present*," says Mark. "Only that it will be your birthday. And now we're in this room. Those two things might be entirely unrelated."

"But you—" I stop. "I feel tricked."

"You were so ready to believe the worst of me when you first came here, and now you're shocked by a little massage-related deception? Your estimation of me must have improved over these last several weeks. But never let it be said that I have no mercy…"

His hands come to my balls, rolling and fondling, cradling and gently moving the testicles inside the skin, and my heels dig into the plastic sheet, but they're now too slippery to find any purchase, and I slide on the table and he laughs. The dark laugh, the one that makes me want to sign my soul away.

"Little slut," he purrs, his oiled fingertips running up my cock one time and then falling away. The muscles in his forearm flex under his tattoo. "My little whore."

"Please," I whisper again, and he gives my erection a hard flick with his fingers. I arch in agony as he steps away from the table.

"Back on your stomach, Tristan. And no peeking. I want your not-a-gift to be a surprise."

I suppress the urge to grumble—I was never a grumbler as a soldier, and the one or two times I've come close with Mark have never had any effect other than earning myself a sore ass—and turn back over. There's not enough residual oil on my erection or the plastic to make pushing against it pleasurable, meaning that even if I rut against the table, it'll be a fight to make myself come.

Cruel of him.

My forearms are crossed and my head rests on them; I don't look up as I hear him approach, although I do tense a little, despite the rubdown I've just been given, because what could possibly require this much oil?

His footsteps stop, and I sense him on my left side, moving slightly. And then—out of nowhere—hot pain drips along my shoulder.

I jolt, the heat already mellowing into a pleasant warmth, the sensation sinking into my skin, and then it comes again on my other shoulder, a small splash and drip, burning and then immediately gorgeous.

Wax.

He's dripping wax on me.

"I remember you saying that you'd have a hard time

staying professional if you saw a wax scene," says Mark casually. There's some movement, Mark picking up something he's set on the table, and then more dripping. Along my spine now, in slow, torturous arcs. I suck in a breath with every flash of heat, shudder out an exhale as it cools and leaves behind hot, angry deliciousness. "And then it occurred to me that it might be fun to do *to* you. Fun for me, certainly."

More wax on my back. And—on my backside, a splash and then an agonizing slide down my crease. I moan as it reaches my entrance, cooled enough not to burn, but still so, so warm.

More comes, dripping down to my balls now and then splashed onto the backs of my thighs and knees and even on the soles of my feet. Flashes of searing heat, followed by unbearable surges of arousal. The cooled wax on my skin adds to it all, layers of sensation, cool and warm and *so fucking hot.* At some point I'm up on my elbows, my head hanging down and my ass lifting mindlessly in the air as he drips on me.

Mark is laughing at me. *Little wax slut,* he says, voice a little cruel, a little affectionate. *Look at you. Look at you.*

When I think I can't bear it without touching myself any longer, he makes it worse. He orders me to roll over, and now I'm allowed to look, and so I see as he alternates a turquoise candle and a gold one to create a beautiful play of colors on my skin. I see as he drips the wax up the line running from my navel to my sternum, as he drizzles it along my belly and chest.

He splashes burning wax on my nipple, waiting for me to settle down after each splash before he does it again and again, until both nipples are tingling with agony and my erection is a dark red bar hovering above my stomach.

And then he sets the still-burning candles in their holders, steps back, and looks at me. The room is lit by wall sconces and the tiny, flickering candles, and his eyes are blacker than the devil's when he rakes his eyes over my spattered flesh. He runs a possessive hand over me, from the wax-bitten soles of my feet to my navel to my throat, his palm lingering there while he bends over and licks my lower lip.

"Open," he murmurs, and I open for him because I will always open for him. His tongue seeks mine, rubbing against it, tasting it, and then he proceeds to map the rest of my mouth in a deep, exploratory kiss. Like for all the times he's kissed me since Morois House, he's never kissed me while I'm covered in wax, and so he has to commit it to memory.

I hope it's a good memory because I'm trembling underneath him, burning alive inside my own skin. I don't know that I've ever been this aroused, with every single part of me prickling and tingling and hungry for more, and the flames are still dancing and he tastes of pepper and citrus and spice, and I'm so hard—I'm so, so hard.

"You've been very patient, letting me play with you," he says against my mouth. He moves his hand from my throat, and I hear the click of a bottle. And then oil, sweet and slippery, drizzles all over my cock.

It jerks up in response, from nothing more than that, and then Mark pulls his mouth away from mine with a fierce oath, like it's my fault that he'd rather keep kissing me than carry on with his scene. My mouth is wet when he straightens up, clicks the bottle shut, and then gives me a series of hard, vicious strokes that has my back bowing off the table.

"Oh God, I'm—"

Mark's hand has already moved away from me, and I have to bite back a series of choice words for him as my orgasm freezes right on the edge.

"If you can come from this, then you can come," he offers, which is one of his favorite games to play, and one which he always wins.

Maybe I win too, depending on how I look at it, but it doesn't feel that way as he lifts up the gold candle and moves it over my hips. The first bite of fear, the first real flicker of *oh fuck, I don't know*, dances through me like the small flame currently guttering above my hips, inconstant and distracting.

Hazel. I've never had to say it, I've never wanted to, but I don't know if I can handle hot wax *there*—

I realize that the long pause, the drawn-out drama of the moment, is so I can say my safeword. He's watching me, not the candle, waiting for me to speak. And if the wax dripped now, it would drip on my upper thigh, nowhere too painful.

Weirdly, knowing it would be that easy to stop him, makes me not want to stop him at all. Makes me want to see how far I can go for him. For me.

"Please," I say. "*Please*."

It's the beauty of the safeword that I can say please and it can mean anything, anything at all, except for *stop*. Only *hazel* means that.

He licks his lip, the knot of his throat moving up and then down, and then I fully appreciate how much he wants this too. There's a subtle hitch to his breath as he looks back at my oiled cock, a hectic thudding of his pulse at the side of his neck. An obscene tent in his trousers.

"You're beautiful," he tells me, right before he tilts his hand and the wax lands on my skin.

I nearly scream, my chest coming off the table, the air driven right out of my lungs. The wax landed right on the tip, a sear of pure, undiluted pain, and is now dripping down the length of my shaft, its progress eased by the oil.

The pain is gone almost the minute it starts, but the after-effects—my pounding heart, my rigid muscles—linger even as the wax cools. I slump back on the table, my eyes going to Mark in some kind of plea. Again the candle spends a long moment over my upper thigh, the wax slowly spilling down Mark's hand instead of on my skin.

But the lingering heat, the hardening wax…it's no longer anything like pain. It's like being touched. Being stroked.

My skin tingles everywhere, still aware, buzzing and receptive to every tickle of cool air. And impossibly, I don't even know how, don't ask me to explain it, my dick is jerking up for more abuse, so swollen it feels like the skin itself might split.

"More," I croak, and Mark smiles.

"More," he agrees, and there's another splash of burning wax, this time on the root of my shaft, dripping down my scrotum.

Again I buck, squirming away from it, squirming toward it, and then still with that devil's smile, Mark tilts the candle a final time.

It lands just below the head, on the soft skin of my frenulum, and this time, I *do* scream. The pain punches right through me, right through my little fears and cravings and secret miseries and untold hopes, and claws something vital and primal right back out.

Even as my scream leaves my throat, my testicles draw all the way up, my thighs clench, and I'm fucking up into the cool air, the hard wax pulling at my crown and my shaft, and then I'm contracting, surging, ejaculating, high and thick jets that land on oil and wax, and I'm still screaming, I think, or something like it, still mindlessly fucking the air, feral as a trapped animal.

The pleasure tearing through me is painfully perfect, barbaric in its bluntness and yet exquisite in its unending torment. It goes on and on, built and layered on itself like the wax on my body, pump after pump of my hips in the air and the semen splattering on my stomach and chest.

Until finally, *finally*, it slowly ends, my body empty, my mind dazed.

I stare at the blurry dance of the candles' flames, unable to form a single word.

Mark's hands on are on me now; I'm back on my stomach, his fingers on my intimate skin. The wax falls away easily, with a single brush of fingertips, and that was what the oil was really for, I think. Not for the added pleasure of slippery skin to massage, but for the ease of removing the wax later.

Except it's not *later* yet; there's more oil drizzled into the small of my back and rubbed farther down, and then I feel Mark on top of me, his trousers gone, his erect penis nestled into the place where my backside splits. Not to penetrate me, but to rock and slide against the hot, thin skin there. To rut against the slick space hard enough to make both of us grunt.

Mark comes fast, faster than I've ever known him to, his arms sliding under me to hold me close as his hips toil and churn and his cock gives a thick swell against me. He starts pumping between us, his seed nearly as hot as the wax he used to burn my skin.

His forehead comes down on the nape of my neck, and his breath is warm and fast against my back.

"Perfect," he says breathlessly. "You are perfect."

And then he kisses the nape of my neck with so much tenderness that I start to cry.

The sole other time I've ever cried during a scene was when he used the binder clips on me, and even then, it was only when he'd taken them off. But I'm crying now.

It is a stunning thing, to be covered in wax and semen and with someone heavy and panting on top of you and to realize that you really are in love. But there it is.

The fall that I've been fighting, the snare I've been slowly cinched in—it's done now. I'm here. I'm lost.

"Oh, sweet Tristan," Mark says softly. He moves to kiss a tear off my cheek. "Let's get you cleaned up."

"Thank you for my birthday not-a-gift," I whisper, and he kisses my cheek again.

"You need only ask, and I'll give you everything. Everything I can."

CHAPTER 19

A SLOVAKIAN BUSINESSMAN IS COMING TO THE CLUB THIS weekend, and we meet with the head of his private security on Wednesday in Mark's office. Mark is there, along with myself, Goran, Nat, and Dinah. It's ten in the morning, the mood is tense, and Mark is already drinking his customary gin on the rocks, which I can tell is irritating the Slovakian security lead.

The lead glances over to Mark, who's sprawled in his office chair, swirling his glass so that the ice clinks along the sides. It's the lazy persona he normally adopts in the club at night, and I don't entirely understand what he's doing right now. This serves nothing except to ruffle Mr. Kulov's feathers.

"I need more assurances that this *open house* will be safe for my client," Kulov says, his eyes narrowed on Mark before he looks back to Goran and Nat. "We were not aware that the club opened itself to nonmembers."

"Once a year, members are allowed to invite up to three guests of their choosing," Dinah cuts in smoothly. "All the guests are background checked by us and screened as they come in. Of course, it is unfortunate that Mr. Drobny is visiting on the same weekend—we couldn't possibly tempt him to move his visit?"

"He will only be in the States for the next week," Kulov says. "His business requires him elsewhere before and after. It must be this weekend."

"Then let me assure you that we will endeavor to make his visit flawless," assures Dinah. "His favorite room will be ready, and any club submissive of his choosing along with it, and we will make sure every security precaution is in place."

"You are bringing in additional security for this open house, yes?" Kulov asks. "For the number of people? We will be with Mr. Drobny, of course, but even with three of us, I worry about the sufficiency of your resources."

Goran nods, opening his mouth to explain, but Mark interrupts, leaning forward in his chair.

"There are a lot of Carpathian resistance sympathizers who are associated with your client, are there not, Mr. Kulov?"

It's so unexpected—and Mark's voice, with the slow, casual drawl of the drunk, is so incongruous with the pointed nature of the question—that the room falls silent.

Kulov's hands flex over his knees and then curl into fists. "It is no business of yours who my client associates with."

"Oh, I think it is," Mark says sadly. "See, we have other guests to look out for, members who'd be very uncomfortable knowing Mr. Drobny brought in a security team that may or may not have a bone to pick with countries allied with Carpathia's legitimate government."

Kulov's hands are still in fists, but I notice that the pulse at the base of his neck is steady. Almost as if he's actually unbothered by this line of questioning. "Are you suggesting that Mr. Drobny's team might behave unprofessionally?"

"I'm suggesting nothing of the sort," Mark says and drains the last of his glass. He puts it on his desk clumsily, crookedly, so that it clunks and rattles. Goran winces. "I'm just saying that of course Mr. Drobny will understand that we'll need to be just as thorough with his team as we are with our open-house guests."

"I will get you the names so you can do your background checks, although you'll find nothing." He stands quickly, his posture hostile, although again, there's a certain calm underneath it all. It unnerves me more than outright aggression. "If that's all you need, then I'll be on my way."

"See you Saturday, Mr. Kulov," says Mark lightly. "Give Mr. Drobny my love."

———

That evening, Mark is having dinner with his twin sister in his apartment, and he gives me the rest of the night off. Tacitly dismissed, I rattle around my own apartment for an hour or so and then decide to finally make use of some of the club's non-sex amenities.

Namely, I go up to the bar on the fourth floor to drink until the obsessive ache in my chest stops hurting.

I'm sitting at the dark wooden bar—having just finished a pea soup with fresh cream and preserved lemon (and the Lyonesse signature of edible flowers), and am eating the soft bread and salted butter that came with the soup—when Goran sits next me.

"Mr. Trevena cloistered with Ms. Trevena?" he asks, reaching over and taking a slice of bread without asking. The bartender sets a glass of a clear golden beer next to him, and he winks at her.

I push the small ramekin of butter his way. "They're having dinner."

"The terror twins," Goran says. "You know, they used to

get sent out into the field together because they didn't need to speak to communicate. They say that the two of them used to be able to dismember and then dispose of bodies without ever having to say a single word."

"Are you saying Melody Trevena is as scary as Mr. Trevena?"

Goran gives me an incredulous look. "Dude, she's scarier. She's still *in*, you know, still at the agency. Except she's the one who calls the shots now."

I try to remember Melody from the wedding. Tall, I think, with the same blue eyes as her twin brother. A sleek, blond ponytail and a pantsuit. A pretty wife with big glasses who talked to anyone who'd listen about storing energy in molten salt.

How the twins are related to sweet, wide-eyed Blanche, I have no idea.

"What do you think they're talking about right now?" I ask.

Goran lifts a shoulder. "She's probably trying to cajole him into divulging some Lyonesse tidbit or other. He's undoubtedly trying to do the same in the opposite direction."

I can picture it now, the two them facing off across the table, blue eyes against blue eyes, plates speckled with flowers and rich sauces and tiny bones set between them.

I like the idea that someone can challenge him, resist him. God knows I can't.

"I'm worried about Drobny," Goran says abruptly and then takes a long drink of his beer. "Real worried."

Same. "Yeah, me too."

"The security assessments came back fine, which almost bothers me more," he admits. "But they were thorough as fuck, so I don't have anything to go on other than a gut feeling."

"It's something about Kulov," I say. "He never got riled

194

up. It's like he was pretending to be offended that Mark didn't trust him, but he expected it."

"If it were any other day but Saturday," Goran grumbles, and I nod. The logistics for the open house are complicated enough—that many guests, that many demonstrations, with rooms and booths booked solid…the place will be a zoo. The whole team will be there, we're bringing in additional security, and all the guests' names have been submitted in advance and vetted—but still.

Like most parties, it'll be a lot more fun for the guests than the hosts.

"At least if it's a clusterfuck, it'll be a fun clusterfuck, eh?" Goran says with a wide grin as he tips his glass to my beer bottle. By this point in my life, I've seen people react to stress in every way imaginable. There are the types who get quiet, the types who get pissy, the types who—like me—get sad. And there are the people who already have big, easy smiles, who slap you on the shoulder, who joke and joke and will probably die joking. Their smiles just get wider when they're barely holding it together, their shoulder slaps harder.

I wave for the bartender and ask for a bourbon, neat. Beer isn't working fast enough.

Goran watches me take the first long swallow with his eyebrows raised. "You okay, kid?" he asks.

I look at him. His dark gold eyes are kind.

"I don't know," I say honestly. I'm surrounded by wood and leather and lighting pendants that have probably been featured in *Architectural Digest*. I'm making more money than I ever could have dreamed, doing a job that's actually pretty easy, and once or twice a day, I'm fucked blind by a man so magnetic that people turn to look at him when he walks through a public park.

I *should* be okay. Being in love with someone who doesn't love me back should be as familiar as the sunset behind the farmhouse. But this time it's not okay at all, and I feel the loving of him like I felt the wax burning on my skin. Dangerous, addictive. Impossible to resist.

"I like you," Goran says after a minute. "A lot of people who get out young—well, there's usually a reason, and that reason can make them hard. Like they've grown an extra skin to protect themselves. Sometimes that skin is as heavy and rank as old body armor. But it's like you've grown a shell of glass instead."

A shell of glass.

Is that what it feels like to be Tristan Thomas now? Like the daydreaming prom king is still there, just in a translucent chrysalis now to keep him and his tender heart safe?

"I killed my best friend," I blurt out. So that he knows. So that he can't mistake my clear and pretty shell for something good, something nobly tragic or whatever. The shell, if it's for anything, is to protect myself from what I have done.

"I know," Goran says, and I guess he would. It isn't a secret—the news stories about me saving the next prime minister of Carpathia are the first things to come up when you Google my name.

"But being here…" I let out a breath. There's music playing from somewhere, a dark, elegant cello. "The shell feels different."

"Because of Mr. Trevena?" Goran's voice is gentle but direct, and I can't help but be direct in return.

"I think I love him," I say quietly.

There's a pause, filled with cello notes and clinking glasses, and then Goran says, "I'm sorry."

It probably means something that an apology is his first response.

"So you're filling Strassburg's shoes now?" he asks after we both take a drink.

Is that what I'm doing? Is that what Mark thinks I'm doing?

The idea of that is worse than jealousy, worse than unrequited love. I'm suddenly miserable. "Yes."

"But you love him."

"Yeah."

He looks down at the bar and then over at me, like he's trying to decide whether he should ask what he wants to ask next. "What—" He pauses, tries again. "What will you do after the…" He makes a strange gesture with the fingers of his left hand, like I'm supposed to fill in the blank, but before I can ask him to elaborate, his phone rings.

He answers and then makes a face as he listens to the person on the other end. "A little fuckery happening downstairs with a Sybian a guest refuses to abandon," he explains after he hangs up. "I better go handle it. But, Tristan, you can talk to me anytime."

His hand lands on my shoulder, heavy and comforting. Not a fatherly gesture, necessarily, but something solid and reassuring all the same.

"Thanks, Goran," I say. He smiles and then goes to rescue the Sybian, and I finish the rest of the bourbon and ask for another.

I think he really does mean it, about coming to him. And it's nice to have a friend who gets it. All my friends are civilians from high school or from the same group of West Point cadets that McKenzie and Sims had also been in. And while I don't think any of them truly judge me for what I did, it also makes casual conversation a little difficult.

Hard to go to them with a problem like being in love with my boss when Sims will never have the chance to love anyone ever again, and I'm the reason why.

I drink until the room glows and it doesn't hurt to

breathe. I check my phone after every swig, every exhale, hoping—

I think I love him.

I'm sorry.

I go upstairs and get ready for bed, stumbling a little, my thoughts full of hot wax and flickering candle flames. And as I fall asleep, alone for the first time in weeks, I remind myself that I survived a war. Four times.

I can survive Mark Trevena.

CHAPTER 20

THIS OPEN HOUSE IS STRESSING ME THE FUCK OUT, BUT SO far, everything is whirring along with perfect, purring dispatch, and everyone who isn't paid to keep the building's occupants safe is having a great time.

The rooms are full of members, guests, and spectators, doing everything from impact play to having full-blown orgies; the bar upstairs is crowded and congenial; and the hall is like something from a movie—packed shoulder to shoulder, lights flashing, music thumping and filling the space with soaring synths the way that hymns fill up a church.

There's plenty of sex and kink happening in here too, but at the edges, in the booths and nooks, not on the dance floor. This kind of dancing—all sound and light and sweat—is its own kind of kink practice, just as important to some members as cuffs or paddles, and I've observed that club etiquette is to leave the floor itself to dancing and dance-adjacent foreplay. Anything more involved should happen along the edges or up in the balconies.

About fifteen minutes ago, Mark gave a welcome speech

that was met with cheers and applause, and now he's at the far edge of the room, caught in a chain of people who want his time and attention. He looks the part of the underworld lord tonight, in an all-black tuxedo with his collar open and the bow tie undone, customary glass of gin in his hand. Only the small earpiece he wears signals that he's something more than a devil at his leisure.

I watch him a moment, smiling lazily at a young man I vaguely recognize as being famous. The celebrity is flushing at Mark's attention, and presumably also at Mark's night-sky eyes and the way a small lock of hair has broken free of its styled hold and is now hanging dashingly over his forehead.

I have to tear my eyes away over and over again, and I'm no better than this flushing celebrity because just being near the knot of his Adam's apple or the slice of his jaw makes me fumble for my own thoughts. And I spent my morning on my knees between his planted feet as he took phone call after phone call, sucking him quietly the way he likes while he's working, only to be hauled over his desk when the calls were done and fucked until I came all over the glass surface of his desk.

So. It's not like I haven't seen him today.

At least Drobny never showed. One less headache tonight.

I'm giving our corner of the hall another scan—easily catching the uniformed silhouettes of the extra guards we hired, stationary forms against a backdrop of dancing hedonism—when the air itself splits.

A snap, loud and unmistakable. The calling card of lead tearing through time and space.

A gunshot.

It's funny how little changes, how instinctive it is to move, run, shield someone with my body. The room is screaming, now a crush of bodies, and I have Mark, my hand fisted in the shoulder of his tuxedo jacket to haul him to safety, and my thoughts are clearer than ever, my mind alert, processing the shouted bits of information coming in through my earpiece.

Can't find the shooter—

Nat, evacuate the playrooms—

Goran, stay at the cameras, Roz will take Isaac and Emily and clear the bar and roof—

And then a noise I've never heard before, a shrill alarm ringing through the earpiece. Mark goes stiff as I'm trying to move him to the doors, and I settle for covering as much of his body with my own as I can.

"Sir, we need to leave!" I shout over the tumult.

"That's the alarm for the basement," Mark says tightly.

"Mr. Trevena, we have a problem" comes Goran's voice over the earpiece. "I can see two men in the basement trying to get into the server room."

Mark's fingers go to his ear. "I need someone there, Goran," he says, but I already know it's hopeless—every single staff member we have is trying to evacuate nearly a thousand people from the hall, playrooms, bar, and every other corner of the club.

"Sir, I can't spare anyone until the guests are safe," Goran says.

Mark closes his eyes a moment. People are rushing behind us, bumping and elbowing, and my back prickles with awareness that the shooter is still in here. "The guests come first," he agrees. But then he opens his eyes and looks at me.

"No," I say instinctively.

"You need to," he says. "You're the only one we can spare. Everyone else is keeping my guests safe."

"I'm keeping *you* safe."

"I'll be fine," he says impatiently. "This is a feint to

distract from what they really want, which is getting into the server room. And if they do get in there, it's possible many, many people will die with the information they find, and that blood will be on *our hands*."

I don't like that any more than he does, but also I can't leave him here, unprotected; the very thought fills my mind with a bright, awful static, and for a second, I see McKenzie's vacant eyes, Sims's pulpy neck.

"Sir," I try again, but Mark is past impatience now. He shakes off my hold on his tuxedo jacket with strength that surprises me, his eyes flashing.

"*Do as I say.*" His words crack through the air like more bullets. "Or I will fucking go and do it myself."

He means it. I see in his carved, tense features that he means it.

With a bitten-off growl of frustration and a feeling of wrongness so strong that I can *taste* it, I go, wheeling around and shoving through the crowd to the elevator banks closest to the backstage area. This is a horrible fucking idea, and I'm going to tell Mark exactly that when I get back, and if something happens to him while I'm down there, then it serves him fucking right—

"I can hear your thoughts from back here," Mark says through my earpiece. "Knock it off."

"I'm supposed to be protecting you. My *job* is protecting you."

"There's enough security here tonight to declare Lyonesse a sovereign nation. And I'm also a combat veteran, Tristan, so I promise I have better instincts than standing still while someone's shooting at me."

I don't answer, at least not out loud, instead venting my irritation in an unending litany of silent swear words and curses, finally breaking free of the crowd and climbing up the stage as I pull my firearm from my holster. I didn't draw it earlier because

I wasn't going to return fire in room full of people, but in the basement, there won't be guests to worry about. I won't have any compunctions about leveling the playing field.

The elevator takes its sweet time coming up, and then even longer to shut its doors and get moving again. The whole time I listen to the chaos happening elsewhere in the club, the evacuations, the head counts. They still can't find the shooter.

I did all my combat in body armor and MCEPs, but you'd think that I'd only ever fought naked like an ancient Celt for how fucking stifling my suit jacket feels right now. I quickly strip the jacket off and drape it over my arm like I'm a gentleman about to walk into a nice restaurant.

"Goran," I say as the elevators tick down. "Tell me what I'm walking into."

"Still just the two. They finished fucking with the electronic lock and are walking through the doors now. If they go anywhere near the servers, it'll trigger the weight sensors and the aluminum security doors and they'll be trapped. There's a clear line of sight from the vestibule into the server room, so if they're paying attention, they'll know you're there right away."

"Got it," I reply. The elevator bobs to a stop on the server room floor. Dings and then opens.

"Good luck, kid," he says, and then I'm in the corner of the elevator, carefully angling myself into the open, gun first.

Nothing.

Jacket still over my arm, I creep forward, the blue light of the vestibule glinting off the glass doors, which are currently hanging open.

"They haven't triggered the sensors," I say quietly to Goran.

"They're on the far wall, sticking to the edges of the room," Goran says. "It's weird. It's like they know not to—"

A shot cracks into the glass just behind me, and I duck into the server room, the heat coming off the machines already pulling blood to my skin. Adrenaline beats through me like a drum.

"Sorry about that," Goran says. "I didn't see him moving until just now. He's using the last row of servers as cover, but he's staying on the edge. His friend is still moving away from the main door…actually, now they're both moving away. Fucking weird."

There are really only two reasons to move away rather than engage: to avoid fighting or to trap me.

I really, really don't want to walk into a trap. Especially since I suspect the trap is the room itself, with its waiting aluminum cage.

I crouch and creep forward until I can see straight down an aisle between two banks of servers. Their lights blink and flash, making it hard to detect anything past the first few rows.

"They're not moving now," Goran says. "Everything upstairs seems to be stable, although we're still nowhere near evacuated. So I can't send you help, but you can take your time. Keep them pinned in place until I can send reinforcements."

I'm relieved to hear that it's stable upstairs—that Mark is okay without me—but something about this whole moment feels wrong. Like these guys aren't interested in the servers at all.

So why come down here?

I creep to the next aisle, and it's a mistake. Several gunshots ring out, going into the concrete wall where I was just crouching a second ago, one hitting a server inside its glass case and sending chunks of glass and metal and plastic everywhere. Sparks spit.

I use the cover to move to the next aisle, and then I see the second man just around the corner.

"I don't want to hurt you," I call. "Just set down your gun."

He spins, already shooting at me, and oh well, it was worth a try. I run right toward him, not interested in our slow-motion game of Duck, Duck, Goose anymore, and as he's adjusting his aim, I fling the jacket I'm carrying over my arm at his face.

In the moment it takes him to bat it away, I shoot him in the knee, like I did Sims. Unlike Sims, though, he drops his hands to catch himself as he pitches sideways, and for a moment, I think it's going to be fine. I'll go over there and kick his weapon away, his buddy will surrender, and by then Goran will have sent the team down—

Gunshots come from behind me, and I only move out of the way just in time, my foot almost grazing the grated floor of the central server area. Not wanting to risk the aluminum trap, I fling myself the opposite direction, turn as I do, and shoot.

It's all luck, what happens next. I'm moving, he's moving, it's dim and hot and lights are blinking everywhere. But my first shot punches into his shoulder and the second, fired right after the first, drills into his temple.

The first guy, the one I just shot in the knee—that's not luck. I hear him move, and years of combat take over. I turn back, and by the time I see his own gun lifting, I'm squeezing the trigger.

And it's over.

"Tristan, you okay?" I hear Goran's voice ask. Even though it's right there in my ear, it feels a million miles away.

The adrenaline makes everything hyperreal, so vivid that time itself feels like syrup sliding down the tines of a fork, and I'm kneeling next to the first dead man before I even really catch up to what's happened. I've taken his gun, I'm searching his pockets, and—

There's nothing.

Nothing at all.

He's wearing tactical clothing, all black, with the labels removed. His pockets are empty, and he's got nothing clipped to his belt save for a knife and a few extra magazines. And I don't recognize him. He's got a ruddy, broken face like a bar brawler, with hair the color of Oklahoma mud. I'd remember him if I had seen him.

The other guy is the same story—tactical clothes with the labels removed, nothing save for a knife and bullets on him, not even a phone. I sit back on my haunches and think, and then tap my earpiece.

"Goran," I say, and I hear his loud exhale of relief.

"Fuck, you scared me, kid," he says. "I could see you on the cameras, but I couldn't tell if you'd been hit or not. Seems like something you'd do, pretend that you weren't bleeding out."

"This feels wrong," I say. "There should be more than two of them. And if they wanted to steal something down here, I don't know how they'd do it. They don't have any drives with them, nothing electronic. Not even phones. Not even earpieces."

"Maybe…" Goran starts and then stops. The channel's dead; he's talking to someone else, I think.

I stand up and holster my gun after checking the magazine. I look at the two men dead on the floor, and then I make myself turn away and walk to the vestibule. I need to go upstairs. I'll need to wait for the police so I can talk to them. I'll need to walk them through the night and its events and how it ended with two dead bodies in the server room.

When I reach the elevators and press the button, I notice for the first time that I have blood on my sleeve. With steady fingers, I unbutton the sleeve and roll it up to my elbow. I do the same with the other side.

I just killed for the first time since the war. The knowledge hangs in my chest like rotten fruit still on the tree. I ignore it.

Turns out you can get really good at ignoring things like that.

I tap the earpiece again. "Goran," I say. "I'm coming up. I think...something's not right."

"I think so too" comes a cool voice, still tight with impatience. Mark. "If there were only two— "

Gunshots, bright, staccato, echo through the earpiece, and then I hear more screams.

"They're in the hall," Goran yells. "Shit, six, seven of them? Eight? I'm coming down—"

"Sir?" I ask wildly as the elevator doors open and I rush inside. "Mr. Trevena? Are you hurt?"

Fuck!

I stab at the button to close the doors and hit the button for the second floor, my heart racing all over again, my blood up, but my thoughts coming fast and clear in this slow-syrup world. I see it all now, the clever mechanism of it, a double feint. Tie up the security team with evacuations, lure attention downstairs to the decoys. And then attack.

"I'm coming, sir," I say, my jaw tight. I'm bouncing on the balls of my feet as the elevator gets moving, gun back out, my skin prickling.

Mark has to be okay. He has to be. If he's not, if he's not answering right now because he's hurt—

I suck in a breath. It's the first panic I've felt tonight, the idea of him being hurt, killed, in danger without me, even though I know he's capable and dangerous in his own right.

"How many, Goran?" I ask as the elevator slows. I back into the front corner as the doors open and then carefully ease my way out. The corridor is empty.

"Can't tell," Goran finally replies. He sounds out of

breath, and there's mayhem in the background, gunshots, screams, grunts. He must have left the office. "I think seven. All armed. Nat's going to take over for Roz, and Roz and Isaac will join us. I can't see Trevena." It's a sign of his stress that he's forgotten the *Mister*, slipping into the military habit of calling everyone by their last name.

"I'm almost there," I say, now running through the empty space to the hall. When I push through the doors, I find pandemonium.

The fresh swarm of assailants has meant that any guests who haven't been evacuated are stuck, pinned down, hiding behind overturned tables and the stairs to the stage. Bullets pop and snap, burying themselves in walls and leather booths, and no one's turned the lights or the music off, so all of this is happening in a steady, engineered scatter and spray of lights. Without the DJ, the music is stuck on the same heady, ethereal loop.

It's in this nightmare that I finally find Mark in the center of the hall with another man dressed all in black tactical clothes, an abandoned and presumably bullet-less gun kicked off to the side.

Mark is fighting.

Badly.

He's too slow. He's clumsy. Out of practice, maybe. His blocks come too late, his parries are too far off-center, leaving him open and unprotected for whole seconds at a time. There's a glint of metal in his opponent's hand—a knife—and he should turn or tuck his shoulder or *anything*, and he's not—he's moving like he's moving through tree sap, and then it hits me.

The gin. The gin he drinks like water, that he was drinking tonight...

He's out of practice and he's drunk and he's going to get stabbed.

I've come in on the second floor, thinking I'd want the better sight lines, and I don't give myself time to reconsider. I tear to the railing as fast as I can, grab it, and swing myself to hang from my hands on the other side. I drop the single story to the dance floor, which is sprung wood and absorbs a decent amount of the shock, although my knees and ankles still yip at me as I start moving again.

Gunshots tear into the balcony where I was just hanging, and they haunt my steps like vengeful ghosts. I can't risk leading the shooter's aim to Mark, and so I take a sharp right, following my intuition to the bar, where I see my attacker. He jerks back and I'm running at him at full-tilt, my own gun up, firing enough to make him duck, second-guess, and I'm tackling him, on top of him, and I squeeze my trigger and then he's dead.

I don't spend a second more there, already stealing his gun and shoving to my feet to run to Mark. I turn just in time to see the flash of his attacker's knife in the club's dizzying lights, just in time to see Mark miss the chance to block it and then stupidly, incomprehensibly, step forward *into* the attacker's range.

I turn just in time to see Mark get stabbed in the chest.

CHAPTER 21

I ROAR, SOME KIND OF PRIMAL FURY AND FEAR GRIPPING hold of me, more than I've ever felt it before, even with McKenzie, even with Sims, and I'm running and shooting my last bullet and the assailant falls dead. I toss my gun aside, lifting the other one as I run to Mark, shooting at someone in the corner who's now started paying attention to me.

He drops, just as Roz and Isaac bust through the doors upstairs, just as Goran appears at the railing on the third floor, pistol out, aim steady. The air is all pops and snaps over the dreamy synth music still playing on repeat. I ignore it all, falling to my knees next to Mark and making a shield of my body the best that I can.

"Sir," I say, my hand on his arm. He's on his side, facing away from me, and I roll him onto his back, expecting vacant eyes or a blood-slicked mouth.

"Fuck. Off," he chokes as I roll him over. He is white-faced and shaking and very, very much not dead. The knife I thought had gone into his chest is actually closer to his shoulder, which is good, but it's buried to the hilt. Which is less good.

Blood is everywhere, his black tux is drenched in it. It's all over my hands now, and I have to blink away the memory of my hands against Sims's slippery neck.

"When you're done panicking, a little help would be nice," Mark bites off in a voice that could flay the skin right off a person's body, and that's when I know for sure that he's not dying.

He's something worse.

He's furious. Two hours later, and I'm in Mark's bedroom with Mark, Sedge, and a small, trim man with light olive skin and a dark beard. The man—Dr. Sutcliff—is currently stripping off his gloves and walking over to the trash can. A shirtless Mark watches him from where he's propped up in bed, his shoulder now stitched and bandaged, his hair tousled and hanging over his forehead.

"You'll need to rest for at least four days," the doctor says. "IV antibiotics the whole time. After that, we can move to oral antibiotics and talk about what you can and can't do. Hint: the last list will be very long."

"Are you still sure we shouldn't go to the hospital?" I ask from my post at the foot of Mark's bed. The knife was buried *so deep*. And Dr. Sutcliff sutured it all on Mark's *dining room table*, with only a chandelier and a headlamp for light.

Mark bore the whole thing silently, mouth wrenched shut, every muscle etched in rigid pain. The only noise he made was a closed-mouth groan when the doctor sanitized the wound.

"The hospital?" Dr. Sutcliff asks. His expression is dubious as his gaze swings back to Mark.

"He was a prom king," Mark says to the doctor in tones of apology. "And he was in the army."

"Ah, a rule-follower," the doctor says and starts gathering up his things. "Well, he'll get used to this way of doing things quick enough."

"As opposed to doing things with, like, scans and operating rooms?" I ask. It's more cutting than I usually like to be, and Dr. Sutcliff is just as competent and skilled as any trauma medic I've ever seen in Carpathia—but also I'm exhausted and I'm worried about Mark. I keep seeing that knife sticking out of his shoulder, keep feeling his soaked tuxedo jacket ooze blood like a pressed sponge onto my hands as I held him.

Dr. Sutcliff finishes packing his bag. "I'd love to take him to the hospital, prom king. Do you think he'd let me?"

I look back to Mark, who somehow looks more dangerous bandaged and propped in a bed than most hardened soldiers I've seen in my time. "Mr. Trevena—" I start.

"No," Mark interrupts. "No hospitals. I've already been stabbed. I don't have the energy to worry about some nurse with too much student loan debt willing to let someone into my room to finish the job for a fee."

"Despite everything, it will be safer here," Sedge points out. "We can ensure more security and more surveillance than a hospital can provide."

I guess I see the logic in it…but what if Dr. Sutcliff missed something? What if I wake up tomorrow and Mark is in horrible pain or his wound is infected or he's dead—

"I'll be back tomorrow to check on you," Dr. Sutcliff says. "Do *not* get out of bed without help, and do *not* rip my stitches."

He leaves, and it's a testament to how fucked up the night has been that I can't even enjoy the experience of seeing Mark Trevena get bossed around by a man who looks like he plays doubles tennis on the weekends and loses.

As the doctor leaves, Goran and Nat come in to the bedroom, their faces grim and tired. Nat has a dried streak of blood along her jaw. I don't think it's hers.

"Well?" Mark says. His knuckles are whitening on the blanket as he looks at them. The morphine has put Mark in a better mood but better than lethally furious is still deeply, *deeply* pissed off. "Tell me."

"None of our members or their guests were killed," Goran says, and Mark's fingers relax a little on the blanket.

"Injuries?"

"A dozen, give or take," Nat says. "Mostly sprained ankles and knees from the evacuation. Three gunshot wounds, none of them critical. We also have seven unidentified bodies in the building, including the two in the server room."

I think back to the hall, the rain of bullets sinking into walls and furniture. "There were more than seven."

Goran nods. "My guess is that the rest of them escaped and blended into the evacuating crowd. It'll be impossible to say until we can comb through the camera footage."

"And Drobny? I didn't see him."

"Never showed."

Mark looks up at both of them. "How did this happen?" he asks. The skin around his mouth is blanched white—with anger or pain, I don't know.

Goran and Nat exchange a look, and then Nat speaks. "Drobny knew we'd be looking into anyone he brought with him. So he seeded the assailants into the guests, snuck them in through the open house."

"And our background checks didn't catch this?"

Goran bows his head. "It seems our standard checks can be fooled with a good enough cover identity. We'll start the process of matching the attackers to the fake identities and then to the guests who sponsored them, and take appropriate measures."

At my stricken expression, Mark gives an irritable sigh. "Expelling them from the club, Tristan. I'm not going to strangle them with my favorite necktie. Yet."

Sedge's phone pings, and he announces quietly, "The FBI will be here soon. They'll want to talk to you, Mr. Trevena."

Mark abruptly looks like a teenager who's just been told to go to the principal's office.

"This night can't get any worse," he mutters.

His reaction is…kind of hilarious, actually. And adorable.

And I can never tell him that I thought of him as adorable because then he might strangle *me* with his favorite necktie.

Together, with Mark growing increasingly drowsy, he, Goran, Nat, and Sedge outline what needs to happen over the next several days. The club will need to be shut down until it's no longer a crime scene, the necessary repairs commissioned, the new furniture ordered, and a thorough audit of all server access to make completely sure nothing was compromised. Dinah will begin a press campaign to manage questions from the public; Andrea will reach out privately to members to assure them that their information is secure and that the club will be reopening with increased safety measures. We will cooperate with the local police and the FBI and hand over anything they ask for, save for the club's proprietary information.

The security team will be pursuing their own leads to find out how Drobny did this—and why.

Goran says this last part, and Mark huffs, making his hair ruffle around his face. "There's no elaborate motive for *why*. He just wanted to kill me."

"But why you, sir?" asks Sedge. His forehead is creased and his mouth is turned down, and I can see a sheen to his pale eyes. He's close to crying.

It hits me then that he cares for Mark. That he's barely holding it together.

Mark drops his head back against the pillows stuffed behind him. "Why not? I probably killed his cousin's best friend's brother-in-law years ago or something like that. I'm at the top of many revenge lists, you know. I made myself quite famous back in the day."

Sedge looks even more upset, and Goran shakes his head. "We'll get to the bottom of it, sir."

Mark lifts a hand, rather feebly. There's an IV needle adhesived neatly to the back of it. "I think I need to be on my own for a while. Everyone go. We'll talk later."

Sedge, Goran, and Nat all leave the bedroom, and I turn to leave too.

A giant exhale. "Not you, Tristan."

Despite everything, my heart lifts at that. He wants me to stay. "Sir."

Mark gestures impatiently at the edge of the bed, like I haven't gotten the hint fast enough.

After I've settled, gingerly, facing him, he looks down at where the blanket is pooled around his naked waist. "You saved my life," he says.

"I thought—" My throat suddenly hurts so much that I can barely speak. "I thought you were dead. I really thought you were dead." I'm shaking now, and I realize how close I've been to actually fucking losing it ever since I saw that knife plunge into his body.

A hot tear tracks down my cheek and I wipe it away quickly.

Mark's face softens. "I'm hard to kill."

It shouldn't have come down to that. If only I'd sensed the deception earlier...never left his side. "I failed you."

His brows shoot up. "You saved my life, protected my club and its treasury. You were astounding. For the last two hours, I've been congratulating myself on hiring you. I'd be dead if I hadn't."

I open my mouth, and he holds up his hand, bringing the IV cord with it.

"I can't argue with you tonight," he says, and he looks so tired, so etiolated and worn, that my heart aches.

"You need to rest."

"I can't." And then lower, more exhausted: "I can't."

"You have to. And I'll wake you up the minute you're needed, I promise."

He's reluctant to agree, but I have an ally in the morphine because his eyelids keep sliding closed without him meaning for them too. They're bruise-colored and delicate-looking, and he's suddenly so fucking dear to me that I just want to gather him to my chest and bury my lips in his hair and keep him there and safe forever.

"Okay," he finally mumbles. His eyes are still closed, the long lashes resting on his cheeks. "But wake me up as soon as the FBI gets here."

"Of course, sir," I assure him. Without asking, I slide my hand behind his back to help him lie farther back. His skin is cooler than it should be but still firm and warm, and I can feel the muscles shifting under my palms as I move him.

He blinks up at me with blue, blue eyes, and there's a fond expression on his face. "A knight in shining armor," he murmurs as I finish settling him on the pillows. I pull the blanket up to his chest, my knuckles grazing the fresh gauze there.

"I thought heroes didn't exist," I say, letting out a long breath as my hands linger at their work, tucking the blanket gently around him.

"I might have to change my mind."

I'm about to force myself to get off the bed when his hand reaches out, snares my wrist.

"Stay," he says sleepily. "Stay close."

He pushes his fingers through mine, and he might as well be pushing his fingers right into my heart, right into its valves and ventricles. He might as well be clutching the tender, bloody thing in his fist.

He's asleep within seconds, his hand cool and relaxed in mine, and I bend over it, pressing my lips to his skin and confessing the words that have been clawing at me since I first felt his blood slick my hands under the dazzling dance floor lights.

"I love you, sir," I whisper against his knuckles and his fingertips and his wrist. "I love you."

I love you so much that I can't bear it.

CHAPTER 22

"WE SHOULDN'T, SIR," I WHISPER THREE MORNINGS LATER AS Mark pushes me to my knees in his shower. The large open space is lined with stone on two sides and glass on the other two, and the damp mineral scent and running water smells almost like Morois House. Almost like him.

I blink up at him, my eyelashes wet, my hand still clutching the washcloth I was using to clean him. "Dr. Sutcliff said no sex."

"I don't need my shoulder for this," Mark says in a low voice, his hand already on my head, twisting in my wet hair. He pulls me to his waiting erection, and I groan in the back of my throat, unable to resist, even when it's for his own good.

It looks too wonderful, standing straight up, his balls heavy underneath, and his hand in my hair is like the hand of God for all I can fight it. I let him guide my open mouth to the crown, plump and soft, and then down the shaft and back up.

He's standing with the spray behind him, and water is

running down his chest and stomach, dripping into his navel and along the line of hair leading down to his sex. The spray makes a soft tapping noise against the waterproof bandage sealed over his wound and hisses against the stone floor, and when he finally nudges me to take him all the way inside my mouth, I hear the rush of his breathing over it all.

A symphony of water, breath, and stone. And as he finishes down my throat, he murmurs my name like a coda, like it was the reason for the music to begin with. His thumb finds my bottom lip and rubs it fondly as I finish swallowing, his gaze going from my mouth to my eyes to my whole face, like he's trying to memorize exactly the way I look right now.

I know he doesn't love me; I know that I'm convenient, available, an animate doll that's happy to be used and toyed with…but *sometimes*.

Sometimes when it's like this, I can pretend.

Finally, he releases me and then looks down at the erection straining between my thighs. He nudges it with a wet, bare foot.

"You can take care of that if you want," he says, with the air of someone being uncommonly magnanimous. And the shame of it is like a drug, humiliation twisting in my guts as I wrap my hand around my cock and start masturbating on my knees. And of course, the humiliation is everything—it's like nothing else; it gets me even harder and it might as well be sweet nothings in my ear for how warm it makes me feel.

It's someone saying *no matter how mindless or messy or weak you might be, I'll still want you. I'll still want you at your worst, your lowest, your ugliest.*

I pant and spurt ropes of cum between his feet, making sure to stroke myself all the way through the climax because I've learned over the last month that I can never predict when Mark will decide that orgasm deprivation is his new favorite thing, and so I need to make every orgasm count.

After I'm done, Mark looks down at my semen like a king looking at his tribute, and prods my cock again with his foot. I hiss. It's sensitive now.

He smiles.

"You can finish washing me," he says, turning to give me his back, the tight lines of his ass and thighs, and I get to my feet to obey.

Mark refuses to discuss even the idea of a nurse, so it's fallen to Sedge and me to take care of him while he recovers. Not that he needs much taking care of—he's been patently ignoring Dr. Sutcliff's orders to rest and striding around the club with his IV catheter unhooked, taking meetings, answering questions for the police, and overseeing the necessary repairs of the club. It was driving us all wild how stubborn he was being. But halfway through the first day, he realized that he could make me play the part of a Victorian valet and concubine all at once, and after that, he became something much worse than a stubborn patient.

He became an infernally needy one.

Tristan, come dress me.

Tristan, bring me another glass of water.

Tristan, give me your hand, I need—yes, that's right. Slower. Slower.

But I love it. I love it so much that I almost wish we could live like this forever, with me being even more than a bodyguard, being his valet and manservant and everything. I love it so much that every time Sedge helps in the slightest— even if it's just to fetch his suit jacket from across the room or to get a pillow to put under Mark's arm as he works in his office—jealousy bites at my stomach, gnaws in my chest.

I hate that Sedge has known him longer, that he can anticipate Mark's needs, that he *looks* submissive, all quiet and unassuming, the kind of person who will take what he's given and never ache for more. I hate that I can't tell if there's any fondness in Mark's voice when he thanks him, and I hate that I care that there could be.

I shouldn't care. I'm the one who gets to run soapy washcloths over Mark's naked body; I'm the one who buttons his shirts and ties his oxfords for him, even though I know for a fact he can do it himself because he seems to have a superhuman ability to ignore pain.

But I do care. I'm still jealous. I want Mark like he was at Morois House—staring at me with naked, possessive owner-ship, refusing to let me leave even to get a new pair of pants. Sometimes I get moments of it here at Lyonesse: when we are together at night, alone; in the mornings, when I wake up to find him already watching me with eyes that shift like the underwater light that fills his room.

But for the most part, his attention is claimed by every-one and everything else that comes along with having a place like Lyonesse: members, employees, money, information.

And occasionally Sedge.

I have no idea what I'll do if he brings back Isabella Beroul to play with. If I'm this jealous of an administra-tive assistant, I don't know how I'll cope with him having a woman tied to his desk again. Fuck.

After the shower, I make Mark go into the kitchen and sit at the table so I can change his bandage and check for signs of infection like Dr. Sutcliff showed me. He makes a noise in his throat when I clean the wound itself but other-wise stays silent.

"Do you want—"

He interrupts before I can finish. "No. It makes my thoughts slow."

I remember the night of the stabbing, when I woke him up from a morphine-laced sleep to talk to the FBI. How lucid and precise he'd been, quick and perceptive. The only sign he'd been injured had been the bandaged shoulder and the occasional tightness of his mouth. The only sign of the morphine had been his eyes, a pinprick of black in a sea of blue.

"It didn't make you slow," I say, although I know it's pointless. He'll keep refusing the medicine and pretending he's not in agony whenever he moves or breathes. I press the new bandage over the neatly sutured wound—which is healing nicely, despite Mark being the most noncompliant patient ever—and seal the edges with my thumbs, being as gentle as I can.

"You're good at this," he says. "Nursing."

"I like it," I reply. In the field, there was only time for combat gauze and a call for help, and that was it. It's nice to be able to do things neatly. Kindly.

I think of my hand against Sims's neck, his last words, bloody and burbling. *Family…ease.*

"Not that you need it," I say, trying to shake off the memory. "Sometimes I think you'd wrap a kitchen towel around it and call it a day."

"I've done worse," he says and gives a slow roll of his shoulder. I know he's worried about keeping his range of motion there, although after seeing him fight in the hall, I hope his concerns are more kink-related than combat-related.

Because, uh, his range-of-combat motion wouldn't be much to mourn.

Together, we go into his room, and I dress him for the day. I help him into his pants and undershirt, and then into the pale-gray shirt he's wearing today, easing it over his bad shoulder and then buttoning it for him. Then the cuff links, my fingers on his wrists, on his palms, brushing, grazing.

He watches me the entire time, his eyes hooded, his breathing steady, even as a muscle flickers in his jaw. I don't need to look down to know that he's hard.

I knot his tie as neatly as I can—and then have to untie

222

it and start over when Mark tells me that it looks like it was tied by a cat batting a ball of yarn between chair legs—and then it's my favorite part, kneeling to put on his socks and shoes. Normally, I dress him with a soldier's efficiency and a submissive's respect, only touching him when necessary and when allowed, no matter how tempting it would be to rub my palms up his back or trace the line where his pressed collar rests against his throat.

But his feet…I can't resist the urge to stroke when he rests his bare foot against my thigh, and I don't. I don't resist. I run my fingertips over the intricate architecture of bone and tendon at the top; I press my thumbs to the sole and knead. I caress his ankle, feeling the crisp hair of his leg and the tight taper of muscle coming down from his calf, and I just stare, wondering how it can affect me so much. Wondering why it feels like a crime and a gift all at once to pull the fine wool sock over it and then the other, followed by his shoes, which I lace with tight, even loops.

"I think I'd like to wear my watch today," Mark says once I've finished tying his shoe. He's forgone the watch since the attack—watches aren't much use if you can't lift your wrist to look at them—but I also sense that he's getting impatient with the pain in his shoulder and with himself for feeling it. And once Mark decides something, it's *done*. Leaving the CIA, fucking me, wearing a watch even though his shoulder vibrates with agony whenever he moves his arm—once he's chosen, the choice is chiseled in stone.

I know this is another thing I can't fight him on and hope to win, so I get to my feet with a sigh. "I'll get it for you," I offer, just as his phone rings.

He nods at me as he answers it with his left hand, walking out toward the kitchen. I go into his large walk-in closet and stare at a section of built-in drawers for a moment, and then start opening them at random. I haven't seen the watch in here while getting socks or ties or cuff links, but it seems like the most logical place to start.

Coming up empty, I walk back out of the closet and go to one of the bedside tables which brackets Mark's oversized bed. The table on the right I'm very familiar with, since it's where lube, condoms, and a handful of Mark's favorite toys are kept. The one on the left I've never opened.

I do now, gratified when I see the watch right away. It rests on a wooden tray inside the drawer…and it's not the only thing there.

Two rings sit in a shallow depression in the wood. Both are a dark metal—tungsten, maybe—each in a different size. The smaller one is polished, with a ring of black stones wrapped around the middle. The larger one is matte and unadorned.

When I nudge them with my finger, I see that both have the same thing etched inside: *1 Samuel 18:3.*

Catholic Sunday School did a good enough job that I know 1 Samuel is in the Old Testament, but that's about as far as I can get without a Google search, and I don't want Mark to walk in and find me snooping. Because there can be no doubt that this is private. As private, maybe, as the dead rose in the drawer at Morois House.

I think they're wedding rings.

I take the watch and close the drawer, thinking of the man in the picture next to Mark's bed in Cornwall, thinking of Mark alone in the library, going there year after year to mourn.

Was he married to that man? And is it strange that I don't know the answer to that already? For the last three months, I've been his shadow; for the last four weeks, I have given everything to him. It is odd not to know if someone's been married after that kind of time together, right? Unusual? Especially when I feel so often like he knows everything there is to know about me, my foibles and nightmares and maybe even my stupid, hopeless obsession with him, and I can't help feeling like it matters somehow, when it comes to him. Like if I can know this about him, then I can expose one of the intricate inner mechanisms that makes him tick.

CHAPTER 23

I'VE SPOKEN WITH THE POLICE THREE TIMES, AND THE FBI four times, and yet I still spend my afternoon in a glass meeting room with two FBI agents, this time going over the security footage from the attack with them, corroborating the video with any details I can recall. Which is nothing that I haven't already said, written, and signed several times over, but I guess the army has given me a deep well of patience for redundancy because it feels very normal to be explaining something for the eighth time, with lots of *no, sirs* and *no, ma'ams* indicating that no, I have not spontaneously recalled the attackers reciting their last-known addresses or aliases as they died.

Mark seems to take their lack of leads as a given whenever it comes up. *FBI*, he'll say in a voice dripping with scorn. *They can't even investigate their way into a suit that fits.*

And indeed, even though we all agree Drobny must be involved, no one can find him or even where he went after he was in DC this last week. He's gone, and the best we can do is hope that Mark's web of information and connections will eventually do what the FBI's can't and help us locate the bastard.

After I'm done with the interview, I'm meant to go up to Mark's office, but I stop by Sedge's office first, taking a moment by the door to shelve my pride.

There is a private humiliation in having to ask Sedge about Mark, about his life, and there is the not-so-private impression that it will surely make. Sedge will know I don't know. He'll know that I care.

But the curiosity is like needles under my skin, pricking at my palms and the nape of my neck. An instinct, the same one that made me aim for a wristwatch glinting in a dark alley, the same one that led me into caves and seemingly empty houses in Carpathia. An instinct saying *there's something here, there's something here.*

Or maybe it's just the old curse, my obsessive nature: I have to know this.

Sedge looks up at me as I enter, and something moves in his pale eyes, something that makes me wonder if he feels about me the same way I feel about him, but it's gone in an instant, replaced by his usual soft wariness.

"How can I help you, Mr. Thomas?"

I am so, so aware of how awkward and unprofessional and exposing this is, but it's too late for anything else. I can see the wedding bands so clearly in my mind's eye now, the way one had been half resting on the other, the light catching the black stones of the smaller ring. I just…

I have to know.

"Has Mr. Trevena ever been married?" I ask, sitting down on the low, armless chair in front of Sedge's desk. "Like before he founded Lyonesse, maybe?"

Sedge regards me. I can see him weighing my reasons for asking. Finally, he answers, "No. Mark Trevena's never been married."

I think of the rings. "Are you sure?"

"If I wasn't before," Sedge says, and I could swear there is a pinch of dryness to his normally inflectionless tone now, "I would have been by fifth time I had to reassure Mark's priest of that very thing so we could get on with the wedding planning."

He says the words together like they all belong together, but they don't.

They don't make any sense.

"Wedding planning," I repeat.

Not as a question but as an attempt to make the phrase legible.

"Yes," Sedge says, eyeing me. "For the wedding. Weddings need planned. Thus the wedding planning."

"There's going to be a wedding."

Sedge's brows have lifted the smallest amount, and he blinks slowly. "Mark's wedding? In two months?" His expression plainly says, *uh, look alive.*

"I didn't—he didn't—" The needles of curiosity are knives now. I'm being cut open by them. "How can he be getting married?"

"Well, I wasn't here for it, but I presume that he proposed to Isolde and she accepted. That's usually how it goes."

Isolde.

I've heard that name before.

Isn't she Irish?

That was her mother.

Other snippets begin surfacing—Goran complaining about a wedding planner, asking me what Mark and I planned to do *after...*

I thought I was going to find out that Mark had been married once and that there had been a tragedy, and the tragedy now lives inside various drawers, in rings and pictures and roses—but no, the tragedy hasn't happened yet; it's *going* to happen. In two months.

Isolde.

The tragedy has a name and it's Isolde.

I stammer out a combined *I'm sorry for bothering you* and *thank you*, and somehow push my way to my feet and out of the office.

I don't know how I make it upstairs to Mark's floor. The knives are cutting and cutting, and I'm in love with someone and he's going to marry someone else and he didn't even tell me. I wasn't even worth the trouble of disillusioning.

He hadn't even taken the time to break my heart himself.

He's not in his office when I get there, and for a minute, I consider leaving.

Just. Leaving.

Going down to my apartment, or even better, leaving Lyonesse altogether. Going for a drive, going to the farmhouse.

Quitting this job where I surrender my soul hour after hour to a man who couldn't bother to mention that he was engaged. To a woman, which I shouldn't care about because I like women too, but I do.

But I don't leave. Maybe because I spent eight years in a job I couldn't quit until I was allowed, or maybe it's because I can't seem to stop flinging myself into misery, I don't know. But instead I walk through the office to the hallway leading to Mark's apartments.

Which is when I hear the swearing.

It's not Mark swearing when I step inside, but Dr. Sutcliff, who is standing in front of a seated Mark, his cheeks a dark scarlet above his neat beard and a bloody hunk of gauze in his hand.

"—if you just would have *listened*, just goddamned listened *for once*—most people would give anything to be told to stay in fucking bed—and I don't even know how the fuck you managed this, you worthless, shit-for-brains asshole—"

I pull up short, shocked out of my fugue by this rant from the doctor, who I'd assumed was more of the *silently judge you from across a Men's Wearhouse rack* type.

"Ah, Tristan," says Mark, noticing me. "I seem to have run into some trouble with my shoulder."

And yes, he has. As I come closer, I can see that somehow the stitches have pulled and several of them have ripped. The skin is a torn and ragged mess, like a gaping maw below his clavicle, and streaks of dried crimson track down his pectoral muscle to his stomach.

Fear and worry join the anger and heartbreak, and there's a cold, choppy storm in my chest of emotions I can't possibly separate. "I was only gone for two hours," I say. "How?"

"I thought I'd carry one of the damaged chairs out from the hall to the lobby," Mark says like it's no big deal, like he's explaining how he got a splinter. "It was heavier than I thought, and it just happened."

"It just happened?" Dr. Sutcliff demands, setting his bag onto the table with a pissy *thunk*. "You are so fucking lucky I'm free today, or I would have just let you suffer. I would have told you to go to the goddamn hospital, I don't care who wants you dead because I *don't have time* to be redoing my work every time you think about playing HGTV in your goddamn pervert clubhouse—"

The doctor's rant continues as he pulls out his supplies, as he rips open sterile packages of needles and filament, and as he starts removing the old stitches to make way for the new ones. He only pauses once—when he's pouring the alcohol over the torn skin and Mark sucks air through his teeth—and it's only to give Mark a vindicated glare.

And then he's off again, muttering and grumbling as he grabs his curved needle and needle holder, and Mark settles on the table in front of him.

"You're going to have a fucking ugly scar," Dr. Sutcliff

says. "And I don't want to hear any bitching about it because I already tried to give you a nice scar, and this is what you get for not listening."

"Do the mafiosos and Russian vory give you this much trouble, Sutcliff?"

"Never," Sutcliff answers crisply, stabbing the needing unceremoniously into Mark's skin. Mark blinks up at the ceiling, giving no outward sign that he feels anything. "You know why? Because they have some respect for my profession. You don't respect anything that can't be turned into a game at your little club."

"Medical kink is very popular," says Mark, sounding offended for the first time. "I own a lot of speculums."

"You," the doctor tells me, ignoring him. "Go get a glass of ice water, a wet washcloth, and a towel. He'll need to get cleaned up after I'm done."

I obey, and I linger for a moment in front of Mark's bathroom mirror, washcloth and towel in hand, my eyes on the drawer between sinks.

Despite the bloody scene just outside, my mind stalls, slicing at itself in midst of the domestic reality of Mark getting married.

My toothbrush is in here, my deodorant. Will he ask me to take them back to my apartment? Will they get shoved to the back of the drawer to make room for *Isolde's* toothbrush? *Isolde's* deodorant?

Will Mark still want me to—

No. No, even he can't be that sadistic. To expect me to give him my mouth or my body, to be available for his needs, when he'll be married to someone else. Even if he is polyamorous and even if his wife is okay with it, I don't think I could ever…share—

The jealousy would eat me alive. It's already eating me alive.

And imagining him bending me over and wedging his cock inside me for a fast fuck while his wife is just a room away…

My cock gives a quick, urgent stir, like it's trying to hoist a flag to get my attention, and I spin away from the bathroom counter and stalk out into the hallway, trying to outpace my body's reaction to the scenario. Even if I were desperate enough to let Mark use me after his deception, I could never be a party to infidelity.

I go out to the large space that contains the kitchen, dining room, and living room, and see that Dr. Sutcliff has finished the stitches and is sealing a fresh, clear bandage over the wound. He pulls out a syringe, vial, and alcohol swab and starts prepping Mark's elbow. I notice that the IV catheter on the back of Mark's hand is gone now, a small bandage in its place.

"You'll need IV antibiotics for the next few days, and since you're so keen to be done with IV bags, I'll come by myself and give you the shots. Not like I don't have better things to do, but patient knows best, right? Make a fist." He pulls the medicine from the vial, presses the plunger to remove the excess air, and then slips the needle into Mark's elbow. He pushes the medicine in slowly, looking at his watch as he does. "You also need to *rest*, and I swear to Jesus, Mary, and Joseph that if you tear a *second* set of stitches, I'm duct-taping you closed next time."

Mark relaxes his hand, and I hate how my eyes automatically track the movement, the strong fingers, the taut muscles lengthening under the inked skin of his forearm.

"How long do I need to rest?" Mark asks. "I occasionally have other things to do aside from having a shoulder, you know."

Dr. Sutcliff doesn't lift his gaze from his watch, his other hand still slowly pressing the medicine into Mark's arm. "I'd tell you two weeks, but I know you won't listen. Give me a week. Just give me a week to make sure we're not going to get an infection that wants to spread to your heart and kill you. Okay?"

A put-upon sigh. "Fine."

Dr. Sutcliff finishes with the syringe, presses a square of gauze to the punctured skin, and then nods to Mark to press his own fingers over the gauze instead.

"So...hypothetically, a three-week yacht trip across the Atlantic," Mark says casually, coming to sit upright on the table. "Starting this weekend. You'd say no to that?"

Three-week yacht trip...

It comes clear as a bell. The mysterious trip to Ireland, the *Philtre D'Amour*. The person with the Irish mother.

Isolde.

"If you are stuck on a boat and that wound gets infected, you will deserve fucking septicemia," Dr. Sutcliff says with the weight of someone laying a curse on a victim. "Stay. Here. And. Rest."

He turns to me and adds, "Make him drink that entire glass of water," and then leaves without so much as a goodbye.

"He's very surly for how much I pay him," Mark observes as the door to his apartment closes.

I step forward and set the towel and the washcloth on the table, hand him the glass of water, and then I take a step backward, away from him. Because he's shirtless, and the slanting afternoon sun is finding the white-gold streaks in his hair, and the dried blood streaking his chest somehow makes him look better, not worse, and I don't trust myself, I just don't. Not around him.

Mark lifts his eyebrows at me. "Got somewhere to be?"

Anywhere. Anywhere that isn't the place you'll be bringing a bride.

"No, sir."

He doesn't drink the water, not yet. He's still regarding me. "Clean me, then."

"You are supposed to drink your water. Sir."

His mouth tilts a little. "I forgot that I have a Dom now too. Very well." He sets the glass to his lips and, without breaking eye contact with me, drinks.

I heroically manage not to watch his throat move as he swallows.

"Now," he says after he finishes and sets down the glass. He takes hold of the damp washcloth and holds it out to me. "Clean me."

I take the washcloth, our fingertips brushing as I do, and hot sparks prickle along my knuckles and palm. They sweep up my arm and settle in my chest, and everything is warm and everything is cold and everything hurts and also I feel nothing at all.

I need to tell him that I know. I need to ask him why he lied.

I need to—I need to end things between us.

Things.

Just fucking. Just kink. It shouldn't feel like I'm preparing to dig out my wet, slippery lungs with my bare hands and throw them in the trash.

I wish it were only the habit of obedience that has me stepping between his legs and pressing the washcloth to his skin, and I wish it didn't thrill me to see the goose bumps pebbling his chest as I work.

He doesn't speak as I clean him, but his eyes are his possessive eyes, his Morois House eyes, watching me with dark, avid fascination. I flush.

I hate that everything feels right when he's watching me like this. I hate that I crave what comes next: his hand on my neck or the sound of a zipper. The slick search of his fingers inside me.

Tell him. Tell him.

I open my mouth, meaning to start with something eloquent, something that puts the last thirty minutes of shock and misery into an excoriating declaration of exactly how fucked up he is, but nothing at all like that comes out.

"Ireland," I say, my voice toneless. My hand keeps moving across his chest, scrubbing carefully at the dried blood. "You were going to Ireland."

Mark's gaze shifts, and there's a different kind of watchfulness to his stare now. "Yes."

"Was it something to do with your bride? Isolde?"

His hand comes up and captures my wrist. To hold me still, I think, so his eyes can search mine.

After a long minute, he asks softly, "You didn't know?"

"Why would I have known?" I ask bitterly.

"It's not a secret, Tristan. Our engagement was announced in five different newspapers. Her uncle is a Catholic cardinal and will be in attendance. Her father, Geoffrey Laurence, is one of the most influential men in international banking."

Geoffrey Laurence. I remember him—compact and well-dressed with silvering hair. Mark had been in a strange, restless mood after lunch with him. And that night, he'd kissed me on the rooftop.

At least one of us should get what they'd hoped for.

"It's been in the works for four years," Mark continues. He's still holding my wrist, still watching me. "It's always been the plan."

"And fucking me? Was that part of the plan?" And then I stop and give a bitter laugh, remembering his words in Singapore. "No, of course not. I was going to complicate things. But what—you just couldn't help yourself anyway? You wanted to fuck me badly enough that it was worth cheating on your fiancée? Risking an engagement that's been announced in five different newspapers?"

His face grows cool. "Something like that."

It occurs to me that someone walking into the room would see two regular lovers right now. Him on the table, me standing between his legs. My hand on his chest with our eyes locked.

But of course that's not the whole story. There's a bloody rag between my hand and his skin; he's holding my wrist tightly enough that I'd need to safeword in order to get away.

And it's not just the two of us—we're not alone. Isolde is a veil between us, a shadow.

"Is she like me?" I ask, and the words are as ragged as the wound on Mark's shoulder. "Will she kneel for you? Let you do whatever you want to her like I do?"

I don't know what I want the answer to be. Is it better or worse if she's not a submissive?

Mark doesn't answer for a moment. "She submits when it suits her," he says, which is more confusing than no answer at all.

"Is she polyamorous?" I ask. "Will the marriage be open?"

"That's up to her," he says mildly, and I could kill him right now, I really could.

"So you don't even know if she would be okay with it, and you still had sex with me?"

"What we do is a lot more than *having sex* and I think you know it." He lets go of my hand, but not to free me. He grabs my tie instead, standing up and looking down at me as I'm held in place by the silk around my neck.

He's only an inch taller, but I feel that inch like a mile.

"What we *did*," I correct him. My voice is quiet now. "I'm done now. I can't be—it would be cheating."

He doesn't like this. I can feel his fingers spasm around my tie, and his mouth is white around the corners.

But he says, "As you like."

Like it's all down to me. Like I'm being the unreasonable one.

"Let go of my tie. Sir."

A muscle moves in his jaw, but nothing else changes. Until—abruptly—he lets go of me and turns away. The bloody washcloth falls to the floor between us, and I bend to pick it up.

"Will you keep working for me, Tristan?" he asks. He's looking out the window now instead of looking at me. "Being my bodyguard?"

"I—"

There's the shelf of World War I poetry he has me read aloud to him on Sunday afternoons. There's the door to his bedroom, the light dancing around the floor from the pool above it.

There's the door to the guest bedroom, a room that Isolde might claim for use of its closet.

There's the kitchen where he's cooked for me; there's the kitchen island where just last week I was naked and trussed up, rope wrapped around my testicles while he jerked my dick until every inch was blood dark and as tight and smooth as stretched satin. I screamed when I came and then Mark had fed my own orgasm back to me, running his fingers over my stomach and then making me lick them clean.

I turn back to him, and he's still looking out the window, afternoon sunlight catching on the gold of his eyelashes.

With dismay, I realize that I'm still his. I'm still cursed. The idea of leaving him is impossible.

But so is staying, so is watching him marry someone else.

"Yes," I finally admit. The word is edged with pain. "Yes. I'll be your bodyguard still."

Mark's shoulders relax, his mouth too, and I realize he was worried about my answer. Afraid to hear it. It sends a small curl of pleasure amongst the agony behind my sternum.

He doesn't want me to quit. It could be because I'm good at my job, or because he doesn't want to train someone else, or because he's hoping he can lure me into being his bodyguard-with-benefits again, but I don't care. He doesn't want me to leave, and oh god, I'm fucked up because that feels almost like love to me.

"Good," he says, and his voice is low and deep, and I think of him burning me with wax until I came. "I need you to do something for me."

"Whatever you require, sir," I say, hoping it sounds professional and not pathetic. Not like I'll still do anything for him because I'm in love with him, because I've made him into a graven image, my own personal god, and it doesn't matter how capricious or cruel he is, I'll still worship him.

He turns and settles so that he's half sitting, half standing against the edge of the table. He carefully moves his shoulder forward, testing how much it hurts. Given the way he pales, I assume it hurts quite a bit. "I need you to go to Ireland and bring Isolde home to me," he says.

I step back like he's just swung at me.

Like I've been shot at.

I stare at him, my eyes wide and my breath coming faster. "No."

"No?"

"I can't go get your bride for you. Don't ask me to do that." *Don't ask me to be complicit in my own heartbreak.*

Mark settles a little more on the edge of the table, wincing at whatever the change in posture does to his shoulder. "It would be an extremely pleasant errand, I assure you. I had planned on flying there, fetching her, and then sailing back on the *Philtre D'Amour*. Three weeks of the best meals and sunsets in the world, just the two of us and a handful of unobtrusive crew members. Unfortunately, Dr. Sutcliff has now extinguished my dreams of ocean-based courtship."

"I won't do it. Have her fly here instead. Or find someone else."

"I've gone to considerable trouble and expense to create this vacation, and Isolde deserves a respite before we're plunged into the politics and headaches of getting married. And the closer we get to the wedding, the more danger she could be in, especially considering Drobny and the events of last week."

"All the more reason I should be here with *you*," I say in frustration. "You need me here to keep you safe."

"I have the whole team here, and she has no one right now. There's no one I trust more than you." He looks down at his hands, and then he looks back up to me. "She is important to me. I don't know that I can state it any more clearly than that. She is quite possibly the most important thing in the world to me right now."

It hurts. I close my eyes and think of how much I would give to be the most important thing in the world to Mark, even after what I learned today, and it hurts. Even knowing he was blithely fucking me while someone else wore his ring.

I hear him come closer.

"I understand you wish you'd known about the engagement."

"Don't make me sound needy. It's a normal thing to know about someone you're having sex with," I say miserably. I don't open my eyes yet.

I can't—I can't look at him.

"Tristan." I feel his hand on my arm, and then my chest, and then around the back of my neck. I crumple, and my face goes into his throat, and he smells like blood and rubbing alcohol and the smallest hint of rain underneath it all. He's so warm and his collarbone against my jaw is strong and smooth.

"Tristan, I'm sorry. Can you forgive me? I'm not…I'm not accustomed to explaining myself, and especially to someone who's new to Lyonesse..." He sighs. It tickles warmly over my ear and jaw. "I'm sorry," he says again.

I can hardly explain that the reason I'm hurt has just as much to do with being in love with him as it does with my principles. I've managed to hide my infatuation with him, my wayward heart, this long, and thank God, because I think if he knew how much this was destroying me right now, I would die. And if he *pitied* me for it, then...

I don't know. I'd die and resurrect myself just so I could die even more horribly a second time.

"You're only apologizing because there's something you want," I mumble into his neck.

I feel Mark smile a little. "Well, obviously."

"I think it's cruel of you to ask me to bring her to you."

There. That's the closest I can allow myself to confessing the truth of the matter. That asking a lover to escort the bride to the groom is viciously unfair, salt in the wound. That every mile I sail closer to America with her will feel like another mile of barbed wire cinched around my chest.

But I know I'm about to cave. I can feel it. He's so close and my lips are resting against his pulse and his hand on my neck is firm and unyielding, and I can't help that I've already surrendered my soul to him. That I would do it again in a heartbeat.

He's just like that somehow.

"It can't be the cruelest thing I've asked of you," he murmurs. "Out of teeth and burning wax and binder clips, surely this doesn't even rank in the top three."

He's hard against my hip, I realize. Because I'm close or because he's remembering being cruel to me, I can't be sure. Either way, it makes me shiver.

"It's the worst and you know it."

"Hmm. You could use your safeword, you know."

I pull back and look at him. He looks back at me, his hand still cupping my neck.

"That's for kink," I say uncertainly.

"And kink is all the time for me," he responds. "Because you are mine all the time."

His words sink into my mind without so much as a splash, racing right down to the very bottom, right to the very seat of my soul.

"Don't say that," I whisper. "Not now."

I search his face, wondering—scolding myself for wondering—but could he...care for me? I'd assumed for him that our arrangement was physical, that I was nothing more than a pet. An affectionately treated pet maybe, but not beloved. Not someone to invest a future in.

You are mine all the time.

"Okay," he says. "I won't say it."

But his eyes blaze.

"I mean it," I say weakly. "I'm not...yours." I am. "We're not anything now." We are.

"You are in control, Tristan," Mark says. "Always. If you change your mind, then rest assured that mine remains unchanged. I want you. Being a groom doesn't change that."

"It should," I mutter.

Mark shrugs. "I'm an uncommon groom. And Isolde is an uncommon bride. This is Lyonesse after all."

I shake my head. I've only been at Lyonesse for a few months, and even I know that kink and polyamory only work with honesty and transparency. Whatever was happening between Mark and me was about something else. But I don't know what, and when I look at Mark, I can't find the answer in his eyes. Only something that looks like...regret, maybe. Pain.

Like he's about to lose me for real, and I have to close my eyes again.

"Okay," I say, wishing my stupid, weak heart were anything but what it were. "I'll go to Ireland for you."

CHAPTER 24

ONE DAY THEY'LL WRITE SONGS ABOUT HOW MUCH I DESPISE Isolde Laurence.

Which is impressive of me, given that I haven't even met her yet, but still. I detest her. She's marrying the man I love, most importantly, but also she comes from some kind of plutocratic banking empire, *and* she has a degree in art history, which is the most pretentious horseshit I've ever heard of.

I know my West Point education came with a literal sword, but still. Art history? What the fuck.

And now, as I'm driving a rented car along the low, green cliffs to get her and escort her to the yacht, I'm looking at my destination nestled above the sea, a manor house of white stone, wide and symmetrical, with tall windows and a circular drive. The lawns around it are a deep green and as neat as a blanket rolling down to the cliffs. On my flight here, I searched Cashel House online and found that there's been some kind of manor house on the site since the twelfth century. So that's Isolde Laurence, then—a pointless degree and a family seat that predates the invention of the chimney.

All of that and she has to take Mark away from me too.

I pull up in front of the house and take a deep breath as I park.

Stop.

This isn't like me—or it isn't how I used to be. The prom king who liked going to Mass just to see everyone, the sort-of-suburban, sort-of-farm kid who loved bottle-feeding the rejected lambs at dawn. I used to meet everyone with a smile on my face, with a hum in my throat. I didn't resent people solely because they were wealthy or had the attention of a certain kink club owner.

And now here I am hating a girl I've never met—jealous of her just like I've been jealous of Sedge for daring to know Mark better than me. Just like I've been jealous of a maybe-dead-man whose picture is in a bedside drawer an ocean away from Mark's apartment.

There is something *alive* about the hatred at least. A breathing inside the jealousy. When I first came to Lyonesse, I felt like a puppet of myself, a collection of traits without anything deeper to animate them: alertness, discipline, longing, regret. A shell of dried sinew and bone and no heart.

I *feel* now. Even if it's misery, obsession, jealousy, I feel them all, and no matter how awfully things have turned out, I can't doubt that Mark had something to do with that. That when we locked eyes in that library at Morois House that day, he poured some kind of life back into me, however primal and desperate.

I turn off the car and get out of it with a new determination to be…

Well, if I can't manage *kind*, then at least fair. At least polite.

Even if it's only for Mark's sake.

Resolved, I make my way to the front door, and I'm about to lift the heavy knocker—a dragon's head with a long, iron tongue hanging from its mouth—when the door swings open.

In the instant before I see her, I see that there's a man in a robe and skullcap standing behind her. I see that the interior is immaculately designed with parquet floors, jewel-toned walls, and a wide, curving staircase.

But all of that melts away, the whole world melts away.

There is only her.

There is only her and she is perfect.

She's wearing slim red pants and a white blouse unbuttoned to just below her collarbone, exposing a long, pale neck. Her hair is blond, almost pearl-colored, and it's pulled back into a low chignon, not a hair out of place. She's too young to be dressed with such contained sophistication, I think, but maybe that's the difference between rich people and regular people. Regular people dress in clothes to get them through the day. Rich people dress like someone's coming to photograph their house for a magazine at any moment.

It's her face that stops me, however, stops my thinking. My speech. When I'd searched her and her house online—a moment of weakness on the plane, brought on by too much champagne and also memories of the last time I'd flown with Mark—the pictures of her had been few and far between. Mostly on her father's arm at social events involving Laurence Bank, and one recent shot of her in her graduation gown and cap. But she'd been only half-visible in those images—a silhouette, a quarter-profile. I'd gleaned a narrow nose and delicate jaw and little else, enough to decide all over again that I despised her for being blond and pretty and wealthy and everything that, when added together, made Mark Trevena's bride.

But in person, she's—

It's not only that she's beautiful; I've seen beautiful people before. I've witnessed symmetrical features, statistically average distances between the eyes, nose, and mouth; I've beheld bright eyes and ruddy lips. Those are common and everywhere, but this, *Isolde Laurence*, seeing her, it's like—

It's like the first time I helped birth a calf and it blinked up at me with giant, black eyes while its mother licked it clean.

Like coming home from my first deployment to see the blown roses crawling up the side of the farmhouse, stupidly soft and oblivious to everything but the summer sun.

Like the Carpathian forest, snowy and frozen and still, sparkling under a pink sunrise. Breathless and beautiful when everything else was scarred with tire tracks and hand-dug graves.

That something like her exists when there's misery and cruelty and war…it's almost painful to see, a grace I'm not worthy of witnessing. The feet that nudged corpses to roll them over should not be the same feet which step closer to her; the hand that was pressed against Sims's slick and pulpy neck should not be the same hand still lifted to rap the knocker on her door.

And these eyes which just two weeks ago watched blood spill around the still-warm bodies of Mark's attackers…these eyes should not be looking at Isolde Laurence now. At her own eyes, dark green with a hint of blue, like the sea lapping at the cliffs below her house. They should not be looking at her ever-so-slightly crooked front tooth or at the freckles dusted faintly across her cheeks. Or at her full lips, with their sharp edges and unusually shallow cupid's bow, lips that look fixed in a permanent pout.

Although I can tell from the careful way she holds herself and the lift of her pointed chin that she probably thinks she's never pouted a day in her life. The thought almost makes me smile, and then like a clap of thunder, I remember where I am and why.

I'm not here to stare at Mark's future bride like she's my own personal revelation. I'm here to bring her home. To him.

"Hello," I manage to say to her and the man behind her, hoping I sound normal and not like the sight of a person I've never met before has my breath stuck in my chest. "Mr. Trevena sends his regrets that he can't travel with Ms. Laurence himself to Manhattan. He's asked me to escort her instead."

Her eyes flicker like she's trying to place me. "I'm sorry. I don't believe we've met," she says.

Oh shit. Right. "My apologies, I should have introduced myself right away." I extend my hand for her to shake, which she takes, and the shock of her warm skin against mine is enough to punch the air from my lungs once again. But despite those delicate, slender fingers, her handshake is as strong as a soldier's. There are calluses on her palms and fingers too.

Must be all that art history.

"I'm Mark's nephew-in-law and bodyguard," I say. "Tristan Thomas, at your service."

Her eyes dip down, her lashes resting on her cheek, long as a doll's, gold as the ring on her finger. How did Mark never mention her, never speak of her? If she were my fiancée, I'd talk about nothing else, think of nothing else.

I almost can't blame him for breaking my heart now, seeing her.

"It's lovely to meet you, Tristan," she says, and I absorb how enchanting her voice is. Not *quite* accented to my ears but almost, a faint crispness to her consonants, a small lift to her vowels. I saw that she went to school in Manhattan despite her father being English and her mother Irish, and so she doesn't sound English *or* Irish *or* American.

She just sounds rich.

"This is my uncle, His Eminence Mortimer Cashel," she adds, because of course there is someone else here with us, watching me with blue-green eyes that don't entirely match each other. I have the simmering worry that he can see the effect Isolde's having on me.

"Hello, Cardinal Cashel," I say with a nod, and then step back and gesture toward the car. "We should go soon, Ms. Laurence. I think our captain is hoping to get out of the harbor before dark."

"Yes," she says. Her throat moves over the open collar of her shirt. A swallow. I wonder if she's nervous about sailing.

Her uncle breaks into a smile, revealing a gap between his two front teeth. It's so cheerful and kind that *I* feel reassured and it's not even meant for me. He pulls Isolde into a fond hug. "I'll see you at your wedding, my child. Have a safe voyage."

I spy two suitcases just inside the hall, and I make myself useful by slipping past the familial goodbye and grabbing the luggage, walking them out to the car with the gravel crunching under my feet. I hear Isolde and her uncle murmuring together, and when I look back, he's making the sign of the cross in front of her. Blessing her for her journey, I think. I am sort of Catholic in the same way that I'm sort of good at singing—something I was born with and am happy enough to exercise if the situation calls for it—but Isolde seems to be really, *really* Catholic.

I think about her marrying Mark, about Lyonesse and the rumors of the priest he killed, and then give up trying to make it all make sense.

The only route to sanity with Mark Trevena sometimes.

Isolde comes over to the car, her shoulders straight enough to measure the horizon against, and I wonder if she's uneasy being around me. Something that would have sounded ludicrous to Before Tristan but that I've noticed happens sometimes with After Tristan. I forget to smile; I forget to relax my body.

Even if I feel safe, I've forgotten how to make other people feel safe too. A little ironic, given my job.

I make an effort to be Before Tristan now, smiling at her as I open her door and then smiling at her uncle, who returns the smile and gives us a small wave.

"I like your ring," she says, before I shut her door.

I look down at the black and silver ring on my pinkie finger. "Thank you," I say. "It was a gift."

I don't say that it was a gift from her future husband, pressed into my palm seconds before I left Lyonesse. Mark's eyes flashing as his strong hands brushed over mine.

Wear it if you want, he'd said. *Just know that I want you to.*

"What does it say?" asks Isolde now, making out the faint etch of words along the band.

"Quarto optio."

"Fourth option?" Isolde translates from the Latin, looking puzzled. "Why?"

"I have no idea," I say honestly. Just like I have no idea why I'm wearing it. Except that I've always liked when he's given me pain, and so seeing this ring on my finger the finger for clubs and guilds and alma maters and not the finger for marriage—bruises me deeper than any binder clip or ruler ever could.

I shut her door, and I get behind the wheel, pressing the button to start the car. And then we're rolling down the gravel drive to the road and then to the harbor.

Then to the sea.

CHAPTER 25

This yacht is ridiculous.

Isolde and I take the speedboat tender to the yacht itself and then board, and the porter shows us immediately to our rooms…which takes an obscene amount of time on the five-hundred-foot-long ship.

We're shown to adjoining suites with a shared door, which is when I realize I'll be sleeping where Mark would have been if he'd come, a mere door away from his betrothed.

There have got to be other empty suites on the boat, and I make a note to ask the porter if I can switch. I don't want Isolde to feel like I'm…I don't know. *Lurking.*

And then we're free to explore. Isolde tells us that she'll unpack and then see me at dinner, and I go to meet the captain and ask her about emergency protocols.

The captain gives me a tour of the ship herself, showing me every fire extinguisher and life jacket station as we pass, as well as the stairs to the tender garage and the fastest routes to the helipad.

"There are six of us on deck crew," she says when we

reach the bridge, "six on interior crew, three on galley crew, and one engineer."

"That's a large crew for just two guests," I say.

Captain Duval gives me a look. She has short, tight curls, light umber skin, and straight eyebrows that she still manages to arch whenever I make a comment that shows I have no idea how boats work.

"It's a sizable craft," she says dryly, and then adds, "and you haven't even seen the movie theater or spa yet."

And indeed, she takes me to all of these places. There're also two pools, a shaded one and one near the prow—that one has a waterfall—three hot tubs, a spacious dining room the size of a restaurant, a library, a small space with candles and kneelers that looks like a chapel, and then a room fitted with mats, kick bags, and a wall full of practice weapons.

Captain Duval shrugs. "Mr. Trevena had this fitted when he bought the ship four years ago. It's never been used that I know of. Same with the little chapel space. I've been sailing for him since he bought the *Philtre D'Amour*, and he's never gone near these rooms as far as I know."

I think of Isolde's uncle making the sign of the cross over her bowed head. "Maybe they're for Ms. Laurence," I say.

"The basketball court probably isn't though." The captain laughs and then leaves me to go back to the bridge.

I'm grinning like a kid when I find the court just two more doors down. It's only a half-court, and the ceiling isn't gym height or anything, but it has a regulation wood floor and a rack of orange-brown balls. I had no idea Mark liked basketball—maybe when I get back, I'll have to see if—

No. I have to stop thinking of him as anything other than my boss now. Even if the idea of us playing ball together—his front to my back as I try to move, his large hands on the ball, him gradually pinning me to the floor and tearing my shorts to my knees—makes my mouth wet.

He's just my boss. Just the person who pays my wages and gives me mysterious rings and who's getting married in two months.

And who am I kidding? Mark Trevena playing basketball? Really? Next I'll delude myself into believing he likes puppies or something.

Grow up, Tristan.

We set sail right before dinner, and as I reach the dining room, I notice that one glass wall has been rolled open so there's only a glass railing between us and the sea. Through the opening, I can see the harbor slowly disappearing behind us.

I want to make sure that Isolde is comfortable and settled here, but then I'll endeavor to leave her alone. Probably the last thing she wants is to be trapped on a boat for three weeks with a stranger.

And anyway, it's my job to blend into the background, to disappear. Not hover over well-dressed Columbia grads.

I wait by the dining room entrance until Isolde silently appears, wearing the same clothes as earlier. Several locks of hair have escaped her chignon to brush along her jaw.

"Tristan," she says when she sees me. "You didn't have to wait for me to eat."

"I wanted to make sure you were doing okay and that everything was to your liking," I say as we walk over to the table. I pull out a chair for her, but after she's seated, I don't take a seat myself. "If there's anything you need, anything at all, just let me know, and I'll make it happen. Or I'll call Mr. Trevena and he'll make it happen. Otherwise, I'll be out of your way and you can enjoy the boat uninterrupted by me."

There's a small press at one corner of her mouth, which after three months with Mark Trevena, I recognize as an aloof person's version of a smile. "Maybe I'd like to be interrupted. Sit, please. I'd rather not eat alone tonight."

I hesitate. "Are you sure? Mr. Trevena had hoped this would be a relaxing trip for you, and it's understandable if—"

She's shaking her head. Pearly hair grazes her jaw as she does, and I am mesmerized. "It hardly makes sense for us to eat apart," she says. "And anyway, I'd feel better getting to hear about Lyonesse from you before I get there."

I sit slowly. "Don't you already know about it?"

The server approaches and hands us the tasting menu for the night, which comes with wine pairings for each course. Normally, I'd refuse, but I decide there's no harm tonight. We're alone with Mark's long-term yacht crew, and the only danger is from storms or Kate Winslet–hating icebergs. It'd be permissible to lower my guard a little.

After the server leaves, Isolde adjusts in her chair. Every movement of hers is graceful, deliberate. It seems like more than good manners because there's an awareness to it that I'm not used to seeing from civilians, like she's conscious of the distance of the chair to the table, of the table to the door, of everything to the open sea just beyond the dining room. It's fascinating.

"I have been to Lyonesse a few times," she says, finally answering my question. "But the visits were brief, and—" A pause. "Specific."

I'm not proud of what flashes through my mind right then: Mark and Isolde, cuffs and wax and him inside her, her tight cunt stretched around him as he ruts into her without mercy…

"And I've never had a chance to see his office or his apartments," she's finishing. "It's just hard to imagine what it will be like to live there. Have a toothbrush there and eat breakfast there and wash my socks there. You know?"

"I live at Lyonesse, just a floor underneath Mr. Trevena,"

I volunteer, hoping it wasn't obvious what I was just thinking about. "I can tell you anything you'd like to know."

She blinks at me with those sea-colored eyes. Outside the dining room, the Irish coast passes by in ragged dunes of green and black. "I want to know everything," she says, her mouth curving apologetically. "Truly."

"And you haven't asked your fiancé?" I tease with a friendly smile back.

Before Tristan. That's who I'm being right now. Playful and kind.

The server comes with our first course, scallop crudo with pink peppercorns, and frisée lettuce, served with a white wine that tastes the same as all white wines. But it meets with Isolde's approval, I think, because she considers it after a small sip and then takes another.

"You know Mark," she says after she's set down her glass. "Casual conversation isn't really his thing."

No, I guess it isn't. But still. "This is hardly casual, Ms. Laurence. This is about where you'll live."

"Call me Isolde," she says. "Please. We'll be together way too much for you to 'Ms. Laurence' me at every turn."

"Okay, Isolde," I say. "What do you want to know?"

It turns out that she wasn't exaggerating when she said she wanted to know everything. What the food is like—delicious and creepy—and if it's loud on the weekends—the apartments are extremely well-insulated from sound—and if it feels like the staff are everywhere—yes but in a way that feels efficient and friendly, like being on base. She wants to know where I do my laundry and if I'm in the hall with Mark at night and how busy he is during the day.

"Very busy," I answer the last. We're onto a course of lamb, kohlrabi, and wild garlic now. The wine is red—and tastes red, about as far as my beer-drinking palate will take me—but it is beautiful in Isolde's hand, a deep ruby color curling in

253

the glass. "Although less busy since the stabbing, obviously. The doctor had to get pretty stern with him about resting and recovering, but I think Mr. Trevena's listening now."

She sets the glass down. She blinks. "I'm sorry, Mark was stabbed?"

"Well, yeah," I say, perplexed. "Why did you think I came in his place?"

She opens her mouth. Closes it. "I thought maybe he was busy. We haven't spoken in a while," she says. And then adds at my expression, "I was hired on at an art and antiquities firm right after graduation, and I've been scrambling a little with my new remote-work schedule."

It's delivered easily, not defensively, but it's still strange. Sure, they're both busy, but being stabbed seems like one of those events that transcends *busy*. And then—*oh God, I'm going to hell*—there's a flare of quick, selfish pleasure at knowing that *I* knew. I knew, and he's been blowing up my phone all day, demanding to know our locations, if we were safely on the yacht, if everything seems to be to her liking. Even if he's only talking to me about her, he's still talking to *me*. It's *my* phone lighting up in my pocket, and it was *my* hands that wiped the blood from his chest, and it was *my* mouth around his cock when he needed release and was still too injured to fuck.

And then as quickly as the pleasure came, it fades away. He's texting me about *her*, he sent me to get *her*. And the whole time I was anything to Mark, he was engaged to Isolde.

I'm suddenly miserable. With myself, with Mark, with how I still ache for him. I'm miserable looking at the elegant woman across from me, seven years younger and yet with a natural self-possession I'll never have. The woman who accepted a blessing from a cardinal like it was as normal as a pat on the back, who seems like she has no idea her fiancé was fucking the man sitting across the table from her.

"There was an attack on Lyonesse last week," I explain. "Mark was stabbed in the shoulder. A businessman with Carpathian rebel connections was responsible."

Isolde licks her lips and looks down. "I thought Lyonesse was secure."

"It was an open house—lots of guests. We thought we'd vetted them all but apparently not. And we're increasing all of our security, background checks, everything." Seeking to reassure her, I add, "You'll be safe there, I promise. I'll make sure of it. I'll take care of you."

She lifts her gaze to mine, and there's an openness to her expression, like I've surprised her. "That's nice of you to say," she says. "I don't—it's been a while since someone's offered that."

I'm surprised by her surprise. "It's my job," I state. "And Mark has told me that you're the most important thing in the world to him. Of course we'll keep you safe."

It stings to say out loud as much as it stung to hear, but I don't think Isolde notices. Her eyes have moved to the side, to the pinks and blues dimming over the dark and broken coast.

"And he's okay?" she asks in a murmur. "Truly okay?"

"Yes," I say, and her expression is too opaque now for me to parse, but I think she's relieved. Of course she is. Mark is her fiancé.

"I'm glad," she says softly, after a long moment. And then the conversation dies until we finish our meal, and she excuses herself to go to bed.

CHAPTER 26

I WAKE EARLY ENOUGH THE NEXT MORNING THAT I CAN SEE the sun lift itself, small and cadmium orange, over the water.

It's been almost a week of waking up without Mark's legs tangled in mine, his arms tight around my chest, and I'm still not used to it. To a bed being cold, to being able to move freely without his thighs wrapping around mine or without being hauled even tighter against his chest so he can bite my neck.

I've given up wondering why it feels better to wake up that way, weighted down and in immediate danger of being nipped at. Maybe years of body armor and war have ruined me for anything else.

I watch the break of day from the balcony of my suite, glancing occasionally at Isolde's neighboring balcony. The curtains are drawn shut over the door, but I see a splinter of light coming through. She's awake.

My mind is on Isolde when I step back inside—whether she's slept okay, what she wears to bed—and I'm trying to drag my thoughts back into *professionally interested bodyguard* territory when my phone rings.

It's Mark. It's still late at night where he is, and I'm surprised I don't hear the noise of the hall in the background when I answer.

"Sir," I greet as I close the balcony door behind me.

"Tristan," says Mark. His voice is rough and a little warmer than usual. Almost like he's pleased to hear my voice.

Which is wishful thinking on my part. Would he be pleased to fuck me? Tie me up and top me? Absolutely. But he doesn't miss me.

Still, I feel that warm tone of voice like a hand spread between my shoulder blades, firm and wonderful.

"I want to make sure everything is going well so far," he says. "The *Philtre* is good? Isolde is comfortable?"

"I only saw Isolde at dinner last night, but I presume she is," I say. I open the wardrobe where I'd unpacked my clothes and stare at the collection of suits I brought.

"I want you to make sure of it," says Mark. "She's very driven—to a fault—and I don't think she's accustomed to relaxing. She'll need your help."

I stare at the neat row of jackets in my wardrobe. "I don't know that I'm good at relaxing either, sir."

A noise, fond, low. Like a laugh. I don't hear anything around him, so I surmise that he's alone in his apartment.

Oh god, I hope he's alone.

"Then do it for my sake. For Isolde's. She won't enjoy the ship unless you make her, and you'll only be able to make her by enjoying it yourself. Just pretend to be me."

Yes, because you're so relaxed, Mr. Ripped My Own Stitches Disobeying My Doctor, I want to say. But I wisely stay silent.

"I mean it. Make her relax. That's an order."

"Yes, sir," I say, and then I almost ask him about—*no, no*, I shouldn't. It's not my business, no matter how much it feels like it.

257

Except Mark knows, somehow, that I was about to say something, because he says, "Yes, Tristan?"

"It's not my business, sir."

"If it involves Isolde, it's *my* business, which then makes it your business because you are my proxy. What is it?"

I hesitate and then forge ahead. "Just…last night at dinner, Isolde didn't know that you'd been stabbed, sir. Actually, she made it sound like you two haven't spoken in a while."

A pause. "Is there a question in there?"

I don't know.

I don't know what I want to ask, what I want to make sure of. And anyway, it's not my business.

"No, sir," I say finally.

"We're both very busy people. I didn't want to bother her with something I'm already handling."

"Yes, sir."

"And we're not in the habit of talking frequently," he says. "It's been about two years since I've seen her."

Two years?

I'm glad that he can't see my face because I'm sure I'm not disguising my shock right now. Even deployed soldiers see their sweethearts more often than that.

There's another pause, and then Mark asks—slowly, almost as if he's willing himself not to, "What's she like now?"

I think of clear, sea-colored eyes, a slender throat. An expression composed enough to rival Mark's at his most reserved. The feeling of the winter sunrise over the snow-covered forest, untouchable sweetness.

"She's lovely," I say. And then the inside of my skin tingles with a hot rush, realizing what that sounded like. "I mean, she seems like a lovely person. A little solitary, maybe, but we just met."

If Mark found my *lovely* comment strange, he doesn't

remark on it. "She's rather solitary by nature," he says. "Her mother died when she was young, and her father was more concerned with decorum than with affection."

"Oh," I say. It's almost involuntary when I add, "Like me."

"Like you. Which is why I think if anyone can coax her into letting her guard down, it's you. And if that fails, just pretend to be me."

Him, the bossiest person I know? "You are awful at coaxing people," I say, and that surprises a laugh of out him.

"Is that so? I seem to recall coaxing you into several interesting situations over the last month."

"I had to coax you first," I counter, and he laughs again, and there's a burning hook in my chest, just behind my heart. I don't think I can handle this, *us*, the teasing, the warmth, like there's nothing behind us but easy, happy sex.

"I should go," I say. "I know it's late where you are."

"Of course," he says. "And I mean it about relaxing. Isolde won't if you don't."

"Right. Just pretend to be you."

"Now you've got the idea. And, Tristan?"

"Sir?"

"I put you in your suite for a reason. I want you to be close in case Isolde needs anything."

I bite back a sigh. I had really wanted to see if I could change rooms today. It doesn't feel…healthy…to be so close to her.

"Yes, sir," I say reflexively.

"Also, I have clothes you can borrow in the dresser. You're on a yacht; you don't need to look like you're dressing for a job interview."

"You're the one who wanted me in suits. Sir." But I go over to the dresser in question and find shorts, linen pants, both short- and long-sleeved T-shirts. They look light and comfortable and tempting.

"Well, I changed my mind about the suits, at least while you're in the middle of nowhere. Since I can't enjoy you in them anyway."

It feels like flirting, but from him, it's just honesty. "Yes, sir," I say, and after I hang up, I dress in a pair of his shorts and a T-shirt.

They smell like him.

———

I find Captain Duval to check in, and I'm assured that everything is running like clockwork—or like *marine chronometer-work*, she adds with an eyebrow arch, letting me know this is a boat reference I won't get—and then with nothing else to do, and it still being early enough that I don't want to pester Isolde with my company, I decide to head to the basketball court and see how bad I've gotten.

I'm walking down the narrow hallway that leads to the gym, the basketball court, and the room with the racks full of wooden weapons when I catch movement. Instinct has me stopping just before I reach the doorway, using the wall-length mirror to see inside without revealing myself. It's an instinct I'm grateful for, because it allows me to stand there and watch the incredible sight within: Isolde Laurence, knife in hand, fighting an enemy only she can see.

Her hair is pulled back in a braid that looks like it started neat and has been trying valiantly ever since, and thin strands of hair cling to her damp neck and forehead as she spins, slices, stabs. She's wearing only a sports bra and bike shorts, and I can see that her rich-girl clothes from yesterday hid *muscles*.

Lean ones, yes, tight and subtle—but for-real, no-shit muscles that any soldier would be proud of.

They flex and lengthen as she moves, every part of her body working in concert to kick or pivot or block. Her feet make almost no sound on the mats, and even though I can see the strength behind each movement, she's not out of breath. There's an case to her, a practiced grace, that makes me think she's done this sequence of movements before, that it's not spontaneous. It doesn't take away from the beauty of it, or the skill—even when the yacht sways, she moves with it, as unbothered as a leaf on a branch in the wind. Her knife flashes in the morning light, and gold glints on either side of her fingers. Some kind of inlay into the hilt.

I catch winks and drops of red —rubies, I think. Her knife has rubies in the handle.

She finishes with one knee drawn up, her other arm extended behind her, and she could be the tiny ballerina inside of a music box, save for the look on her face, which is deeply, if beautifully, grim.

Well, that and the knife.

I wait until she puts her foot on the mat and makes a small bow at the air before I step inside.

I see the moment she senses me, her spine lengthening and her eyes finding mine in the mirror.

"So this room was all for you," I say with a smile. "The captain and I weren't sure."

"It was kind of Mark to have it here for me," she says. Her voice is neutral, her face too. It's not *distant* necessarily, her demeanor, but it's so self-possessed that it's close. "I wouldn't have thought to ask for a space like this on a yacht."

"The whole boat is nonsense," I agree. "There's a basketball court. And a *spa*. And that's a really cool knife."

I don't mean to say the last part, it just comes out, but now that I'm closer to it, I can see the intricacies of gold and ruby in the hilt, the wavy patterns in the steel blade, and it's like nothing I've ever seen.

"It was a gift from Mark, for my birthday," she says. She flips it easily in her hand, catching it by the blade with alarming confidence, and then holds it out to me.

261

I take it and trace my fingers over the pattern in the hilt.

"Honeysuckle," she says. "It's supposed to bring good luck to a marriage."

I look up at her and hand it back with a smile. It's so easy to smile at her, easier than it's been in years. I'm not sure why, since it's not like she's smiling much back. "And if it doesn't bring good luck, you can always stab him with it."

"A shame he seems remarkably resilient to stab wounds then," she says, and there's the tiniest flicker of her eyebrow.

My smile widens. Her dry riposte, her eyebrow—it feels like a victory somehow, like the rush of taking a hill in the forest or a contested bridge over a river. I'm ready to plant a flag here between us, right in front of her bare, delicate feet.

Her gaze drops to my mouth, and then her eyebrow lowers again. She turns away, walking over to where the knife's sheath rests on the mat near the mirror.

"You looked lethal as hell, doing all that earlier," I say, not wanting this moment to be over. "You could give Mr. Trevena lessons. He could have used them when Lyonesse was attacked."

She picks up the sheath and slides the weapon inside as she stands, every shift and gesture as graceful and deliberate as her movements earlier, when it was just her and the mirror and the knife. "Did you see the attack? When it happened?"

"Yes." I go to lean one shoulder against the mirror, my hands in the pockets of Mark's shorts. "I was too late. Mark was trying to fight the guy off, but he was—" I pause, loyalty to Mark stilling my tongue. "Well, he's been retired from the CIA for a while," I hedge instead.

Her lower lip catches briefly on her teeth, like she's trying to make sense of this. "I've only sparred him once, but he was incredibly good. *Unfairly* good," she says, and there's a tinge of irritation to her voice, like this still stings. "It was a long time ago, though. These things can change."

"I suppose." I glance out the window, where a light drizzle has started. "What are you going to do with your day? I'm under strict orders to help you relax, you know, so please don't say work."

"My firm is able to spare me for a bit," she says, "since I've just started there. So no work."

"Good. I've always said that everyone needs a break from art history once in a while."

She's doing that mouth corner thing again, the almost-smile. "You're not wrong," she admits. "I actually wanted to major in theology. Well, truthfully, I didn't want to major at all because I wanted to become a nun after high school. But my father was not so keen on the idea."

"A *nun*?" I'm fascinated. It's a quite a step from *nun* to affianced to Mark Trevena.

The almost-smile deepens "Yes, a nun. But my father convinced me otherwise. He wants me to take over Laurence Bank one day, and that would be difficult as someone who'd taken a vow of poverty. So…college. A double major in business finance and art history: finance for my father, and art history for me, because if I couldn't be a nun, I still wanted to have a part of what I love about my church—the history and the beauty. I'll get to spend every day looking at religious art and artifacts and making sure they're finding the right homes."

"And the bank?" I ask, desperate for her to keep talking. It's the most she's said at one time since I met her. "Doesn't your father want you to come work for him and not for… Catholic artifacts?"

She's drifted over to a window ledge now, unscrewing the top from a glass bottle of water. She takes a drink before she answers, and I look down at my feet on the mat. Cross my ankles, one foot propped on the toe of my shoe. Because watching her throat when she drinks feels like the uncleanest prurience right now.

"He does," she says once she's swallowed.

She screws the cap back on the bottle with a quick, practiced spin, and tucks it into the crook of her elbow so she can slide the sheathed knife into the waistband of her shorts. Like she wants her hands free as much as possible, which is a preference I share. Old habit from my combat days.

"He wants me working there yesterday," she continues. "But I've told him it needs to wait. I've already compromised enough by not going into the church. He doesn't get to take the rest of my life away too."

"But you wouldn't have joined the church anyway," I remark as I join her and walk out of the small dojo space. "Because you met Mr. Trevena and fell in love."

She pauses as we step into the hallway.

"Very true," she affirms after a beat, like I've made an interesting, if irrelevant, point. "But as it stands, I still don't want to be a banker. It's an ongoing argument."

I look at her, damp and flushed from her training, that strangely pretty knife shoved into her shorts. "No, I can't say I see you as a banker myself."

"What will you do with the rest of *your* day?" she asks. It's still in that polite voice, like she's dispensing with whatever social obligation I represent, but her eyes are on me and she's turned toward me too. I have her full attention, which feels good.

"If it stops raining, I might try the pool," I say. "It's heated, supposedly, so it should be quite nice. Otherwise, I'm going to check out the library."

"I really want to swim," she says with a glance through the doorway to the window. "But I didn't pack a swimsuit."

"Have you checked your room?" I ask. "This yacht is like the castle in *Beauty and the Beast*. It will provide anything you need—dojo, chapel, swimsuit."

"The yacht will provide. I like that." Another almost-smile. She's still looking at the window.

I decide that I've hovered long enough and make one of those *I should get going* sighs, even though I have nowhere to get going to. Lunch is served buffet-style for us and the crew, and dinner isn't for hours yet—and it's not like I have a date. But as much as Mark wants me to put her at ease, I don't want to smother her with attention. "I think I'm going to check out the basketball court and then maybe the gym, see if I can manage a treadmill on the waves."

"Let me know how it goes," she says. And then her eyelashes dip, once, and she looks at me. "Tristan?"

"Yes?"

"You weren't hurt during the attack or anything? You're okay?"

It's not something I expected her to ask—or anyone to ask. No one asks if a bodyguard is okay because the whole point of a bodyguard is that they're willing *not* to be okay for someone else.

"I'm okay," I reply, not sure what to make of this, if I like it or if I'm vocationally insulted by it. "I wasn't hurt. But it hardly matters, because Mr. Trevena was."

"It still matters. But I understand."

The yacht rolls gently under our feet. It's a big boat, but we're in the open ocean now, the dark coast of Ireland having disappeared behind us sometime in the night, and the rain has brought rougher seas with it.

"I didn't think I would have to kill anyone after I came back from Carpathia," I say, and I have no idea why I say it, because surely she doesn't care, and it doesn't matter. Those men are dead, and I would have done nothing differently anyway.

And I'm bad at talking about these kinds of things with civilians. How do you talk about killing people when it's part of a job? Like paperwork or replacing a tire—except it's paperwork that gives you nightmares, and a tire that you sometimes see in front of you when there's nothing actually there?

"You were protecting someone you care about." When she meets my gaze again, her eyes are clear. "And killing is a part of a life, as far back as Cain and Abel."

"Which is a story about how killing is bad."

"It's a story about how ancient Israelites thought pastoralism was morally superior to farming and city-building," she says.

Uh. "That doesn't seem like a very religious take on things," I point out. "Maybe this is the real reason you're not a nun."

She doesn't seem offended, although her shoulders move ever so slightly. A stifled sigh. "Maybe. But I know this: you kept people safe that night in the club, including my fiancé, and I have to think that was by design. Sometimes," she adds solemnly, "God needs us to do his work for him."

CHAPTER 27

ANOTHER DAWN, ANOTHER CALL FROM MARK. I STEP IN from the balcony, not wanting the sound to carry through the neighboring balcony doors to Isolde, who is certainly awake again. She's an early riser like me, although she doesn't seem interested in the sunrise. Her curtains stay shut even after her light comes on, and even though I watch them as much as I watch the sun, they never so much as twitch.

"You should be to the Azores in five days," Mark is saying. "After that the satellite connections aren't great, so we won't speak again until you get to Manhattan."

Manhattan. Where he and Isolde will see each other for the first time in two years. "Have you spoken to Isolde since we boarded? Sir?"

A pause. Tonight I hear some voices behind his, and a breeze. I think he's on the roof with some guests.

"I haven't," he replies.

"You should call her."

"Every day you're away from me, you grow bolder," he

says. But he sounds amused, not annoyed. "You let me worry about wooing my bride."

"Yes, sir," I say, although I don't think he's worrying about it enough.

As if he can read my mind, he says, "I'm already doing it, in fact. Right now. You're there in my place to woo her for me."

"That's the stupidest thing I've ever heard. Sir."

"Bolder and bolder," he says. Ice clinks. He's holding a drink. "But it's not stupid at all. Make her pliant. Make her smile. And by the time she arrives in Manhattan, she'll be ready for her fairy-tale wedding to me."

I frown. "I'm not good at things like that."

There's another pause, and I hear laughter, a playful shriek.

Mark's voice is like silk when he speaks again. "I think you underestimate your ability to disarm people, Tristan."

The heat crawls up from my chest to my cheeks. I can't think of what to say back to him, but it doesn't matter.

He says goodbye and hangs up anyway.

———

Breakfast on the yacht is served continental style: fresh pastries, yogurt, cut fruit. I treat myself to a lingering meal on the deck, the cool morning breeze toying with the light zip-up of Mark's I'm wearing, the crew milling behind me as they eat as well, and then I take the wide steps down to the second level to the dojo, to see if Isolde's there.

She is—this morning she's whaling on a freestanding bag, her hair once again escaping her braid to stick to her neck. It's the same combination that she's doing over and over again, punch *jab* kick, punch *jab* kick, the punches landing with heavy smacks, the kicks rocking the bag back on its stand.

The rain is gone today, but the skies are still gray and the water is still choppy, meaning the yacht is still bobbing and rolling with the water. And every time she kicks the bag and it rolls backward, it doesn't roll forward on its own and she has to grab it and resettle it back onto its base.

"Want some help?" I volunteer, walking inside. I kick off my shoes before I get on the mats, the smile spreading easily across my face when she looks at me. All she has to do is look at me and I smile, like her gaze is enough to lift weights from my shoulders.

I smiled at the sunrise in Carpathia too, at the sight of roses blooming along the side of the farmhouse.

Isolde pushes her braid off her shoulder, unsticks some hair from her neck. "I'm sure you have much more interesting things to do than hold a bag," she says politely, but I'm already to the item in question now, shifting it forward so I can stand behind it and hold it in place.

"It's either this or bother Captain Duval some more. I think I know which she'd prefer."

Isolde studies me a minute, like she's trying to sort out which would be better manners, to object or to relent. I don't give her a choice, leaning in to brace my shoulder against the bag.

"Come on," I say. "Let's see what those art history muscles are made of."

This earns me a determined little huff—something I file away for later, that this quiet, mannerly heiress has a competitive streak— and then she's back in position with her guards up. Punch *jab* kick, punch *jab* kick. Each strike solid enough for me to feel through the bag. She's *strong*.

"How long have you been doing this?" I ask. "Martial arts?"

Her rhythm doesn't break as she answers. Punch *jab* kick. "Karate since I was twelve. Jiujitsu and Krav Maga since I was eighteen." Punch *jab* kick.

"Why?" I ask, even though that's a stupid question to ask because obviously the answer will be *because I like it.*

But she doesn't act like it's a stupid question at all. She stops striking for a minute and stands up straight, dropping her guard. She looks frozen by it. Like I've just asked her to solve a Diophantine equation without a calculator.

"I think," she starts, and then stops. Tries again. "I was enrolled after my mother died. It was the only thing that made sense for a long time. Not school, and not home, because she wasn't at our home anymore. But I'd go to the dojo and there was this thing that was as easy as moving your body left or right, up or down. It carried me through those years."

Everything she's saying about martial arts is in the past tense. "Is that still why you do it now? Because it makes sense?"

She's looking at her hands when she answers. "No. No, that's not why anymore."

But she doesn't clarify, doesn't say anything else, and I don't press her.

Whatever's on her mind, I don't think she'd tell me anyway.

———

A faint guttural noise, like a wounded animal, ruptures the night.

I sit up in bed, having gone from fast asleep to heart-poundingly awake in an instant, already getting to my feet. I almost reach for the knife I've been keeping in my bedside table when I hear it again. Through the door connecting to Isolde's room.

I lunge for the door, and to my surprise, it opens easily at my touch—it's not locked from her side. Pushing that unnerving knowledge away, I'm already crossing the small sitting room to her bedroom, scanning for danger, my skin humming with awareness, my pulse kicking with adrenaline. I don't know how someone could have gotten on the boat this far out from the Azores, which means that whoever's hurting her is with the crew—

Except when I make it into her bedroom, she's alone. She's alone, in bed, her eyes shut and her hands flexing against the blanket. Her chest is rising and falling in short, rapid jerks. I hear the noise again, the miserable, helpless moan, and it all comes together.

A nightmare.

She's having a nightmare.

It doesn't occur to me to leave, to let her endure this on her own. I know all too well the torment crouching inside the shadows of night; I know how impossible it is to endure, to wake from. I stride over to her bed and crouch beside it, taking her hand.

"Isolde," I say softly. "Isolde, it's Tristan."

She snaps awake with a gasp that doesn't seem to work because her shoulders curl and her eyes are wide and panicked, and I also know this too well. Without thinking, I order her in the same hard voice Mark ordered me: "Breathe."

Her eyes slide to mine, and I see her try, try to drag the air in, but nothing's working right; she's too disoriented, too shot full of adrenaline.

"Breathe," I command again, this time splaying my hand over her chest. "Here. Breathe here."

Her skin is clammy under mine, but soft, so soft, and her eyes are shining in the dark as I feel her chest lift a fraction, and then all the way, shuddering into a noisy inhale and rushed exhale.

"That's right," I praise. "That's exactly right. Just feel my hand. Right there."

Another breath, still rushed and shaky, and I move my

hand over the blanket to her stomach as I move to sit on the edge of the bed.

"Can you breathe here for me?" I ask. "Can you lift my hand with your breath?"

She gives a small nod, and this time her breath goes deeper, all the way in. I see the minute her brain finally registers how to breathe on its own again, that her body accepts she's not in danger. Her lips part and her shoulders uncurl. Her eyes close.

"I'm sorry," she says, still sounding breathless. "I have... bad dreams. Sometimes."

I don't move my hand from her stomach, even though I'm suddenly very aware of every quiver and lift as she breathes. I'm a living seismograph for Isolde Laurence's inhales and exhales.

"I have bad dreams too," I say. My words are quiet in the dark. "Keep breathing."

She does, and the only sound in the room is her and the ocean outside. The occasional creak of the boat. My eyes are adjusted to the dark now, and I can see that she's wearing a thin white tank top—expensive looking but not delicate or indulgent—and I can see the furled tips of her breasts pressing against the fabric.

Heat rises in my groin, and I fight it back, lifting my hand from her belly and turning away.

"Better?" I ask, managing to sound normal.

"Better," she says. She hesitates, and then adds, "I'm sorry I woke you. This is embarrassing."

The admission is enough to make me turn and face her, even though a smarter man would have fled the room already. Her eyes are already on me, and her hair is liquid silver on her pillow. She could be a fairy tale princess if not for her mornings spent slicing imaginary people apart with a honeysuckle knife.

"Don't be embarrassed," I tell her firmly. "I once had to have Mark to do the exact same thing to me on an airplane."

I don't mention that he's also been able to drive away my nightmares by using me as a human body pillow.

And then I add, "Do you want to talk about them? The bad dreams?" I do wonder what nightmares could possibly haunt someone like Isolde Laurence. Her life seems easy and charmed, as graceful as she is.

Isolde shakes her head on the pillow. "I'd rather not," she says tightly, and I nod.

"I never want to talk about mine either."

She breathes out, her eyes flicking up to the ceiling. "I've had them for years. But every time is like the first time."

"Yes," I say quietly. "I know."

She looks at me. "I'm sorry that you know."

"You might have to come into my room one of these nights," I tell her with a small smile. "And help wake me up."

There's something like a smile back and then her eyes drop to my chest—which is bare. I'm wearing only loose pajama pants, and she's in just a tank top and then whatever's underneath the blankets, and we both realize at the same time how inappropriate it is, because her cheeks go dark and I scramble to my feet.

"Anyway," I say too casually. "I'm just through there if you need me. Or if I need you," I joke weakly, but it comes out sounding like it's not at all about nightmares and more about something else.

Something wrong.

"Okay, Tristan," she says softly, and I retreat back into my room like a general abandoning the field.

A general who knows he was about to lose if he stays.

CHAPTER 28

BY THE TIME ONE OF THE AZORES COME INTO VIEW ON THE horizon, green and mountain-peaked, Isolde and I have created a little ocean routine.

In the mornings, I go to the dojo with her and do whatever she needs—hold her bag, wave a rubber knife or rubber gun while she practices disarming me, do push-ups and squats with her and cheerfully win whatever unspoken calisthenics competition we're in...although not by much. Then we split off, and sometimes I treat myself to a massage and sometimes I go to the basketball court and sometimes I go to the library, which has the now-predictable shelves of Owen and Sassoon and Rosenberg...and murder mysteries about crime-solving cats and Edwardian Egyptologists and chemistry-set-owning sleuths in postwar England. It also has all of my favorite fantasy novels—ones I read as a kid and forgot about and ones I've reread a million times, and it even has new books that are simply perfect for me. I read about quests and dragons near the library's glassed-in fireplace, and sometimes I read up on the deck with the wind ruffling my hair, and sometimes I read at the prow, braced against the railing with sea spray flecking the pages.

And sometimes I just watch the waves, the swirl and the froth, and my mind drifts to Isolde, gleaming with sweat, a blade flashing in her hand.

My mind drifts to the man waiting for her in America and what it felt like to have his hands in my hair, on my throat, bruising my hips.

How he looked when he burned me with wax.

It's usually around this time that I have to go to my room and masturbate, the black and silver ring Mark gave me rubbing against my flesh as I do.

Isolde and I meet again for dinner, and we eat food that reflects the "terroir of our destinations" or something pretentious like that. I'm almost used to it, after months with Mark, but sometimes I'll be looking down at a plate of foie gras with mint gel or roasted pigeon with sweet red fruits scattered everywhere, and I'll remember that it was less than a year ago that I was eating DFAC food scooped out of a hot metal pan.

It was less than a year ago that Simo was stealing my Pop-Tarts.

And then usually whatever conversation Isolde and I are having goes quiet, me lost in memories and her lost to something too. After dinner, Isolde takes a drink and goes out to the prow alone, her back straight and her eyes on the sea. I don't join her because by that point in the day, I've started not to trust myself.

War memories, and missing Mark, and Isolde's mouth with its barely there dent on her upper lip, and the gorgeous, twisting thresh of the sea—it's all added up by then into something dangerous.

I lock myself in my room and stare out the balcony window until the ship is asleep, hardly knowing myself. And then I wait for the tortured whimpers, the soft noises of the sleeping damned, and I go into her room and wake her up. I press a hand to her chest and then to her belly until she can breathe, and we both ignore the points of her nipples poking through her top, and we both decline to talk about what we see in our dreams, and eventually I tear myself away and go back to my room.

We don't say much in these moonlit moments, but sometimes our eyes meet and they stay met for too long and it feels like we're speaking anyway. Together in whatever perdition that turns sleep into a haunted circus of memory.

And so it's like this that we reach the Azores, gliding into the unreal turquoise and teal arms of São Miguel.

We're only here for a day, to provision and refuel ourselves for the rest of the way across the Atlantic, but time seems indifferent here. Mist hangs in the air, rainbows shimmer over volcanoes, and the occasional spit of rain haphazardly dances along the decks while the sun beams from the other direction.

We refuel closer to shore and then move back out into the harbor, the interior crew and captain taking the tender to the marina to handle provisioning and paperwork. I grab a beer—a Żywiec, *the yacht will provide* indeed—and stroll out to the main deck, intending to enjoy the view.

And stop short, because I'm greeted by an entirely different view than green island slopes and clear water.

There had been a swimsuit in her room after all, because Isolde is swimming in the pool.

It's shockingly modest: a white one-piece with long sleeves, more rash guard than swimsuit. But then again, Mark knows her, and anyone who's spent any time with Isolde can tell that she's not the type for micro-bikinis or mesh.

No, she'd want something that deflects attention, that draws no notice…so it's a shame for her then that this suit does the absolute opposite.

The contrast of the fabric and her now lightly suntanned skin is the contrast between white and pale gold: white-clad arms and slender, gold hands, white-clad hips and taut gold legs. And the cut of the swimsuit over the contours of her rump—deceptively indecent. Because it's not cut high, not tailored like a thong, nothing so obvious as that. But on *her*, on that toned, luscious part of her, it's more obscene than wearing nothing.

Her body carves through the water with ease—strength and timing both—and even though she's not tall, her legs look long and powerful as she kicks through the water. Her hair streams behind her, and then when she kicks off from the wall, turning underwater, it billows into a silky cloud, like some kind of mermaid's.

All this I see before good manners and loyalty to Mark—and basic fucking morality—slam into me like a wave breaking on a steep shore.

I'm staring. I'm staring and that's wrong and I'm going to go drink my beer somewhere else.

Except that's the moment she sees me. The moment I'm turning away is the moment she stands up and gives a wave, gesturing for me to wait as she climbs out of the pool.

And oh my God, what the fuck, Mark is going to hell, the hell reserved for evil fiancés, because that swimsuit is the furthest thing from modest, the furthest thing from demure.

When she is out of the water, it is absolutely fucking see-through. A thin glaze of white over a toned stomach with an oval navel, over high breasts with roseate nipples. Over a darker delta between her legs.

And she has absolutely no idea. Her bearing is the same as always, upright and deliberate, and she's not making any move to cover herself, and she's walking toward me with a larger almost-smile than usual. The swimming has put her in a good mood—or maybe it's the

Azores, the shimmering mist and lush mountains—or maybe it's that we only have two weeks left until she's home and with Mark.

"The yacht did provide, you were right," she says, and reaches up to twist her hair into a platinum rope, squeezing out more water. It drips onto her breast, wetting the fabric even more. I don't look, I don't look, *I can't look*, but I don't need to. Even in my peripheral vision, her nipples through the swimsuit are conspicuous, unmistakable. I could precisely recreate the diameter of her areolae, the amount of time it takes for the tips of her breasts to grow stiff in the air outside the heated pool. I could draw the exact geometry of her navel, the triangle between her legs. Just from that one instant.

Her, in this swimsuit, is now forever etched into my mind.

Fuck. Me.

And I can't move from where I'm standing, which is behind a half wall that separates the pool deck from the shaded bar and the glass doors leading to the dining room.

I mentally curse Mark for only having linen pants and shorts in his room for me to wear—the kind of soft, loose clothing that makes no secret of my weakness.

"We should eat lunch together. I've thought of some more questions about Lyonesse," Isolde says, and Mark would be so happy right now that she's thawing, that she's seeking out company—but I'm not happy, not happy at all, because she's coming closer, and it's only the giant bottle of Żywiec in my hand that blocks my groin from view as she passes to go to the stairs. She turns back after she's on the first tread. "Would that be okay? I'll go change real fast and then I'll be ready to eat."

"Yes," I say. Rasp. "That would be okay."

278

Thank God she's going to change. I hope she doesn't get to her room and realize what the suit reveals and then feel embarrassed; I also hope she sees immediately what's happened and never ever wears this suit again.

I wait for her to get most of the way up the stairs before I move to follow—the stairs lead up to the shaded deck where lunch is set out, and it's a mistake, it's a *fucking mistake*, because just as I'm commending myself for having escaped the moment unscathed, I look up to see her run a finger along the inside of her swimsuit bottoms to adjust them. A natural gesture, an unconscious one, to straighten the bunched fabric between her cheeks. And in any other situation, it would have been a *modest* instinct, to make sure her bottoms were covering every possible part of her.

But this is not any other situation. And she's at the top of the stairs and I'm at the bottom, and she has one foot on the topmost step and her thighs are parted, and when she tugs the swimsuit back into place, it pulls aways from her skin for the briefest moment. And I see pink.

Pink.

Wet and tight and disappearing into shadow and then covered once more.

I freeze, and she's already gone, and my blood is rushing hot into my belly, and my mind is whispering profanity, utter fucking profanity. And my chest feels like someone's kicked it in, because I just saw my boss's fiancée's cunt— off-limits *rich girl who likes knives* cunt—and I'm so fucking done for.

Because I want it. I want it so badly that I might have to lash myself to the fucking mast of this boat, might have to pitch myself overboard.

I want to look at it; I want to feel the inside of all that pink. I want to taste it.

Fuck, I want to taste it.

I want to slide my way inside and pump myself empty.

And I have to go have lunch and answer questions about Lyonesse's washing machines or whatever and pretend that everything is normal and that I'm not trying to strangle my own thoughts.

I have to pretend that after months of seeing people screw onstage, of seeing sex and torment in every shape possible, a flash of pink isn't enough to unravel all my fucking control.

CHAPTER 29

THE NEXT MORNING, I SPEAK WITH MARK FOR WHAT WILL BE the last time until we get to Manhattan. I reassure him of the usual things, that Isolde is content and enjoying the yacht, and I try to keep my voice steady, like someone who's slept a deep, untroubled night's sleep, and not like someone who didn't sleep at all. Not like someone who jerked themself raw thinking of the pink between Isolde's thighs while the bed smelled like damp stone and rain, and then had to go into her room and wake her from a nightmare and act like everything was normal and platonic and fine.

But Mark hears something in my voice because of course he does.

"Is everything okay, Tristan?" he asks. "You sound strained."

"Everything is fine," I lie. "Just a little groggy still."

It's a bad lie, such a bad lie, because I'm never groggy in the morning, but he makes a little hum of acknowledgment.

"That's good. Take care of Isolde for me. Give her everything she needs."

"You should call her, sir. Before the signal's bad."

I say this every morning. And every morning he says the same thing.

"Why would I do that when I have you there to be me in my place?"

I am either lucky or outright damned that he has no idea how much I want to be in his place right now. Almost as much as I want to be in her place.

Jesus Christ, I'm a lost cause.

"One last thing," he says. "Someone came to Lyonesse looking for you today."

I'm at a loss. "Looking for *me*?"

"Seems they asked your father for your current address. Wanted to speak in person, not over the phone or over email. A sister of the soldier you killed in Carpathia."

"Oh," I say. Faintly. Dizzily.

"Reception didn't write down her name, only his," Mark goes on. I already know the name he's going to say before he says it, but it still feels like a hammer to the face when he does.

Aaron Sims.

———

Dinner is a delicate affair of things like crustacean foam and olive oil powder, and when we finish dessert—light, cloud-like farófias with tangerines—I finally accept that I've barely tasted any of it.

My mind is on Sims, just as it has been since Mark's call this morning, my memories sawing against each other in the same jagged grooves for hours and hours.

His death, and the usual memories of his blood, hot and wet against my fingers.

His burial.

I didn't mean to go to the service—it wasn't right for me to go—and yet I'd found myself outside that Pennsylvania cemetery anyway, white-knuckling a bottle of bourbon I planned to leave at his grave once everyone had cleared off.

And *everyone* had been a small group. There was no uniformed detail for Aaron Sims, Traitor, after all. No flag, no taps. Just a handful of family and friends staring down at the rectangular hole in the dirt that I had no small part in making.

Had both his sisters been there? Chloe had been there, but had Cara been?

No, Cara wouldn't have gone. No one had heard from Cara in years; last Sims had known, she'd gotten herself tangled up with some Mob-adjacent boyfriend and skipped town. It had made him sick with worry. No, it must have only been Chloe.

Sims had wanted me to date Chloe when we were at West Point. He was the kind of person who wanted everyone in his life connected, and he was especially determined to see his sisters married to his friends. Whether he thought that would make his sisters safer or make it so his friends couldn't drift away from him, I never figured out. Either way, I hadn't dated Chloe, had only met her a few times. Last I heard, she was a kindergarten teacher in Erie.

Imagining quiet, unassuming Chloe standing at the glass gates of Lyonesse is impossible. God, what she must think of me, working at a kink club…

And then I want to stab myself in the eyeball with my farófias spoon because of course she doesn't give a shit where I work now. She's got bigger things on her mind when it comes to me. Like that I killed her brother.

What could she want?

She'd be right to scream at me, hit me, cut me into pieces and drive those pieces to the National Aquarium in Baltimore to feed the aquarium sharks. If this were biblical times, she'd consider herself within her rights to kill me. *I'd* consider her within her rights.

I'm very close as it is, because even though Mark was

right when he told me I'd done the necessary thing, it still doesn't make it the *moral* thing. It doesn't erase the hole in the world that used to be filled by Aaron Sims.

I scrape my hands over my face, shame and foreboding filling me, a heavier dinner than actual food could ever be, and look up to see that Isolde's no longer at the table but at the prow one deck below.

She's wearing a white jumpsuit tonight, rolled up at the sleeves, cuffed above her ankles, fitted so well to her body that I can see the slope of her waist and the wings of her shoulder blades. Dressy sandals have been abandoned in favor of bare feet; the relentless breeze is tugging her hair from its habitual braid, but she doesn't reach up to brush it away from her face.

There's this way she stands when she thinks no one is watching her, so different from her usual erect posture. Shoulders pulled in, head bowed. Like something injured trying to protect itself.

A shell of glass.

Goran had said it about me, but I see it in her, around her. Snow White in a glass coffin, a priceless jewel in a vitrine.

A heart behind walls.

Her awareness, though, that's still there. Like me, like Mark, there is no sneaking up on her. By the time I make it to the railing next to her, her shoulders have straightened and her head has lifted and she's back to looking like a ballerina waiting in the wings.

A soft mist sprays up from the sea. I can taste it when I breathe.

"Do you regret killing them?" Isolde asks after several minutes of us standing there together, and I know it's not the subtle pitching of the deck that has me off-balance.

How could she know I was thinking of war, of death, of Sims—

"The people who attacked Lyonesse, I mean," she clarifies when I don't answer right away. "The ones trying to kill Mark."

"Oh," I say, thrown for a moment. "No. At least I don't think so. Wait, are you withdrawing your reassuring words about Cain and Abel from the other day?"

I know I manage some kind of smile, but she isn't looking at me to see it. She wraps her hands around the railing and stares at the water.

"No," she says. "Not withdrawing. Just…it's been on my mind. Killing."

Oh no. "Isolde, Lyonesse is safer more than ever, and if you're worried about—"

She shakes her head. "That's not what I mean." It takes her a minute to speak again, and when she does, her voice is low. "I was thinking about killing in general. When is it good. When is it bad. What it means if there's not a clear answer either way."

"What brought this on?" I ask.

"Oh, you know," she says with a sound that could be a laugh if it weren't so strangled. "Art history."

I study her out of the corner of my eye, not sure what to make of this Isolde, this mood she's in. Her fingers are gripped tight around the railing, and her face is tilted up to the sky. To the waxing moon with its full belly.

"I killed my best friend in Carpathia eight months ago," I say, and then wish I could scrape the words back into my throat. I don't want her to know this about me; I don't want her to guess my nightmares. I want her to think that I'm good and noble and—*yes*—heroic. I want her to look at me with trust in her eyes. I want her to be one person that I can start fresh with, without my past rotting around my neck like an albatross.

She doesn't react to my statement, but it's a near thing, I think, because it takes her a moment to respond.

"Why?" Her voice is low still, but uninflected. She could be asking me why I chose the shirt I wore today.

I blow out a breath. "He tried to kill the people we were protecting on a diplomatic escort. Two of them were kids."

Her chin lifts the tiniest bit, but she doesn't do what most other people do when they find out. She doesn't swear. She doesn't say *Jesus Christ* or *what the fuck?*

She just says, "That's evil." Like a statement of fact.

And it's so reassuring to hear, because *yes*, it was fucking evil. Even if Sims wasn't. Even if he looked desperate and strange and afraid of himself. He might not have been evil, but he was about to do an evil thing.

"And you never found out why?" Isolde asks. "Why he was going to kill them?"

I put my own hands on the railing. It's wet and solid under my palms. "The official report said he'd been bribed into it by rebels. Paid off. There'd been a transfer into his bank account the day before from somewhere untraceable."

"Does that sound like him?"

"No." The answer is immediate. Of all of us, Sims was the most zealous about Being a Solider. It was his whole identity. As was taking care of his mom and sisters, but being a soldier was how he did it, and he was so fucking proud of that. So fucking proud of being in the army, being patriotic, never harboring doubts about our mission. If the army had told him to fight a group of Girl Scouts, he would have done it without question and then left their corpses smoking in a pile of smashed Thin Mints and loose merit badges.

There's no way he would have done anything for the rebels, no matter how much money they offered. He was too loyal.

"He must have had a reason," muses Isolde.

I tell her the same thing I've told myself every day for eight months. "It doesn't matter. His reason wouldn't change anything."

"But don't you want to know?"

"Of course I want to know," I reply, my hands lifting from the railing briefly to emphasize the word *want*. "But how *can* I know? And even if I do know, his death is far from the only blood on my hands. There were more that I killed over there. Many more."

"Enemies," Isolde says.

"Yes, but—" I look up at the moon. "People. People with favorite colors and songs they hated and aunts they couldn't stand. And sometimes I'd be glad to kill them, you know? Like you're shooting from some village street and they're trying to pin you down, trying to kill you first, lobbing shit at you, trying to smoke you out or flash-bang you, and I'd feel this…like, *fuck you, motherfucker, you can't kill me* feeling, and I'd be so hopped up on adrenaline, and I'd finally kill them. And there'd be this surge of…triumph. I'd be sick with how good it felt."

Her voice is quiet when she speaks. "Like being drunk."

She doesn't know how right she is. "Exactly like that. But then…later—much later— my blood would cool, and I'd start wondering why they were there at all. Who they were. Why this was the fight they picked to fight. And I'd still be sick with it, but in a different way. Like there was mold growing inside me and only I could see it."

The ocean is a bit rougher now—lines of wave-foam and chunks of light. Like someone tore up the moon and scattered the pieces over the water.

"And then, other times," I say, my voice barely louder than the water, "I'd feel sick from the very beginning. Like I could taste the mold in my mouth from the minute I lifted my gun to start shooting back. And the only way to get rid of that feeling was not to think about it. Was to pretend it was normal. And I think that must be what people mean when they talk about heroes. Heroes are the ones who can pretend the shame away, at least long enough to fool everyone else."

This can't be what Mark meant when he said to court Isolde, to give her everything she needs. Dumping war trauma on her seems like the exact opposite of courting.

And yet, she's listening intently. She seems to understand.

"Maybe that's what's heroic about it," she says and looks at me. "You did it knowing that you'd have to give something up. That it would feel like a corrosion, like bits of you were being clipped off every time you drew breath and remembered."

I look back at her. I don't have to see my own face to know that my smile is sad. "Mr. Trevena would say that there are no heroes."

"Mark is wrong," she says, suddenly fervent. "He has to be."

"You'll get to tell him yourself in two weeks," I say.

A low breath, gusted out quick. She looks away. "Right."

I wonder if she's thinking of the wedding, of going home to Manhattan.

But then she surprises me again, asking not at all what I was expecting. "You said you were Mark's nephew-in-law," she says. "How are you related?"

"Mr. Trevena's older sister, Blanche, married my father."

Her hands twitch once on the railing, like she's pushing herself to say something, so I add, "My mother died when I was in high school," so she doesn't have to be the one to ask.

"I'm so sorry," she murmurs. She looks at me again. "It was awful when my mother died."

"I'm sorry too."

Isolde's eyes go back to the water, back to the torn-up pieces of moon. "Do you still miss your mother?"

"Sometimes," I say. "Do you?"

"Yes. She was—" A breath tears out of Isolde's throat. It could almost be a laugh. "She was good. Not everyone in my family is. But she was."

"My mother was good too. But that's why, sometimes, I don't miss her. Because—"

I can't finish. I can't find the words.

But Isolde finishes for me. "Because if she were alive, she'd see you now." Her eyes are on the water. Sea spray has dampened her face—it's caught in her eyelashes and is gleaming along her cheekbones. And at the fullest curve of her lower lip, it's gathered into a single drop. When she speaks again, the drop falls. "She'd know the person you've become. And you can't be sure if that would be a good thing or not."

I am suspended in the air like the spray, weightless and flashing in the night.

No one, *no one*, has ever guessed this about me. And the shock of it, the relief of it, is annihilating. Someone knows. Someone can *see*.

Someone understands that sometimes I'd rather my mother still be dead than be alive to see what I've done.

And then I wonder how Isolde could have guessed that, that horribly specific kind of grief that makes grief itself a lie. "How did you know?" I whisper.

She turns to face me, and water is beading on her lower lip again. I have the absurd fantasy of leaning forward and licking it off.

"I know," she says, "because I feel the same way."

I want to know why. I want to know if it has anything to do with why she can't sleep without nightmares, why she needs someone else to help her breathe in her own bed. But I don't get a chance to ask. Before I can even part my lips, she's pushing away from the railing and disappearing into the glowing belly of the ship.

CHAPTER 30

THERE IS NO PHONE CALL FROM MARK THIS MORNING. I expected it, but it still feels strange to start the day without hearing his cool voice. Unsettling, and it's like the world knows and the world agrees because the rough weather has continued and the yacht is pitching under my feet as I stand at my balcony door.

But there is something beyond missing Mark's voice, and as I watch the drizzle-washed sea outside, I return to memories of last night. Of Isolde at the prow of the ship, salt water glistening on her mouth.

I feel the same way.

It is nice to be seen. Understood. Especially about as ugly a thing as killing. As being glad your dead mother can't see what you've become as an adult.

I still don't know why *Isolde* feels that way though. Maybe it is the nun thing. Maybe her mother wanted her to join the church more than anything and would have been horrified at her marrying Mark.

Curiosity burns bright in my mind as I finish getting

ready for the day and eat a quick, efficient breakfast while rain patters on the deck. I'd like to ask Isolde about it directly, but something makes me think that it wouldn't work, that the inner workings of her are like a masterfully cut gem, and the facets of her will only flash in precisely the right light, and only then with a patient hand.

I wonder if Mark was drawn to her because he saw a puzzle, something only cleverness and perseverance could work open. A challenge. Not like me, who was begging to be fucked into the carpet at the first opportunity.

I'm jealous of Isolde in a brand-new way as I walk down to the dojo after I eat. Of course, I'm still miserable that she gets to marry Mark, share his life and his attention and his bed, but now I'm also jealous of *who* she is. *How* she is. Elegant and crisp. Contained and mysterious. I want to be those things so badly, instead of the tortured, needy mess that I am.

No wonder I'm no one's fiancé.

Isolde is already in the dojo when I get there, holding a rubber knife by the blade. She extends it hilt-first to me. "Want to spar today?"

I don't take it. Instead, I eye her, slender and short. She barely comes up to my shoulder, and for all those tight muscles of hers, there's no doubt in my mind that I have almost a hundred pounds on her.

Plus—okay, Mark would scoff at this—but sparring a woman feels wrong. There were no women in my BCT group, and I've never mock-fought a woman before. The only women I've fought were Carpathian rebels, and we were actually trying to kill each other.

Isolde correctly interprets my hesitation. "I'll be fine, Tristan," she says with an almost-smile. "I promise."

"Isolde…"

"You'll pull your strikes, right?"

"Well, yeah, but—"

"Then I'll be fine," she insists. For her part, she looks like she means it. She also looks like she thinks I'm being very parochial right now.

I rake a hand through my hair, trying to make her understand why it's a bad idea. "Mr. Trevena will kill me if I hurt you."

"How is he going to kill you? I thought you said he was no good at fighting." Then she pauses, tilts her head the tiniest amount. Her braid moves over her shoulder as she does. "Do you call him Mr. Trevena in your head too?"

"In my thoughts, he's Mark," I admit. And then feeling like that exposes too much, I revert back to our original subject. "I don't have a cup on."

Isolde's eyebrow lifts. "I'll be mindful of future Thomas generations."

That was almost like a joke. I feel like I've pried a pearl from an oyster, or a gem from a hunk of cold rock. And then I reach for the knife. I have no resistance to her when she's playful and entreating.

Her lips press, like she's trying to hide a real smile now, and then she goes to find another rubber knife.

"Why knives?" I ask. "Why not spar empty-handed?"

"I like knives," she says simply as she returns. Leave it to Mark to marry a little thing who says *I like knives* the same way most people say *I like ice cream.* "Don't you?"

"I guess I haven't really thought about it."

"More of a gun guy?"

"More of a whatever gets the job done guy," I state, and she gives me a long look, like she's trying to figure out whether or not I'm lying. I'm really not—the job is the job, and whether the job requires guns, fists, or the seven-inch bayonet the army gave me makes no difference.

She bows to me and I mimic her, and then we both shift

into a fighting stance. Hers is almost balletic—light and agile, her free hand up in a gesture that reminds me of the way her uncle blessed her before she left Cashel House.

I feel like an oaf in comparison, more used to fighting in boots and body armor than sidling barefoot on cushioned mats, my tread heavy and obvious as we start to circle each other. But even so, my shadow stretches over her, and each of my steps is like two of hers. It would be nothing for me to take her down, so I remind myself to be slow, be careful, and—

Like a sprung snare, she's snapped forward and struck me, rubber poking hard into my stomach.

I blink at her. What the fuck?

She's already resettling in her stance. Her pulse isn't beating any harder in her neck. "I told you I'd be okay," she says, tossing the knife into reverse grip and lifting her guard again. "I'm not made of sugar."

Well. Fine, then.

This time, I watch her differently. I watch her shoulders, her hips, the sources of her striking power. I see her guard dip ever so slightly and then lunge in—only to have the rubber edge of her knife drag across my throat.

A trick.

Shit.

We step back, and this time, it's fucking on. I stop seeing her as a refined little doll and start seeing her as a real opponent. "I thought all this shit was about fitness," I say as we circle each other. "But you're really scary, you know that?"

That pleases her, I think.

"I'm sure you're a better shot than I am," she says, like she's trying to soothe my ego.

"I don't mind you being better than me," I tell her with a grin. "I promise."

"Do you think I'm better than Mark?" she asks.

I remember him that night in the club. Even subtracting the effects of the gin, I still think Isolde would smoke him. And I don't think he'd mind either. "You'd win for sure."

This pleases her too.

We begin again, and I'm dying, dying, dying, countless fake rubber deaths. Fighting Isolde is like fighting smoke, ephemeral and curling. Indifferent and impervious to strength.

Because I *am* stronger. I feel it every time we make contact; I feel my solidity, my size. But she's faster—and cleverer. No matter how spontaneous my strikes, no matter how instinctual, she's always three moves ahead. I'll still be following through with a stab that I'm *sure* is going to make contact this time, and then I'll feel the gentle tap of a restrained kick to my head. A heel hook to my kidney. Her small fist popping into my ribs.

And goddamn if it doesn't have me slowly stiffening in the compression shorts I stole from Mark's drawer. Her nearness, her fearlessness. The full mouth set in a look of deadly concentration.

And her scent—sweet, sweet, earthy. Like honey glazed over a fingertip to be licked off.

So it's luck when I finally take her down to the mats. Pure fucking luck.

We hit a wave right as she's kicking me, and I'm making to tackle her, something she's danced away from a hundred times this morning, but we both lose our balance as the yacht pitches hard to port and the world slants sideways. Down we go.

We land with me on top, and it's a soldier's instinct that has me grabbing her wrists while she's stunned into pliancy, securing her weapons, so to speak. Except the effect is that the ship rights itself, and I'm sitting on top of her and pinning her wrists to the mat.

And then I'm suddenly, horribly aware of every single detail of Isolde Laurence.

Her sweat-slick throat and collarbone. The slightly crooked upper tooth.

Her breasts, heaving under her sports bra.

I remember again that I'm not wearing a cup. I need to get off her before she notices her resident bodyguard has an erection from being fake stabbed over and over again.

She's trying to catch her breath—the fall knocked the wind out of her. I realize I'm squeezing her wrists too hard and ease up, preparing to climb off her and apologize, but then she shifts, quicker than I would have thought possible before this morning. She plants her feet and bucks her hips, and suddenly I'm the one on the bottom with my wrists pinned.

She's straddling me, and I'm not wearing a cup.

I'm not wearing a cup, and she's sitting on me with her thin bike shorts, and I can feel the heat of her cunt through our clothes. That pretty pink cunt that I saw for myself on the stairs, that's been haunting my thoughts ever since, and it's on me now. Against me. Three thin layers of fabric away.

Fuck *fuck*—

"You win," I say desperately, before she can recognize that the bulge she's sitting on is a cock. A swollen one that's currently begging to be touched. "Let me up."

She doesn't move. She's staring down at me with a dazed expression. The fall must have been harder than I thought.

"Isolde," I say, my voice tight. "Honey, you need to move."

The endearment slips out without me meaning for it to, but I'm too panicked to care. There's a lot worse than an endearment currently wedged between us, and I'm just a bodyguard, and she's engaged, and I'm in love with her fiancé. I'm in love with her fiancé, and I'm hard underneath her.

I try to move from underneath her—it's not a matter of strength but of finding a way that doesn't make it very, very clear that I'm painfully turned on—but the minute I try to shift, to nudge her off, I end up driving my arousal harder against her core and she lets out a low, shuddering gasp.

We both freeze.

Her eyes meet mine, blue green and nearly black with pupil. "Tristan," she whispers.

"I'm sorry," I breathe. "I'm so sorry, I didn't mean—"

She moves her hips over me, once. Hard. On purpose.

And pleasure skates right down my shaft to my balls, and it's my turn to suck in an agonized breath, and I stare up at her, my thoughts driven away by the pressure of her sex sitting directly on me. I can feel the shape of her through her bike shorts.

Fuck it now, some silky instinct coaxes. *Expose her cunt and push into it and fuck.*

The ship does the next part for us, rolling over a wave, the gravity pressing us together again, and she shivers, goose bumps creeping everywhere on her skin.

She's looking down at me with an expression I haven't seen before, beyond dazed, beyond stunned. It's *naked*, almost—vulnerable. Lids hooded, eyebrows up, like they're frozen in a question. Mouth parted and lips wet. She still hasn't stopped shivering.

Almost like she looks when I've rescued her from a nightmare, but somehow so, so different.

"Do you need it?" I hear myself ask, and I have no idea where the words come from. I just know that they need to be asked. "Do you need it right now?"

She nods, quick and miserable, her braid moving over her breast as she does.

I get why she's miserable. I'm miserable too. Because here I am on Mark's yacht, wearing his clothes, with his

296

pretty bride's pussy rocking over my erection. Because I had righteous things to say about *cheating*, about how he and I had to stop because otherwise it would be wrong, and yet here I fucking am, not with him but with *her*. And this is cheating, there can be no doubt.

When Mark told me that I should take his place, that I should give her anything she needs, I know he didn't mean this.

But I look up at her parted mouth, her pert tits moving with ragged breaths, and I think of the salt water dripping off her lip. I think of how she said *I feel the same way.* I think of her in that sinful white swimsuit, of her whipping around this space with her honeysuckle knife flashing in her hand, and of the nights spent with my hand on her chest, helping her breathe in the dark.

And God, it's wrong, *it's so wrong*, but somehow knowing that she belongs to Mark, that I can feel his ring on her finger digging into my wrist—it makes me into someone or something I don't recognize.

Filthy, greedy, angry.

Whether it's to get closer to him —or to punish him—I don't know. But I say to Isolde in a rough growl, "If you need it, honey, take it. Take it fast."

Her mouth falls open even farther, that one crooked tooth, that wet, pink tongue, and her brows are pinched together even more, like she doesn't know what I'm saying, but her body does, her body knows, and she grinds down on me with a twist of her hips.

She twists again, searching for something, her eyes never leaving mine, and then she finds it, a low moan escaping her lips.

She lets go of my wrists and braces her hands on my chest and starts riding me, hell-for-leather, rutting that needy pussy hard enough to drive the breath from both our lungs.

And every twist, every rock and thrust, has me straining underneath her, my neck arching, my fingers digging fruitlessly into the mats by her knees. My balls are full, so fucking full, and my mind is full of fantasies about emptying into her—that pink place, that wet mouth. All over her goosebump-covered tits and her sweet ass.

Fuck, I want to see that ass. I want to see the tight little button there. I want to grab one cheek and pull—spread—and see everything. Slick cunt and cinched opening and soft folds and plump clit. I want to come all over it. I want to fuck it—God, I want to fuck it.

And because I'm lost to her, to the needy little movements of her hips, her worried brow, her open mouth, my mind goes to darker places, worse places.

I want to come inside her and then have Mark *know*. I want to come inside her and then watch Mark come inside her too, his way slicked by my seed. I want us both in her bare, so bare, pulsing and breeding, and then I want Mark to punish me for daring to use what's his, to shove me down and hurt me until I'm crying, and then wedge his cock inside me until I spurt all over the floor.

Maybe it's because I'm thinking of him that I notice the change in Isolde above me, the way her fingers twist restlessly in my shirt, the way her eyes go round and worried, her whole face pleading as she moves faster and harder above me.

She can't get there.

Even though her nipples are bunched so stiff that they're stretching the fabric of her bra, even though she's getting my shorts wet through her own clothes, she can't get there. And it's just a guess, just a whisper, a whisper in Mark's voice maybe, but I reach up and grab her hips and dig my fingertips in hard enough to bruise.

The noise that leaves her then is brutal in its filth, wholly animal. She shudders above me, her fingertips digging into my chest in return, a hectic flush crawling up her stomach to her chest.

She needs—I don't know if it's surrender or if it's pain—but whatever it is, she needs it to finish.

And I'm here to serve.

With a grunt, I flip us back over, the impact sending a short breath from her lungs, and I'm between her thighs immediately, rutting, humping, shameless as I brace myself with one forearm and slap her breast as hard as I can.

She shrieks and arches against me, writhing.

"Don't want to—leave a bruise—" I pant above her. "He might see if I do. Slapping is better."

She nods, her hair moving on the mat, stray locks cracking with static electricity. "Again," she gasps. "Do it again."

I slap her breast again, harder, hard enough to make her sob. Her breath hitches against my lips, and my eyes go to her mouth, so soft and pink below mine. That upper lip with its shallow philtrum. Those corners that naturally tug down into a pout.

I want to kiss her. I'm going to kiss her. I'm going to slick my tongue against hers and taste that soft mouth for myself, and I don't even know what I'm doing. I've never done this part, and it's pure instinct to pump my hips, to slide one arm behind her back to hold her tight and thrust and thrust, to lean down and—

She rolls her face to the side before I can put my mouth to hers, but her hands are still fisting in my shirt and she's closing her eyes and saying *more more more*, and I'm hurt that she won't kiss me, and I'm so—*shit*—I'm so close, and I slap her tit again, hard as I dare, and her back comes off the mat as she comes with a silent scream, her mouth open and her eyes wide and unseeing.

Her thighs are tight around my waist, and I can *feel* the pulse of her cunt on my cock, feel everything get a little bit wetter through our clothes, and then she reaches up, still desperately trying to fuck herself against me, and pulls my hair so hard I see stars.

The pain shoots down my spine, hot, needed, and for a moment, Mark is there with me, in the torment, in the dirty need that follows. With a gasp, I erupt, wrapping both arms around her head and fucking my way through the pleasure like a knight fucking a princess he knows he'll never get to touch again.

Warmth spreads between our hips: my spend, slick inside my compression shorts, pumped out with hard, grunting thrusts against her. Again and again.

Until slowly, inevitably, I'm empty. Empty on top of a flushed and sweaty Isolde.

I unwind my arms, feeling dizzy, feeling outside of myself, my arms shaking as I lift myself up to check on her.

Her eyes are round when she stares up at me, her cheeks scarlet, as is what I can see of her left breast. She's breathing in slow, shaking breaths that she's obviously trying to bring under control, and her throat is working over and over again to swallow. From the waistband of her bike shorts to her backside is a giant wet spot, slick enough to let me know that most of it is semen.

I settle back on my heels, my hands falling by my side. I go from euphoric to horrified in an instant.

"Fuck," I mumble. "*Fuck*."

CHAPTER 31

Isolde doesn't come out of her room for two days.

I knock on our shared door, which is now locked; I call the room's phone from mine. I ask the butler delivering her meals to let her know I'm here if she needs me—which doesn't earn me the skeptical expression it should, since Isolde's told everyone she's not feeling well, and he seems to assume I'm just being a considerate fellow passenger.

"Isolde," I say through our adjoining door on the second day. "I'm sorry I didn't... I'm just—"

My head falls against the door. "I'm sorry."

I should have done so much more after I pushed myself to my knees in the dojo and realized what we'd done. I should have made sure she was okay; I should have apologized for the whole episode the minute I found my voice. But instead, I'd knelt there, frozen with guilt, while she'd scrambled, wild-eyed, to her feet and then fled. And I didn't even try to follow her. I'd just stayed there on the mats, shorts wet, heart pounding, ashamed and wanting more and strangely alive with all of it. Pulsing, tingling, rushing. It reminded me of being at Morois House, of being Mark's, being so thoroughly inside my own skin that the world itself seemed sharper and brighter.

But there was no untangling that feeling from how I'd got there. From what I'd done to get there.

And so now Isolde doesn't answer me through the door, and I don't blame her.

We cheated on Mark. There's no getting around that.

But she also deserves to know about Strassburg and about Isabella Beroul and about me. She deserves to know so that she doesn't feel like she was the first to break the trust between them.

I close my eyes and think about the semen all over her shorts. Her wide eyes and her pert breast slapped red. Despite everything, blood surges to my groin.

I want to do it again.

I want to do it again and do more. I want to feel her naked pussy. I want to kiss it. I want to kiss *her*, kiss that soft mouth, see if she tastes like she smells, like honey and earth. I want to sift her hair through my fingers and run my nose over her neck. I want to hear her tell me more about ancient pastoralism in that rich girl voice; I want her to feed me more of those low, heartbreaking observations about myself.

And ah God, I feel it, I feel it, that curse of mine, twisting its vines around my ankles and up through the spokes of my ribs, seeking out my heart, my central nervous system, my brain.

No—*fuck*. No.

I'll beat it back. Falling in love with Mark was one thing, but his bride too? Being in love with a husband and wife both?

Lunacy.

Torture.

I step away from her door, drag in a breath, and then

go down to the gym to burn away the vines already winding their way to my heart.

———

The next day dawns clear for the first time in what feels like forever, and I stare at the soft sunrise for a long time before I go into my room and get ready for the day.

I want two people.

I'm not able to have either of them.

How did I get here? I keep asking myself. *How did I get here?*

I don't try knocking on Isolde's door today. I subject myself to a punishing workout in the gym, and then after I shower and change, I pace the small space of the library, trying to gather my thoughts.

Two things become clear amidst the noise in my head.

First, I have to get Isolde to talk to me. I need to know if she's okay, and I need to apologize for my behavior. There's no excuse for it, none at all, because as much as this yacht feels like a little vessel of timeless paradise, I'm still on the clock. I'm still working for Mark.

Which leads me to the second thing…

I have to quit this job.

When we get back to Manhattan, I'll get Isolde to Mark and then I'll—well, I don't know how much Isolde will want him to know, but I also don't know if I can lie.

Either way, I can't claim to be a good bodyguard when I'm currently two for two on having sex with the people I'm supposed to be protecting.

And I've proven myself unable to be trusted in the most egregious way.

Isolde's not at dinner, and so I'm required to eat suckling pig in peppercorn sauce on my own, and after I finish, I drain a glass of whiskey for courage and go to knock on her hallway door.

There's a tray by her door, with a metal-lidded plate and a glass filled with ice water and covered with plastic wrap. Dinner that she hasn't brought inside yet.

Worry scratches at me. I give our shared door another try—locked—and then I go out my balcony door to the balcony itself, and give myself two seconds to accept that I'm about to do something extraordinarily stupid.

I climb onto the balcony railing and jump.

It's an easy jump, and I make it without issue. I try not to think about how long it would take someone to notice that I wasn't on the boat if I'd missed.

I'm more worried about *Isolde* having gone missing, and sure enough, when I slide open her balcony door, her room is empty. I observe the tightly made bed, the rosary on the table next to it, wrapped in neat coils around the sheathed honeysuckle knife. Everything is in its place, except for the wardrobe and its contents. The doors are hanging open to show several dresses that I'm almost certain she didn't have room for in her two compact suitcases.

I check the bathroom, also empty, and feel time ripen into a slow, vivid thing, palpable as the deck moving gently beneath my feet.

Ten minutes.

If I can't find Isolde in ten minutes, I'm raising the alarm. I mentally calculate how long it's been since she's been definitively seen, how long in the water that might translate to.

Cold water. Open Atlantic.

Help would have to come from the Azores—planes at first—and another boat would take at least three days—

I bite off the panic, swallow it, move quick as my thoughts move quicker. First the dojo, then the chapel. Then everything else on that level. Then the library and spa. After that, I'm alerting the crew to search their quarters, and then it will be time to declare a passenger overboard.

With so many other likelier spots, I almost don't bother checking the aft deck on the lower level. It's not a pretty space, and its only purpose is for climbing on and off the moored tender when the ship is in harbor. But I duck back there anyway, the part of my mind that thinks in grids and sectors needing to check it off my mental map.

And then I stop, my ribs frozen midbreath.

She's here.

She's okay.

Isolde is here and in a green dress and she's safe. She's not drifting facedown in the Atlantic.

But my relief curdles in an instant.

She's huddled in a corner, her back to the wall and her shoulder against the deck railing, with her knees drawn up to her chest and her hair loose around her shoulders. Taffeta is spilling everywhere, shifting from emerald to sage to chartreuse, and it's spattered with ocean spray. The hem is caught around one of her thighs, leaving one leg uncovered, and I can see that she's barefoot.

Tears are tracking slow and clear down her cheeks. When she slides her defeated gaze to me, I get the impression she's been crying for a while.

While there's plenty of mist and splash this close to the water, the deck is sheltered from the wind and out of the way enough to be a good hiding place. I see why she chose it. I just want to know why she *needed* to choose it.

I squat down next to her, careful of the skirt.

"I was worried," I say. "I couldn't find you."

She leans her head against the wall, exposing her throat and collarbone. The dress has a low neckline and no sleeves; a row of small buttons the same color as the dress marches down the middle, leading to a thin sash tied at her narrow waist. The surfeit of silky fabric in the skirt, the immaculate tailoring of the bodice…it's sumptuous and rich. Even barefoot, even without any jewelry other than her engagement ring to set it off, she's redolent of money.

"I dressed for dinner," she says, her eyes closed. "I thought—I thought I was ready to see you. But I wasn't. I came here instead."

This is my fault. Her crying in a dinner gown on a yacht deck—my fault.

I open my mouth to start my apologies, to ask how I can make it right, but before I do, she speaks, her voice a whisper.

"I think I'm losing my mind."

It's like a kick to the throat. "Isolde," I whisper back. "I'm so sorry."

Her eyes are still closed. The thin lids are purple tinged, sleepless and miserable.

"It's not you," she says. "It's him. It's Mark. He's in my head, and I think, *I always think*, I'm guarded against it, but—" She opens her eyes, staring straight ahead at the sunset-orange sky and the water disappearing behind us. Her fingers find her neckline and dance over it. With every breath, her breasts swell against the fabric. "This dress was in my quarters. There's a whole closet of them, and they all fit perfectly, and they're all exactly what I would choose if I could. There's a dojo and a chapel. That swimsuit, which…"

I blush remembering the swimsuit, and I see a blush on her cheeks too. She must have realized when she got back to her room how revealing the swimsuit was after a swim.

Isolde looks at me. Her eyes are still so wet, her gold lashes spiky with tears.

"It was all by design, this whole trip. To break me down and get in my head. And it's *working*." The spray has left dark dots of green on her skirt, glistening streaks on her calves and feet, and her tears drop to her bodice, leaving matching spots there too. "The only thing that hasn't worked is him being here to see it working."

Is this what Mark imagined when he pictured Isolde wooed? Pliant? Did he imagine her sobbing and wet from the sea?

She pushes her legs down so that they're stretched in front of her. The farthest edge of her skirt is caught by the air and flutters at her ankle. Her eyes are searching mine, questioning.

"It's not real, you know," she says, finally looking away.

"What's not?"

"Anything to do with him. Anything at all." An exhale. "But I mean the engagement, the whole marriage. It's not real."

I stare. "Like in a philosophical sense, or…"

She gives a rueful laugh. "I wish that my only problem were that the institution of marriage is ridiculous. No, I mean that the marriage is arranged. It's a transaction."

Arranged.

A transaction.

"I don't understand."

"My father wants me to marry Mark to grow Laurence Bank's reach, and Mark agreed for the same reason but in reverse. Lyonesse's information coupled with the financial power of Laurence Bank. It would make everyone happy."

I look at the girl in her ocean-mottled dress, her tear-streaked face, and her shoulders slumped against the wall.

"Everyone except for you," I say.

"Everyone except for me," she agrees.

It's starting to make sense now. The reason why she and Mark barely talk, the reason why they haven't seen each other in two years. Why Mark never spoke about her.

What he did with Strassburg and Isabella Beroul. And me.

I sit next to her, pressing my back to the cool wall. "Mark never said anything about... I had no idea. He spoke about it like it was real."

"We want as few people as possible to know the truth," she explains. "It's more effective that way."

Betrayal is a pinprick right to the heart, slipping between membranes and muscle fibers to puncture some vital inner mechanism.

Why wasn't I immediately one of those few people? Why would he let me believe it was real? Why didn't he say anything when I told him things had to end between us?

Would I...would I still have ended things between us if I'd known his marriage was arranged?

And then I look at Isolde, at the hair tangled around her shoulders and at the soft creases of her lips, wet with tears, and know the question is infinitely more complicated than it would have been two weeks ago.

"Isolde," I say slowly. "You should—you should know that he's been with other people."

I can't decipher her expression when she rolls her head along the wall to look at me.

"It's not a real marriage," she says woodenly. "It doesn't matter."

"So he can just fuck whoever he wants while you wear his ring?" It's absurd that I'm being defensive of her given my history with Mark, but still. It doesn't feel fair.

"No, he—" She stops, lifts a hand, drops it in her lap. "He doesn't want any perceived gap between us. No lover or affair that could be used as a wedge because it would make leveraging each other's power and connections less effective. So he wants me to be faithful after we marry, and he's promised to be as faithful as I am. And as far as our agreement is concerned, the wedding day is Day One. The beginning of fidelity."

"So nothing before the ceremony counts?"

It still feels enormously unfair that Mark has been indulging himself without reserve, and here's Isolde miserable in a pile of crumpled taffeta.

"He asked me once if I wanted him to stop playing with other people," she says. "I told him no."

I watch her. The defeat in her curled shoulders, in the limp nests of her hands.

"Did you want him to stop?"

She rolls her head back so that she's staring at the ocean again. "Yes."

"Then why didn't you ask him to?" Mark is many things, but he's also the most direct person I know. He wouldn't have asked if he wasn't ready to hear whatever answer she might have given him.

"I was already not going to be a real wife or a real submissive, and it felt selfish asking him to stop when I wasn't going to be giving him myself in return, at least not in the way he wanted. And I wanted to hate him! I didn't *want* to want him to stop playing with other people. I didn't want to feel anything about him at all, but…"

She stops. There are so many tears spilling now.

"He infected me," she says after a long minute. "None of it mattered because he infected me anyway."

Recognition comes, dizzy and certain. Because I know this, don't I? The torment of having Mark Trevena inside your mind, your body, twisting you into someone you barely know.

I know this because Mark infected me too.

"I thought I was ready this time," Isolde murmurs. "I thought that two years away was enough to make me strong. Impervious. But here I am, lost all over again. A week and a half, and I'm completely, *stupidly* lost. And he's not even *here*."

I close my eyes. The waves slap against the hull, pushing and rocking the yacht. I try to push away the fresh, puncturing pain that Isolde has fallen for her future husband. Knowing the marriage is arranged should make it better, right? So why doesn't it?

Why does it feel worse?

And why do I want her undivided attention when I myself am still in love with Mark? What kind of greed is that? Especially when I know the kind of man Mark is, the effect he has on pride and sanity and need. There's no fighting him.

Isolde's voice is as opaque as the water when she asks, "How many people?"

I turn my head to look at her, dread pooling in my stomach. I can see from the haunted look in her face what she means.

"How many people has he fucked?" she asks.

I was the one who wanted her to know, who wanted to alleviate her guilt about what we did. But I still feel miserable when I answer. "Three that I know of. Strassburg, his former bodyguard. A submissive from Montreal named Isabella. And"—a long breath—"me."

She looks back at the ocean, blinks. Shakes her head. "I should have—of course." A pause as she inhales slowly. "Will it end at the wedding?"

"It's already ended," I say quickly. "When I found out he was engaged, I told him it was over." Which is hardly a moral high ground after I came all over his fiancée, I know.

"Are you in love with him?" she asks, voice still frustratingly opaque.

She's been so honest tonight, and I owe her my honesty in return. "Yes."

"Are you loyal to him?"

That is a more complicated question, with a complicated answer. "Yes, but…"

"But?"

"He's made it clear that you are a part of him and his world." I roll forward to my knees and face her so she can see how serious I am about this. "My loyalty is to you too, Isolde."

I can't tell if she believes me or not. Her lips roll together, and they're wet, because through all this, she hasn't stopped crying.

I touch her hand. It's cool and wet with tears or maybe water that's splashed up from the waves. "Can I ask you something?"

She gives a quick, jerking nod.

"Why did you say yes? To marrying Mark?"

"I told you," she replies. "My father wanted me to."

I study her. "Is that really it?"

Her jaw is tight when she looks away. "It's enough. And I can't fuck this up. Too much is riding on this marriage. People need me to make it work."

"I won't tell Mr. Trevena. About what happened between us."

Although privately I worry he'll be able to tell anyway. Or that I'll confess after one cold, blue glance.

"It's none of his business," she says suddenly, furiously. "Nothing until the wedding day is anyone's business, and if it's true for him, then it's true for me too."

Nothing until the wedding day…

My stupid body kicks to life at that phrase, at the layers of meaning that could be tucked behind it. What if she… No.

Better not to go there, even in my mind.

"What happened the other day still shouldn't have happened," I say. "I'm sorry. Even if this whole marriage is arranged, even if nothing matters until the wedding day. I was trusted to take care of you, and I—"

"Don't say *took advantage*," she interrupts. She gets to her knees, facing me, and in the barely there light of late evening, I can see the goose bumps covering her arms and the tops of her breasts. I can see the shine of stars in her eyes and the fresh tear tracks and the places where the tears have dried on her skin.

"You're a good man," she says, and when I open my mouth to argue, she presses her fingertips to my mouth.

I go still, transfixed. She could make me do anything if she touched my mouth like this.

"I know you don't think you are," she continues. "I know you think you're corrupted and stained, but you *are* good, Tristan, and when I'm near you, I feel like I can be good too. I feel like I can be brave. And I want to protect you. Take care of you."

Two days ago, I had her pinned to the floor, *slapping her*, and she wants to protect me?

But her eyes are completely serious, even if they're still spilling slow, heavy tears.

I stare at her, feeling the curse blooming inside my chest, twining and thickening its roots. A wave comes, an abrupt pitch of the boat with a heavy spray surging up from the water and showering us both. We ignore it, our eyes locked.

"I don't love you," she whispers.

My lips move against her fingertips as I speak. "You don't have to."

And then she's leaning in, I'm leaning in, and she drags her fingers from my mouth and replaces them with her warm, wet lips.

I can't taste the difference between her tears and the sea.

CHAPTER 32

SALT IS BRIGHT AND LIGHT ON MY TONGUE AS I brush my lips over hers.

Her hand finds my shirt, fists in the fabric, and holds me close —as if I'm going anywhere. As if I'd ever fucking leave.

Her lips are soft enough to stop a person's heart. And then they part and allow me inside.

I lick once, twice, seeking her tongue and grunting when I find it. It's slick, velvet and sliding, and then my hands come up to sift through the silky ends of her hair. It spills over my fingers like water, and I can't get enough. I have to push my hands into her hair and feel it on my palms, my wrists. I have to grab and pull just enough that she gasps into my mouth.

A sharp, raw thrill stabs right down to my cock at that noise. Is this what Mark feels? When he's controlling someone? Like every whimper and moan is wired straight to his system? I don't know how he can stand it, how he can think straight when he's got someone under his mouth and their head in his hands.

And Isolde just…lets me. She lets me twist my fingers in her hair and slide my tongue over hers. She lets me trace her teeth and rub against the roof of her mouth, and she lets me steal every pant, every breath.

There are no words for what that's like.

I slide my hands from her hair to her neck, my thumbs pressed against her jaw and tilting her face farther up to mine.

"You're beautiful," I say roughly. "You make me—" I don't finish because that's the whole sentence. *She makes me.*

She makes me mean and brutal in my hunger; she makes me a different Tristan, a new Tristan. It's fucking exhilarating. With Mark, it was like floating, like breathing, but this—this is like *burning*.

This isn't the thrill of danger; this is the thrill of being dangerous.

"Tristan," she breathes as I break from her mouth to nip at her chin and then her throat. "Oh god. I've wanted this since the moment I saw you."

Satisfaction, fierce and amoral, floods through me.

"I wanted you too," I rasp, licking back up to her mouth, which is already open for me.

Who am I? Who is this animal that has already given his heart to another? She said I was good—I want to be good—but all of that is hazed over now. I'm gone. I'm feral.

My only comfort is that she's strong enough to withstand my storm of gripping fingers and relentless teeth.

I reach for her dress, search through the taffeta to find a lithe sweep of thigh. I slide my hand up farther and she widens her knees. She does it instinctively, and I shudder out a pleased breath. I did the same for Mark and would again in a heartbeat, and here I am with someone else doing it for me, and I don't know how to make sense of it. How can I be both Tristans in equal measure? But I am, and God, her thigh is so warm, so smooth, like nothing I've ever felt, and then I reach the place where her leg joins her body. I pause, dropping my forehead against hers.

"I want to touch it so bad," I mumble. "Let me touch it. Please."

She is breathing hard against my mouth. "Until my wedding day, it's yours to touch."

I move my thumb first, my fingers still on the inside of her thigh. Her underwear isn't lacy or silky, but it stills feels expensive. Like her. Like her cunt, a cunt so costly that Mark is paying his whole kingdom for it.

She shivers at each pass of my thumb, and then has to grab on to my shirt with her other hand when I press my palm to her.

"Oh God," she moans. And when I rewrap my hand around her throat to hold her still as my fingers slide into the top of her underwear, she inhales so quickly that she's almost hyperventilating.

My hand on her throat isn't that tight, so it's not an airflow problem. I look at her, my hand pausing in her panties, about to ask—

"Hyssop," she says on a quavering exhale. "That's my safeword. I'll say it if I need you to stop."

I can't stop the smile that quirks my mouth. "Mine is hazel," I say.

And her mouth tilts too, and for a moment, we're still. Smiling like fools over these twin possessions of ours, and I see a new understanding in her eyes too. That Mark and I weren't just ordinary lovers, that I was *his*. His in the way that required a safeword.

I push my hand all the way into her underwear now, the stretchy material caught around my wrist as I skate my fingertips over the hauntingly perfect center of her. And my smile fades as the dark thrill of having her like this returns. My hand around her throat, my other hand up her dress.

It would take nothing for me to spend right now. Just a couple rocks of my hips, and the friction of Mark's borrowed linen pants would do the rest. But I'm also so, so aware that I've never done this. I've never stroked a pussy, touched it, hoped to make it come. And I've never been in control of a moment like this. With Mark, I was his plaything, his fuckdoll, and I have a fresh appreciation for how intense it is to be in charge, for the pressure of it. I want to make it perfect for her; I want to feed this new beast inside me.

How to do both?

The fabric of her skirt is gathered on my forearm and bunched at my elbow as I stroke a long path from her clit to the hot skin of her back entrance. She takes in a long breath as I continue exploring, feeling for myself her soft curls and then her wet, slick flesh.

Oh god. So…so fucking wet. I didn't know what it would feel like, feeling someone else's *wet*, but it's like being burned from the inside out, like being stroked on the inside of my skin.

My thighs are clenched to keep my climbing orgasm at bay.

I bend my face to hers and map her above as I map her below—tongue along teeth as I rim my finger around her soaked entrance, tongue against tongue as I caress the swollen knot at the front of her.

And then as my kiss dips deep, I do the same with my first finger. I push it into her, all the way to the last knuckle, and I—

My mouth breaks from hers, and I'm fighting to keep from erupting right now. My whole body is trembling, transformed, by this tight channel, slick and silken. So hot that I don't know how I'm not tasting flames in her mouth.

For a long moment, we stay like this: me fighting for control, her shivering and breathing and shivering. Me feeling the inside of her under the stars, her kiss still tasting like tears.

And I think: *this is Mark's bride.*

"Can I tell you something?" I say as my thumb finds her clitoris and presses against it.

She's trembling. "Yes."

"I've never done this before."

"You're"—more trembling—"doing great."

It isn't enough to do great. I want her to make my whole hand wet. I want her like she was the other day—shameless, wicked. I want her to feel just a fraction of what I've felt at Mark's hands, like the happiest, most wrung-out slut who ever drew breath.

"Take my hand," I command, pleased when she lets go of my shirt and reaches between her legs. I'm even more pleased when I feel that it's shaking as it rests over my own. "Make my hand do what you do when you're alone."

Her eyes close. "*Tristan.*" It's a moan.

"Do it."

Her hand is still shaking, but she obeys, her fingertips pressing to my fingertips, guiding me, *using* me. She uses my fingers but it's her, her making the slow circles, the gradually quickening strokes. Her clitoris is so hard now that it's practically pouting for attention. I wonder if I could get my mouth around it and suck it like a dick. I want to try.

Her hand falls away as she grows more and more rigid against me, and I press my forehead to hers as I work her eager flesh, drawing in her every exhale as my own inhale, savoring the small noises that eke from her chest. Treasuring the gasped words—*yes—close, I'm close—Tristan, faster, make me, make me—*

I know the last ingredient. My other hand drops to her thigh, my thumb seeking out the slope of her quadriceps muscle, and then slipping down to dig hard against the nerve

317

buried alongside it. Enough pressure to make her feel it, not enough pressure to contuse.

She detonates on a silent scream, her eyes wide, her hands clawing at my chest as her thighs try to clamp around my hand. I grab one thigh to keep her spread, and the minute I feel her start to relax, I push two fingers inside her to feel all that wet quivering for myself.

A primal growl rumbles in my chest. The fading pulses, contractions, what I made her do. I want it again, I want more of it, and I'm not a sadist, I don't get off on hurting her, but I love *making her*, I love using her roughly, and I shove the heel of my palm against her clit, my fingers still buried deep.

"Ride it," I tell her, and she shudderingly obeys, fucking my hand so obediently that I can't believe this is the same girl who plays with knives in her spare time.

I grab her jaw and tilt her up for a deep kiss, satisfying myself with tasting her mouth for a long moment before I take her lower lip between my teeth and bite.

Hard.

She comes again with an animal noise, her lip still between my teeth, her thighs wide as she desperately humps against my hand, her dress everywhere, just fucking everywhere, and my cock hurts so much, my whole body hurts. I let go of her lip and lick at it as she continues to convulse around my fingers, and then I pull back to watch her.

She's an absolute mess right now, tangled hair and red eyes and drenched pussy, and oh my God, I can't believe I never thought to imagine this, a wrecked heiress riding my hand like her life depends on it.

When she finally goes still, inside and out, I withdraw my fingers and then suck them clean. I nearly die at the taste: salt and honey and something else that has no name because it's just *her*.

She watches me with hooded eyes, and then I push my hand into the bodice of her dress. I find a stiff nipple and tease it with wet fingers. I tug just enough to make her whimper again.

"I want to fuck your cunt," I hear myself say.

"I've never done that before," she confesses.

"Even though you have a safeword?" I ask. Given that Mark had me facedown on a rug within weeks of meeting me, I'd assumed he and Isolde had done all sorts of things together, everything together.

She shakes her head. "The safeword was a precaution. Everything we did, we did as a performance, to sell the story of our marriage." A shadow crosses her face. "Except for one time."

I think about this, about where this leaves us.

"I haven't done this either," I admit. "I might be really bad at it."

She glances down to my hand in her dress, to her spread thighs. Her cheeks are pink. "I think we've just established that you're pretty good at things you've never done."

I laugh a little, letting go of her breast to band an arm around her waist and haul her against me. I can't stop touching her, grabbing her. There's so much of her I want, and I want it all at once.

"Mark keeps his room well-stocked," I say, running my nose over her cheek, burying it in her hair. Her hair smells like honey too—sweet, sweet, sweet. "He has condoms in there."

And then I pause, realizing I never actually asked. "If you want."

"I want you inside me," she says against my collarbone. "And I have an IUD."

"That's not very Catholic of you." My hands are busy, grabbing her waist, smoothing her hair, squeezing her ass through her dress.

She huffs out a noise. "It's not like a condom is any better, at least according to the pope."

"What he doesn't know won't hurt him," I say, and I reluctantly let go of her to get to my feet. But she stops me with a hand on my wrist.

"I don't think you understand what I'm saying. We don't need a condom," she whispers.

Images of my orgasm all over her fill my mind. Of my semen dripping from her, white from pink. My dick jerks against the linen, my balls pulling tight to my body, and I groan. Mark's words from months ago echo through my mind.

Breeding kinks.

Yes, it's a thing of mine. To breed and to be bred. But exchanging fluids like this isn't a small thing. At Lyonesse, I've heard of partners waiting years to do it. Mark and I haven't even done it.

I pull back, cradling Isolde's face in my hands so I can see her expression. "Are you sure?"

Her face is open like I've so rarely seen it before tonight. The moonlight catches the lighter threads in her irises and turns them silver. "I'm sure," she says softly, and I groan again.

"I want it so much," I say, and I'm already reaching for her skirt again, ready to lay her down on the deck and crawl between her thighs.

"Here?" she asks before I can.

"I can't wait." And then I take her hand and press it to my throbbing cock, hissing as she wraps her hand around it. I don't know how long I'll last inside her cunt. Not long, I think.

"I have an idea," she says, and then presses a kiss to my jaw.

———

A few minutes later, and we're in the chapel one floor up. It serves our needs perfectly—only a door and quiet set of stairs away, much closer than our suites, and the crew is accustomed to giving it complete privacy since it's where Isolde comes to pray.

The chapel is small, lit by artificial candles on the small table in front and more fake candles in a recessed nook, and by the moonlight coming in through the window. Two short pews with attached kneelers fill the space.

I turn and look at Isolde, who is staring up at me with dark eyes, her mouth swollen. Here in the enclosed space, I can hear the rustle of her dress as she moves.

I suddenly—perversely—wish Mark were here. To see her like this. To see me like this.

I tremble just thinking about it.

Isolde steps close, rustling, rustling, and presses her hand to my heart. My cock is an obscene thing between us, brushing against the skirt of her gown as she looks up at me.

"What are you thinking about?"

"You," I whisper.

Her eyes miss nothing. "And Mark?" she guesses.

I can't lie. I give a reluctant nod.

"You really love him," she says quietly.

I don't answer, but I don't need to. I think of what she said before she kissed me.

I don't love you.

But here we are anyway, wet and swollen and already gone too far. I'm here because I can't seem to stop myself from falling for cold, deadly people, but I don't know why she's here. Am I a way to punish Mark? To prove something to herself?

Or am I simply scratching an itch before she gets married and has a duty to be faithful?

The curse doesn't care. It's used to being lonely, to aching

321

for what it can never have. And if I'm alone in falling for her, then she's made me feel not alone in so much else. Grief. Nightmares. Being snared by the dark gravity of Mark's world.

We're together. Whatever else we are, we're together.

I seize her waist and pull her in for a hard, quick kiss.

"How do you want it?" I rasp.

"I want it how you want it," she breathes.

I search her face. Her eyes reflect every candle in the room, and her pulse rushes in her throat. "Are you sure?"

A small smile, like I'm being very precious right now. "Make it rough, Tristan. Like you mean it."

I hesitate. "It's your first time."

"It's not my first time having *sex*, just my first time having sex like this. And my first time was with Mark, and you better believe he fucked me like he meant it. I can still feel the imprint of his fingers inside me."

She says it with a flash of her eyes and a toss of her head, and static dances in front of my eyes.

"You're goading me," I manage to say.

"Maybe. Is it working?"

I could laugh if jealousy wasn't stuck in my chest like a sword. I push her backward to a pew, biting her lips, her jaw. I spin her around, bend her over the back, and shove her dress up to her hips.

She is still finding her balance as I yank her panties—black, soft, label-less—to her ankles and then shove them in my pocket to use privately later. I kneel a moment so I can take in my new favorite thing, the gold curls and pink petals. She's flushed and wet from my fingers, and I can see all of her like this.

I take her ass in both hands and spread her apart, and then press my tongue inside, burying my nose in her as I do.

Ah God, she tastes so fucking good. My tongue slips

through her with no resistance, and then I lick a hot stripe up to her back entrance, which is just as tight and pretty as I imagined.

She jolts, fighting me, a panicked whine in her throat as I test the muscled rim with my tongue, but I dig my fingers in and keep her spread, returning back to her core. I swirl my tongue as deep into her channel as I can, and then I find her clit and polish it with the tip of my tongue.

Her knees are buckled and she's panting when I stand up and wipe my mouth with the back of my arm.

"I want you to sit on my face," I say, shoving the waistband of my pants down and pulling out my dick. "I want to trap you there, with my hands on your hips, and my mouth wherever I want it, and I want to feel your clit on my tongue. I want to suck it. I want you to come on my face so I can taste it." I wrap my fingers around my aching length and shudder at my own touch.

I'm not going to last long, I think. I need to make this count, make her climax again.

God, the thought of her fluttering on my cock, impaled and squirming...

"Tristan," she says, looking back over her shoulder. Her eyes are burning in the dark. "I need it now."

"Fuck, honey, me too." And I fit my crown to the slick cove of her cunt, hissing as our two needs meet. The center of her is so hot, so wet, and the sight of my tip pressing into such a pretty, pink hole—

"Oh," she whimpers. "Oh God."

Oh God is right. I'm having to jam my way in, the muscles in my thighs and ass and stomach working to push me into her wet little glove, and she's stretching around me, each new inch I take inside of her like some kind of primal victory.

But it's toil, sweet toil, to wedge inside, and I have to

find her hips to hold her steady as I do it. Each stroke is a velvet caress on my flesh, sending ticklish sparks of heat up my organ and into my belly, into my balls, which are embarrassingly tight. Ready to breed.

And I'm not even all the way inside her yet.

"You feel so good," I groan. "Fuck, I'm not going to make it."

"Come inside," she whispers. "I want to know it's because of me."

I'm finally all the way in, and I look down at where we're joined. My cock swells as I appreciate the sight: her rosy skin wrapped around my thick intrusion, clinging as I withdraw a glistening inch and then shove back in.

Her pretty asshole. Her firm ass.

The fabric of her sumptuous dress rucked up around her hips.

"Okay, honey," I finally say. "I'll come inside."

I let go of every good thing in me, and I follow my instinct to rut, to mate. It doesn't matter that I haven't done this before, it doesn't matter that it's ridiculously brief, because I'm going to fuck her hole until I come, and it's every fantasy I've ever been ashamed to have.

The only thing that would make it better is if someone were going to come inside me too.

Fuck, this is it.

I pump faster, harder, crueler, like she's something I found and pinned down for this very purpose, and she's whimpering, moaning, trying to push back to meet my thrusts and failing since I still have her hips in my hand.

"Here it comes," I groan, going even faster. "It's coming, it's coming."

The climax claws up my thighs, chews through my belly. It surges through my groin with tight, vicious waves of heat, making me grunt with the agony of it, the incredible, beautiful agony of releasing into the bride currently bent over a chapel pew.

She's moaning too, a low, musical hum, and I'm shivering as I fill her up. As I give her all of my need, all of my lust, all of this new beast inside me. All of my twin curses, her and Mark both.

It's slick and every pulse of my dick makes it slicker, until I feel it running down my balls and smearing over my lap. But I don't stop until she's had every single bit of it. Every last fucking drop.

I pull out slowly, and she makes a wounded noise. She didn't come, and I'm going to fix that, but first—

I look down at what I've done, at the mess I've made of her. Cum is everywhere, wet and crude, and dripping out of her in gleaming pearls. I gather it with my fingers and push it back inside her, the sight unbelievably pornographic.

I shudder as I do it, my fingers moving faster and faster, and now she's rocking back to meet me. "I want to come again," she's panting, "please, please, please—"

If my cock wanted a break, it doesn't anymore. It's already raring back to life with my semen and her arousal drying on the hot skin. My erection juts lewdly between my hips as I take a final look—as I memorize the sight, knowing I might never have it again—and then I'm grabbing her, hauling her up and pushing her to the floor.

She knows what I want—or maybe it's what she wants too—and she's already gathering her skirt up to her hips and spreading her thighs. I'm greeted by glistening pink, by my seed still visible there.

I move between her legs and mount her immediately.

"Fuck," I curse as I'm swallowed again by liquid heat, my passage eased by what we just did. "Fuck, baby."

I find her wrists and pin them above her head, my whole weight on her now, and her throat is arching underneath me.

I thought coming would take the edge off, give me longer to enjoy being inside her, but there's nothing that could have prepared me for having Isolde Laurence like this. Writhing underneath me with her cum-wet pussy speared by my cock, her throat bared to my teeth.

I grind my lap into her, seeking the right kind of friction and feeling her quiver underneath me when I find it. When I find the perfect angle to rub against her clit as I fuck into her. And all that's left is to run my tongue over her pulse, to bite and suck where her throat meets her shoulder until she moans.

My hips churn, roughing my cock in and out of her, and then I lift my head to watch her. To watch as her eyelids flutter and her mouth parts, as her hands claw and flex above my grip, as she whispers my name.

Tristan.

She quakes underneath me, her hips seeking, and I push in to the hilt and let her rub herself on me as much as she can while she's pinned to the floor. Her head thrashes and her shoulders lift as she breaks apart, satin quivers, and I'm fucking done for.

I sink my teeth into her collarbone and pulse, letting loose for the second time, trying to push deeper and deeper and deeper as I jet my release into her body.

And finally she goes still underneath me, her eyes closed and her hands limp. Her ribs are moving fast, hard, and her mouth is twitching into a smile.

"You were pretty good at that too," she says, and I let go of her wrists to tickle her sides.

"Pretty good?" I mock growl, dipping my head to kiss the smile off her face.

"I mean—" She's laughing and it's the most beautiful sound I've ever heard and also every laugh is squeezing me inside her and it's killing me. "You might have to do it again for me to judge properly."

"That can be arranged," I murmur, moving my face so I can nuzzle her hair, nose into the corners of her jaw and throat. Drag my mouth over the tops of her breasts. When I meet her eyes again, she's still smiling and I'm smiling, and I think we both realize at the same time that we're just…happy.

She presses her hand to the side of my face. "I love your smile."

I turn my face to kiss her palm. "I love yours."

Her eyes are searching my face. "You deserve to smile more, Tristan."

"This seems like a stones and glass houses situation."

"Maybe we just need more reasons to do it," she replies.

I kiss her palm again. She's right, but also there's no erasing our lives as they are. Dead mothers, war, unwanted marriages, being in love with Mark Trevena—it's all here to stay.

I lift all the way off her. My cock slips free with a rush of fluid, and we both take in a sharp breath.

"Will you stay here for a few minutes?" I ask as I rise to my knees and fix my clothes. "I'm going to get something to clean you up."

She hesitates, her delicate face strangely vulnerable, but then she nods.

"I'll be back," I say, wanting her to know I mean it. "Please don't go."

"I won't," she replies softly, and I get to my feet and rush out of the chapel.

Even though it takes me less than three minutes to dart to the spa, find a robe, a washcloth and a bottle of water, I'm still terrified that I'll open the chapel door to find it empty. That she'll have realized the monumentally stupid thing we just did—*again*—and she'll have fled to her room to get away from me. Because even if nothing counts until the wedding day, surely that excludes the bodyguard? Mark's own former lover?

But when I open the chapel door, she's still there. She's sitting with her knees drawn up to her chest and her eyes on the crucifix on the wall, her hair hanging down her back.

She's lovely and lonely and my heart hurts just looking at her.

I step inside and shut the door and go to her. I unscrew the bottle of water and make her drink while I kneel behind her and slowly start unzipping her dress.

"Do you regret it?" I ask softly, not knowing what I'll do if the answer is yes. Not knowing what I'll do if the answer is no…because I don't know what the answer is for me yet. Only that, regrettable or not, this was inevitable.

From the moment I saw her and thought of blooming roses and frozen forests, this was inevitable.

"I regret that we have to weigh our regrets," Isolde says. I peel the dress from her body, and she looks over her shoulder. Her eyes are rimmed red, but they are clear now, and dry. "I would do it again, just so you know. The other day. Tonight. Whatever else is to come. I would do it all again."

The clarity in her voice matches the clarity in her eyes, and I'm reminded of her words on the deck. That she wanted to protect me.

I might have been the soldier, I might be the bodyguard, but I am growing increasingly aware that when it comes to fortitude, to focus, Isolde is the stronger of us.

In fact, she reminds me of no one so much as Mark.

I kiss her naked shoulder and take the water bottle from her hand. I guide her to lie down on the rug, tugging her dress all the way off her body until it's a green pile on the floor by the altar.

And then I take a minute to savor her, to enjoy the sinful

display. Her hair in a gold halo around her head and her swollen mouth and the pink tips of her breasts.

All of her, save for the soft handfuls of her tits, is lithe and lean, and as she shifts under my gaze, I can see subtle lines of muscle move in her stomach.

But there's something delicate about her too—in the architecture of her collarbone and the crescents of her ribs, in her slender feet, with their unpainted nails. The soft gold covering her sex. She reminds me a little of her knife, the one with the gold-and-ruby hilt. Far too pretty for something so dangerous.

"Tristan," she murmurs, stretching a little. "What are you doing?"

"Looking my fill," I say as I kneel between her legs. "I want to see every part of you. Every slope and curve. Every inch."

The corners of her mouth tilt, but she's still looking at me with that serious, certain gaze. "It's yours to look at."

"Until your wedding day."

I don't know why I repeat her earlier words—I meant it teasing, but it comes out mournful and mean. But she doesn't flinch.

She just nods and says, "Yes. Until then."

I duck my head to hide my face, not sure what it might be revealing. I find the warm, wet washcloth I stole from the spa, and I bring it slowly and gently over the place I just used.

And then her thighs clamp together as she giggles, rolling to the side. I watch, fascinated, as the muscles move in her stomach, as her teeth flash in a wide grin, as she tries to stifle her laughter and then snorts as a consequence and then giggles even louder.

She's ticklish between the legs after she comes.

I file away this information for later and then roll her onto

329

her back and pin her with a spread hand on her stomach. She squeals the whole time I clean up my mess, and I'm laughing too, until finally I toss the washcloth aside and lay my body over hers. I cover as much of her as I can, not wanting her to be cold. Not wanting a single inch between us.

"Why do you like it?" she asks after I've kissed the laughter out of her. "Your cum in me, I mean."

I brace myself on my forearms to look down at her. "I think there's something depraved about it. About it being messy, risky, a way to claim you. But if I'm being truthful, I'm not sure there's anything behind it. It just gets me off." I tangle my hands in her hair, rubbing the strands between my fingers as I stay propped above her. "What about you?"

"Me?"

"What gets you off?"

Something changes in her expression. "I think you can guess what it is," she says.

"The pain?"

She nods. But she doesn't offer anything about why she likes it, and I don't push.

I lift off her and find the robe I brought from the spa. I help her into it and then tie the belt snugly around her waist.

"Can I meet you in your room?" I ask. I don't want tonight to end. I want to shower with her, cuddle her, sleep with my arms around her.

She kisses my jaw. "Yes."

———

Thirty minutes later, and we're in her shower, which is palatially sized considering we're at sea, and we're trying to hush our laughter as the motion of the waves occasionally sends us pressing into each other.

I'm busy massaging shampoo into her scalp when she says, "Don't quit when we get to Manhattan."

My hands go still.

She turns to look at me, tilting her chin up to meet my eyes. Soap runs down her shoulders. "That's what you're planning, isn't it? To quit working for Mark once we arrive. To martyr yourself to your own sense of loyalty."

I frown. "I wouldn't call it martyring."

She doesn't respond to that. Just continues to look at me.

I sigh and frame her face with my hands, using my thumbs to wipe away stray bubbles of shampoo. "Yes, I'm considering quitting," I say. "I think it's the right thing to do."

"You do?"

"Isolde, I've fucked my boss's fiancée a few times now. I'd like to do it some more. I don't think that makes me very employable."

"Even if fidelity isn't expected of me until I marry him?" she asks quietly. Her gaze hasn't broken from my own.

I sigh and push my forehead to hers, briefly, before pulling back to rinse the shampoo from her hair. "Mark knowing you might have sex with other people before your wedding is one thing. But for it to be with his bodyguard, who would be around after the wedding? His bodyguard, who was supposed to be doing one thing on this trip and that was ensuring your safety? Isolde, he should never trust me again. And if he can't trust me, then I can't do my job right. And if I can't do my job right, then he deserves a bodyguard who will."

Isolde looks down as I finish rinsing her hair, her eyelashes almost to her cheekbones as I turn her and reach for the conditioner.

"And if I want you to stay?" she asks.

Softly. Not looking at me.

Vulnerability is etched into her voice, into the curl of her shoulders and tight line of her jaw. I rub the conditioner in her hair, not answering, my heart torn into chunks just like the moon on the sea.

Her request, raw and quiet, bruises me with its transparency, with what she's admitting by it.

And the curse hearkens to it, seeking her, whispering *Yes, yes, she wants you. She wants you like you want her.*

But what can I do about my own feelings? My own sense of morality? What can I do about still loving Mark and knowing that sleeping with Isolde might worry him or displease him?

Wound him, even?

I rinse the conditioner from her hair, and then she turns. We don't touch, just look at each other, and I stare down at this woman who lost her mother and then lost her dream of joining the church. Who's about to lose so much of her freedom just to make her father happy.

I'm kidding myself if I think this is a real choice.

All she has to do is ask, and I'm hers.

"If you want me to stay," I say and bend my lips to hers, "then I'll stay."

CHAPTER 33

"Shh," I tell Isolde as she moans. "Be quiet or I'll have to stop."

It's the middle of the day, when most of the staff are taking a break after lunch, and Isolde and I are tucked behind the waterfall of the yacht's largest pool, pressed into a nook just wide enough for two people to fit inside. I scouted the nook thoroughly yesterday, checking every sight line, watching as the boat rocked and the waterfall moved with it just to make sure. The nook is dark enough and the waterfall wide and rushing enough that anyone standing behind it is invisible.

Necessary reconnaissance, as Isolde has taken to wearing that godless swimsuit every day, swimming long laps in the pool as I pretend to read fantasy novels on the deck, until I finally give up and stalk back to my room to jerk off.

She thinks it's very amusing.

But today I'm making her pay for it, and as she swam close to the waterfall, I darted out from behind it and grabbed her, hauling her back like a marauder as she struggled against me. Struggling which only lasted until I pushed the crotch of her swimsuit aside and buried my fingers in her cunt.

And now she's panting against me, her back to my chest, her hips moving to fuck my hand. Heaven.

"Teasing me all week with this goddamned swimsuit," I growl in her ear. I band my free arm around her front, reaching up to fill my hand with her breast. Weighing it in the water. Scraping my fingernails over the translucent fabric covering the furled tip. "Making me need it, honey. Making me need it so bad."

All the while my fingers work underwater, scissoring slowly inside her to stretch her, sliding up to stroke the knot of nerves at the front, teasing once or twice at the tight hole in back.

"Then take it," she whimpers, echoing my words in the dojo that day. "If you need it."

I press my face against the side of hers and breathe her in. I taste salt. I'm already pulling down the waist of my trunks and fishing out my cock. Pressing the head against her center and penetrating.

"I don't know how you do it to me," I whisper, squeezing her breast. The water is buoyant, resistant to force, and I have to hold her tight to me to wedge into her cunt as hard as I'd like. "We just fucked this morning. I spent all night with my face between your legs. How can I still need it *so bad*?"

"If you figure it out, let me know," she says, gasping. My fingers find her clit and start rubbing again. "I think about it all the time. How to get you alone, how to make it not matter if we're *not* alone. Last night I was seconds away from taking your hand under the dinner table and pushing it between my legs."

I groan—quietly—my orgasm already locked and loaded at the base of my cock.

"Gonna come, honey," I mutter, and she arches against me.

"Inside me," she begs, as if there were any other thing I'd rather do. "Inside."

I release with a grunt, spurting ropes of heat into her, biting her neck from behind before I tear myself away, not wanting to leave any marks, any trace of this.

Or rather, *wanting* to but knowing it's a terrible idea.

I come until my balls are drained, my craving soothed temporarily by the snug channel inside her body, and then I slip out and replace my dick with my fingers, giving her two and the heel of my hand to ride, one of her favorite ways to come.

She curls in the water as she does, convulsing around my hand, her thighs closed tight, and I keep her pinned against my chest, growling at every single pulse she gives me. "Fuck, you're so sexy," I praise. "You make me so hard. You make me feral. I want to fuck you every single moment of the day. I don't know how I'm gonna stop—"

My voice falls quiet as her body gives up the last of its pleasure, and we just stay there for a moment. My fingers are still inside her as she turns in my arms and wraps her arms around my neck and her legs around my waist.

"I don't know how I'm going to stop either," she confesses, her voice a husky melody over the waterfall, and feeling something vital inside me tear open, I grab my newly hard erection and slide it inside.

We screw facing each other, my hands on her hips, moving her up and down on my dick as easily as I'd move a toy or my own hand, and we don't say a word as we stroke ourselves to our next climax.

What else is there to say?

We don't know how we're going to stop.

———

I'm obsessed with maps.

Specifically the maps in the bridge with the blinking dot

showing the yacht and how far away it is from Manhattan. Every morning, I meet with Captain Duval on the bridge, and my eyes are fixed on the screens in front of the bridge windows, watching as we pull ever closer to shore.

"Should be tomorrow afternoon," she says confidently. "The forecast is clear and we'll be approaching well away from the shipping lanes, so it'll only be noncommercial boat traffic to worry about. An easy final leg. Is Ms. Laurence ready?"

I glance over to the captain and am relieved to see that her expression betrays no suspicion, no subtext. As constantly as Isolde and I have fucked, there's no erasing my years as a soldier, my experience as a bodyguard. I've been careful, discreet, sure that any time we're together, we're not raising conjecture. Making sure we still give the appearance of pursuing our own interests and recreation, all the things we did before, on the first half of the trip.

I'm almost disappointed at how adept I am at deception.

And Isolde thought I was a good man.

"She's known this day was coming and made all her preparations. And I'm excited to be on solid land again," I add. I speak as much truth as possible, since lying aloud is still hard for me.

Which is oddly relieving. At least there're traces of my morality still left.

I give the map one last look, let the captain know that I'll be ready to deliver Isolde to Mark tomorrow, and go to the basketball court. I take shots until my arms hurt and sweat drips into my eyes, and then I go to my room to shower and change.

And then I go stand at my room's balcony and watch the waves move under the afternoon sky.

The ocean is endless. There is no way to make sense of where you are on it, no terrain association, no dead reckoning. It's just a vast, blue bruise that defies logic, at least without the sun or stars, without panels of screens, without satellites and GPS transponders. On its own, it's the opposite of a place.

It's no place.

And here it felt like I could be no one—for the last week, I've been no one. Not a bodyguard, not a man with morals.

Not a man still in love with Mark Trevena.

Tomorrow that changes. Tomorrow, we will see the shore, and we will anchor, and we will take the tender to the marina.

We will be back in *a place*. A place where I am no longer no one.

I brace my hands on the railing and hang my head between my shoulders, breathing in the cool, wet air.

The door to the balcony next to mine slides open, and I don't need to look up to know it's Isolde. Out of the corner of my eye, I see her come to her own railing, her hair in a white-gold braid.

"You didn't come to the dojo this morning," she says.

"I know."

"Or the chapel after."

"I know."

She lets out a breath. I look over to find her staring at the waves.

"You're ending it, aren't you?" she asks. Her words are so flat, so dull, that I know she's already gone somewhere deep inside herself. The place she's lived inside of for years to cope with her mother's death, with her father's plans for her future. And I hate it. I hate that I'm the cause of that voice—I hate that I'm the one sending her to that place.

But she's right. I am ending it.

I exhale with an unrelenting tightness in my chest. "Yes."

"Why? Why when I can do whatever I like until the wedding? A wedding which is weeks from now?"

I turn to look at her fully, but she stays as she is, her eyes on the water.

"We'd have to stop anyway. It's better we do it before we get home to Mark."

"Because you're worried about him finding out," she says tonelessly.

"Because I love him." My voice is quiet, tired.

Sad.

And she does turn to look at me now.

"I have to be loyal to my own feelings," I explain. "And there's more, because while you might be free until your wedding day, I'm not. If I'm going to stay at Lyonesse, then I have to be worthy of his trust. I have to be worthy of my own. I can't sleep with his bride behind his back, no matter what her own freedoms are."

"So this is the cost of you staying for me," she says. Her eyes are wet, but the tears haven't fallen. I don't think she'll let them fall. "If you stay, then we have to end things now."

"It's for the best. Besides," I add in a self-wounding attempt at comfort, "you told me yourself that you didn't love me. So this was just temporary for you, you know. Just fun."

Her jaw flexes once.

"Just fun, that's right," she says, voice devoid of inflection. "No harm done."

"Well, maybe some harm done." I pass a hand over my face. "I know what you do before the marriage isn't Mark's business, but I'm not convinced it's the same for me, especially since I'll be working there after the wedding too."

It makes me sick to say out loud but it has to be said. "Are we…going to tell him? Or keep it a secret? And hope he never finds out?"

When I look back, her arms are wrapped tight around herself, and I want so much to jump over to her balcony and pull her close. I want to comfort her, soothe her, drive away any fears or worries. It only adds to my misery right now that I can't.

That I shouldn't.

She doesn't love you, I tell myself. *This is hurting you far more than it's hurting her.*

Still, though. The idea of her hurting any bit, any little bit at all, is excoriating.

"I don't like lying any more than you, Tristan, although I think I might be better at it. But I suppose—if I were thinking with a clear head, which I admittedly haven't done much of recently—it would be smarter to keep it between us until after the wedding. I shouldn't risk the marriage, not when we're so close. And then—after the papers are signed—we can think about it some more."

It all makes sense, and I nod.

"As you wish," I say, and pray that I'll become a better liar in the next twenty-four hours.

I put my hand on the door to my room, sliding it open to step inside.

"Tristan."

I look at her, slender and steely against the bright blue sky.

"This week was the best week of my life." She swallows, and before I can reply, she spins, yanks her balcony door open, and disappears into her room.

CHAPTER 34

THE TENDER IDLES UP TO THE MARINA, AND RIGHT AWAY I see Mark. The breeze plasters his suit against his lean frame, toys with his hair. Behind him, the Manhattan forest of glass and steel looms large.

Next to me, Isolde folds her hands in her lap. She's been nearly silent all day, speaking only to reply in elegant, little snippets. Not brisk enough to be rude, of course not, but reserved enough to deter small talk with the staff.

Or conversation with me.

We haven't spoken since my balcony, not even when I came into her room last night to wake her from her nightmares and she jolted awake before I could touch her. She'd waved me back into my room, where I'd lain in my bed, staring at the ceiling almost until dawn, wishing I were a different kind of man. One who could shuttle between the beds of a bride and a groom without needing the promises of a future and honesty and love.

The tender docks, one of the crew members hopping up to lash the boat to the dock, and I step out of it and turn to help Isolde out as well. She's wearing a white bodysuit and white trousers today, her hair in a low ponytail, and her lips a shell pink. She looks radiant, a vision, as she takes my hand and allows me to help her to the dock.

Warmth ripples through me at the touch, and I fight the urge to shiver. It's the first time we've touched since two nights ago when I made an Isolde-shaped dent in her mattress.

She pulls her hand free the moment she has her balance on the dock, and I have to force myself to let go.

We ended this. I'm in love with her, but we ended this.

It's for the best.

Even if it feels like bleeding right into the bay, one hot drop of blood at a time.

I look up to see that Mark isn't alone. Sedge is behind him, pale eyed and inscrutable, and then Goran is behind them both, grinning and friendly.

And then Mark looks at me and our eyes meet, and it's like being shot clean through the chest.

Three weeks. It's only been three weeks, and he'd become like a myth in my mind, hazy and godlike. But in the flesh, *here*, he's something more than godlike. That high forehead and once-broken nose and full mouth—brutal beauty.

His lips tilt in a smile, a smile *for me*, and I drag in a breath through my lungs.

I have to be steady. I have to be so steady around him. At least until the marriage, he can't know the truth about me and Isolde, and it will be very hard to keep it that way if he's already making me want to kneel to him here on this dock.

You were careful with Isolde, I remind myself. *So careful. Our secret is safe.*

Mark is extending his hand to his affianced now, and Isolde takes it with a grace that speaks of manners, of living

341

in a world where such gallantry is normal. And as she takes his hand and their eyes meet, sapphire and turquoise, I can practically see the electricity arc between them. The tension rippling through both their bodies.

It's not hostility—although I can't say it's affection either. Whatever it is, it's physical, and I think of what Isolde told me on the boat, about Mark being her first.

I can still feel the imprint of his fingers inside me.

The jealousy is going to eat me alive.

I realize I'm scrubbing a hand over my chest as I watch Mark kiss Isolde's hand like I can rub away the wretched envy. I knew it would be torture to be in love with them both, but fuck, fuck, this is worse than I could have imagined.

"Welcome home, my queen," Mark murmurs over Isolde's hand, and then lifts his head to meet her eyes again. Whatever passes between them then, unspoken, has Mark's mouth flickering in a smile.

He looks like he's just been presented with his favorite thing: a dare.

We all start heading toward the end of the dock, toward the waiting vehicles. Mark, Isolde, and I will stay in Mark's Manhattan penthouse while the others stay nearby in a hotel. My mind is fretting over the potential torment of being trapped in a home with the two of them when Sedge comes up alongside me.

I look over at the assistant, slender and neatly dressed in a button-down shirt and periwinkle shorts, his chin-length hair tucked almost shyly behind his ears.

"A word of advice, Tristan," he says, and despite his appearance, his voice isn't shy at all. It's edged with something I don't understand. "Maybe make sure there aren't cameras on the *inside* of the yacht before you use it for any old thing you like."

And with that Sedge strides off, his meaning detonating behind him.

He knows.

And if he knows…

It won't be long until Mark knows too.

If he doesn't already.

And just at that moment, Mark looks over his shoulder at me, his hand on the small of Isolde's back.

"Come along, Tristan," he says calmly. "There's much to discuss."

ACKNOWLEDGMENTS

Salt Kiss has been nipping at my fingers to be written for years now, and I have bucketloads of gratitude to everyone who took a chance on my sweet bébé Tristan and the two monsters he falls in love with. (Yes, Isolde is a monster too. Shh, it's fine.)

Firstly, a huge thank-you to Christa Désir, who not only brought me into the Bloom family, but didn't hesitate a second when I told her what I wanted to write and gave me all the space and grace I needed to get Tristan on the page. And secondly, I owe so many thank-yous to the entire Bloom Books/Sourcebooks team, who've been as generous as they are innovative: Dominique Raccah, Letty Mundt, Pam Jaffee, Madison Nankervis, Katie Stutz—and Jennifer Sterkowitz, who once gallantly saved me from a publishing pickle!

I also have to thank my doughty agent, John Cusick, for charting me through publishing waters both calm and stormy, and my crew of cheerful marketing and admin experts: Candi Kane, Serena McDonald, Melissa Gaston, and the entire GSC team. A loving squeeze goes to Erica Russikoff, who helped me dial into the world of Lyonesse with all its kinky, stabby goodness!

I owe a huge debt of time (and liquid comfort) to anyone who's had to listen to me talk about these three characters for *checks watch* almost six years now. Thank you to Julie Murphy, Ashley Lindemann, Nana Malone, Natalie C. Parker, Tess Gratton, and Kenya Bell for being there for plot problems, sprints, and minor nervous breakdowns. (Extra thanks goes to Nana Malone, who kindly listened to *many* VMs about bodyguard logistics and fielded far too many questions about how earpieces work.)

I also have to thank all of my writing and non-writing friends for propping me up during a season that was the deadline equivalent of the episode where Lucy and Ethel work at a chocolate factory: Kate Fasse, Ashley Brown, Ian Pearce, Juliet Naumann, Kennedy Ryan, Nisha Sharma, KA Linde, and Skye Warren.

I also have to thank the tireless Mr. Simone and our hilarious, salty kids for surrendering me to the Words, over and over again. Thank you for putting up with YouTube ambience channels and empty coffee mugs everywhere.

And finally, thank you to anyone brave enough to scoop up this book without knowing what kind of mayhem I was going to get up to. You are the best, and I promise there's plenty of mayhem (and spanking) to come.

ABOUT THE AUTHOR

Sierra Simone is a *USA Today* bestselling former librarian who spent too much time reading romance novels at the information desk. She lives with her husband and family in Kansas City.

Sign up for her newsletter to be notified of releases, books going on sale, events, and other news here: subscribepage.com /sierrasimone

Website: thesierrasimone.com
Facebook: TheSierraSimone
Instagram: @thesierrasimone
Twitter: @TheSierraSimone
TikTok: @thesierrasimone